THE DEATH OF KINGS

RENNIE AIRTH was born in South Africa and has worked as a foreign correspondent for Reuters. The first novel in his John Madden series, *River of Darkness*, published in 1999 to huge critical acclaim, was shortlisted for four crime fiction awards and won the Grand Prix de Littérature Policère in France. *River of Darkness* was followed by *The Blood-Dimmed Tide*, the CWA Ellis Peters Award short-listed *The Dead of Winter* and *The Reckoning*. *The Death of Kings* is the fifth novel in the John Madden series.

RENNIE AIRTH

THE DEATH OF KINGS

MANTLE

First published 2017 by Mantle
an imprint of Pan Macmillan
20 New Wharf Road, London N1 9RR
Associated companies throughout the world
www.panmacmillan.com

ISBN 978-1-5098-1732-0

1 3 5 7 9 8 6 4 2

A CIP catalogue record for this book is available from the British Library.

Typeset by Ellipsis Digital Limited, Glasgow
Printed and bound by CPI Group (UK) Ltd, Croydon, CR0 4YY

For Ronald Vance

For God's sake, let us sit upon the ground
And tell sad stories of the death of kings

William Shakespeare, *Richard II*

THE DEATH OF KINGS

PROLOGUE

Kent, August 1938

WHEN SHE HEARD the stair creak beneath her foot, Portia stopped and stood frozen. Her heartbeat quickened with excitement.

She didn't want to be seen. She planned to slip out and then return to her room in time to appear for tea as though nothing had happened; as though she had been resting, which was what she had told the others she would be doing when she had left them in the drawing room after lunch.

But there was always the danger that he might be spying on her; keeping a watch on her movements. She knew that he didn't trust her any longer. He suspected that she might be trying to take matters into her own hands.

'What is this game you're playing?' He had come to her room the night before after the household had gone to bed. 'Are you out of your mind?' His face, which so seldom showed any feeling, had been stiff with rage. 'Do you think you're on the stage? Must you always be the ... *actress*?' He had spat the word out as though it left a bad taste in his mouth. 'Leave this to me. Just do as you are told.'

She had tried to calm him, telling him not to worry. 'They're in a safe place,' she had assured him. But she had resented the tone of his angry accusations and the evident scorn he felt for her. As if *he* wasn't the one playing his own game! She still didn't know what he was up to – what his scheme involved – only that she had a part in it and would be rewarded in due course.

Or so he had said. But she no more trusted him than she did any other man. And as it happened, his suspicions were justified. Unknown to him she had already put her own plan into action and he was helpless to stop it. The stage had been set; all that was required was for the curtain to go up.

She knew her lines – she had written them herself – and before leaving she had stood before the full-length mirror in her room taking in not only her appearance but also the expressions on her face as she rehearsed the scene she was about to play.

She had dressed with care, choosing a simple skirt and blouse, and covered her red hair with a silk scarf. Although the occasion hardly called for a display of jewellery, she had put on the pair of earrings she had been lent for the weekend and then, unable to resist the temptation, had slipped the pendant around her neck as well. Carved in the shape of the Buddha, it was made of jade and deep green in colour – the shade most valued by Chinese emperors, she had been told. She had already removed the paint she had put on her nails the night before – that had been purely for show, and to draw attention to her hands as she played with the pendant – and having examined her reflection in the mirror she went one step further, wiping the lipstick off her mouth. She meant to display a new image of herself, one about which there could be no mistake: that of a woman with a serious purpose, not a plaything to be used and then cast aside at will. As if by reflex she reached for the small leather handbag that was hanging by a strap from her shoulder. Searching for the clasp, she opened it and slipped her fingers inside. Yes . . . everything she needed was there.

Now, with the house as silent as a tomb around her, she resumed her descent of the stairs, reaching the empty hall below with its echoing paved floor and then crossing it on tiptoe, padding softly as a cat. Her goal was a long corridor that ran the length of the house and when she came to it she turned right and made for a door that gave onto the garden.

She had almost reached the end of the passage when a figure appeared from one of the doorways ahead of her and she slowed her pace, unsettled at being discovered. But it was only one of the maids, who stood aside, bobbing her head as Portia went by. The door was a few paces further on and as she opened it and slipped out into the blazing hot afternoon a wave of relief washed over her.

Although she didn't want to admit it – even to herself – she was afraid of him. The men she had known in her life, and there were many – too many – had been mostly of a type and she had learned what to expect of them, which was little enough. But *he* was different – unreadable, unknowable – and she had sensed that his silent presence and cold, ever-watchful eye signalled a more dangerous and less predictable nature than any other she had encountered in the past.

The door she had come through gave onto a path that stretched the length of the garden. Walled on either side by high yew hedges whose topmost branches had been trained to meet overhead, it offered a shield against prying eyes – even those who might be watching from the bedroom windows above – and once she had entered the long, cool tunnel she was able to relax and focus her mind on the business ahead. She was already a good ten minutes late for her appointment (deliberately so – she would not be the one kept waiting) and when she came to a wooden gate in the high brick wall at the bottom of the garden and saw a party of a dozen or more people, both men and women, strolling along a path that crossed the expanse of common land beyond it, she paused and waited while they made their slow way towards the tree-covered knoll which was visible from the terrace of the house behind her and which she had been told bore the name of Holly Hill. She assumed that the casually dressed group were hop-pickers; the harvest was in full swing and driving down from London the day before she had seen the fields surrounding the village busy with pickers. But since today was Sunday she knew they wouldn't be working and didn't want the rendezvous to which she was heading disturbed by passers-by.

As soon as the last of the party had disappeared into the wood she went through the gate and made her way swiftly across the field on a path less trodden than the one they had used. The two paths met on the far side of the meadow just short of the wood and when Portia got there she glanced over her shoulder to make sure she was not being followed before continuing in the wake of the group whose voices she could hear in the distance ahead of her; plunging into the gloom of the wood whose deep shadow was in stark contrast to the bright sunshine she had just stepped out of.

She was treading unfamiliar ground. She had never been invited to the house where she was a guest before, so its surroundings were new to her. But she had been given directions easy enough to follow: some way into the wood, near the top of the slight rise she was ascending now, was the ruin of an old hermit's hut. It was situated a little way off the path, but easy to spot. They were to meet there. As she neared the top of the knoll she began to scan the surrounding trees and presently caught sight of the stone structure. Overhung by a towering beech, it was without a roof; only the walls still stood.

She stopped to peer at it and as she did she heard the sound of movement behind her. It might have been no more than a twig breaking, but she stood still for long seconds peering into the shadowy depths of the wood, waiting until she was sure no one was there. Only when satisfied did she turn back to peer at the ruined hut again and almost at once caught sight of a figure moving about inside. One moment it appeared at the single window, the next it was standing in the doorway, barely visible in the deep shade cast by the branches overhead.

Poised to move forward now, she hesitated. Was she going too far? Had she overreached herself? She knew what *he* would say; it was why she had kept it a secret from him. Still she felt a tremor of doubt, and for a moment her nerve faltered.

Then anger came to her rescue, the deep rage that had been building inside her – for years it seemed. She had been used once too often; humiliated in a way she was no longer prepared to tolerate. It was time someone paid the price.

An actress, *he* had called her, and standing there motionless in the wood, she couldn't help but picture herself as a character in a play, or perhaps a film: a woman of mystery, a woman with a secret. It was the sort of part she had always longed for, and while there were no cameras, no lights adjusted so as to catch her face half in shadow as she waited, she could still comfort herself with the knowledge that hers was the leading role in the drama that was about to unfold.

Her moment had arrived, the one she had dreamed of, and her only regret was that there was no one to record it, no director standing hidden in the shadows somewhere behind her ready to shout the magic word.

'*Action!*'

PART ONE

1

London, August 1949

'I'M SORRY TO BE the one to tell you, John, but it's no go. Not on the available evidence. Cradock won't go along with it, and I see his point.'

Sitting at ease in his shirt sleeves, with his tie loosened and his cuffs rolled up, Detective Chief Superintendent Chubb settled back in his chair with a sigh. A man whose drooping jowls and moist, dog-like eyes had earned him comparison with a bloodhound in his younger days together with the nickname Cheerful Charlie, the chief super's naturally mournful expression was well suited to the role forced on him that morning as the bearer of bad news.

'He even went so far as to refer to a can of worms, which is not like him at all.' Chubb shook his head regretfully. 'For one thing, there's no proof as yet that these two pendants are one and the same, and even if they are that doesn't necessarily mean that a mistake was made in the original investigation.'

'How's that, Charlie?'

Madden cocked an eye at him. Old colleagues in the distant past, they were sitting facing each other across a desk in the chief superintendent's sun-filled office at Scotland Yard. For nearly a week now London had been sweltering in a heatwave and with August not even half done and no sign of a change in the weather, it seemed likely the capital would continue to suffer for a while yet.

'Come on, John.' Chubb looked discomfited. 'You know as well as I do that there are nearly always loose ends in any inquiry; it's rare that all of them are tied up. Just glancing through the file it seems to me there are any number of ways that pendant might have gone missing. For one thing some-one else may have picked it up and simply pocketed it; for another it may still be lying around somewhere in the wood. We've only the word of this anonymous correspondent that the one he sent to Derry once belonged to Portia Blake.'

He awaited the other's reaction. Madden was considering his response.

'Well, I'll pass on what you say to Angus,' he said finally. 'But he won't like it.'

'I'm sure he won't.' Chubb winced. The man they were speaking of, Angus Sinclair, formerly a chief inspector, now retired, had once been their superior, and while Chubb was willing to admit that he had learned all he knew under Sinclair's stern tutelage he was also wont to claim, only half humorously, that the experience had left him scarred for life.

'He's very upset about this, Charlie.' Although Madden, too, had suffered on occasion from the chief inspector's acid tongue during his time as a detective with the Metropolitan Police, now long past, the two men had become friends during the years they had worked together and on retiring Sinclair had chosen to settle in the same Surrey village of Highfield where Madden and his wife lived. 'He thinks there may have been a miscarriage of justice. As you're aware, the man they arrested was eventually hanged. And we all know how Angus feels about capital punishment.'

Chubb grunted. 'I never shared his views, mind. If you take a life, you deserve to swing. That's my opinion.'

'Yes, but what's bothering Angus now is whether this man, Norris, was in fact guilty. Or was the wrong man sent to the gallows? He won't rest easy until he's satisfied on that point.'

The chief super's sigh sounded a long-suffering note. Fanning his face with a sheet of paper taken from the file in front of him, he turned to the third person present at their meeting.

'What's your opinion, Inspector? You've read this.'

Billy Styles hesitated. A detective for close on a quarter of a century now, he owed his early opportunities not only to John Madden, under whom he had cut his teeth in a still-famous murder case, but also to Sinclair, the senior officer in charge of the investigation, who had overlooked his inexperience at the time and given him a chance to show his worth. He would have preferred to take their part, but like the chief super he had his misgivings.

'I agree that initially we'd have to show that these two pendants are one and the same – at least as far as the AC is concerned.' Assistant Commissioner, Crime, Eustace Cradock was their immediate superior and a man with whom Charlie Chubb had never enjoyed the easiest of relationships. 'He won't budge otherwise. But actually, after thinking it over, I feel there are one or two other questions that need answering.'

'Do you?' Chubb eyed the younger man in feigned astonishment. 'This is the first I've heard of it.'

'Well, for one thing, why did she go for a walk, this Portia Blake? There didn't seem any good reason for it; not right after lunch in the heat of the afternoon. And why did she go alone?'

'Why shouldn't she?'

'I just thought it strange, her being an actress and all, and a good-looking young woman, too.' Billy scratched his head.

'I must be slow, Inspector.' Chubb's gaze was stony. 'You'll have to explain that to me.'

'I think what Billy's saying is that it seemed out of character,' Madden intervened. 'I thought the same when Angus told me about the case: and so did he, apparently – at the time.'

'Then why didn't he do something about it?' The chief super was losing patience.

Madden rubbed his chin.

'The whole trouble with the investigation – and Angus is quite ready to acknowledge that now – is that it was resolved too quickly; too easily. This man Norris was arrested almost at once; all the evidence seemed to indicate he was guilty.'

'It still does. And correct me if I'm wrong – but didn't he confess to the murder?'

'He did; although he later retracted his confession. But that was part of the problem, you see.' Madden strove to clarify the issue. 'Once the Kent police were persuaded they had their man, there seemed no need to continue with the inquiry and the investigation was wound up, leaving certain questions, as Billy says, unanswered.'

Clearly unhappy with what he was hearing, Chubb growled.

'All right. Let's say I accept that for the moment. What about this actress? What was so strange about her behaviour?'

'Well, as Billy said, for a start it was a very hot day, yet she chose to go out shortly after two o'clock without telling anyone and when her hosts and the other guests were either resting or otherwise occupied in their rooms. If she hadn't been spotted by a maid she would have slipped out without anyone noticing. It could be argued that was her intention.'

Madden frowned.

'She was an attractive young woman with no shortage of admirers and one can't help but wonder whether she wasn't on her way to meet one of them. Why go out in the blazing heat of the afternoon otherwise? It might not have been so surprising if she had stayed in the garden. But she left it to walk across a field and into a wood, which was where her body was found.'

'And just who might she have been going to meet?' Chubb cocked an eye at Madden. 'Has Angus any ideas about that?'

'Not that I'm aware of. But if she was headed for a rendezvous it was most likely with a man.'

'And you – or rather Angus – now think this imaginary bloke could be the real murderer?'

'It's possible.'

The chief super shook his head again. A rumble of discontent issued from his lips.

'Possible maybe, but not good enough, John, and you know it. It's guesswork. Don't blame Cradock. For once I agree with him. We all know what will happen if he consents to reopen the case. All hell will break loose. It was bad enough the first time round, what with an actress getting herself topped and the Prince of Wales's name being batted about like a ping-pong ball. We won't want to go through all that again if we can help it.'

He peered at his listener.

'Look, Styles here said you were planning to go down to Kent to have a word with Tom Derry and take a look at this pendant. Fine. I've no problem with that. In fact, if you learn anything interesting you might pass it on to us. But if you're going to ask any more questions, for heaven's sake be discreet. I don't want this thing suddenly blowing up in my face; and neither does Cradock.'

He paused to lend weight to his words.

'As for Angus, he'll just have to swallow it. I'll write him a letter explaining why we can't take it any further; not as things stand.' He cocked an eye at his visitor. 'How is he generally – in good spirits?'

'I wouldn't say that.' Madden prepared to get up. 'His gout's playing up again. I left him growling like a bear in his cave.'

'Then like as not he'll bite your head off when you give him the news.' Chubb chuckled.

'I shouldn't be surprised.' Madden rose to his feet. 'Look, I understand your position, Charlie, and I'll do my best to explain it to Angus. Thank you for giving me your time. Helen sends her regards and says she hopes you'll pay us a visit again soon. I'm sure Angus would like to have a word with you as well.'

'I'll bet he would.' Chubb rose to bid his visitor farewell. 'So he can bite my head off too.'

'I'm sorry it's turned out this way, sir.' Billy Styles walked with his old mentor down the corridor from Chubb's office to the head of the stairs. 'I'd like to have given you more support, but . . .'

'But Mr Sinclair doesn't have a strong case.' Madden patted him on the arm. 'Don't worry, Billy. I knew I'd be batting on a tricky wicket. I told Angus I would try, but I didn't really believe we could persuade either Charlie or Cradock to act. It'll take more than that pendant to get them to reopen the inquiry.'

'Mr Sinclair must know that.' Billy was puzzled. 'I just wonder why he's stirring things up. I know he was in charge of the investigation, but only nominally, to judge by the file. It was almost all over by the time he got down there. The Canterbury police arrested the bloke the next day.'

'Yes, only nominally, as you say, but he was still in charge.' Madden paused at the head of the stairs leading down to the lobby. 'And the man was hanged: that's the point to remember. That's why Mr Sinclair is so upset. If he thinks for a moment that they were wrong – that he played some part, no matter how small, in sending an innocent man to the gallows – it'll go on tormenting him. He's always hated capital punishment. He thinks it's barbaric.'

Billy reflected.

'I'm surprised he didn't come up to London himself.' He grinned. 'Then Charlie would have had to face him. He wouldn't have enjoyed that.'

'Oh, he would have come. You can be sure of that. But he's immobilized at the moment. As I told Charlie, it's his gout. Helen has told him he's not to budge from his cottage until his gout eases a little. Even then, I doubt he could manage a trip to London. He's quite crippled at the moment.'

In her role as Highfield's doctor, Madden's wife had overseen the former chief inspector's health ever since his retirement four years earlier.

'Since I was coming up to town anyway I offered to have a word with Charlie in person. Mr Sinclair wrote to him a week ago. He's still waiting for a reply. I'm sure he'll get it in due course – but it won't be the one he was hoping for. I'll have to ring him this evening and give him the bad news.'

Madden started down the stairs, but paused when he caught the look in Billy's eye.

'I was just wondering.' The younger man scratched his head. 'Isn't there something I could do? I'd like to help Mr Sinclair if I can.'

'No, don't do anything, Billy, not for the moment.' Madden was quick to discourage him. 'Charlie's a good sort, but he won't take kindly to having his orders ignored. And

15

as it happens, it's no inconvenience for me to slip down to Kent. I'll be up in London all this week and probably next week too, but not fully occupied. I'm rather looking forward to seeing Tom Derry again. You remember him, don't you?'

'Of course.' Billy grinned in happy recollection. 'That was when we went down to Maidstone together.'

The visit he was recalling had occurred more than a score of years earlier when he had worked under Madden on an investigation into a series of brutal murders that had begun in Highfield but taken them far afield in search of the killer. Their travels had included a trip to Maidstone where the then local CID chief, Tom Derry, an old friend of Sinclair's, had proved to be of particular help.

'Derry was transferred to Canterbury in the Thirties, which is how he came to be involved in the Portia Blake murder. He's retired now, but it was his letter to Mr Sinclair that got the ball rolling. I rang him yesterday and explained about Angus being laid up at the moment and that I was coming down in his place. Derry's also worried that they may have arrested the wrong man.'

'Well, if both of them feel the same way there may be something to it.' Billy frowned.

'Perhaps. I'll know better when I've talked to him.'

Madden started down the stairs.

'Before then, though, I'm going to have to ring Angus and give him the bad news.'

He glanced back over his shoulder.

'Spare a thought for me, would you?'

2

'YES, ANGUS. I see. No, really, I understand. Not at all, Angus – I was happy to be of help. Yes, of course I'll give you a full report when I get back. By the way, are you feeling any better?'

Madden listened with the receiver pressed to his ear; and then, like Chubb earlier in the day, he winced.

'I'm sorry to hear that. Helen did say it might take some time to wear off.'

Again he was silent as he listened to the voice at the other end of the line.

'Quite so. It sounds most unpleasant. We'll talk again very soon. Goodbye for now.'

As he replaced the receiver Madden looked up and saw that his daughter, Lucy, was standing at the bottom of the stairs listening. He hadn't heard her come down from her bedroom upstairs. She was shaking her head.

'Poor Angus.'

'Yes, poor Angus.' Madden scowled. 'But he's certainly making a meal of it.'

'You're being very hard-hearted,' she observed piously.

'Am I?' Madden led the way into the sitting room. 'According to your mother he's the worst patient she's ever had, and I can believe it. I thought he'd be pleased when I told him I was going down to Kent tomorrow. Not a bit of it. He said I should have been more insistent with Chubb, made him see reason.'

'Poor Angus.'

'Will you stop saying that?' Madden caught her eye and she laughed. He stood back to take in her appearance. 'What a lovely dress. Did you make it yourself?'

'Sort of.' Lucy turned slowly about so that he could appreciate the full effect of the tight-waisted, bouffant garment. Cut well below her knees in the so-called New Look – a fashion that like so many had come from Paris (and been much derided by killjoys when it first appeared as a waste of scarce material) – it swirled about her graceful figure in a shimmering blue wave. 'It's an old evening dress of Mummy's which I cut down and made some alterations to. Can you remember her wearing it?'

'Yes, now that you mention it.' Madden's gaze softened. 'You're really very good at this. Are you going to make a career of it?'

It was more than a year now since Lucy had come up to London with the idea of finding a job, and to her parents' surprise had accepted a lowly position in the salon of a well-known dress designer (somewhat to the disappointment of her mother, who still nursed the hope that her unpredictable daughter might eventually realize she had a good mind and try for university).

'But that's what I'm doing, in a way.' Lucy had sought to console her. 'I'm studying, learning things. I'm a bit of a dogsbody at the moment, but that'll change, you'll see.'

'Perhaps I'll have a famous daughter one day.' Madden mused agreeably on the thought. 'We'll all be invited to view the new Lucy Madden collection.'

'You never know. It might happen.' Lucy was busy checking her reflection in the mirror above the mantel. 'I feel I'm abandoning you tonight,' she said. 'Are you sure you'll be all right?'

'I expect I'll manage. I've got Alice to look after me.'

'Dear Alice. She hardly knows what to do with herself now that Aunt Maud's gone. She talks to me about her all the time.'

It was the recent death of Helen's aunt – and Lucy's great-aunt – Maud Collingwood that had brought Madden to London. Surviving well into her nineties, the old lady had passed away peacefully in her bed – as she had always sworn she would – two months earlier and when her will was read Helen and Madden found that she had left them her house in St John's Wood.

'It's not that surprising, I suppose – I was her closest living relative – but what on earth are we going to do with it?'

For a while Helen and her husband had toyed with the idea of letting the house. But the problems of absentee land-lordism had finally persuaded them to sell it.

'We can use the money to buy a flat which Lucy can use,' Helen had pointed out. 'And it can be somewhere for Rob to stay as well when he's in London.' Their son, a naval officer, was presently serving on a cruiser in the Indian Ocean.

The decision having been made, Madden had set himself the task of finding an estate agent to handle the sale and of disposing of such furniture as they did not wish to keep while Lucy, who had been camping with friends in an over-crowded flat in Knightsbridge, had moved to St John's Wood.

'I'd rather not leave Alice in the house on her own,' Helen had explained.

Aunt Maud's long-time maid and companion, Alice Penny had made plans to spend her retirement with her sister and brother-in-law at Hastings, on the south coast, but her move had been delayed by the alterations that would have to be made to their home before they could take her in. In the interim, Helen had insisted that she remain in her late mistress's house and Alice in turn had decided that she would continue to serve as cook and maid there for as long as the Maddens might need her.

Lucy, meanwhile, was busy in front of the mirror putting last-minute touches to her make-up.

'Could you help me with my dress, Daddy? It's those buttons at the back. They're so hard to reach. I don't know how Mummy used to manage. Did she have a maid to help?'

'I should think so. People did in those days.'

Madden came up behind his daughter and began the painstaking job of fitting each small cloth-covered button into its appropriate slit. Glancing at the mirror he saw their faces – Lucy's fresh glowing complexion and his own weathered visage where the lines around his eyes were deeply carved now and his dark hair streaked with grey. As always in summer, when his skin grew tanned, the scar on his forehead – a legacy of the months he had spent in the trenches during the First World War – showed white against the brown skin. She caught his eye in the mirror and smiled.

'When you took me to dinner at Rules the other night we were spotted by a friend of mine, Polly Manners. She rang me next day wanting to know who my madly attractive escort was and did I know any other fascinating-looking older men like him I could introduce her to.'

'Madly attractive!' Madden spluttered. 'What a ridiculous thing to say. And you're much too young to be thinking about older men.'

'Correct me if I'm wrong, but isn't that what's called a contradiction in terms?'

She kissed him on the cheek, and then stood back to examine her reflection in the mirror.

'Don't wait up for me. I won't be back till late.'

'Dancing till dawn again, are you?'

Madden regarded his lovely daughter wistfully. Lucy had inherited not only her mother's looks but also so many of her mannerisms that there were times when he seemed to be seeing Helen in her youth reborn in the golden-haired girl before him.

Lucy shook her head. 'You keep forgetting I've got a job. I have to get up in the morning. You're confusing me with Mummy. It was she and Violet who used to dance the night away. Literally. Violet has told me all about it, how they would gather in Piccadilly at the end of a ball to have breakfast at one of those mobile kitchens. "Ah, the times your mother and I have seen the sun come up over Green Park."'

One of Helen's oldest friends, Lady Violet Tremayne was a fixture of Highfield life.

'Of course, Mummy denies it furiously. She says Violet exaggerates everything. But I know which one of them I believe.'

Lucy put on her stole.

'I wish I were staying in with you tonight. I'd much rather hear about this case of Angus's and what happened at Scotland Yard today. You must promise to tell me all about it when you come back from Kent. I want to know what you find out – every last detail.'

To Madden's surprise, when he had told his daughter about the mission Sinclair had entrusted him with she had reacted instantly to one of the names he had mentioned.

'The Portia Blake murder! Of course I remember that. When I was at St Clare's we used to smuggle copies of the *News of the World* into the dormitory and read it by torch-light under our sheets. She was an actress, wasn't she? She looked lovely in her photographs. It was awful to think of her being strangled that way.'

In the course of her chequered scholastic career Lucy had spent some months at a boarding school in Dorset, one from which her parents had hurriedly removed her when it became apparent from letters sent by the headmistress that she was about to be expelled for persistent misbehaviour.

'We always thought there was more to it than met the eye, the other girls and I. The trouble was the police made an arrest almost at once. It was over so quickly.'

At that moment the bell rang – it was the taxi she had telephoned for earlier – and Madden accompanied his daughter to the front door.

'Oddly enough, that's exactly what Angus says,' he told her as she kissed him goodnight.

3

'IF ONLY SHE hadn't been an *actress*.' Tom Derry scowled at the word. 'It was all Fleet Street needed to start licking its lips. We'd hardly had time to shift the poor woman's body to the mortuary slab in Canterbury when more than a score of them descended on us from London – reporters, photographers . . . the lot. They pretty well laid siege to the house.'

He muttered to himself, as though the memory still had the power to rile him.

'And, of course, it wasn't only that. It was also because of where she was staying: her host, Sir Jack Jessup, was a big name. "Black Jack Jessup" – that's what the newspapers used to call him. Actually he was christened with your name, John. But he was always known as Sir Jack, and preferred to be called that. He'd been quite a lad in his younger days, always in the public eye for one reason or another, and later on he became "one of the Prince of Wales's set", as the press liked to put it then. I don't know how much truth there was in that, though Edward did come down here to stay a couple of times before he abdicated. But it meant the papers could put it all together – actress, Prince of Wales, murder! Well, I don't have to draw a picture for you. It was meat and drink to them.'

He fell silent for a few moments as a flock of sheep materialized on the narrow lane in front of them and he was forced to steer a careful path between their woolly bodies.

'That's also why Angus was sent down from London. As

soon as our chief constable heard about the murder – and that was within an hour or two – he was on the blower to the commissioner in London. He could see what lay ahead and wanted any brickbats that might be coming our way from the press or public spread around, with the Yard getting its fair share. At least that's my opinion.

'And the irony was she had never been much of an actress anyway, Miss Portia Blake. I looked into her background and found she'd only been in a handful of West End plays and one or two films, and always in walk-on parts, never as a lead or anything close to it. But the press boys weren't going to let a little thing like that spoil their party.' He snorted.

Madden glanced across at his companion for the day. Not surprisingly, the former Kent detective had aged with the years. Now quite bald, Derry had also shrunk, at least in Madden's memory as he recalled the lanky individual he had first encountered in Maidstone all those years ago. Like Sinclair, he had retired from the force at the end of the war with the rank of superintendent. But he seemed as alert as ever and had greeted Madden warmly when he had arrived at his cottage on the outskirts of Canterbury earlier that morning.

'I remember the day you came down from London as though it were yesterday,' he had told him. 'Whatever happened to that young cub you had with you?'

'He prospered, I'm happy to say. Billy Styles is his name. He's a detective-inspector at the Yard now and he sends his regards.'

Although Madden and his wife had visited Canterbury more than once to stay with a cousin of Helen's who was married to a local solicitor, they had not done so since the end of the war, when the couple had moved away, and Madden had been shocked by what he'd seen as the taxi from the station had borne him through the city. Accustomed as he was to the sight of bombed-out buildings in London, where the snail's pace of post-war reconstruction had left much of the city still in ruins, he had not expected to see damage on a similar scale in the much smaller confines of Canterbury.

'The Germans used us as a target for any bombs they failed to drop on London,' Derry explained to him later. 'Canterbury was on their way home and they just unloaded whatever they were still carrying before they crossed the coast.'

Luckily the famous cathedral, like St Paul's in London, had survived relatively unscathed, and Madden had turned to look at its imposing spire rising above the town as they set off for their destination.

'You might be interested to see the spot where the murder took place,' Derry had suggested. A widower now like Sinclair, he had provided his visitor with a cup of tea on his arrival and handed him a buff-coloured folder.

'That's a copy of the file the Canterbury police have in their records. They were kind enough to make one for me after I raised the issue with them. I put the letter I got in there. I expect you'd like to read it.'

Madden had removed the envelope from the folder and taken out the letter which was typed on cheap notepaper and addressed to 'Chief Inspector Derry'.

I have reason to believe that the jade pendant accompanying this letter is the same one that disappeared from Miss Portia Blake's body in August 1938.

It had started without ceremony.

Rather than tell you why I suspect this I will leave it to you to establish the truth of the allegation. It should not prove difficult. As you may have noticed there is a slight flaw in the stone. That should be sufficient to identify it.

Since the piece could not have been stolen by the man who was hanged for Miss Blake's murder, the question arises: who else could have taken it?

And why?

I leave the rest to you.

The letter was unsigned.

'Chief inspector?' Madden had examined the piece of notepaper closely to see if it had a watermark. 'Was that your rank then?'

Derry nodded. 'Either the writer knows that or he got it from newspaper files.'

'Could I have a look at the pendant?' Madden had asked.

They had been sitting facing each other in armchairs in Derry's small parlour and without replying the former super-intendent had reached into his pocket and pulled out a velvet bag tied with a drawstring. Turning it upside down, he had leaned across and emptied the contents into his visitor's hand. He had watched as Madden held the stone up to the light. Deep green in colour and suspended from a gold chain, it was carved in the shape of a seated Buddha.

'Yes, I can see what your letter writer means about it being flawed. Mind you, it's hardly visible. And it doesn't spoil the look of it.' Madden had pointed to a line hardly wider than a hair in the plump stomach and paler than the dark green around it. 'How do you plan to check whether it's the same pendant? Is there someone you can ask?'

'Not really. Both Miss Blake's parents died when she was still quite young and she was brought up by an older sister who lives in Ipswich. It was she who collected Portia's things after she died. I spoke to her on the telephone, but she wasn't able to help. She didn't know anything about any pendant.'

Derry shrugged.

'But there is one other possibility. Miss Blake had a flat-mate called Audrey Cooper; another actress. I found her address and phone number in the file and rang her. Unfortunately, she was out of town, but I managed to get hold of some other woman – a flatmate, I gathered – who told me Miss Cooper was on tour in the provinces with a theatrical company. She'll be back in London next week. I thought I'd wait until then to talk to her.'

'But this pendant resembles the one Portia Blake had?'

'Oh, yes. We were given a description of it. She was wearing it at dinner the night before she was murdered and the housemaid who saw her as she was leaving the house next day said she had it on. I can confirm it wasn't among her effects when we searched her room later.'

Madden had studied the note again.

'The wording's strange, isn't it?' he remarked. '*I have reason to believe . . . rather than tell you . . . the question arises . . . I leave the rest to you.* If whoever wrote this had any information regarding the case, why not just come forward and say so? What did you make of it?'

Derry shrugged.

'My first thought was that the writer was playing the fool with us. But although the tone is odd he – or she, though I get the impression the writer is a man – seems to know something; or wants us to believe that he does.'

'But to what purpose, I wonder?' Madden frowned. 'It seems clear that the writer wants the case reopened. But if so, why not point a finger at someone? It's far more likely the police would be interested if they were given a name.'

It was at that point that Derry had suggested they drive out to the village of Burnham, near to where the young woman had been killed.

'You'll understand what's bothering Angus and me better when you've seen the actual murder site.'

Derry had assured his visitor their journey wouldn't take long – the village was only a few miles from Canterbury – and soon after they left the outskirts of the city Madden found they were in the midst of open countryside, a gently rolling landscape which in other parts of England might have been covered with wheat or barley but here was planted with field after field of hops. He saw that the plants had turned from green to yellow, a sign that they were ready for harvesting.

'This is the time of year, the same month in fact, when the Blake woman was murdered.' Derry gestured at the land on either side of them. 'The fields around here were full of hop pickers, just as they are now. Owen Norris, the man convicted of the murder, was one of them. He was an itinerant farm worker; he'd come here for the harvest, same as the others. At the time I thought it was a crime that was unpremeditated; that Norris had come on Miss Blake by chance.'

He glanced at Madden.

'Now I'm not so sure.'

'That's where she left the garden.'

Madden followed the direction of Derry's pointing finger and saw a green wooden gate set in a high brick wall overhung with trailing creepers.

'You can't see the house from here. We'll have to wait until we get higher up into the wood.'

They had left the car in the village half a mile away and walked along a narrow road bounded by the same wall until they reached the field they were crossing now on a path that branched off from the road. Ahead of them was a wooded hillock which Derry had already identified as the spot where Portia Blake had met her end.

'There's another path that leads from the gate.' Again Derry pointed. 'It joins with this one further on and it's the one she took. The strange thing is there were people around when she was killed, and quite nearby, too. If there was someone waiting up there in the wood to do her in – and that's only speculation, mind – then he was certainly taking a chance.'

'People?' Madden glanced inquiringly at him.

'Hop pickers. A party of them had walked here from the village. It was a Sunday, not a working day, and they had been having a drink at the pub and must have crossed this field at almost the same time as Portia Blake came out of that gate. They walked up through the wood and out the other side to where they were camping. Norris had also been at the pub, and drunk too much as usual, or so the landlord said. He'd wanted another drink at closing time but been sent on his way after an argument. He followed the same route as the others – the one we've just taken – but they were some way ahead by this time and he never caught up with them.'

Derry paused to lend significance to his last words.

'Might he have seen Portia Blake entering the wood?' Madden asked.

'He might . . . though he said not.' Derry shrugged. 'Let's go on, shall we?'

They continued, crossing the field and passing the point where the path Portia Blake had taken joined the one they were on, and then walking up the slope to the wooded knoll. When they came to the first of the trees Derry stopped and turned round. Madden followed suit.

'There – now you can see it. That's the house. It's called Foxley Hall. It was bought by one of Jessup's forebears in the last century from a family that dated back to the Conquest. Originally it was a Norman manor, one of the oldest in the country, but it was sacked and burned during the Civil War and then rebuilt in the Dutch style; or so my architecturally minded friends tell me.'

Madden shaded his eyes. It was after midday and the overhead sun was bright. It glinted on the many windows at the front of the house and brought a glow to the red brickwork which was topped by a line of triangular gables, all clearly visible now above the tall garden wall. They were high enough that he could also see the flagged terrace in front of the house and below it, descending in shallow steps, several other terraces decorated with lawns and flower beds, one of them containing a wide lily pond.

'She went out by a side door – that's where she was seen by the maid – and must have come down that yew alley you can see at the edge of the garden.' Derry's pointing finger had shifted. 'She wouldn't have been spotted walking down – the hedges form a tunnel – so it doesn't look as though anyone in the house could have noticed her.'

'Is the house empty now?' Madden asked. He could see that the ground-floor windows were shuttered.

Derry nodded. 'Sir Jack died here in 'thirty-nine, shortly after the war started. The lady he lived with moved out soon afterwards. He only had one child, a son named Richard – Sir Richard now – and he was away on active service for most of the war. When it was over he decided he didn't want to live here and the house was let to tenants. Lately he's decided to sell it and I'm told it's going to be turned into a school. Apart from a caretaker, no one lives here now. You can see that the garden's been allowed to go.'

Madden nodded. He had divined as much from the untrimmed hedges and empty borders.

'The lady Sir Jack *lived* with, you say?'

'A Mrs Castleton, she was, Adele Castleton.' Derry smiled.

'I wouldn't say she was notorious exactly, but she'd certainly had her name in the papers often enough before she hooked up with Jessup. He was still married, but his wife wouldn't give him a divorce. I believe he and Mrs Castleton had been together for some time, living as man and wife, but not legally hitched. I must say I thought her a damned attractive woman when I met her. Not young any more, but I could understand any man losing his head over her.' He shook his head in rueful memory.

Madden had turned from studying the house to listen to him. 'I'd be interested to know who was staying with them that weekend,' he said. 'Do you still have the names?'

Derry nodded. 'They're in the file. We interviewed them all briefly. Initially, we just wanted to know where they were when the murder took place. We were going to question them again, in detail, but when Norris was arrested – that was only two days after the murder – the investigation was wound up and we never got to do it. They weren't a particularly interesting bunch. But one in particular did catch my eye: a Mr Stanley Wing. I don't mind admitting I didn't like the look of him. He was a business associate of Sir John's, some kind of oriental; not pure Chinese; a half-breed I would say. He certainly had a touch of the chink about him. I don't know if you're aware of it, but the Jessup family fortune was made in Hong Kong.'

Madden nodded. 'Jessup's are one of the great trading companies out there – *hongs* they're called. You were telling me about this man Wing . . . ?'

'There's not much to tell.' Derry shrugged. 'As it happened, I interviewed him myself. He said he had come down from London for the weekend at Sir Jack's invitation and had brought Portia Blake with him. There was nothing to tie him to her murder, no obvious motive. But as I say, I had a feeling about him. He seemed to me the sort of man you wouldn't put anything past.'

'Were they together, he and Portia Blake – as a couple, I mean?' Madden frowned.

'I don't believe so.' Derry shook his head. 'You can check it in the file, but my recollection is he simply said they were acquainted and that he had driven her down from London at Sir Jack's invitation to spend the weekend.'

'Where was he when she was murdered?'

'In his room, resting, he said. So were most of the other guests. As I told you, we never got round to checking their alibis.'

'What was it about him that you didn't like? Was it something he said?'

Again Derry shook his head.

'No, it was the man himself. He didn't seem bothered by Miss Blake's death. In fact, he didn't show any emotion at all. He just stared at me with those black eyes of his.'

He clicked his tongue in irritation.

'The trouble is, this all happened over ten years ago. The people who were in the house that weekend, staff and guests, are mostly scattered; and as you'll see from the file, some of them are dead.

'Here we are, then.'

Derry took off his hat and wiped his bald pate with a handkerchief. Their walk from the village along the road and across the sun-bruised meadow had been warm work.

'This is the spot. She was found lying inside that ruin; so whoever murdered her – whether Norris or some other man – must have either killed her there or else dragged her body inside with the idea of hiding it. But it turned out to be visible from the path; it was spotted through the doorway by these young boys. They were the ones who raised the alarm.'

The former superintendent paused to give his companion time to take in the scene. Madden looked about him. Out of the bright sunlight now, they stood in the dark shadow cast by trees in full summer leaf. Hard beside them was an old stone wall, part of a ruined structure that had once been a small hut, though little remained of it apart from the walls and the uneven brick floor. They had followed the path through the wood until they had reached the crest of the knoll, at which point Derry had veered off it and Madden had spotted the ruin through the trees.

'These lads – there were three of them – had come from the opposite direction; they were on their way to the village and one of them saw something lying just inside the doorway.' Derry pointed to the dark recess. 'He was curious enough to come over and have a look to see what it was. As I say, her body was lying inside the hut but close to the doorway. It must have been her face that he spotted; it was pale enough to show up in the dark.'

'The killer was careless, then.' Madden frowned. 'If he'd taken the trouble to drag the body into a corner it probably wouldn't have been found for hours, not until after a search for her had been made. That sounds more like the man you arrested, more like the act of a casual killer rather than someone who was lying in wait for her.'

'True.' Derry nodded. 'But it could be that these boys forced the killer's hand. They told us they had been chatting as they came up through the wood, and being young lads they were probably making a racket. The murderer, whoever he was, would have heard them and he may have decided to get moving while he still had a chance to escape unobserved.'

He put his hat back on and then paused to reflect.

'Let's look at this first from the point of view of Norris being the killer,' he said. 'Let me explain how we came to arrest him and charge him so quickly. We knew by calculating how long it would have taken him to walk from the pub that he would have been a few minutes behind Portia Blake when she began walking up the path into the wood. It's possible he could have spotted her from the road and quickened his pace to catch up with her. We also know that Miss Blake got no further than this ruined house; if she had gone on, the boys coming up the hill from the fields on the other side would have seen her. So if Norris killed her it must mean he caught up with her at the top of the hill and probably dragged her off the path and into this hut. We believed that he meant to rape her and was probably trying to silence her by choking her, using her scarf to do it. But he'd overdone it, we reckoned, and killed her by mistake, after which there was nothing he could do but make himself scarce.'

He glanced at Madden, as if to gauge his reaction.

'I expect Angus told you, but the reason we were able to arrest him so quickly – it was only two days after the murder – was because he tried to sell some earrings Miss Blake was wearing to a Canterbury jeweller. They were also made of jade, carved in the shape of dragons, but paler in colour than the pendant, and we knew they were missing from the body because the maid who had spotted her going out remembered she was wearing them. Norris was trying to sell the earrings to the jeweller together with the girl's wristwatch, which was also missing. We'd already put out a description of the earrings and the jeweller simply got his assistant to call the police and kept Norris there long enough for them to turn up and arrest him.'

Madden pondered.

'Am I right in thinking he denied the murder at first?' he asked.

'That's correct.' Derry nodded. 'His story was that he'd spotted her body from the path just as the boys had and simply stolen the stuff off it; nothing more. Well, we didn't believe him for a start, and even less so when we checked with Central Records at the Yard and discovered he'd done time for attempted rape. He'd been caught in the act of assaulting a young woman near Pontypridd, in Wales. There was no doubt about it, either; he'd torn off most of her clothes and was on top of her when her cries were heard by a couple of farm workers who came to her rescue. Norris was given eight years. He'd only been out for a few months when this happened. We reckoned he must have been ready to try again after all that time in stir. But as I say, he denied murdering her or trying to rape her. He would only cough to the theft at first. But after we'd interrogated him for a day or two he changed his mind and signed a confession.'

'In other words, he cracked?' Madden's voice was sharp and Derry caught his eye.

'I know what you're thinking.' He scowled. 'We all know that people can be made to confess to things they didn't do if they're denied sleep and questioned without a break for long enough. But that didn't happen with Norris.' He looked hard at Madden. 'I'm not saying we didn't push him, but I made it clear to the team of detectives I had with me – and Angus can confirm this – that he wasn't to be bullied and browbeaten into saying anything he didn't mean.'

'I accept that.' Madden nodded. 'But it does seem to me he changed his story rather suddenly.'

Derry shrugged.

'The truth is right from the start he seemed ready to give

in; half a dozen times he appeared to be on the point of confessing and that only made us more sure that we'd arrested the right man. I had the impression he didn't want to go on with his denials; that he was tired of the struggle; that he wanted to end it. So when he agreed to sign a confession – this was two days after we'd arrested him – I wasn't surprised. I'd been expecting it.'

'But now you don't feel the same way?'

'I wouldn't go that far; not yet.' Derry grimaced. 'I just wonder now if it wasn't life he was sick of; his own, I mean; if he hadn't had enough of it. His family had disowned him after the attempted rape conviction – I learned that later. They were Chapel – very religious. They didn't want anything to do with him. None of them came to his trial at Maidstone.'

'Yet he went back on his confession later.'

Derry nodded. 'At the trial he did, but the judge wasn't having it – he made that clear in his summing-up – and Norris seemed to accept it. I remember watching his face when the jury returned its verdict. He shut his eyes when he heard the foreman's words. That was all. Then he seemed to sink back into himself. He didn't speak again. He was hanged at Pentonville the following January. Angus and I were both there. It's a nasty business, a hanging. Thank God neither of us has ever had to attend another.'

While he'd been talking Derry's stoop had grown more pronounced and now he moved away from Madden and went to the single window aperture in the wall behind them. Brushing off the ledge he sat down.

'I can't stand for too long these days,' he explained. 'I need to take the weight off my old pins.' He fanned his face with his hat.

'Tell me about the pendant now.' Madden frowned. 'What part did it play in the investigation?'

'Not much, as it turned out.' Derry had given some thought to his answer. 'But one thing I can tell you is that Norris didn't take it. At first we assumed he had, along with the other stuff, but he was adamant; it was the one thing he stuck to. Quite simply, he didn't know what we were talking about. We had to explain to him what it was – a green stone hanging around her neck. He swore he had never seen it and by the end I believed him. He'd confessed to everything else, after all, so why not that? His defence counsel raised the point during his trial. He said the fact that the pendant was missing suggested that someone else might have killed the girl. But the judge wasn't buying it.'

'What did you think had happened to it? At the time, I mean?'

'That it must have been lost, torn off in the struggle she'd most likely had with him. She had a small handbag with her when she left the house; it was hanging from her shoulder by a strap. The maid who saw her told us that. We discovered it lying in a bush near the hut. It looked as though it had fallen or been thrown there. Norris said he couldn't remember seeing it and we were inclined to believe him since there was a gold compact with an enamelled top inside it, a pretty thing that he certainly would have taken and tried to sell if he had seen it.'

'Did he tell you they had fought?'

Derry shook his head. 'The fact is he didn't have much to say, not off his own bat. Once he'd confessed to the killing he seemed to think that was it and he needn't say anything more. We had to keep prodding him. It was mostly a matter of question and answer. We would ask him, for instance, if he had grabbed her from behind and he would nod. Then we'd have to insist he say the word "yes" so that it could be written down for the interview. It was the same with most of the other details. Did he drag her to the hut, and so on? Each time we had to get him to agree it had been so.'

'So in effect you wrote his confession for him?'

'You could put it that way.' Derry looked displeased.

'Go on about the pendant, would you?' Madden spoke after a moment.

'Well, the area around the hut had been searched as a matter of course, but after it became clear that it was missing I widened the area considerably and made sure every inch of ground was gone over, but without result. So we still couldn't explain for certain how the pendant had disappeared. But it wasn't crucial to the inquiry. It was possible she had lost it somewhere else in the wood: perhaps she managed to break free from Norris and he had to chase her and it came off. We thought it might still be lying here somewhere, hidden by dead leaves.'

'Charlie Chubb suggested that might be the explanation.' Madden grunted. 'For what it's worth, he pointed out that it wasn't uncommon for investigations to end with a few questions still unanswered.'

Derry nodded in agreement. 'That was what we told ourselves – Angus and I. And it's what's bothering us now. Did we make a mistake in shrugging it off as just one of those things? If this turns out to be the same pendant' – he tapped his jacket pocket – 'then perhaps we did.'

Madden took off his jacket. He slung it over his shoulder. Derry had put his hat back on but was not yet ready to move from his seat on the window ledge. He sat there gnawing at his lip.

'Let's consider the alternative,' Madden said. He stirred the dead leaves at his feet with the toe of his shoe. 'Supposing it was someone else who murdered her – how could he have managed to do that, given there were so many people about? How is it nobody saw him?'

'I've wondered that myself.' Derry mopped his face. 'You might even say the question has been occupying my mind to the exclusion of all others since I received that note.'

'The suggestion has been made that Miss Blake might have gone out that afternoon to meet someone: that she had a rendezvous arranged in the wood or somewhere near it and that whoever she went to meet might be the person who murdered her.'

'Angus and I discussed that possibility. We spoke on the phone a few days ago. If she was coming here to meet a man he could well have been waiting for her in this hut.'

Madden frowned. 'If Norris was no more than a few minutes behind her, as you say, that wouldn't have left much time for the murderer to act. He must already have had it in mind to kill her.'

'That's a fair assumption.' Derry nodded.

'And that would make him a very different kind of killer.'

The Kent detective shrugged.

Madden continued to stare at the ground; he was lost in thought.

'The next question then is how did he escape?' He looked up. 'What route would he have taken?'

Derry rose from his seat and looked about him.

'Well, he didn't use the path, obviously, or he would have run into either Norris or those young boys who were coming from the opposite direction. He must have made his way through the wood, which would have meant crossing the path and going straight on until he hit the road, which is over there.'

He pointed over Madden's shoulder.

'But he could equally have taken the other direction, slipping out the back of this hut and going on until he came out of the trees into the fields, where he might well have been noticed by some of the hop pickers. On balance, I think he would have headed for the road. But where he went after that is anyone's guess. He might have had a car handy; or he might have strolled into the village. Once he had put some distance between himself and Miss Blake's body he would no longer have been an object of suspicion. Depending on how he was dressed, he could even have passed as just another picker.'

Shrugging, he glanced at his watch.

'But I see it's after twelve. What do you say to a bite of lunch in the pub? We can talk about it some more there.'

'I remember you,' Madden said. 'I saw you fight at the White City before the first war. Nineteen twelve, was it? Your opponent was a Frenchman. You knocked him out in the fourth round. You weren't Mr William Batty then.' He nodded to a wooden board on the wall behind the bar where the legend *Wm. Batty, prop.* was depicted in faded gold lettering. 'You were Kid Cannon.'

The landlord's battered face broke into a broad grin. Though he looked to be in his sixties now, with short grey hair, a crooked nose and a belly that threatened to overflow his trousers, he was still recognizable as the fresh-faced young man pictured in boxing trunks standing with his fists raised in a photograph hanging beside the board.

He slid the pint of bitter he had just pulled across the bar.

'That's for remembering, sir. It's on the house.'

'Thank you, Mr Batty.' Madden raised the glass to his lips, but then paused when he caught the other's eye. The landlord was giving him a strange look. 'What is it?'

'I wouldn't have taken you for a copper,' William Batty said.

Madden smiled. 'Well, you're half right,' he conceded. 'I used to be with the force. But I quit years ago. How did you guess?'

'I recognized that old fellow you came in with.' Batty nodded towards the back of the pub where Derry had wandered off a few moments earlier in search of a lavatory. 'I remember him from when a young woman was murdered here before the war. He took a statement from me.' He paused. 'I was just wondering why he'd turned up again. There's not more trouble, is there?'

Madden shook his head. 'Mr Derry's retired. He was just showing me where that murder happened, taking me over the ground. We worked together on another murder case years ago. That's how we got to know each other. I was down in Canterbury and he offered to drive me out here.'

He thought for a moment.

'Incidentally, do you recall the man they arrested drinking in your pub on the day of the murder?'

'Too right, I do.' The old boxer's friendly grin showed where two of his front teeth were missing. 'He was always the last to leave, always wanting one more beer. That day was no different and since I'd already called time, I told him to hop it.'

'Did he ever give you any trouble?'

'Was he violent, do you mean – up for a fight?' Batty's grin widened. 'Not a chance. Not him. He was the whiny sort. He used to sit in a corner drinking on his own. He never joined in. I thought he looked sorry for himself.' He shrugged. 'Maybe he had reason.'

'Were you surprised when you heard he'd been arrested?'

'Surprised?'

'Did you think it likely he could have killed someone? Did he seem to be the type?'

'Would I have taken him for a murderer, you mean?' The landlord stroked his cropped head thoughtfully. 'No, I don't think so. But then you can never tell, can you? You can never be sure.'

'Sure?'

'You think you know people, but you don't.' Batty shook his head ruefully. 'Not really.'

Derry had reappeared while he was speaking. Madden turned to acknowledge his companion.

'I've been explaining to Mr Batty here that you've been giving me a Cook's tour of the murder site. He's wondering why you're taking the trouble.'

'Is he now?' Tom Derry favoured the landlord with his flat copper's stare. 'Well, let him. And in the meantime he can draw me a pint of whatever it is you're drinking – I seem to recall they serve a good brew here – and put up a plate of sandwiches for us while he's at it.'

They had walked from the wood back to the village, a distance of less than a mile by the road but somewhat longer by the route they had followed after Madden had asked Derry if he could show him where the hop pickers were at work.

'I'm a farmer now. I'm curious. I've never seen a hop harvest in progress.'

Returning to the path, they had continued along it, eventually coming out of the trees to find that on this side of the wood the hop fields stretched into the distance as far as the eye could see. Soon they were walking along a deep lane flanked by long lines of trailing plants where the pickers were busy filling bins with the cone-like flowers that contained the resins and oils used to impart an agreeably bitter taste to ale and beer. The scent of them was overwhelming in the hot summer air.

'It's like a pilgrimage every year.'

Derry gestured at the lines of pickers, many of them wearing straw hats against the hot sun. Men and women seemed equally represented and Madden saw that there were children working there as well, their small fingers nimble and well adapted to picking the flowers.

'Whole families turn up, many of them from London. They do it to escape the heat in the city and although the work's hard it's something of a holiday, for the kids at least. They go swimming in the river when they get the chance. By the end of the summer they're as brown as berries.'

Proof of his words came a few moments later when they reached the end of the field and turned into a much wider avenue where a line of huts with corrugated-iron roofs stood and where a group of younger children, some no more than three or four years old, were playing in a circle under the eyes of a grey-haired woman busy herself at a washing-tub.

'A lot of these kids get conceived down here, too, I've been told.' Derry had grinned. 'Hopkins, they're called. Everything's rough and ready and if the weather's fine like it is now a lot of people sleep out. There's no telling what goes on under the stars.'

'And Norris was a part of all this, was he?' Madden had been curious.

'Hardly. These are families. They stick together. Like I say, he had no one. He probably slept rough, got his food where he could, did his work and then drank his wages away at the pub.'

'After he'd stolen that stuff from the body, where did he go?' Madden had paused to look up and down the long line of huts.

'Not back here. He was never seen again by the team he'd been picking with. When we caught him in Canterbury he was dirty and unshaven and said he had slept out the two nights preceding. His story was he had realized what a fool he had been to take the jewellery off the body and panicked. He knew if he was caught he wouldn't be believed, not with his record. In the end he had decided to try and get rid of the stuff as quickly as he could and scarper. What worries me now is that he may have been telling the truth.'

Madden had been silent at that point. Running the facts as Derry had reported them through his mind he had hit on what he thought was a snag.

'Assuming that Norris wasn't the killer, he must have come on the body *after* the boys found it' – he had finally given voice to his doubts – 'after the sound of their voices had scared off the real murderer. But is that possible?'

'I'm afraid it is.' Derry had looked glum. 'After their discovery the lads ran to the village to alert the local bobby, an officer called Duckworth: he retired a few years ago and went to live in Maidstone. I've spoken to him: there's nothing new he can add to what we know. The boys didn't think to leave one of their number behind to stay by the body and it must have been all of ten minutes before they came back with Duckworth.'

'But if Norris was innocent surely they would have run into him on the way. He was coming *from* the village after all.'

'Not necessarily.' Derry shook his head. 'Before we even got to the question of the murder, while we were still establishing his movements, he told us he had stopped for a leak in the wood on the way back from the pub, which sounded reasonable given the amount of beer he'd put away. Later, when we questioned him about the boys, he said he'd left the path and gone into the bushes to relieve himself and didn't see or hear them when they ran past, and given the fact that he was the worse for wear from drink at the time that may well have been true.'

'That's agreed then, is it? You'll take the pendant back to London with you? It'll be more use there than down here.'

Derry weighed the velvet bag in his hand.

'If you can find the time to show it to that woman Portia Blake shared a flat with you'd be doing Angus and me a favour, and saving me a trip to London. As I said, she'll be back next week, and her phone number is in the file.'

He handed the bag to Madden, who loosened the drawstring and drew out the pendant. Their conversation inside the pub had been interrupted by the arrival of a party of pickers, a noisy group eager to down as much beer as they could in the short lunch break allowed them. At Batty's suggestion the two men had taken their glasses and the sandwiches he had made for them outside into a small courtyard where tables and chairs were set.

Derry watched now as Madden held the pendant up before his eyes. The green stone glinted in the sunlight.

'The fellow who sent that to me – could he be the killer, do you think?'

Surprised by the question, Madden stared at him.

'It's the teasing tone of the letter. I can't get it out of my mind. It's almost as though he wants to play games with us.'

'Now . . . after all this time?'

'Maybe he's bored,' Derry suggested. 'Perhaps he thinks he's so far separated from the murder in time that he can afford to have some fun at our expense.'

Madden weighed the question.

'But would he really take such a chance simply to amuse himself?' he asked. 'Surely it would be better to let sleeping dogs lie.' Pondering the question, he chewed his lip. 'But he's playing some sort of game, isn't he?'

Derry snorted. 'In that case, I wish he'd be kind enough to tell us the rules.'

Madden glanced at his watch.

'We'd better be getting back to Canterbury. My train leaves in half an hour.'

He put the pendant back in its bag.

'I will take this with me if you like. I'll ring that woman Portia Blake shared a flat with next week and try and arrange to show it to her. There's no point in us racking our brains until we know whether it's the same pendant. Let's hope she can help.'

'And take this, too, while you're at it.'

Derry pushed the file across the table.

'I've done all I can from this end.'

4

BILLY STYLES SAT BACK from the table with a sigh. He rubbed his stomach appreciatively.

'My word that was good, sir! Pheasant, you say?'

'But only out of a tin.' Madden was apologetic.

'Still . . .' Billy sighed again. 'The truth is I can't remember what the real thing tastes like. It's been so long,' he reflected. 'You keep thinking it's going to end, don't you, the rationing and the queuing and the shortages, but it just goes on and on. It's like the war never ended. At least, that's what Elsie says.'

He was referring to his wife, whose complaint was one heard often these days. Towards the end of the preceding year the government had suddenly relaxed controls on a wide range of products, prompting hopes that the corner had at last been turned: that the relentless burden of economic austerity which a war-weary Britain had borne since the end of hostilities in 1945 would finally be lifted. And so it had seemed – for a while. Then, in March of that year, the meat ration, pitiful though it was, had been cut yet again, and while sweets had come off the ration the following month, to the delight of millions of children, they had gone back on the restricted list almost at once thanks to the huge demand for them. In the circumstances, Madden couldn't help but feel guilty over the relatively sumptuous meal he had been able to offer his old protégé whom he had invited to dinner at St John's Wood after learning that he was living a bachelor life, Elsie having taken their three children up to Bedford to spend a fortnight of the summer holidays with their grandmother.

'It's time I confessed to knowledge of a grave offence which I've kept silent about for years,' he said now as they rose from the table. 'I'm sorry to say Aunt Maud was a shameless exploiter of the black market. There's a cupboard in the kitchen full of questionable items. I've never had the nerve to tell you. You might have felt obliged to arrest her. I did raise the issue with her several times, but to no effect. She seemed to take the view that at her age she was safe from the clutches of the law.'

'She was probably right.' Billy chuckled. 'I can't see anyone having the nerve to haul an old lady like her into court. Mind you, it's turned into something of a joke now, rationing; a bad joke, that is. It's not only spivs who break the law; regular grocers do the same if they think they can get away with it. Elsie says she's seen them slip stuff under the counter to favoured customers. It used to be that everyone was prepared to go without – it was the patriotic thing to do. Not any longer.'

Madden sighed. 'Be that as it may, I must get rid of this stuff before the estate agents start showing the house. I'm going to put it in the hands of a couple of them starting at the end of the month. You wouldn't care for a tin or two of caviar, would you?'

'I don't think so, sir.' Billy's grin widened. 'For one thing, I've never tasted the stuff; for another, Elsie would want to know where it came from and next thing the neighbours would be talking about it and then the whole street would know.'

'I see your point. But there's a fine Stilton sitting in there which I hope you'll take home with you when you go. Elsie won't object to that, I'm sure. And I can offer you a glass of good cognac now. Aunt Maud bought only the best.'

Madden led the way into the sitting room and having seated his guest in one of the two armchairs that still remained – the process of getting rid of the furniture was already under way – busied himself at the drinks tray.

'I must say Lucy's looking lovelier than ever.' Billy smothered a yawn. 'She's what the Yanks call a knockout.'

Madden's daughter had joined them earlier for a quickly swallowed meal before going out. She had been collected by a young man driving a sports car.

'Is that the boyfriend?' Billy had asked. Treated since time immemorial as one of the family by the Maddens – he had held their baby daughter in his arms – he felt entitled to ask the question.

'Oh, I don't think so.' Madden had dismissed the notion. 'He's not special so far as I know. None of them seem to be.' He mused on his words. 'Just between us I think she takes after her mother. According to Lady Violet, Helen had a string of admirers when she was Lucy's age; all full of hope, all doomed to disappointment.'

'She was waiting for the right man then, was she?'

Billy caught his old chief's eye and smiled. Madden handed him his glass. Billy sniffed the rich fumes.

'Before I go, sir, can we have a last word about this Portia Blake business? I'm still not sure what you think. Do you agree with Mr Sinclair and Mr Derry that the investigation should be reviewed?'

Although they had talked about the case at length over dinner Billy felt he still hadn't plumbed the depths of Madden's mind on the subject. His old chief had been open enough about the former superintendent's misgivings following his return from Canterbury, but had given little indication of his own views.

'I'm quite ready to raise the matter again with Mr Chubb if you think that's on the cards. But I should warn you he'll need something more than that pendant if he's going to change the AC's mind.'

Madden picked up the object from a low table beside him and held it up to the light. Earlier he had shown the small jade Buddha to Billy and pointed out the faint flaw in the dark green stone.

'I realize that,' he said, 'and to answer your question, I'm still not sure. Derry seems to feel that, if we can show it's the one that belonged to Portia Blake, that should be enough to get the wheels of the law moving again. But I don't agree. It doesn't necessarily follow that they arrested the wrong man. It all depends on who sent the pendant to Derry and how the sender acquired it in the first place. One can't rule out the possibility that whoever is behind this has no connection to the original police investigation: that having come into possession of the pendant in some way and being familiar with the details of the case, he has either seen a way of using it to his advantage or is simply bent on making mischief. But let's stick to the facts.'

He put down the pendant and picked up the folder Derry had given him.

'Assuming we can establish that this is Miss Blake's pendant, the next step would be to look at the guests who were staying at the house that weekend. Their names are all in this file. I imagine you'll find them in your own records. If Cradock changes his mind and gives the go-ahead for the investigation to be reopened I can hand it all over to the Yard. But it might be as well in the meantime if we try to ascertain now just who these people are and where they are living.'

'I could help,' Billy said. 'It wouldn't be going against orders just to locate them, and we can do that a lot more easily than you can.'

'Most of them should be easy enough to find.' Madden had the file open. 'They include a Lord and Lady Cairns and a Mr Rex Garner. I don't know who they are but Derry said they were all society figures. Garner's wife was there with him, but she died during the war. Sir Jack's son, Richard Jessup, was present at dinner on the Saturday night. He had come down from London, but he didn't stay the weekend. He left directly after lunch the next day; at that point Portia Blake was still alive. The local vicar and his wife were dinner guests, but he passed away during the war according to Derry. Sir Jack himself died in 1939, but the lady he lived with – a Mrs Castleton – is still with us. She might be worth talking to, and the son as well, Sir Richard as he is now. He took over the chairmanship of Jessup's before his father died. They've got an office in the City.'

He looked up.

'As I said, if Cradock has a change of heart I'll leave it all to you. But if he keeps digging in his heels I might have a word with one or two of them myself, particularly if they're here in London. Angus will expect it of me. I hope Charlie won't take offence.'

'I'm sure he won't.' Billy tossed off the last of his cognac. 'He hasn't said so, but I get the feeling he'd like to move on this. He just needs a good reason.'

About to rise, he paused. He saw that Madden had something more to say.

'There's one more name in here and I've left it till last.' He tapped the folder again. 'He's going to present the biggest problem, but unfortunately he may turn out to be the most important from your point of view. His name is Stanley Wing.

He was a business associate of Sir Jack Jessup's, an oriental, part Chinese. Derry took against him. He didn't like his manner. While that might simply have been a reaction to the fact that he was foreign and had "a touch of the chink about him", as Derry rather indelicately put it, I think there was more to it than that. Tom Derry had a lifetime of experience in dealing with criminal types. If he felt there was something off about this man Wing, I'd be inclined to take him seriously. The trouble is, the Jessup family's business is based in Hong Kong and I suspect that's where Wing is most likely to be found. That might involve sending an inquiry to the police there. You'd have to check with Charlie before you could do that.'

'Did Mr Derry have any reason to suspect him?'

'Not that I'm aware of. But he brought Miss Blake down from London with him. What's not clear is how well they knew each other. Derry was shocked by how little reaction he showed to her death. But that may just have been his way.'

'The inscrutable oriental, you mean?' Billy grinned.

'Something of the sort.' Madden's tone was dry. 'Anyway, if this inquiry is reopened he's bound to figure in it one way or another so we'd better try and locate him. As Derry pointed out, there's been a war since Miss Blake was murdered and, among other things, Hong Kong was occupied by the Japanese. Most of the Europeans living there were interned in camps; a number of them didn't survive the experience and there's no telling what might have happened to Wing, where he might have ended up. He was closely associated with them.'

He put down the file.

'There's no evidence he was involved in Portia Blake's death. But it was he who brought her down to Kent and one has to wonder why. She wasn't well known as an actress; not a name to conjure with. And it's unlikely that she knew Jessup personally; she wouldn't have been part of his set.'

He looked at Billy.

'So what was she doing there? Perhaps Wing can supply the answer. But you'll have to find him first.'

5

'You didn't waste any time, did you, George?'

Madden's voice held a wistful note. He cast a regretful glance over the scene before him.

'You've certainly been busy in my absence.'

When last he had stood where he was, beneath the arched entrance to his stable yard, the surrounding fields had been gold with ripened corn. Now harvested, but not yet ploughed for next year's crop, the bare, stubbled acres wore a desolate look.

'We couldn't wait, sir.' George Burrows, his farm manager, was apologetic. 'There was no telling how long the fine weather would last. We didn't want the harvest spoiled.'

'I understand. And you were quite right. I was stuck in London. I couldn't get away.'

'It was a better year than last, sir.' Burrows sought to cheer his employer. 'And we'll be getting a good price for it.'

That much at least was true. With food subsidies still high up on the government's list of post-war priorities, farmers remained a pampered segment of the population. But Madden's personal satisfaction derived from humbler roots. Like a boy with a new toy, he had been looking forward to watching the Deere harvester they had bought in the spring, an American machine shipped to England during the war, second-hand but with relatively little wear and tear on it, go about its work. Now he would have to wait for another year.

He glanced at his watch. Although it was only mid-afternoon, too early to think of going home, he felt the prick of conscience. He had returned from London the previous day and with the excuse of having much to catch up with both at home and here at the farm had managed so far to avoid dropping in on Angus Sinclair, who he knew would be waiting anxiously for any news he might have brought back.

'I've really nothing to pass on to him that he doesn't know already,' Madden had told his wife. Helen had been at the station to meet him and Lucy when they had returned home for the weekend. 'He's bound to be disappointed.'

Later that evening, at supper, he had brought them both up to date on the inquiries he had been making on the chief inspector's behalf.

'Did you ever know Jack Jessup?' he had asked Helen. 'He must have been a figure in society before and after the First World War. I was thinking you might have run into him.'

'Daddy's being diplomatic,' Lucy had interrupted. 'He means when you were going to all those parties with Violet.'

'Thank you, my dear. I'd never have guessed.' Helen smiled sweetly. She turned to her husband. 'No, I don't think I did. He would have been quite a lot older than the people we went around with. But I remember what they called him: Black Jack Jessup. He was supposed to cut rather a dashing figure.'

'And you wouldn't have known his son, of course?'

'He would have been too young. He can't be much more than forty now. Why do you ask?'

'I may have to go and see him, though I want to talk to Angus about it first. As things stand there's really nothing more than that pendant to indicate that they might have arrested the wrong man, and it's not enough in itself. The Yard won't move on this unless something more turns up.'

'Then why are Angus and Mr Derry pushing so hard to get the case reopened?' Helen had put the same question that Billy had asked earlier. 'They must know that.'

'I'm sure they do.'

'Then *why*?' Lucy had persisted with the query.

Madden had hesitated before replying. It was a question he had asked himself, and he was still not sure he had the right answer.

'It's not that easy to explain,' he said, 'and I may be wrong. But it's to do with the feeling they both have that they may have made a mistake. Bear in mind these were two very experienced detectives who had every reason to believe at the time that they were dealing with an open-and-shut case. Norris wasn't just the obvious suspect: he almost begged to be arrested and charged. He was close to the scene of the crime; he admitted to stealing jewellery from the victim's body; he had a record that appeared to single him out as precisely the kind of violent criminal they were looking for; and to cap it all, he confessed. In the circumstances there can't be many detectives who wouldn't have come to the same conclusion as they did. I know I would.'

'Even though this man Norris tried to retract his confession?'

'Even so. Remember that only happened when he came to trial, and as every policeman knows – and judges too – it's a ploy criminals often try. That wouldn't have been enough to sway me.'

'Then what's behind it?'

'Something they both find hard to put into words, though Derry gave me a clue to it when we talked. It's Norris's confession – not the fact of it, but the way in which it came about. He wasn't bullied into talking. Derry assured me of that and, even if he hadn't, I worked with Angus long enough to know he would never have permitted such a thing to happen. Derry was convinced Norris *wanted* to confess – that he was just waiting for an opportunity to do so. Now he wonders – and perhaps Angus does too – what brought that on? Was it simple guilt, as they assumed at the time, or something more complex? His life was in ruins, after all. His family had disowned him. Had he come to the end of himself? That's what Derry wondered. Had he had enough?'

Madden paused to let his words sink in.

'What I think is that Norris's behaviour may have left a seed of doubt in both of them, something they weren't really aware of at the time, something subconscious. It's been lying there all these years and the pendant turning up this way has reawakened it. Now they both want the investigation reviewed, and if it turns out they were wrong it can only do harm to their reputations. Yet they still insist on it. That fact alone speaks louder than words.'

He shrugged.

'But it's only a supposition, and I'm not going to put it to Angus. For all I know I may be wide of the mark and I don't want to upset him even more. All I can tell him at present is that Chubb and Cradock are both aware of the situation, and that Charlie at least is open to any suggestions. However, I doubt that will be enough to improve Angus's mood and I expect to be hauled over the coals when I pluck up the courage to go and see him.'

'Don't be too sure. You may be in for a surprise.' Helen smiled. 'I'm hoping you'll find him chastened. I told him this morning he had to stop behaving like a bear with a sore head, snapping at me every time I looked in on him. That I had no magic wand I could wave to make him feel better. He would just have to be patient.'

Not altogether encouraged by her words – patience had never been his old friend's strong suit – Madden had contrived to avoid passing by his cottage on his way to the farm that morning. But now, with no further reason to delay, he waved goodbye to Burrows and set off down the winding road that led to the bottom of the valley where there was a stream with a path running alongside it that passed by the chief inspector's abode.

'Wing, you say? The oriental gentleman? I didn't speak to him myself, but Derry took a dislike to him, I recall. He was planning to question him again, and in more detail. But then Norris was arrested.'

Seated in the shade of an apple tree, with his right foot, encased in a loose felt slipper, resting on a well-cushioned stool, Angus Sinclair frowned.

'We had nothing on him. Other than the fact that he'd brought the Blake woman down to Kent with him, there was no reason to connect him to the murder. Has Derry got some new information?'

Madden shook his head. 'It was just a feeling he had at the time. He thought Wing was a dubious character. And he didn't like the way he reacted to Miss Blake's death; or rather that he didn't react. He seemed unmoved by it.'

'The Kent police had already done the preliminary interviews by the time I got down there,' the chief inspector explained. 'The guests had all been questioned. I did have a word with Sir Jack Jessup, but he wasn't able to help. He was too upset. He seemed to take the view that he was personally responsible for the safety and well-being of anyone staying under his roof. I felt sorry for the man.'

Shifting in his chair, Sinclair grimaced with pain. Madden waited for the explosion he was sure would follow. Instead, to his surprise, a pained grin appeared on the chief inspector's face.

'I can see you're holding your breath. Have no fear. I'm a reformed character.'

He resettled himself carefully.

'I got a fearful wigging from Helen yesterday. She said I was behaving like one of those gout-ridden colonels in a *Punch* cartoon whose toe has just been stepped on. I was reduced to shamefaced silence.'

Madden had already noted that his old colleague seemed in better spirits that day and had attributed the change to the presence of his daughter – a great favourite of the chief inspector's – whom he had found setting the garden table for tea when he arrived. Lucy had walked down from the house with a plate of freshly baked scones and accompanied by the Maddens' basset hound, Hamish, another welcome visitor and one with whom Sinclair was wont to claim a special tie, though admittedly only on the basis of the dog's name.

'You will admit,' he had said to Helen once, 'that while he never ceases to dig holes in your garden, he has always left mine untouched. It's clear he accords me special dispensation as a fellow Scot.'

The chief inspector was especially proud of his roses, now at the height of their full-blown summer beauty, and before Madden sat down to have tea with them both, he had spent ten minutes watering the beds under the approving eye of their temporarily stricken owner.

Her duty done, Lucy had departed, rousing Hamish from his deep sleep on the grass beside Sinclair's chair so that he could accompany her. Before leaving she had warned both of them that she expected to be kept fully informed on the progress of their inquiries.

'You're not to keep this case to yourselves,' she had told them sternly. 'It's much too interesting. If two heads are better than one, then three are better than two. I'm sure if you let me put my mind to it I'll come up with some good ideas.'

Seated in a cane chair now, with the sun lower in the sky, but the day still warm, Madden ran through the main points of the meeting he had had with Chubb at Scotland Yard.

'He's not dead set against reopening the case, Angus. But as Billy Styles says, he needs a good reason to do it. Cradock may be more of a problem. He's afraid of raking it all up again; he dreads what the papers will make of the story. We'll have to tread carefully. I promised Charlie I'd be discreet.'

'What have you got in mind?' The chief inspector had listened patiently while he made his report.

'Well, first off, I'm going to ring this woman Portia Blake shared a flat with, an actress called Audrey Cooper. We need to know if she can identify the pendant.'

Madden had brought the jade figurine with him and Sinclair had been examining it while he listened, holding it up to the sunlight and tracing the faint flaw in the green stone with the tip of his finger.

'If she confirms that it's the same one, we need to decide what to do next. My own feeling is I probably ought to talk to some of the other people who were staying at the house at the time of the murder. But that carries a danger with it.'

'What danger?'

'I don't want the fact that we're looking into this case to get out. It wouldn't be fair to Charlie Chubb. He's being as cooperative as he can be. He's ready to consider anything new we come up with. It would seem like a stab in the back if he were to find the story suddenly splashed across the front page of a newspaper. We should think carefully about who we approach.'

While he was speaking, Sinclair had made another cautious move in his chair.

'Have you any suggestions?' he asked, having completed the manoeuvre successfully.

Madden nodded: 'Since his father's no longer with us, I thought Sir Richard Jessup would be the best person to approach. He didn't stay the whole weekend, but he was present at dinner the night before Miss Blake was murdered. He could tell us something about the other guests and where they are to be found now. And, most important, he would have a strong interest in keeping this business out of the newspapers, from the point of view of both his family and his company. If you agree, I thought I'd write him a note and request an interview. He can always refuse, of course. But my guess is he would want to know what's afoot. How the note is worded will be important: this is not an official inquiry, after all. I'll draft something over the weekend and show it to you before I go back to London.'

He reflected for a moment.

'And I'll have to cook up some sort of story to tell Audrey Cooper, as well. I don't want her thinking that the police are about to open a new investigation.'

The chief inspector looked troubled.

'I'm starting to feel guilty about this, John. You've already done too much. The truth is this case has become something of an obsession of mine since Derry wrote me that letter. It troubles me.'

'And it never did before?' Madden probed cautiously.

'What do you mean?' Rather as he'd feared, Sinclair responded sharply.

'This particular investigation, it never bothered you?'

'Did I ever wonder if we'd sent the wrong man to the gallows? Is that what you're asking?'

The chief inspector had arrived all too quickly at the question which Madden had asked himself, and which he had decided it might be best to avoid.

'The way Derry described it to me made me wonder if there had been any uncertainty in your mind at the time about the way Norris's confession came about. How he suddenly caved in. Derry said he had had the feeling all along that Norris wanted to confess, and had taken it as a sign of his guilt, but that now he wondered if there hadn't been some other reason behind it.'

He waited for the other's reaction. Sinclair's frown had stayed fixed. But he was biting his lip now, seemingly uncertain of his reply.

'Not at the time.' When he spoke finally, it was in a decisive tone. 'I was satisfied we had the right man. As for the speed with which the whole business was wrapped up, there was nothing unusual about that. As you well know, most murder inquiries are resolved quickly; they seldom drag on. The identity of the killer is usually clear from the start, and it certainly seemed to be the case with Miss Blake's murder. I will say this, though: I was disturbed by Norris's manner. There was something about it that didn't seem to fit the circumstances. It was almost as though he was no longer concerned with the questions being put to him; as though he had withdrawn into some private part of his mind. Then again, murderers behave in all sorts of ways when they're arrested. Over the years I've witnessed everything from defiance to abject grovelling. I was convinced of Norris's guilt. But it left me troubled, mainly because I'm so opposed to capital punishment. I thought he was a weak-minded man who had almost certainly killed Portia Blake in a moment of panic, and probably by mistake when she tried to cry out. His execution, at which I was obliged to be present, was far closer to cold-blooded murder than any act of his. So if you're asking whether it bothered me over the years – yes, it did. And when I received Derry's letter with the news about this pendant I felt instinctively that I wanted to get to the bottom of it. If we made a mistake, let the world know about it. If nothing else, it might make people question whether hanging is a just and civilized punishment, or merely society's way of exacting a brutal revenge; and beyond that to the moral problem posed by executions that turn out to be mistaken, as this one may well do.'

He stopped. Observing his old friend's flushed and angry face, Madden kept his peace. It was left to the chief inspector finally to break the silence between them.

'But to go back to what I was saying before, I don't want to drag you any further into this business. If you can get Miss Cooper to confirm that the pendant is the one Portia Blake owned, that would be a great help. It might even be enough to persuade Cradock to reopen the inquiry.'

Madden shook his head. 'I'm afraid not, Angus. Charlie has already made that clear. The assumption we've been working on – the one the sender of this letter to Derry is trying to sell us – is that if Norris wasn't the killer, then the pendant must have been removed from Miss Blake's body by the real murderer, presumably because he thought it might incriminate him. But as Charlie said, there are other possible explanations for its disappearance. I think he was echoing what Cradock had said to him, trying to break the bad news to me gently: telling me we were going to need more than that.'

Sinclair's growl on learning this came as no surprise, and Madden quickly went on.

'Let me do as I suggest. First, I'll speak to Miss Cooper and, depending on what she tells me, try and see Sir Richard after that. To tell the truth, after spending a morning with Derry going over the ground I've become rather fascinated with the case. Quite apart from the question of the pendant, there are other aspects that make me think it might be worth persevering with: the character of Portia Blake, for one. We really know very little about her, other than that she was an actress of no great distinction. Before going any further we ought to try and find out more. Miss Cooper could be of help there.'

'You think there might be a reason she was killed?'

'There might. And that's reason enough to go on, at least for the time being.' Madden smiled. 'Besides, Lucy would never forgive me if I dropped out now.'

'Well, if you're determined . . .' The chief inspector tried unsuccessfully to mask his satisfaction. 'Is there anyone besides Jessup you feel you should speak to?'

'Yes. Mrs Castleton. I take it you know who I mean?'

'Of course.' Sinclair seemed mildly surprised. 'Jack Jessup's companion – or should I say, mistress? But why her, in particular?'

'She can probably give a better account of the guests than anyone else. She was the lady of the house, after all. And women are generally more observant than men.'

'*Are* they?'

The chief inspector's feigned astonishment was a sign that his good humour had been restored.

'You've waited all these years to tell me that?'

6

'So you think this might have belonged to the fair Portia?'

Audrey Cooper picked up the pendant. Gaunt, with cropped, greying hair and deep grooves along either side of her mouth, the actress's raddled cheeks, untouched by rouge or powder, showed the scourges of time. Dressed carelessly in slacks and a stained and crumpled blouse, she had clearly made little effort over her appearance. But her glance was sharp enough.

'That's what I'd like to find out,' Madden said.

He had rung her the day before, and having explained why he wanted to see her had been invited to call the following morning at her flat, which proved to be situated on the top floor of a house at the bottom of the King's Road in Chelsea. Sunlight pouring through a grimy picture window illuminated an untidy sitting room cluttered with books and what looked like scripts piled on tables – with a dirty plate here or there resting on top of them – and hung with framed posters and photographs of faces, most of them well known and belonging to the theatrical profession. They were sitting facing each other, Miss Cooper on a chaise longue upholstered in some faded rose-coloured material shiny with age and wear, Madden on a straight-backed chair that creaked each time he moved.

'Or rather, Mr Derry would.' He went on, 'He was one of the detectives who oversaw the investigation. He's retired now. He lives in Canterbury and since he knew I would be in London for a week or two he asked if I could help. I'm a farmer, but I used to be with the police. That's how we come to know each other.'

'You said on the phone you were just helping to tie up loose ends.' Miss Cooper spoke in a hoarse voice that Madden had fancifully associated with the cigarette burning in her fingers – it was the third she had lit since his arrival – until she apologized for her croaking and explained that she had all but lost her voice as a result of appearing recently as Lady Bracknell in a production of *The Importance of Being Earnest*.

'I'm afraid my dulcet tones and Oscar's deathless wit were lost on the cloth-eared worthies of Scarborough. They like their comedy more earthy oop north.'

Although Madden had handed her the pendant some minutes before, she had not yet done more than glance at it. It was as though she wished to examine his credentials first before giving serious attention to the matter that had brought him to her door.

'What do you mean by loose ends?' she asked, eyes narrowing. 'As I recall it, a man was hanged for Portia's murder. Is there some question about that now? And if so, why are you making this inquiry, and not the police?'

'Well, to answer your last question first, the police are aware of the existence of the pendant, but they don't feel it's significant in itself. Even supposing it is the same one, there could be various explanations for its turning up like this. They certainly don't think that it justifies reopening the investigation.'

'But your friend, Mr Derry, feels differently?' Miss Cooper expelled a lungful of smoke.

'Not at all. He was surprised to receive it, of course. It arrived out of the blue along with a note saying the sender believed it might have belonged to Miss Blake. Now it was known that she had a pendant similar to this one – she was seen wearing it during that weekend – but it disappeared when she was murdered, and what Mr Derry wants to know is whether it's the same piece of jewellery.'

'And that would be what you call "tying up a loose end"?' Extinguishing her cigarette, she reached for another.

'In effect. It's the sort of thing old detectives obsess about. Mr Derry thinks what might have happened was that the pendant was torn off Miss Blake's neck when she was assaulted and has been lying in the wood ever since. It's possible someone picked it up and sent it to him; someone who thought it might interest the police, but doesn't want to get involved.'

'And Mr Derry won't rest easy until he knows the truth?' Her tone was disbelieving. 'That's what you're telling me?'

'I wouldn't go that far.' Madden shifted uneasily on his creaking chair. The fiction he was offering Portia Blake's old flatmate had been concocted by none other than Lucy, who continued to take a lively interest in the inquiries he was making, and the longer he went on with it the less convincing it sounded to his ears. 'What really concerns him is that if the pendant did belong to Miss Blake, then it ought to be returned to her family. I'm told she has a sister living in Ipswich.'

'Has she? I wouldn't know.' Miss Cooper shrugged. 'Portia never talked about her family: she made no bones about wanting to leave her past behind.'

'You must have met the sister, though, surely. Didn't she come by to collect Portia's things?'

The actress stared at him.

'Yes, of course she did.' It had taken her a second or two to collect herself. She clicked her tongue in irritation. 'I remember now. I helped her clear out Portia's room. But that was the only time I ever set eyes on her.'

She had recovered well enough, but just for a moment Madden thought he'd detected a false note in her voice, and he wondered what had prompted it. Now, however, as though deciding on a change of strategy, the frown of suspicion creasing Miss Cooper's brow faded. She looked thoughtful as she picked up the pendant and held it to the light. He was startled to see her put down her cigarette in an ashtray and pick up a monocle from the table beside her. She fixed it to her right eye.

'This is not an affectation, I assure you,' she said, as though reading his mind. 'I'm as blind as a bat in one eye and long-sighted in the other. It's made for some uncomfortable moments on the boards, I can tell you.'

She studied the green stone carefully, turning it this way and that to catch the light until it seemed she had found the right angle, at which point she held the pendant still and peered hard at it.

'Well, I can't swear that it's the same piece.' She lowered the stone. 'But it is very like the one Portia had. I can see it has a slight flaw and the same was true of hers. I happen to know that because she kicked up a fuss about it.'

'A fuss?'

'She thought she'd been short-changed by the gentleman who gave it to her.' Miss Cooper's smile was scornful. 'She was sensitive about things like that; though not much else.'

Madden weighed the remark. It seemed he was being invited to probe further.

'It was a present from a man, was it?'

'Like most other things Portia possessed. She was – how shall I put it – *acquisitive*.' Miss Cooper's smile had turned wintry. 'Her other outstanding quality was ambition, which is a terrible thing to be burdened with when it's not allied to talent.'

'I take it you didn't care for her.'

'Is it that obvious?'

She handed the pendant back to him. Madden slipped it into his pocket.

'I just wonder why you had her as a flatmate.'

'Do you, indeed?' Miss Cooper removed her monocle. 'Well, I don't mind telling you. I was rather taken with her charms, and being a shrewd little minx, at least where that area of life was concerned, she led me to believe that she wasn't wholly opposed to the idea.'

She regarded him quizzically.

'Are you shocked?'

'Not at all.'

'What she actually needed at the time was a place to stay, and she probably also thought that I might be of some help to her in the business. She still harboured ambitions as an actress at that stage in her career.'

'At that stage? Did her ambitions change while she was staying with you? Was she looking to make her mark some other way?'

The question seemed to intrigue Miss Cooper. She drew back to study her visitor.

'For someone who is just doing a favour for an old colleague you seem remarkably interested in the late Miss Blake; and better informed about this business than I would have thought possible.'

'I spent a fascinating day with Mr Derry down in Kent.' Madden contrived to look apologetic. 'Although I wasn't expecting it, he showed me over the ground where the murder took place and explained how it came about. I wondered what Miss Blake was doing there; why she was included in Sir Jack Jessup's house party.'

'A nobody like her – is that what you mean?'

'I wouldn't put it that way. She just seemed out of place. According to Mr Derry she had been brought down from London by a business associate of Jessup's. But they don't seem to have been a couple in any sense.'

'You're referring to Fu Manchu?'

Seeing the look on his face, she laughed.

'Or should I say, Mr Stanley Wing?'

'Did you know him?' Madden spoke after a pause.

'Hardly.' She shrugged. 'I only saw him once when he came here to pick her up. My Chink, Portia called him. Once she actually did refer to him as Fu Manchu and said he was a wily oriental and she didn't trust him an inch. As far as I could gather they had some sort of business arrangement.'

'Do you know what that was?'

She shook her head. 'Only that it had to do with jade. Portia had been wearing various bits of jewellery for some weeks, but they didn't belong to her. They had been lent her by Mr Wing. He took her to some parties and functions. She was showing them off for him.'

'Was the pendant one of those pieces? I thought it belonged to her.'

'So it did.' She lit a fresh cigarette.

'Do you know who gave it to her?'

Miss Cooper shook her head again. 'We didn't share confidences. In fact we were never really on friendly terms, and after a few months I told her she ought to start looking for other lodgings.'

'Could it have been Mr Wing?'

'Possibly. Although he didn't sound like the sort of man who gave girls presents. The other kind were more Portia's cup of tea and she had no scruples when it came to making them cough up.'

Her laugh had a cruel edge.

'Early on in our brief acquaintance she admitted that she'd put it over on one of her swains by telling him she was pregnant. He gave her not only money to take care of the problem, which was wholly fictional, but also a lovely wristwatch from Cartier by way of consolation.'

She was watching his expression as she spoke.

'Just because Portia was a rotten actress didn't mean she wasn't gifted in other areas. It's true her fair limbs never graced my sheets, but they certainly found their way into other beds; or so I deduced from the hours she kept. She'd had a brief liaison with some lordling before I met her and managed to claw her way into society. She got invited to parties, and when we were still on speaking terms she would drop names like confetti, the sort you might see in the gossip columns. Little idiot!'

Miss Cooper spat out the words in disgust.

'She thought she was one of them. But the men were just passing her around.'

'Did you ever meet any of them?' Madden asked.

'Why? Does it matter?' Her glance had sharpened.

'Not really. I just wondered.'

'Did any of them spend the night here? Is that what you're asking?' She laughed. 'Not to my knowledge, though there were times when I was away in the provinces. As far as I know her assignations took place elsewhere and didn't always last all night. I used to hear her coming in at three or four in the morning, so I imagine it was often a case of, "Thank you, my dear, that was delightful and here's five pounds for the taxi."'

'They were not what you'd call affairs, then?'

'Affairs . . . ?'

'They didn't last long?'

'About as long as the average mayfly's earthly existence.

71

Poor little Portia. She was out of her depth. One moment she'd be riding high, talking about Buffy, or darling Ferdie, and telling me how they were about to take her to Paris, or to go skiing in the Alps; the next she'd be dropped like a hot potato and retire to her bed in tears.'

'Still, when you said she had other ambitions, is that what you meant?'

She picked up the monocle again and fixed it to her eye.

'How quick you are, Mr Madden.' She studied him. 'Not *quite* the farmer, are we, or not altogether? Are you sure you're not with the police still?'

'Quite sure.' He held her gaze.

'Yes, Portia's ambitions had shifted from the stage by then. I think she saw herself as married to one of these sprigs of the aristocracy she met at the parties she went to; she began to picture herself in tweeds managing a great country house; Lady Muck in all but name. I told her she was losing touch with reality, but I don't think she listened. She would have hated to hear me say it, but underneath it all she was still little Sadie Mott from Ipswich.' She caught her questioner's eye. 'Yes, that was her real name, but she ditched it early on. She must have found it hard to picture in lights.'

Madden was silent. He was thinking about what she had told him.

'Do you remember when she was given the pendant?' he asked, after a pause. 'Was it around the time she met Wing?'

'I really couldn't say.' Miss Cooper stifled a yawn. 'The only time I saw it was just before she went off to Kent with him. She was wearing it. I hadn't noticed it before and she showed it to me. That's when she complained about the flaw. "You'd think he could have afforded something better," she said. She was quite put out.'

'But you don't know who "he" was?'

This time she didn't bother to hide her yawn.

'I've already told you I don't. By that time I was simply putting up with her presence until she found new digs. We seldom exchanged more than a few words.'

She put out her cigarette and removed the monocle from her eye.

'So? Is that it? Have you tied up your loose end?'

'I believe so.' Madden made to leave.

'What are you going to do now?'

'Return the pendant to Mr Derry and tell him what you've told me: that it could be the one that belonged to Portia Blake. It'll be up to him to decide what to do with it.'

'And you're sure there's nothing more you require of me?' Her tone was mocking.

Madden hesitated.

'There is one thing I'm curious about,' he said. 'How did Portia come to meet Stanley Wing?'

'I'm afraid I can't help you there. I never asked her. Does it matter?'

'Can you describe him for me? What was your impression of him that time when he came to collect her?'

'Now that *is* an interesting question.'

She reached again for her cigarettes.

'He was here when I got back from wherever I had gone that afternoon. I found him waiting while Portia got ready. They were going somewhere together. She had mentioned him before so I wasn't surprised when he introduced himself. From what Portia said I had thought he was pure Chinese; but it was obvious from his features that he had European blood in him. His eyes were very dark, almost black. He made little effort to converse with me. He wasn't rude exactly, but his manner was dismissive. My presence was an irritation to him. He kept looking at his watch as though every moment he was forced to spend in my company was tedious and distasteful to him. It was a memorable few minutes.'

Her laugh was hollow.

'There I was in my own sitting room being quietly despised by a male of dubious origin. I had half a mind to ask him to leave, but he hadn't *quite* given me cause. Then Portia appeared with a flurry of excuses and apologies. She'd been delayed somewhere and had been late getting back to change. It was plain she was nervous in his presence.'

'Nervous . . . ?'

'I'd never seen her like that with anyone before. On the whole she tended to hide whatever insecurities she felt behind a mask of pretended confidence and she certainly thought that she knew how to deal with men – the kind she mixed with, anyway – flirting with them one moment and scolding them the next. But it was plain Mr Wing was a horse of another colour. He didn't respond to any of her chatter. He simply looked at his watch and said: "You are late." And with that they left.'

She drew thoughtfully on her cigarette.

'I say "nervous", but I think I'm being overly generous to Portia. I had the distinct impression that underneath it all she was just the teeniest bit afraid of him.'

Audrey Cooper stood on the landing listening to the footsteps of her visitor as he went down the stairs. After she had heard the street door open and close she went back inside. Lighting another cigarette, she stretched out on the chaise longue and stared at the ceiling.

'I *wonder* . . .' she mused aloud.

Just then the door at the rear of the sitting room opened and a young woman stuck her head in.

'Has he gone, Aud?'

'Like the wind, my sweet. Were you listening?'

'No, of course not.'

The young woman came in. Pretty in a doll-like way, with blonde curls and bee-stung lips, she wore a blue cocktail dress cut lower than was customary, showing the rounded tops of her breasts.

'Who was he?'

'A farmer, he said, though I found that hard to swallow.' Miss Cooper drew thoughtfully on her cigarette.

'What did he want?'

'I'm not sure. I didn't know what to make of him: a bit of a dark horse, our Mr Madden. Very polite on the surface; but I can't help feeling there was more to him than met the eye. And more he could have told me, as well.'

Miss Cooper expelled a long plume of tobacco smoke into the air. The girl came around the chaise longue and stood in front of her. Born Gladys Wainwright, she now went by the name of Pixie du Pre and until its recent demise had been dancing in the chorus of a West End musical.

'Good God!' Audrey Cooper's eyebrows went up. 'Why are you dressed that way? You look like a tart.'

'I told you. I'm going to Bobby Bishop's party. Hugh Grantham will be there. He's casting *Fortune's Child* next week and it'll be a chance to meet him.'

'Well, you won't catch his eye in that get-up, darling. Hugh dances at the other end of the ballroom. I know whereof I speak. And take some of that lipstick off, for heaven's sake, or he'll think you're auditioning for a corner on Curzon Street. Here – you can use my handkerchief.'

She drew the somewhat soiled object from her shirt pocket and held it up. The girl snatched it from her.

'Ooh, you can be nasty.'

She went to a mirror hanging on the wall at the side of room and set to work on her face.

'And just because dear Hugh's eye will be occupied elsewhere, don't imagine for a moment that there won't be other men on the prowl, or women come to that, with quite different thoughts in mind. Behave yourself.'

'You know I will.' The girl glanced over her shoulder. 'You can trust me.'

'Can I, my little Pixie?' Miss Cooper yawned. 'Funny how that word always brings betrayal to mind.'

Without warning she got up suddenly and went to a writing-desk in a corner of the room. Sitting down in front of it she began to go through the small drawers, pulling them out one at a time and scrabbling through the contents.

'I'm sure I put them here,' she muttered to herself. 'I couldn't have thrown them out.'

'What are you looking for?' The girl was examining her reflection in the mirror.

'Nothing you need bother your pretty little head about.' Miss Cooper slammed the last drawer shut.

'Damn!'

She sat scowling at the wall. Then her face changed.

'Hang on, though . . . !'

Springing to her feet, she strode across the room and disappeared through the door which Pixie had left open. The girl, meantime, had finished with her face. After a last glance in the mirror she took a light coat from a hook by the front door and slipped it on.

'I'm going now, Aud,' she called out.

Miss Cooper reappeared. She had a small wooden box in her hands. Clearing a space on the table in the middle of the room where the scripts lay piled she emptied the contents on to it. They proved to be an assortment of costume jewellery – rings, bangles, necklaces – plus some odds and ends in the shape of loose beads, a broken wristwatch and a bunch of keys. She stared at them for a long moment.

'I don't *believe* it.'

Unsure what she was supposed do, Pixie hovered by the door. 'Aud, I have to go . . .'

'Shhh . . . !'

Miss Cooper's frown came back, fiercer than before.

'Let me think.'

She lifted her gaze from the table and stared out of the window. Then with a gesture that might have been rehearsed for the stage she slapped her forehead audibly.

'But of course . . . you *idiot*, Audrey!'

She picked up the box, an ornate object whose lid was decorated with a leafy intaglio design, and searched with her fingertips along its bottom edge until she found what she was looking for. There was a pause, and then, like magic, a shallow drawer slid out of the box. Miss Cooper stared at its contents for a long moment. A smile came to her lips.

'Bingo!' she said.

Late getting back from Chelsea – at that hour, near the end of the working day, taxis were hard to come by – Madden returned to St John's Wood to find the pavement outside Aunt Maud's house crowded with pieces of furniture which were being loaded by three men into a removal van bearing the name of an auction house painted on its panelled sides. Alice stood on the doorstep with her arms folded watching them with an eagle eye.

'This is the first lot from upstairs, sir,' she told Madden when he had picked his way through the clutter and joined her. 'They'll be back next week for the heavy stuff. I've told them to leave our beds until last.'

His daughter was already home from work and impatiently awaiting his return.

'What did she have to say? *Is* it Portia's pendant? Are we on the right track?'

Busy in the kitchen choosing a supper for them from among Aunt Maud's hoard of contraband delicacies, Lucy paused in her examination of the tins she had lined up on the table to interrogate her father.

'Did she swallow your story about Mr Derry wanting to send the pendant back to Portia's family?'

'As I remember, that was *your* story,' Madden replied stiffly. 'And I thought for a moment she'd seen through it. It would have served me right for telling fibs.'

'Well . . . ?' Lucy waited impatiently. Her father had disappeared into the larder. 'Did you like her? Miss Cooper, I mean? Was she another glamorous actress, like Portia Blake?'

'Far from it.' He reappeared with a bottle of beer in his hand. 'She was spiteful and mean-spirited . . . and dressed like a scarecrow to boot.'

'Oh, dear . . . !' Downcast for a moment, Lucy bit her lip. 'But what did she have to say? What did she tell you?'

'Oh, I can't go into that.' Frowning, Madden removed the cap from his beer. He searched for a glass. 'It wouldn't be proper.'

'Not *proper* . . . ?'

'It was too squalid for your tender ears.' Smiling, he took a glass from the cupboard and began to fill it with beer.

'Daddy . . . !' There was a warning note in her voice.

'You don't want to know about the seamy side of life. Not yet.'

'For heaven's sake!' Lucy exploded. 'What makes you think I don't know about it already?'

Madden drew back. 'I'm glad your mother didn't hear you say that.'

'Daddy, *stop it*.' She circled the table to get closer to him.

'Well, all right.' He held up a hand to check her advance. 'But you must promise to be discreet.'

'I'm always discreet.'

'I'm sorry to have to tell you, but it seems Portia Blake was no better than she ought to have been.'

'What does that mean?'

'She had a lot of men friends.'

'What's wrong with that?' Lucy bridled.

'They gave her presents . . . jewellery and the like.'

'Oh . . . I see.' Her face cleared. 'Was the pendant a present?'

'Apparently. But Miss Cooper doesn't know who gave it to her. She knows something, though . . .'

Madden took a sip from his glass of beer. He reflected on his words.

'What do you mean . . . something?' Lucy fought to curb her impatience.

'I don't know . . . she didn't say.'

He was remembering the actress's slight hesitation.

'But all at once she changed note and started telling me all sorts of malicious stories about Portia – and before I'd even asked. I think she was trying to distract me.'

'From what?'

'That's what I'm not sure about. I must have missed something.'

Madden shrugged.

'I also heard a lot about this Chinese fellow, or part

Chinese, Mr Wing, and the more I learn about him, the more mysterious he seems to be. I can't make him out. I still don't understand what role, if any, he played in this business.'

'What are you going to do now?' Lucy asked.

'Have a word with Angus. I'll ring him later. This is his affair. I don't want to do anything without consulting him first.'

'What do you think you *ought* to do?'

Madden pondered.

'Well, although I haven't managed positively to identify the pendant – all Miss Cooper could tell me was that it looked like the stone Portia had – I think it's probably the same one. She remembered it had a flaw. So the best thing now might be if I sent Sir Richard Jessup that letter Angus and I worked up requesting an interview with him.'

'And then?'

'Wait and see if he's willing to talk to me.'

7

'RICHARD JESSUP? Well, if you have any problem there, let me know, John.'

Ian Tremayne beamed from his place at the head of the table. A rumpled looking figure, Lady Violet's husband was given to wearing torn sweaters and old jackets patched at the elbows on the weekend; as a relief, perhaps, from the more formal garb required by his position as a senior official at the Foreign Office. Though a rare visitor to Highfield in the early years of their marriage – he'd been frequently posted abroad – he had lately been occupying a desk in London, and he and his wife had been dividing their time between their flat in town and Lady Violet's ancestral home of Stratton Hall.

'I see him at the club quite often. He's very approachable.'

'Yes, but he may not want all this dragged up again.'

Still awaiting a reply to the note he had sent Jessup, Madden would not have chosen to discuss the matter at the lunch to which he and Helen had been invited that Sunday along with their daughter had not Lucy taken it into her head to air it.

'Daddy's got involved in a fascinating old murder case,' she had announced as they sat down at the table. 'It was one of Angus's and what everyone's wondering now is whether they hanged the wrong man. Angus would be looking into it himself if he wasn't immobilized, poor thing, so Daddy's doing it for him. And I'm helping.'

The subject having been raised, there was nothing Madden

could do but direct a scowl of disapproval at his daughter in the vain hope that she might be persuaded to curb her tongue; a wasted endeavour, since Lucy had contrived to avoid his glance while treating the company to a colourful review of the case as she saw it together with a full account of the dramatis personae involved.

The name Jessup – when he heard it uttered – had done more than ring a bell with Ian Tremayne.

'I know him quite well,' he told Madden, 'and not just from seeing him at the club. We spent a few months in Hong Kong after the war, Violet and I. Richard was there for some of that time getting the company back on its feet after the Japanese occupation. I was very impressed with him. The old boy, Jack Jessup, left it in bad shape. I was told they nearly went under. But Richard seems to have done a good job and I'm given to understand that the business is prospering now.'

'That's perfectly true.' Lady Violet had been paying close attention to what her husband was saying. 'But you're leaving out the most important part,' she said.

As slender as a reed in her youth, Helen's childhood friend had acquired over the years a figure more in keeping with mature middle age; without, however, losing any of her taste for mischievous gossip.

'It's what made all the difference, really.'

'I expect you're referring to his marriage.' Ian turned to his wife with a faint, but detectable sigh.

'Of course I am. You can't pretend it didn't have any effect on the company's fortunes. Sarah Temple was a very wealthy young woman. Marrying her was one of the cleverest things Richard ever did.'

This time her husband's sigh was more audible; it bore a long-suffering note.

'One could put it that way,' he said. 'Except you make it

sound calculated and cold-blooded when it was nothing of the sort. By all accounts they were smitten with each other. And just to put the record straight, it wasn't Sarah's money that went into Jessup's: it was her family's – her father's, to be precise – and he made a business decision. Richard had already begun negotiations with the investment group Temple headed before he and Sarah ever met.'

'If you say so, dear.' Violet's smile suggested she knew better.

'They were married shortly before the war started.' Ian turned back to Madden. 'Richard was away a lot of the time, on active service, but Sarah stuck it out in London throughout the Blitz. We met her in Hong Kong when they came out. She immediately got involved in relief work with refugees. She's a woman of strong principles. The Temples are a Quaker family.'

'You make her sound rather formidable.' Helen's interest had been roused.

'Then I've given you the wrong impression.' He turned to her. 'She's not like that at all – at least, not in my opinion – just . . . just *upright*. And very attractive. Richard's devoted to her.'

'And there's someone else you *must* talk to, John.' Lady Violet was just warming to her subject. 'You'll have heard the name Adele Castleton, I'm sure?'

'It's been mentioned.' Madden frowned. His reluctance to pursue the topic seemed to have escaped their hostess.

'La Belle Dame Sans Merci!'

'The *what* . . . ?'

'That's what she was called in her heyday.' Violet's eyes sparkled. 'Men used to go mad over her. They would lose their senses, poor things, and when she was done with them, which was soon enough, they'd be found alone and palely loitering, like that poor man in Keats's poem.'

'Honestly, Violet.' Helen was laughing. 'What nonsense you talk.'

'It isn't nonsense at all. It's perfectly true. In fact, if I were you I wouldn't let John go anywhere near her unescorted.'

'What was she like?' Lucy was enthralled.

'Well, whenever she arrived at a party a hush would fall.' Violet turned to her. 'Then the whispering would start. Was it true she'd been having an affair with the Duke of so-and-so? Had she actually abandoned him in Deauville, like they said, and run off with a jockey?'

'What did she look like? Was she lovely?'

'Not beautiful exactly, but striking: dark-haired, dark-eyed, and with a doomed air.'

'A doomed air . . . !' Lucy echoed the words with a sigh. 'Is that something you can cultivate . . . with practice, I mean?'

'No, and don't let me catch you trying.' Helen fixed her daughter with a stern parental eye. 'And don't listen to Violet either. She's exaggerating, as usual. It's true a lot of men fell for Adele Castleton, but she wasn't like her reputation. I met her once – properly, I mean, not just to be introduced. It was at one of those parties. We happened to find ourselves alone and we sat down and talked. All I can tell you is she couldn't have been nicer.'

'Don't spoil my story,' Violet pleaded.

Madden saw Tremayne roll his eyes in despair. For his own part he had given up any hope of diverting the conversation into other channels.

'I spent a morning down in Kent last week talking to the detective who worked on the case with Angus, a man called Derry.' He addressed the remark to Ian. 'I was surprised to

hear that Sir Richard was selling his father's house, particularly since it's been in the family for generations.'

'So was I,' Ian agreed. 'In fact, I asked him about it once.
We dine together at the club now and then. The answer was
quite simple. He's never thought of it as home.'

'Why is that?'

'Well, I don't know if you're aware of it, but his parents
separated when he was very young and he was brought up
by his mother.'

'Derry said something of the sort.'

'She lived in Hampshire, not far from Petersfield, and
Richard always loved their house. When he took Sarah there
she said at once it was where she wanted to live. Jack Jessup
was very ill at the time, and Richard kept their decision from
him. But once the war was over he let the house in Kent
to tenants and then, later, decided to get rid of it. The last
I heard there was a plan afoot to turn it into a school.
Richard's mother died only a year or so after Jack passed
away and he and Sarah settled in Hampshire when the war
was over. From what he's told me they seem to be very
happy there.'

He reflected on his words.

'He's an impressive fellow in all sorts of ways, Richard
Jessup. He had an outstanding record in the war, as well.
He started with a commission in the Guards, but he got himself transferred to the Parachute Regiment and was highly
decorated. I didn't get that from him, incidentally. He never
talks about it. But I know for a fact that he jumped at
Arnhem and managed to get what was left of his company
back across the Rhine when the Germans had our chaps surrounded. I hope you manage to talk to him. It'll be well
worth your while.'

*

'I know, I know – I shouldn't have done it. I can't imagine what came over me.'

Lucy buried her face in her hands.

'I suddenly realized when I saw you scowling at me. Is it that serious?'

'That all depends.' Sitting in the front seat of the car beside Helen, Madden had to twist his body round to look at his daughter, who was seated in the back. 'You've just blurted out the whole story to one of the biggest gossips in England. Before we left I had to ask Ian – *beg* him – to speak to Violet: to make sure she understood that she simply mustn't talk about this case to anyone. The last thing we want is to see it plastered all over the newspapers. But if Violet has her way that's exactly what will happen.'

Madden fixed her with what he hoped was his fiercest scowl.

'And only the other day you were telling me how discreet you were.'

'I just thought it was something we could talk about at lunch.' Lucy appeared genuinely stricken. 'Have I really done something terrible?'

'We'll have to wait and see. Ian will try his hardest, I know, but one can't trust Violet an inch. She's incapable of keeping anything to herself.'

'Oh, dear . . .' Lucy covered her face again.

Helen brought the car to a stop. She cleared her throat.

'Here we are,' she announced brightly. They had stopped in front of one of the cottages on the outskirts of Highfield village. 'Oh look – there's Mrs Tomkins waving from the window.'

She turned to her husband.

'Lucy's going to make a dress for her,' she explained. 'She has to measure her up first.'

'Mrs Tomkins . . .' Madden's laugh was bitter. 'There's another chatterbox.' He glared at his daughter. 'Try and restrain yourself this time. Keep your mouth full of pins, or whatever it is you do when you measure someone up.'

Lucy dropped her hands.

'That's a *horrible* thing to say,' she said. 'You're being sarcastic. You're *never* sarcastic. Not with me.'

'Yes, all right, I'm sorry.' Knocked off balance by the unexpected angle of attack, Madden was momentarily robbed of words. 'But you see what you've driven me to.'

He watched as she opened the car door.

'And from now on we're not going to talk about this case any longer; we're not going to discuss it. I'll do what I can for Angus, and that'll be the end of it.'

Choosing not to reply, his daughter climbed out of the car. Head held high, she walked down the short path to the front door of the cottage, which opened as she reached it. In a moment she had disappeared inside.

'Oh, Lord . . . !' Madden groaned. 'I've upset her.'

Helen's face was a study.

'Are you trying not to laugh?'

'I'm sorry, my dear.' She put a hand to her mouth. 'I'm just wondering how long that particular resolution will last.'

'What resolution . . . ? Oh . . . I see.' He scowled. 'You mean you think she'll talk me out of it?'

'Heaven forbid.'

'That's what you're implying, though, isn't it?'

Helen was mute.

'You think I'm putty in her fingers.'

'Have I ever said that?'

'Yes, as a matter of fact you have. I remember the occasion distinctly.'

Madden had given up trying not to laugh himself.

'You said Lucy had always known how to handle me, and when I protested and said that wasn't true, you corrected yourself. Not *always*, you agreed. That wasn't fair. She hadn't really got the hang of it until she was six.'

'So you think this man Wing may be the key to the problem. But is there a problem? You've been at it now for a while, John. What's your feeling?'

Angus Sinclair shifted in his chair. Given the warmth of the day, Madden had expected to find his old friend outside. He had come prepared to help with any chores that might need doing only to discover that another of the chief inspector's willing helpers had anticipated him.

'I thought I'd give the hedge a trim,' Will Stackpole announced from the top of the ladder where Madden had found him perched when he came in through the garden gate.

Clad in rough trousers and a flannel shirt, rather than his customary blue – it being a Sunday – Highfield's bobby had ascended a set of rickety steps to a point where he was able to ply the shears he was wielding to and fro along the top of the tall laurel hedge flanking the small garden. Madden had paused to talk to him – and to inquire as to the chief inspector's whereabouts.

'He was sitting out here until ten minutes ago.' Will nodded at the cane chair positioned under an apple tree. 'But he said it was getting too warm for him, so he went inside.'

'How is he moving now?'

'Better, I reckon.' The constable's tone was judicious. 'He's still not walking as such. More like hobbling, I should say. But don't tell him I said that.' He grinned.

'Helen says it'll likely be a couple of weeks before he's properly back on his feet.'

'Ah, well, she would know.' Will accepted the verdict with a solemn nod. His lifelong admiration for Madden's wife, dating as it did from the time when they had played together as children, had never wavered. His face brightened. 'I bumped into Lucy in the village yesterday. She tells me she's helping you with these inquiries you're making for Mr Sinclair.'

'Gave you a rundown on the case, did she?'

'I wouldn't call it that, exactly.' Will scratched his head. 'But she said you were learning some interesting things, the pair of you.'

'The pair of us . . .' Madden growled. 'Listen, Will, I've told her she's not to go around chattering about this business. If the papers get wind of it they'll turn it into a story in no time. Some of the people involved are well known to the public. If Lucy so much as mentions it to you again you're to speak sternly to her. Tell her she's meddling in what could be official police business. Be firm.'

'With *Lucy*?' Stackpole appeared to find the prospect unnerving. 'Well, if you say so, sir . . .'

'I do, Will. I do.'

Leaving the constable suitably awed (or so he hoped), Madden had gone inside then to find Sinclair seated in an armchair with his foot resting, as before, on a cushioned stool. A pile of books stood on the low table beside him and he had one open on his lap.

'I'm finally acquainting myself with the crimes and follies of mankind,' he announced, as Madden made his entry. 'A little late in the day for a retired chief inspector, you might think. But I persevere. This is Gibbon's *Decline and Fall of the Roman Empire*.' He patted the tall pile beside him. 'I'm barely into the second century AD and already I'm appalled by the depths to which human depravity can sink. Speaking of which, have you anything new to report?'

Madden had earlier given his old colleague a brief account by phone of his meeting with Audrey Cooper and they had decided there was reason enough for him to send the letter the two of them had already composed to Richard Jessup requesting an interview. Now he enlarged on what the actress had told him during their talk, with particular reference to what she had had to say about Stanley Wing.

'Is there a problem?' He echoed the chief inspector's question. 'Do you know, Angus, I still can't make up my mind. I think that pendant is probably Portia Blake's. But was it found in the wood some time later: was it a chance discovery? Or was it taken from her body by someone other than Norris – by the real killer in fact? That's what the person who sent that note to Derry would like us to believe. But how did it fall into his hands? And if he's trying to incriminate someone else, why not point a finger? Why not say who the alleged guilty party is?'

Madden paused to let his words sink in.

'Because either there is no guilty party – he's making this up – or he knows something but doesn't want to reveal it.' He answered his own question.

'So what's his motive then?' The chief inspector frowned.

'I don't know.' Madden shook his head. 'We'll have to wait and see. Somehow I don't think we've heard the last of him.'

Sinclair grunted. 'You're saying the pendant and the letter to Derry are only his opening gambits.'

'That's how it looks to me.' Madden shrugged. 'But to get back to Wing, I still don't understand what he was doing in England at that time, what he was up to. I can't place him in any recognizable context. We're told he was an associate of Jack Jessup's. But what does that mean? And then there's the effect he had on people.'

'What effect?'

'Look at Tom Derry, for example. He took against Wing the moment they met, and for no good reason other than that he didn't care for his manner. Miss Cooper had a similar reaction. She positively disliked him – and on very short acquaintance. Yet there he was, an invited guest at Jack Jessup's dinner table. It doesn't add up. At the very least it needs explaining. As does Portia Blake's presence in the house that weekend. There's also their relationship to consider – if you can call it that. Audrey Cooper said they had a "business arrangement". What did that involve, I wonder?'

'What you require, then, is someone to explain all these mysteries to you.' Sinclair eased a stiff muscle in his back.

'In a nutshell.'

'Someone like Sir Richard Jessup. I take it you haven't heard from him yet?'

Madden shook his head. He rose from his chair.

'I gave him my London address in the note I sent him, and the phone number, too. But there's been no reaction from him so far. I rather thought he'd want to see me. By rights he ought to be curious, human nature being what it is.'

'Human nature?'

With a sigh the chief inspector resettled himself in his chair. He opened the book on his lap.

'Well, as to that, I feel bound to tell you that Mr Gibbon, for one, had a very low opinion of it.'

8

'HERE NOW, WATCH what you're doing. You'll take a piece out of the wall if you're not careful. There's no rush.'

Alice stood at the bottom of the stairs, her stern gaze fixed on the two workmen who were manhandling a large oak wardrobe down the stairway. They were moving very slowly, only a few inches at a time, but still too quickly for Alice's disapproving eye.

'Miss Collingwood wouldn't want to see any damage done,' she confided to Madden, who was standing in the hall a little way off ready to offer help if it was needed. 'She was very particular about marks on the walls and suchlike.'

Since there was little he could say, other than to point out that having quit this world for the hereafter, Alice's late employer was unlikely to be taking any further interest in earthly matters, least of all the state of her walls, Madden restricted his response to a grunt. The workmen were employed by the firm of auctioneers assigned to dispose of the furniture not wanted by Helen or by Alice, who had been told to take her pick of any of the pieces she wished to retain for her own use when she decamped to Hastings. Alice had opted for a pair of bedside tables, two standing lamps and a painting of Westminster Bridge at sunset which hung in the hall above the telephone and which she confessed to having a particular liking for.

'I always stop when I'm dusting to look at it.'

Nearly a week had passed since Madden had posted his

letter to Sir Richard Jessup and, with no response to it received as yet, he was starting to wonder whether he ought to consider advancing the inquiry in some other way, though the prospect was hardly appealing. While it might be perfectly possible to track down the other guests who had been present that weekend, it would be difficult to approach them without some kind of introduction, which Madden had hoped Sir Richard might supply him with. There was no reason to think they would be willing to respond to questions put to them about a long-ago murder by someone with no official backing; one who could not even claim to be a licensed private detective.

'If he decides not to reply to my note, or turns me down, we may have to think again,' he had told Sinclair. They had spoken on the phone the previous evening. 'The trouble is, Richard Jessup is the one person who can smooth the way for us. If he's willing to cooperate then presumably any of the others I might want to speak to will find it hard to refuse.'

'Let's wait until the end of the week,' the chief inspector had advised. 'Let's see where we stand then.'

The wardrobe, meanwhile, had descended to the foot of the stairs and was making its slow way down the short passage to the hall and the front door beyond it. Alice was backing away before it, keeping an eye on the object and obliging Madden to retreat in the same manner until he was forced outside and on to the pavement. The rest of the procession followed at its own snail-like pace until finally the operation was completed and the wardrobe stood by the side of the road, ready for loading into a van parked nearby.

Leaving Alice to oversee its final disposition, Madden went back inside. Earlier that morning the telephone had been unplugged and, together with the table on which it stood, had been removed from the hall to the sitting room to give the men leeway as they shifted the various pieces of heavy furniture brought from upstairs. Now Madden retrieved the instrument and plugged it back into its socket. As he did so – and at almost the same instant – it rang. He picked up the receiver.

'Excuse me, sir.' It was a woman's voice. 'Have I got the right number?' She read it out.

'That's correct.'

'And am I speaking to Mr Madden?'

'You are.'

'Oh, I'm so glad. I've been trying to get you all morning, but there seemed to be something wrong with the line. I'm Sir Richard Jessup's secretary. Miss Harmon is my name. He has asked me to apologize for not responding to your letter sooner, but he's been in America for the past fortnight and only got back to London yesterday. He'd be happy to see you, he says, and wonders if you would be free to call on him at our offices in the City this afternoon. He realizes that it's short notice, but since he'll be away again next week he thought you might like to take this opportunity of talking to him.'

'I would.' Madden didn't hesitate. 'And it's very thoughtful of him. Would you thank him for me?'

'Certainly, sir.' She sounded relieved. 'Our offices are on Cheapside, quite close to the Mansion House tube station. Would two o'clock suit you?'

'The building was in Watling Street. You can see the place from here. It was destroyed during the war.'

Sir Richard Jessup pointed.

'It was during the Blitz and luckily it happened at night

when there was no one in the place. I managed to rent these offices from one of the big insurance companies but we're going to rebuild our old headquarters. It's just a bomb site now, as you can see, but I'm hoping we can get construction started in the New Year.'

With a full head of dark hair and blue eyes that seemed to carry an electric charge, Jessup had been at the window in his office looking out when Madden entered and had turned at once to shake his hand and draw him over to the spot where he was standing. They were on the fifth floor of an office block on Cheapside and the view that Madden found himself looking at took in the great dome of St Paul's Cathedral on one side and the distant silhouette of Tower Bridge on the other. The site Jessup was indicating, one of many in that part of the City damaged or destroyed by bombs, was situated directly in front of them. It was only a little way off, and by chance Madden had walked up that way from the tube station, passing through narrow streets lined with gaping pits like empty tooth sockets. Small enterprises had once flourished in these lanes, rubbing shoulders with the great banks and financial institutions: jewellers, hatters, glove makers, suppliers of stationery. All were gone now, blown to oblivion.

'Come and sit down.'

Sir Richard led his guest away from the window to a low table a little apart from his desk and surrounded by easy chairs.

'Let's make ourselves comfortable. I'll get Miss Harmon to bring us some coffee.'

In spite of his distinguished appearance – he was wearing a well-cut suit with a silk handkerchief showing at his lapel pocket and a Brigade of Guards tie – Jessup still managed to project an air of informality, and given what he already knew about his host it came as no surprise to Madden to find himself warming to the man. Although clearly at ease with his lofty position as head of a great international concern, Sir Richard seemed disinclined to make much of it and from the outset his manner had been open and friendly. Almost as tall as his visitor, his good looks were enhanced by high cheekbones that lent his face a hawk-like aspect; but if there was something of the fierce predator in the swift glance he had shot Madden's way as he was shown in, he had nevertheless crossed the office without a moment's delay to shake his hand warmly, moving with the long, easy strides of an athlete.

'It was good of you to come on such short notice,' he said now as they sat down. 'As you might imagine, I found your letter intriguing and I'm more than curious to discover what this "informal inquiry" you are making involves. To say that I have qualms at the thought that the investigation might be reopened would be an understatement.' He grinned. 'Neither my family nor my board of directors would welcome it. I can still recall the fuss the papers made ten years ago, and I don't imagine they would be any more discreet second time around. But you'll have guessed that already, and what I want to say is if it turns out there is more to this business than met the eye at the time you can count on me not to put any obstruction in your way. I would rather know the truth.' He looked directly at Madden. 'As my dear wife would say, "let the chips fall where they may".' He smiled again. 'Sarah is American. But perhaps you already know that.'

'I do, as it happens.' Madden returned his smile. 'We have an acquaintance in common – Ian Tremayne. He's married to one of my wife's oldest friends.'

'Imagine that.' Jessup's face lit up. 'I first met Ian in Hong Kong just after the war. Did he tell you—?'

He broke off as the door opened and his secretary entered

carrying a tray with the coffee things on it. During the short interval that followed Madden had an opportunity to take in the spacious office and to admire the handsome Persian carpet underfoot which gave the room a sense of intimacy it might not otherwise have had. His eye was caught by a number of framed portraits hanging on the walls; all were of men, some bewigged and garbed in the clothes of an earlier age, others dressed in more up-to-date apparel. Leaving it to his secretary to pour their coffee, Jessup had been observing him.

'The gentleman you see in that painting behind the desk is our firm's founder,' he said, 'and as ambitious and fly a young scoundrel as ever took ship for the Orient. Jeremiah Jessup was his name. He worked for the East India Company originally and was one of their agents in China when it became apparent in the early nineteenth century that the company was about to lose its monopoly on trade with India and the Far East. Along with some other bright young fellows, he struck out on his own and like most of them made his first money in the opium trade. When that came to an end he branched out into other fields and began trading in cotton, tea and silk. Later on the company expanded – into shipping and cotton mills and construction – all of which we are still actively engaged in. The faces you see up on the wall are of the men who have managed the firm's fortunes since. Nearly all of them are Jessups. That's my father over there: as you see, he's the only one with a smile on his face.'

The painting he was indicating had already caught Madden's eye: the features of the man it portrayed were so like Sir Richard's that he had assumed they must be closely related. Sir Jack was pictured sitting at ease behind a wide desk. The smile his son had referred to seemed somewhat rueful, boyish even, though to judge from the older Jessup's grey hair and lined face he must have been well into middle age when it was painted.

'We had a curious relationship. At first it was distant – my parents separated quite soon after they were married and my mother wanted nothing to do with him or his set – but later it improved and by the end, when he died, we'd become very close. He was a man of enormous charm, but quite unpredictable, a gambler at heart. People who knew him all thought he was wonderful company, my mother excepted, but as a businessman he was quite hopeless. His tenure at the helm of Jessup's alternated between periods when he would take off on one of his many jaunts – to Africa, South America, Alaska; to wherever his fancy beckoned – and other times when he would focus all his energies on the company. And it was a toss-up as to which of the two was more perilous. One way or another, he very nearly did for the firm.'

He laughed without restraint.

'But you didn't come here to listen to me going on about my forebears. Before you put any questions to me – and I'm sure you have a few – could you tell me briefly how this all came about? You mentioned that pendant in your letter and explained that you were acting on behalf of one of the two detectives who had charge of the case. But could you be a little more explicit? And take all the time you need. I've cleared my afternoon of appointments.'

In reply, Madden spoke for the next twenty minutes without interruption, explaining first about the anonymous letter Tom Derry had received and then describing his visit to Kent and his subsequent interview with Audrey Cooper. At that point he paused to take the pendant from his pocket along with the letter and passed both across the table to Sir Richard.

'As you can see from the flaw, we've established that that's probably the same stone as the one Portia Blake owned.'

Jessup held up the piece to the light. He examined it closely, turning it this way and that.

'Fascinating,' he said.

'But there's still no explanation for how it came into the hands of whoever sent the note to Derry. Or what his motive was for doing so. Always supposing it was a man. It could equally have been sent by a woman.'

There was no immediate response from Jessup, who was now studying the note Madden had just handed him.

'The wording's peculiar, isn't it?' he said. '*I leave it to you to establish the truth . . .* Does that mean he doesn't know himself if the pendant has any significance? He's just trying it on – seeing if he can stir up some trouble?'

'That's one possibility,' Madden agreed. 'As things stand, the officers I've spoken to at Scotland Yard have no intention of reopening the investigation, and I see their point. There simply isn't enough to go on. I might add that I have no personal stake in this. I used to be a police officer, but that was a long time ago. I'm acting purely on Mr Sinclair's behalf. He's unable to get about at the moment. But he's an old friend and I'd like to help him if I can.'

'And his reason for wanting this matter looked into again – is it only because of the pendant turning up in this way?' Jessup put the letter down. 'Or has he got other doubts as well?'

'Of a sort.' Madden considered his words before replying. 'It's my opinion that both Mr Sinclair and Derry were left puzzled by Owen Norris's behaviour during his interrogation. He was the man arrested and ultimately convicted. They felt they had never got to the bottom of him – they were never sure what was in his mind when he first confessed to the murder and then denied it later on at his trial. On top of that, Angus Sinclair is strongly opposed to capital punishment and the thought now, even though it's only a suspicion, that he may have been party to sending the wrong man to the gallows has been enough to spur him into action. And before you ask, I've formed no conclusions myself about this case. It's quite possible Norris was guilty as charged. But I've come to agree with Angus that there's still a question hanging over it.'

'Why?'

The question was shot at him like a bullet, and the hawk-like glance that accompanied it was Madden's first intimation of the searching intelligence that lay behind his host's engaging personality. Once again he had to ponder his reply.

'I can't give you a simple answer,' he said finally. 'I can only say that I suspect it wasn't by chance that Miss Blake found herself at your father's house that weekend: that in all likelihood her visit was arranged, though I don't know how, for a reason, and that the person behind it was Stanley Wing.'

'Ah . . . !' Jessup expelled his breath in a long sigh. His piercing gaze remained fixed on his visitor. 'I've been sitting here listening to you, Mr Madden, and wondering why you had come to see *me*. What it was you thought I could tell you that might help with your inquiry. Now I understand.'

A smile played about his lips.

'Stanley Wing . . .' His tone was thoughtful. 'What can I say? Only that I'm not surprised.'

Without warning he stood up and strode to a table in the corner of the office where a collection of framed photographs stood. Selecting one of them, he brought it back and handed it to Madden.

'That was taken in 1935. My father's there in the middle of the group. The men on either side of him were the senior staff in our Hong Kong office at the time. It was his birthday. He'd invited them to his house. Wing is on the right at the edge of the picture. You can see he's not really one of them. He's standing apart. But that was Stanley Wing all over. He was always the fly on the wall, the lizard on the rock . . . always watching . . . waiting his opportunity . . .'

Madden studied the photograph.

The men, all Europeans apart from Wing, and all dressed informally in shirt sleeves and straw hats, stood in a loose group on a lawn in front of a sprawling house painted white and fronted by a long veranda. Wing, wearing a black suit and tie, stood a little away from them and, as Jessup had said, at the very edge of the photograph. Slim in build, with black hair plastered so close to his head that it resembled a skull cap, he was observing the group through narrowed eyes. The other men, conscious that they were posing for a snapshot, were smiling.

Madden handed the picture back.

'All I've been told so far was that Wing was a business associate of your father's,' he said. 'That doesn't sound as though he was an employee. But if he didn't work directly for Jessup's, what was his position exactly?'

'A good question.' Sir Richard laid the photograph down. 'And to tell the truth I was never entirely sure myself. He and my father went back a long way. Officially he was one of our consultants. But even that doesn't begin to cover his many . . . activities.'

He had hesitated over the word – as though he might have chosen another – and then continued, shrugging as he did so.

'Look, there's a great deal I could tell you about Stanley Wing. But I'm not sure it has any bearing on this business. He was never a suspect, was he?'

'Not that I'm aware of,' Madden replied. 'But then neither was anyone else who was staying at the house that weekend. What I mean is none of them was ever questioned in any detail by the police. Norris was arrested almost at once and confessed soon afterwards. What bothers both Mr Sinclair and Derry now is that the case might have been wrapped up too quickly.'

'Are you saying one of *them* might be under suspicion?' Jessup reacted sharply.

'I wouldn't go that far.'

Surprised by his host's response, Madden sought to reassure him. Up till that moment Sir Richard had seemed relaxed and at ease with the conversation they were having.

'It's more a matter of widening the original investigation. I've mentioned Wing's name. But there were other people staying as your father's guests, weren't there? I was wondering if you could tell me something about them, including where they are now, in case I need to get in touch with any of them. And also whether you could give me a picture of that weekend, what impression you had of it.'

'That's an odd request.' Jessup seemed intrigued by the question. 'Have you asked anyone else about it, anyone who was there?'

Madden shook his head.

'Well, first of all you should know that, properly speaking, I wasn't one of the guests. I had been coming down to Kent from London to see Father nearly every weekend that year. He hadn't been well for some time – he had a heart complaint – and he'd been in the process of handing over the company's reins to me. Although I wasn't due to take over as managing director until the following year, I was already acting in that capacity, and we had a great deal of business to get through. And there was a further complication, if you can call it that.' He smiled. 'My marriage to Sarah was set for September. The wedding was to take place in America, and we had agreed to take a full month's honeymoon afterwards. So there was the pressure of time, and since my father couldn't come to town – he simply wasn't well enough – I had got into the habit of going down to see him regularly, and the fact that he and Adele had guests that weekend was neither here nor there. We simply got on with our business, which was detailed and burdensome.'

He paused. 'I take it you know who I mean by Adele?'

'Mrs Castleton?'

Jessup nodded. 'I must say when I arrived shortly after lunch and she told me who was there I was taken aback. I couldn't imagine what had possessed my father to invite Wing. The previous year I had spent some months in Hong Kong going through the company's books and looking into all its business dealings, and among the conclusions I came to – the most important in many ways – was that we had to sever our ties with him. I'd prefer not to say anything more about that. It doesn't concern the inquiries you're making. But the upshot was that I finally persuaded my father that we had to cut him loose and he wrote to Wing informing him of our decision and also gave appropriate instructions to our management in Hong Kong. They were to have no more dealings with him. You can imagine my surprise then at discovering that he was one of the guests that weekend.'

'Did you know that he was in England?' Madden asked.

'Oh, yes. I'd heard that he was in London, and happened to bump into him at a party earlier that summer. Our encounter was cool, as you might imagine, but he told me he was over here on private business and I guessed it was linked to his interest in jade. I happened to know that he had been active in that area for some time.'

'Selling jade jewellery?' Madden asked. 'Is that what you mean?'

'Not exactly; no.' Jessup eyed his listener. 'Though he let

me think he was. One of the things I discovered when I went out to Hong Kong – it was more in the nature of confirming a long-held suspicion – was that Wing had been dealing on his own in the procurement and sale of jade antiques from the mainland, objects of historical interest and value that had almost certainly been pilfered from graves. The trade was illegal and, although our company hadn't profited from these dealings, Wing had had no scruples about using Jessup's name and his own connection to the firm to further his business.'

He laughed.

'I hadn't intended to tell you that, but you might as well know. And it was only one of the areas he'd been active in, using Jessup's name whenever it was useful to him, and only one of the reasons I had for getting rid of him. When I met him in London he claimed to have gone into the jewellery business and said he was trying to interest local dealers in buying jade pieces from him. I didn't believe a word of it. I thought it very likely he was renewing old contacts with collectors, people to whom he had sold antiques in the past in order to reassure them that the fact he was no longer connected with Jessup's made no difference: that he was still in business.'

He shrugged.

'I hasten to say I've no evidence of that. It was only a guess. But I certainly didn't credit his story about selling jewellery. Jade has never been a particularly popular stone here and the prices it commands are relatively low. He was up to something else, I'm convinced, but I doubt it ever got off the ground, given that the war started the following year and probably put a stop to any scheme he had.'

Jessup frowned.

'I'm sorry. I'm digressing. You don't want to hear all this.

What I meant to tell you was that when I ran into Wing at that party he had Miss Blake with him. She was wearing various pieces of jade and Wing gave me to understand that she was working for him, displaying the pieces at parties and functions to which he'd been invited, stirring up interest in them.'

He rolled his eyes.

'Well, if you could believe that, you would believe anything. I certainly didn't. But since we were no longer affected by what he was doing I didn't give much thought to it. I heard later on that he'd appeared at several social functions during the summer and each time he had had Miss Blake with him.'

'What was their connection, exactly?' Madden asked. 'They weren't a couple, were they?'

'Good heavens no.' Jessup laughed. 'It's quite impossible to imagine Wing in that role. I don't know if one can ever truly say of anyone that they're sexless, but Stanley Wing certainly came closest to it. He seemed to belong to another species. I had no idea then or now what stirred his blood, what might have set his pulses racing. He was an enigma to the last.'

'You've not seen him again?'

'Not since that weekend, in fact. I heard later that he had gone back to Hong Kong. Then, as I say, the war came. And when I finally got out there later – I mean after the Japanese occupation was ended – he was already in prison.'

He saw Madden's startled look.

'You didn't know? I assumed the police here must have told you. But perhaps *they* don't know. After all, why should they?'

He mused on the thought for a moment; then he shrugged.

'He was arrested soon after the Japanese occupation

ended. He was charged with collaborating with the enemy and pleaded guilty. I gathered he'd been up to his old tricks, selling jade art to the occupiers, but also assisting them in other areas, some of which were regarded as vital to the war effort. He was sentenced to six years in prison. He's still inside.'

Jessup smiled wryly.

'Forgive me. I've gone off on a tangent again. You wanted to know about that weekend. I didn't see any of the other guests when I arrived, which was shortly after lunch. My father and I settled down to work in his study. But I already knew from Adele that Wing was there and after I'd changed for dinner I sought him out and we had a brief conversation alone, out on the terrace. I was blunt with him. I asked him what the devil he was doing there. He was smoothness itself. He said he had simply come down to pay his respects to my father. There was no question of any recriminations. He accepted that he was no longer a part of Jessup's and only wanted to express his thanks to the man who done so much for him. It was very much the sort of act I had come to expect from him over the years and I decided to take it at face value. No more was said and we went inside to join the others.'

He paused to collect his thoughts.

'You'll want to know about the other guests, I expect. Besides Wing and Miss Blake they were Lord and Lady Cairns, old friends of Father's, and a younger couple called Rex and Margaret Garner. Harry Cairns died in 1946. I don't think they can be of any interest to you. Rex Garner I've known since boyhood. He and Margaret had got married a couple of years earlier. The local vicar and his wife were also dinner guests. I'm afraid I can't remember his name, but he was quite an elderly man and I was told he passed away during the war.'

He took a deep breath.

'And now we come to the dinner itself, which I imagine is what you've been waiting so patiently to hear about.'

'Have I?' Madden laughed. 'I wasn't aware of that.'

'Do you mean you know nothing about it?' Jessup looked startled. 'I thought you were bound to ask me about it. No one's mentioned it to you?'

'I've only spoken to the two detectives I've told you about – Derry and Mr Sinclair – and to Miss Cooper. She couldn't have known anything about that weekend.'

'No, of course not . . . I hadn't realized.' Jessup bit his lip. 'Well, then I'd better set you straight. Not to beat about the bush, it was a nightmare; hideously embarrassing; and the cause of it all was Portia Blake. Earlier she had appeared in the most extraordinary dress. Not just revealing: the degree of *décolleté* was breath-taking. She was a pretty girl with a good figure and the effect, on all the men, at least – and I won't exclude myself – was deplorable. We simply goggled at her. What's more she was wearing that infernal pendant, and when we sat down at the table she proceeded to play with it throughout the meal, leaning over the table, revealing even more of herself, dangling the thing between her breasts.'

He shook his head in wonderment.

'As I say, I'd only encountered her briefly before, when I met Wing at that party, but I remembered she had been a little too loud then, a bit too sure of herself, talking too much and acting as though she were one of us, which she wasn't.' He grimaced. 'That's a cruel thing to say. But you know what the English are like. You either belong or you don't, and even though she seemed to know a number of people there, particularly the men, she was obviously a fish out of water; and the same was true of that evening at Foxley Hall. She was all wrong, and the sad thing was she hadn't the faintest idea of the effect she was creating.'

He bit his lip.

'The dinner seemed to last an age, and the person who bore the brunt of it was Rex. He was seated opposite Miss Blake and she spent a good part of the meal flirting with him in a rather clumsy way and dangling that pendant in front of his eyes like a hypnotist's toy. By the end he actually did seem mesmerized. His wife, meanwhile, had got more and more angry with the way Miss Blake was carrying on, and heaven only knows what Harry Cairns and his wife made of it, never mind the vicar. I think the only person who enjoyed the performance was my wicked old father. I could see him chuckling.'

He spread his hands.

'So, there you have it. That was the prelude to the poor young woman's death, her last performance you might say, though I can't imagine it had anything to do with her murder.'

'Nor can I,' Madden agreed. 'But I'm interested by your choice of word. A *performance*, you say. Is that how it struck you?'

'Not at the time: not in the sense you mean.' Jessup cocked an eye at his visitor. 'You're wondering if she was deliberately putting on an act.'

'Yes, and was Stanley Wing behind it? He was the one who brought her down there, after all. That's something that's puzzled me from the start. She seemed out of place. What was she doing there?'

Madden's question hung in the air between them. Jessup had fallen silent. He seemed to have drifted off for a moment.

'Do you know, I asked my father that same question the following day.' He collected his thoughts. 'He simply laughed it off. He said Wing had rung him a few weeks earlier and asked if he could come down and see him. He confirmed what Stanley had told me the day before. He had simply wanted to pay his respects to my father before he returned to Hong Kong. They had set a date for the visit, but then a week before Wing was due to come down he had called Father again and asked if he could bring a young lady with him. My father, like me, had never associated Stanley with a woman and he was so intrigued by the notion that he immediately agreed and said she would be welcome. Quite simply, he was curious. He couldn't wait to see what Wing would produce in the shape of a female companion, and he allowed that he'd been well entertained by the goings on at dinner the previous evening.'

Jessup's smile was rueful.

'But that, I'm sorry to say, was my dear old parent all over. He had a mischievous side.'

'Did you see her the next day – Miss Blake?'

'Only briefly. I had spent the morning with Father – we still had some business to get through – and I'd intended leaving immediately to drive back to London. I didn't fancy witnessing a repeat of the previous night's antics and in any case I had an engagement in town. But Adele begged me to stay for lunch. She thought my presence would help to keep a lid on things. But as it turned out Rex had had a similar reaction. He had left the house soon after breakfast to drive into Canterbury, telling Adele that he was going to look up an old friend. Just before we were due to sit down he rang to say he wouldn't be back. He was lunching with his friend. I think our American cousins call it "chickening out".' Jessup smiled bleakly. 'So lunch passed off peacefully and I left as soon as it was over without waiting for coffee to be served. I got back to London in mid-afternoon. I had a place at the Albany then and when I arrived I found that the hall porter was holding a message for me. It was from Adele. I was to ring her at once. When I did she told me about Miss Blake's murder, and I turned round and drove all the way back. The house was full of police. They were taking statements from everyone – guests and staff – with the aim of finding out where each and every one of them had been during the afternoon. I gave my statement to one of the officers – it was brief, obviously – and then went in search of my father. I found him in bed, quite broken up, shattered. He was appalled by what had happened to the poor girl and felt he had somehow failed her. She had been under his roof, after all. It was very like him.'

Jessup bowed his head.

'I spent the night there and the following two days, mainly to comfort Father and do what I could for Adele, who had to cope with everything. I did have a brief word with Wing, but he professed to know nothing about what had happened. He had last seen Miss Blake at lunch, he said, after which he had gone to his room to rest.'

'Did he show any emotion?' Madden asked.

'Good heavens, no.' Jessup's laugh was harsh. 'But then I'm not sure I ever saw Stanley Wing display feeling of any kind. His face was like a mask. You never knew what he was thinking.'

'You said he and your father went back a long way: what did you mean by that?'

Jessup hesitated. For the first time he seemed reluctant to reply.

'It wasn't something my father liked to talk about, and I've tried to respect his wishes,' he said at last. 'What's more,

I'm sure it has no bearing on this case. Do you really want to hear it?'

'Please.'

'Well, if you insist . . .' He paused, gathering his thoughts, it seemed; or perhaps choosing his words. 'They met when Wing broke into my father's house in Hong Kong.'

'Good heavens!' Madden was astounded.

'It was, as I say, years ago. Stanley was just a boy, no more than twelve or thirteen. He'd been living on the streets, keeping himself alive through petty thieving. My father caught him as he was forcing a window, and then had to hold him at gunpoint, because Stanley was armed with a knife and seemed quite ready to use it. "He was as quick as a cobra and twice as dangerous," was how Father put it when he described the incident to me. Any other man would have called the police, but Father always did things his own way. He made Stanley sit down and he began to question him. To his amazement he discovered that the boy spoke fluent English, and when he learned the reason why he was as good as hooked.' Jessup smiled bleakly. 'Stanley's mother had been an English governess employed by a wealthy Chinese businessman to raise his children. Unfortunately for her she caught the eye of his younger brother and their affair, if you can call it that, ended when she became pregnant, at which point her employer dismissed her and she was left to fend for herself. For whatever reason the prospect of returning home didn't appeal to her and she had her baby in Hong Kong. My father never discovered precisely how she survived after that but it seems that both communities – British and Chinese – turned their backs on her and eventually she was forced into prostitution. Still, somehow she contrived to raise her son until she died quite suddenly of what sounded like typhus and Stanley was cast adrift. With no home any longer he was forced to take to the streets, and from then on he lived by his wits.'

Jessup caught Madden's eye.

'My father was a very lovable man,' he said. 'He had a big heart and a bottomless well of generosity which could be extended to almost anyone, but particularly to those he felt were in need. Without any further consideration, and starting that same night, he took Stanley under his wing. Although he didn't formally adopt him, he found a Chinese family for him to lodge with – needless to say they were well rewarded – and sent him to a good school. And although he was away from Hong Kong for long periods, he took care to keep in touch with the boy and when Stanley turned eighteen he took him into Jessup's as a trainee. He probably saw this as just another act of charity, but it came to seem like shrewd judgement on his part.' Sir Richard smiled. 'Stanley turned out to be very bright. Perhaps his earlier life on the streets had taught him things you can't learn at school, but he soon proved adept at dealing with the local administration where he developed the kind of relationships that were invaluable when it came to steering lucrative contracts our way.'

He stroked his cheek; pensive now.

'I have to be careful here,' he said. 'Doing business out East has always involved a certain amount of what we might call corruption, but can also be seen as simply acts of gratitude in return for favours granted. There are times when one simply has to turn a blind eye to whatever's going on. It would be fair to say that the management at the time – and I include my father – were well aware that we were sailing close to the wind and must have decided that the risk was worth it. In the event, we ran into trouble eventually with the authorities and had to pay some heavy fines. The reputation of the firm suffered and in the years leading up to the war it got into serious difficulties, though none of that affected Stanley Wing, who had managed to feather his own nest quite successfully by then and had already moved on to the next stage in his career, leaving the mess he had been partly responsible for behind him.'

'The next stage . . . ?'

'He'd been working for Jessup's for a dozen years or so when he decided to branch out on his own, and proceeded to do so with my father's blessing, which went so far as to grant him official status as a consultant of Jessup's and allow him to put that on his business cards; a grave mistake, in my opinion. It wasn't easy convincing Father later on that his protégé had turned out to be no better than a crook and right to the end he continued to harbour the illusion that Wing had simply been unlucky. He died in 1939, so he never knew about the Japanese occupation of Hong Kong. But he continued to worry about Stanley and asked often if I had any news of him.'

'And did you?'

'Not at that stage, no.' Jessup shook his head. 'I was called up early when war broke out. Earlier I had toyed with the idea of a military career. I had a commission in the Guards and was on the reserve list. The management of the company passed into other hands. Of course I kept in touch with them as much as I could, but I had more than enough to worry about without inquiring after Wing.'

He fell silent again, and this time Madden took the opportunity to put a question he'd been waiting to ask.

'I can't quite square the picture you've given me of Stanley Wing with this person who seems to have been quite at home in London society. You say you bumped into him earlier that summer at a party. How did that come about?'

'I should have explained.' Jessup acknowledged the

question with a nod. 'During the years when Stanley seemed to be doing so well for the firm – gaining us contracts and helping to expand the business – Father took him back to Europe with him on several occasions and introduced him to some of his business colleagues and friends in London. Knowing Father, I believe it was out of genuine goodwill towards Stanley. He meant to treat him as he would any promising young man regardless of his background. Unfortunately Wing took advantage of it in the worst possible way: it was during those early visits that he made the contacts he was able to exploit later.'

'You're referring to the sale of pilfered antiques?'

Jessup nodded. 'They were mostly rich men, collectors and antique dealers, and it was through them that Stanley gained access to society in a more general way; it was how he got invited to people's homes, and even to some of their parties. But from what I heard he was never remotely at ease at them; I knew from others that he was regarded as an oddity.'

He grimaced.

'I realize you're curious about him. But do you really believe he might have had a hand in Miss Blake's death?'

'Oh, no.' Madden shook his head. 'Or rather, I have absolutely no opinion on the subject one way or the other. I still think the man they arrested was the most likely killer. But Wing seems to be a dubious character at best, and we still don't know why he took Miss Blake down to Kent with him.'

He hesitated.

'Are you sure he's still in prison?'

'I've no reason to believe otherwise.' Jessup shrugged. 'My people out there have standing orders to let me know the moment he's released. I don't fancy the idea of Stanley Wing running around free without my knowing what he's up to. But why do you ask?'

'Based on what you've told me about him, I'd say he's the most likely person to have sent that pendant and the letter to Derry: the one most likely to have cooked up a scheme like this.'

'I see what you mean.' Jessup ruminated in silence. He caught his visitor's eye. 'I take it the British police won't be making any inquiries about Wing?'

'Would they get in touch with the Hong Kong authorities, do you mean? Would they try to have him interviewed in prison?' Madden shook his head. 'I very much doubt it. They have no reason to. Of course it would be different if the investigation were reopened.'

'That's what I thought.' Jessup nodded. 'Look, if you feel it's worthwhile I can ask my people in Hong Kong if they have any news of him.'

'That might be helpful.' Madden bowed his head in thanks. 'And while we're on the subject of Stanley Wing, do you happen to know if it was he who gave the pendant to Miss Blake?'

'No, I don't.' Jessup shook his head. 'I mean I've no idea. But I rather assumed it was, given that it's jade. Are you sure it belonged to her? Couldn't it have been one of the pieces she was showing on Wing's behalf?'

'Miss Cooper seemed certain it was Portia's. She didn't know who had given it to her, though.'

'Then I'm sorry – I can't help you.' He spread his hands.

Madden glanced at his watch.

'I've only one other question,' he said. 'I hope you won't take it amiss.'

'I'm sure I won't.' Jessup smiled. 'And may I say that all in all this has been a fascinating afternoon. You've forced me to delve into my memory. These are things I haven't thought about for years.'

'I was wondering if Wing and your friend Rex Garner were acquainted. Had they met before that weekend?'

'Is that what's bothering you?' His host seemed amused by the question. 'Yes, they had. Rex worked briefly for Jessup's when he was a young man. We were friends from our days at Eton and Father knew him well. He was sent out to Hong Kong as a trainee and spent a year there. I remember him talking about Stanley when he came back. "That Wing fellow of yours," he said, "he's an odd bird, but useful."'

'What did he mean by that?'

'I didn't care to inquire.' Jessup's tone was dry. 'I knew enough about Stanley Wing to assume it was probably disreputable.'

He saw the look in Madden's eye.

'Yes, all right. I'll be more explicit. The key to Stanley's success has always been his ability to acquire whatever it is that his customers want. He's by nature a *procurer*, and since I also knew that Rex liked to have a girl on hand and wasn't too particular in that respect, I didn't care to delve too deeply into whatever sort of relationship they might have struck up. But I had a pretty good idea what it involved.'

'Garner only stayed there for a year, you say.' Madden had taken a moment or two to digest the other's reply. 'Why was that?'

'Well, to put it bluntly, he was no good. Rex has never been one to put his shoulder to the wheel. He rather expects things to fall into his lap. The management out there said they couldn't rely on him for anything: that quite often he didn't even bother to turn up for work. In the end it was gently suggested to him that he might seek his future elsewhere.' Jessup smiled. 'Why are you asking me about him?'

'It occurred to me that if Portia Blake was putting on a

performance that evening, it seems to have been directed at him. I was also going to ask, too, whether *they* knew each other?'

'Rex and Miss Blake? You mean, was there anything between them?' Jessup bit his lip. He seemed unhappy with the question. Madden watched as he sat frowning and rubbing his chin. Finally, he spoke. 'Not that I'm aware of: though I admit I did wonder at the time. Margaret had been away in Scotland for a few weeks during the summer and I knew how Rex's eye tended to stray when she was out of town. I even asked him about it, but he swore to me that he only knew Miss Blake casually. He'd run into her once or twice at parties; that was all. He said he'd been embarrassed by the way she had gone at him over dinner. He had no idea why she'd done it, but he'd decided to make himself scarce the following day. He didn't want a repeat performance at lunch. I told you about him driving into Canterbury.'

'What time did he get back?' Madden asked.

'Around mid-afternoon, I gathered. By then Miss Blake's body had been discovered. You're not thinking . . .'

His expression changed.

'No, that's absurd. People don't go around murdering other people just because they're put out. Rex was cross with her, certainly, but that was all.'

His bright gaze stayed fixed on Madden's face. It was as though he were trying to read his thoughts.

'Given the way Miss Blake behaved at dinner, might Garner's wife have suspected that they had had an affair?' Madden asked.

'I can't answer that. I've no idea. But it wouldn't have surprised her . . . not eventually, anyway.'

'Eventually . . . ?'

'The marriage was always troubled. Rex was a rotten husband. He only married Margaret for her money and he was never faithful to her for long. She was very unhappy. Rumour had it she was going to divorce him, but then she died suddenly. That was in 1944. Rex was home on leave and they had a flaming row – or so he said – and she ended up taking an accidental overdose of sleeping pills.'

He was silent for a moment.

'People were surprised when they got married. Margaret was a shy girl, and quite plain. But if you knew Rex as well as I did then I'm sorry to say it made perfect sense. He was on the look-out for a rich wife. It was as simple as that. We were great friends when we were boys, but all that's past I'm afraid. Sarah can't abide him, and I can understand why. Truth to tell, we don't see much of each other now. And when we do, it's usually because Rex wants to borrow money from me. He's managed to go through most of what Margaret left him – and it was a lot – but he still tries to keep up appearances, play the part of a rich man about town. It's all a front, though.'

'Does he live in London?' Madden asked.

'He's got a house near Shepherd Market; heavily mort-gaged, I believe. Are you planning to talk to him?'

'I might. It rather depends on whether Mr Sinclair thinks this inquiry is worth pursuing.'

'You're welcome to mention my name if you do,' Jessup said. 'I'll get Miss Harmon to give you his address and tele-phone number.'

He rose to his feet. Madden did the same.

'I'd like to thank you for being so frank with me,' he said. 'I've got a much clearer picture now of that weekend.'

'I'm glad to have been of help,' Jessup responded, with the open smile that Madden had come to expect from him.

'And please feel free to get in touch with me again if you need to.'

About to move to the door, he checked his stride. He saw that his visitor had something further to say.

'There is one more favour I'd like to ask of you.' Madden had hesitated before making the request. 'Could you possibly put me in touch with Mrs Castleton? She's someone I'd like to talk to.'

'But of course. I should have thought of that myself.' Jessup's smile broadened. 'Nothing could be simpler. She lives near Kew Gardens. She'd been staying at our house in Hampshire taking care of the children while Sarah and I were in the United States, but she's home again now. I could have spent another hour talking to you about Adele. She's a wonderful woman – and far and away the best thing that ever happened to my father. In the few years they were together she made him happier than he'd ever been in his life and I'm glad to say she's still very much a part of our family. Sarah thinks the world of her, and so do the children. As far as they're concerned she's their real grandmother, and I dread the day when I'll have to tell them that she's not.'

He chuckled.

'Unfortunately I'll be away on the Continent for the next fortnight on business. But I'll write her a note before I go telling her who you are and that I fully support the inquiries you're making. I'll give you her address and telephone number, too, so that you can get in touch with her. I'm sure you'll find her helpful.'

'It wasn't just that I liked him, Angus. I was impressed by him. It must be a huge responsibility, running a concern like Jessup's. Yet he carries it all so lightly.'

'And you don't feel he was keeping anything back?'

'About Rex Garner? No, I don't. He doesn't believe Garner could have had anything to do with Miss Blake's death. He made that clear. But he was quite open about his womanizing.'

They were speaking on the telephone. Madden had rung the chief inspector when he got back from the City and was standing now in a hall stripped of all furniture save for the small table where the phone rested. Even the painting that had hung on the wall above – and which Madden was accustomed to gaze at whenever he used the instrument – had disappeared. It was the study of Westminster Bridge which Alice had claimed for her own, and it appeared that she had already taken possession of the object. In its place now there was only the ghostly outline left by the frame on the wallpaper behind it.

'I was interested to learn that Garner also knew Wing,' Madden went on. 'That might be a line of inquiry worth pursuing.'

'Why?'

'We still don't know why Wing brought Portia Blake down to Kent with him. But bearing in mind that scene at dinner, and the way Miss Blake carried on, it's possible it was somehow linked to Rex Garner being there at the same time.'

'Would Wing have known that: before he got there, I mean?'

'I don't know. But it's something I can ask Mrs Castleton when I see her. And I've a lot more to tell you about Mr Wing . . .'

Madden broke off at the sound of footsteps above. Looking up he saw Lucy coming down the stairs.

'Yes, go on.' Sinclair's voice sounded in his ear. 'What about him?'

'Look, if you don't mind, I'd rather not talk about it now,' Madden replied after a moment. 'I'm a bit caught up at present. Let's discuss it at the weekend. We'll have plenty of time then.'

'Was that Angus?' Lucy asked when she had reached the bottom of the stairs and Madden had replaced the receiver. 'I'm sorry. I wasn't listening in.'

'Listening in . . . ?'

'Only I wouldn't want you to think I was eavesdropping.' Lucy's blue eyes were the image of her mother's and at that moment her gaze was guilt-ridden and apologetic. 'I know you don't want to talk about this case in front of me any more and I understand why. I shouldn't have babbled on in that way.'

'My darling, I don't want you to feel shut out . . .'

Madden was at a loss for words. In the wake of the events of the previous Sunday he had been suffering from an attack of guilt: he felt he had been too harsh with his daughter and Lucy's uncharacteristic meekness since then, the burden of sackcloth and ashes she wore, her penitent's expression, had only added to his feeling of remorse.

'It's just that . . . that . . . I prattle on without thinking, I know. I *must* be more careful in future. This has been a good lesson for me.'

She took his arm.

'I've given Alice the evening off. I'm going to make you dinner. You probably don't know, but she managed to squeeze two pork chops out of the butcher this morning. Such riches! Let's go into the kitchen and decide what we're going to do with them.'

She paused when she saw the look on his face.

'Don't worry, Daddy. We're going to have a lovely evening. And I don't want you to think you have to say a *word* about Angus's case. We've lots of other things to talk about.'

'So you see if Rex Garner and Portia did have an affair in the past, it would change things. Of course, it may not be important – she seems to have had a lot of men friends – but he also knew Stanley Wing from years back. Angus and Tom Derry didn't know that: they never had a chance to find out. There may be some significance to it.'

'It's a triangle, isn't it?' Lucy's face lit up. 'A love triangle!'

'Oh, I doubt that.' Madden dismissed the notion. 'Wing wasn't one of her lovers: that's for certain. No, the question is, was Portia just flirting with Garner to amuse herself, or was there some meaning behind the performance she put on with that pendant, dangling it in front of his eyes? By the end of dinner Garner looked quite mesmerized, or so Sir Richard said.'

'I think it meant something.' Lucy was reluctant to abandon her suspicions. 'Otherwise why was the pendant taken from her body?'

'You could look at it that way.'

As though prompted by his own words, Madden paused to study the wine in his glass. The remains of their meal lay about them on the kitchen table. His daughter was a surprisingly good cook – surprising only because she had the gift of never seeming to take pains over anything, yet somehow managing to achieve a level of skill beyond mere competence; and all that with flair and style. Despite having observed her closely throughout her life, he still didn't know how she managed it, any more than he understood why he was talking so freely about the inquiry to her now. It wasn't as though Lucy had raised the subject herself. It was he who had chosen to refer in a casual way to the call he had received from Jessup's secretary earlier that day, a remark that had led with seeming inevitability to the conversation they were having now.

'But it still depends on the two factors being linked.' He dragged his mind back to the present. 'I mean Portia's performance the night before and the disappearance of the pendant. But if someone just happened to find the pendant – if it was torn off her neck in the struggle and picked up later in the wood – then the whole idea of a connection between them falls away.'

'So it could be just a red herring?' Clearly unhappy with the notion, Lucy frowned.

'Yes, and there might be nothing to any of this,' Madden felt bound to point out. 'We have to bear that in mind. All these interviews I'm having – they may be a waste of time. It could be that we'll decide at a certain moment that they were right all along, Angus and Derry. That there's no need to reopen the investigation.'

'Oh, I hope not.' No longer able to restrain herself, his daughter gave vent to her frustration. 'It would be such a damp squib.'

'I'd hardly call it that.'

'Well, you know what I mean.' Catching his eye, she smiled; and then stretched. 'I must get these things washed up before I go to bed.'

'No, don't worry. I'll clear the table.' Madden returned her smile. 'I'll put the dishes in the sink. Alice will see to them in the morning. And thank you for dinner, my dear. It was delicious.'

He watched as she rose and came around the table.

'I'm so glad we talked.' She bent to kiss him goodnight.

'I hated everything being so stiff and formal between us. It made me so unhappy. You don't realize how important it is for me to know that you're always there and that I can say anything I want to you and you'll understand.'

She kissed him again and then went to the door; pausing to glance back at him.

'Why are you looking at me that way?'

'It's something your mother said. She seems to think I'm putty in your fingers. I can't think why.'

'Well, it's not true.' Her smile dazzled him.

'I'm relieved to hear it. Goodnight, my darling. And sleep well.'

9

'THAT TIME YOU met her at a party – what did you talk about?' Madden asked.

'Me, mostly. Of course, I knew who she was and I was rather in awe of her: we all were. But as I said, she turned out to be quite different: not at all what I expected.'

Helen turned to smile at him, her face bright in the morning sunlight. They were sitting on a bench on the platform at Highfield station waiting for the train that would take Madden to London, where he had an appointment to meet Adele Castleton later that day. Wanting to form some sort of picture of a woman about whom he had heard just enough to make him curious, he had asked Helen to describe her and she had been doing her best to recall the details of their brief encounter.

'It was one of those parties in London that Violet and I went to that autumn; there seem to have been dozens, though there can't have been that many. All I remember is that I was starting to get tired of them: the same faces, the same partners, the same dance bands. I had gone to the bathroom and was on my way out when I caught sight of Adele sitting on her own in a small room off the passage. She was smoking a cigarette. I was going to walk by, but she called out to me. "Come and sit down," she said. "Helen, is it?"'

She told me she had noticed me dancing earlier and asked who I was. I felt tremendously flattered. She was older than I was, of course, and a figure in society: not beautiful exactly, but tremendously attractive, with dark hair and pale skin. And something more: it was in her manner, the way she carried herself. I suppose you would call it "presence". She only had to enter a room and all eyes would be drawn to her. That was partly because of her reputation, of course. There were endless stories about her and although half of them probably weren't true, you could tell just by looking at her that she was different; and that she didn't care what people thought of her. I was nervous – I couldn't think what I was going to say to her – but I needn't have worried. As soon as I sat down she began asking me questions. She wanted to know who I was and where I came from and what I was doing with my life. They were quite intimate questions, but I didn't mind because I could see she was really interested, and so I told her that I was getting tired of the social life we were all caught up in, the never-ending parties, and that I'd applied to study medicine at London University, but I wasn't sure whether I'd get in, being a woman. I thought it might sound pretentious to her, but I couldn't have been more mistaken. She said it was a wonderful idea and I should do it. And then she said something I've never forgotten. "Don't be like me and find yourself sitting on your own at a party one night wondering what to do next, and whether it even matters."'

Helen sighed.

'We were going to meet again. She said she would get in touch with me once she had sorted out a few things in her life – that was how she put it – and we could have lunch together and talk more; but I never saw her again. She went to America soon afterwards. I read about it in a gossip column. She was with some man. But I got into university, as you know, and I always hoped that the news might have reached her wherever she was. Will you give her a message from me? Say I remember meeting her and that I'm sorry we lost touch after that.'

A whistle from down the track alerted them to the approach of Madden's train. He had not been up to London that week, preferring to stay at home and attend to work at the farm, leaving his daughter to see to the gradual disposal of Aunt Maud's furniture. Lucy had decided to remain in the house at least until the end of the month while she looked about for a suitable flat for them to buy.

'I'm glad you two have patched things up,' Helen said as they rose from the bench.

'Just as you predicted, you mean?' Madden drew her to him. 'And you're quite right. I won't deny it any longer. I am putty in her fingers. And yours, too, I suspect.'

'Nonsense. Whatever gave you that idea?'

Laughing, she kissed him on the lips. Then she drew back.

'You won't forget my message, will you?'

'Of course not.'

'I wonder if *she'll* remember . . .'

Acting on Jessup's advice, Madden had waited for a few days after their meeting before ringing Adele Castleton.

The interval had also given him an opportunity to discuss the case further with Sinclair, whom he had found in notably better spirits and moving about gingerly with the help of a cane. They had spent an hour together after lunch on Sunday sitting in the shade of the chief inspector's apple tree while Madden gave his old friend an account of his conversation with Sir Richard Jessup; in particular what he had learned about the fateful weekend when Portia Blake had lost her life.

'There was certainly something going on,' he said.

'Whatever the reason behind it, her behaviour at dinner sounds artificial to me. So was she put up to it, and if so, by whom? Stanley Wing would seem to be the obvious candidate. But even if that's true, what possible motive could he have had for stirring things up? And let's not forget there's still no reason to suppose that that scene had anything to do with her murder the next day. That still looks to me more like a chance killing than anything else.'

Sinclair's muttered growl in response had suggested he was not yet ready to accept the proposition, and his next words lent force to that impression.

'But we still haven't heard what Mrs Castleton has to say, have we? Let's suspend judgement until then.'

The lady in question had received Madden's telephone call in what had sounded like a friendly spirit – it was clear that Sir Richard Jessup had been in touch with her – and they had fixed to meet at her house.

'I live near Kew Gardens,' she had told him. 'You can come down by tube if you like, or there's a bus that will drop you at the Victoria Gate. I'm only five minutes' walk from there.'

Of the two alternatives offered him, it was the train Madden chose, and having been deposited at Kew station a little after four o'clock he made his way through leafy suburban streets to the address given him, which proved on arrival to be a small, neat-looking villa standing in its own patch of garden and shielded from the street by an ivy-clad wall.

'I was in love with Kew when I was a child,' his hostess told him later. 'My father was an amateur botanist. Plants were his passion; he seized every opportunity to visit the gardens, and once he discovered that I shared his interest he used to take me with him. We would wander through the park and the greenhouses hand-in-hand. My happiest memories of childhood all have to do with the hours we spent together. When Jack died and I knew I would have to leave Foxley Hall there was only one place I could think of living; which is why you find me here.'

Madden's ring on the doorbell had been answered by a maid of similar vintage to Alice – they were becoming a rarity in post-war England – who had led him through the house to the garden behind it where Mrs Castleton awaited him. Dressed simply in a tweed skirt and workaday blouse, she had been kneeling on the grass, digging in a border with a trowel when he was ushered through a pair of French windows on to a small paved patio, and had risen at once to greet her visitor.

'I've been so looking forward to meeting you, Mr Madden.'

Removing the gardening gloves she was wearing, she had offered him a hand bare of rings to shake. Slight of figure and with short grey hair now – no trace remained of the dark locks that Helen remembered – she appeared to be in her late sixties with a delicate bone structure that gave more than a hint of the looks that must once have drawn men to her; and might still have done so had she wished it. But it was the intense quality of her gaze that seized Madden's attention – her eyes were deep and dark; that and the sense she gave at once of being at ease in his company while not caring what impression he might have of her. He guessed this was what Helen had meant by the word 'presence'.

'You made a great impression on Richard. He wanted to know more about you, he said, but was obliged to spend the time you had together answering *your* questions.'

She had let a few moments go by before speaking again.

It was as though she wished to give each of them the opportunity to appraise the other.

'I felt it was the other way round,' Madden replied. 'I'm still in awe at the thought of what it must take to run a concern like Jessup's. I know that the war interrupted Sir Richard's business career, but if I understood him right he must have felt ready to take on the responsibility when he was still in his early thirties.'

'When Jack had to relinquish control of the company, you mean?' She nodded. 'Of course, he wasn't well, but even so he felt it was time he handed over the reins to someone younger.' She smiled. 'Poor darling, he really was no sort of businessman, and he knew it. And as you say, Richard was more than ready to take command.'

There was a table with some chairs standing in a corner of the patio and she led him to it, turning to her maid as she did so.

'You can bring us our tea now, Agnes.'

She waited until they were alone again before continuing.

'Richard has told me why you went to see him. I do find it extraordinary that this dreadful business should be brought up again after all this time. But he explained about the pendant to me and said all he wanted was to see the matter cleared up once and for all. He asked me to help you in any way I could, which, of course, I'll do, though I doubt there's much I can add to what he's already told you.'

'It's very generous of you both.' Madden bowed his head in thanks. 'But before we begin, I've a message for you. It's from my wife. She wants me to tell you that she went ahead and did what she said she would do. She studied medicine and became a doctor. She wonders if you remember her telling you that. It was a long time ago.'

Plainly astonished, Mrs Castleton stared at him open-mouthed. They sat like that for several seconds, neither saying a word. Then, without warning, she tossed her head back and laughed.

'*Helen!*' she said. 'Is that her name? It *must* be.'

Madden nodded.

'Of course I remember. I can see her now. She was such a lovely young woman, so open and engaging. It was at a party in London. We sat and talked. I was so envious, hearing what she wanted to do with her life. I remember wishing I had done the same; not studying medicine, but something I really cared about . . . botany for instance; or natural history. We were going to meet again, but then . . . oh, let's not talk of that. It depresses me just to think of it.'

She shuddered.

'Helen . . .' She murmured the name again. Then, still clearly struck by the memory he had stirred, she drew back a little in her chair as though to underline the importance of what she was about to say next.

'Tell me, Mr Madden, when you married her did you feel you had won some great and undeserved prize in life?'

He looked at her in wonder.

'How on earth did you know that?'

'I told you – I *remember* her.' Her dark eyes held him captive. 'But tell me more, please. When did you meet?'

'It was after the war – the first war. I was a police officer then, a detective, and I was assigned to a murder investigation in the village where Helen lived. I had served in the army and when it was over I returned to my old job at Scotland Yard. But it wasn't the same: *I* wasn't the same. I hadn't recovered from my time in the trenches.'

'And did you fall in love with her at once?' Mrs Castleton checked herself. She put a hand to her cheek. 'Forgive me,

Mr Madden. It's none of my business. My friends are always telling me I'm too direct. Don't answer if you'd rather not.'

'I'm sure that I did.' Madden had no hesitation in replying. 'Although I wasn't aware of it at first.'

Even as he spoke, he was struck by the extraordinary sense of intimacy she had created between them in the space of only a few minutes. He saw, too, that it was this same gift that must have been at the very heart of the fascination she had held for so many people.

'Quite simply the thought seemed impossible. I couldn't imagine I might ever mean anything to her.'

'Why was that?'

'It was the war. I thought something had broken inside me. I couldn't feel any more. I was numb. A lot of men who came back from the trenches had the same experience. I couldn't see any future for myself. I felt I was damaged goods.'

He had never talked this way to anyone but Helen, yet the words seemed to flow naturally, as though from a hidden source.

'But she saw through all that? Is that what you're saying?'

'As if it were in plain sight.'

The memory of those days – so precious to him – was still fresh in his mind. It was as if he were speaking of yesterday.

'I didn't have to tell her anything. It was as though she already knew. It still seems like a miracle to me.'

'Dear Mr Madden . . .' There were tears in Adele Castleton's eyes. 'I do believe you and I are two of a kind. Jack Jessup was my saviour. I met him in Kenya in 1930.'

She was interrupted by the rattle of crockery behind her, signalling the arrival of the tea trolley, and for a while she was occupied with pouring their tea while her maid hovered over the table, first handing Madden his cup and then offering him a choice of biscuits or cake, both of which were carried on a stand. Only when she had left them did Mrs Castleton resume speaking.

'I was there with friends and we were invited to visit a farm in the highlands. I was already wishing I hadn't come – to Africa, I mean. It seemed like just another pointless holiday: and a holiday from what? I'd been drifting for so long that I'd lost all sense of direction. Jack was staying with the family on the farm. I knew who he was, of course. Black Jack Jessup, the papers called him. He was said to be a friend of the Prince of Wales. He was about to go off on safari the next day and was only there, at the farm, for that one night. I was feeling ghastly.' She put a hand to her cheek. 'Not unwell, but simply despairing. I lost my husband not long after we were married. He was quite rich, but he wanted to be a racing driver and was killed in a crash. After that I seemed to lose my bearings and went from one man to another until I reached the point where I couldn't see any way of escaping from the mess I had made of my life. I sat up late on my own in front of the fire – it was the end of summer and the nights were getting cold – and Jack found me there. He had come down in his dressing-gown and pyjamas to look for a book, but instead he sat down beside me and asked me what the trouble was.'

She smiled.

'I didn't want to talk to him. I didn't want to talk to anyone. I was too miserable. But he wouldn't be put off. He said he wasn't going to leave me. He would sit there all night if necessary. And so after a while we began to talk: that is, I began to talk and he to listen. We sat there until nearly dawn and then he said I had to go to bed. I needed to get some sleep, he said, but since he was leaving later that morning

I would have to be up and ready to go by ten o'clock at the latest.'

She laughed.

'I told him he was mad, but he was absolutely insistent. There was no way he was going to leave me behind. I had to go with him on his safari. He would show me Africa – the real Africa – and we could continue talking. "Don't you see?" he said, as though it were the simplest thing in the world and how could I not understand it. "We've so much to say to each other. And we've hardly begun."'

She smiled again.

'I'll spare you the details – my protestations and so on. Suffice to say when the moment came for the lorry that was carrying Jack and his gear to leave I was on it. I remember waving goodbye to my friends and thinking what an addition this would make to the catalogue of scandalous behaviour that had attached itself to my name over the years.

'I told myself I was setting out on another of my foolish adventures – Lord knows there'd been enough of those – but all the same I had a feeling that this time it would be different. I had already sensed a quality in Jack Jessup that I wasn't used to finding in the men I'd known: a deep strain of kindness. It was what had kept him sitting up with me all night. He had seen that I was in pain and had set out to heal me if he could. Of course, he had no way of knowing that what he was about to show me – the wildness of Africa, the animals, the wonderful unspoilt country – was a dream I had carried in my heart since childhood. I don't know what Dr Freud would have made of the attraction I felt for this man who reminded me in so many ways of my father and who had appeared as if from nowhere to take me by the hand. But we didn't become lovers for some time: not on the safari, and not when we returned to Nairobi. It was only on the voyage back to England. But by then I knew we weren't going to part.'

She was silent for a moment, lost in memory.

'Jack had told me from the very beginning that he couldn't marry me. His wife wouldn't give him a divorce – it was her last way of punishing him – and he was too much the English gentleman to divorce her on grounds of desertion. I told him it didn't matter; and truly it didn't. I had long since lost any desire for respectability. All I wanted was to remain with him for the rest of my life; or his, as it turned out.'

She shifted her glance away from Madden to the sun-dappled lawn beside them and they sat in silence. Then she faced him again.

'We settled down at Foxley Hall and from that moment on we were seldom separated for more than a day or two. I soon realized that, like me, he was also trapped in a way of life he had neither sought nor wanted. I mean the company – Jessup's. It was something he had inherited, something he couldn't get rid of: until Richard grew up, that is, and was able to take it off his hands.'

'He told me he didn't see much of his father when he was young.' Madden was absorbed by the tale he was hearing. 'Was that because of his mother?'

Mrs Castleton nodded. 'As I say, she wanted to punish Jack, and keeping his son away from him was the best way of doing that. But when he got older Richard wanted to know him better, and by the end they had developed a close bond. It made an enormous difference to Jack's last years: not only because of the personal link, but also because Richard proved to be such a strong ally when it came to dealing with the company. He seemed born to take over the business and Jack came to lean on him more and more.

'They were alike in so many ways. I don't know how I

would have coped with the loss of Jack if Richard hadn't made it plain from the outset that as far as he and Sarah were concerned I was as much a part of the family as if we had been married. It's been a great blessing to me, and one I hardly feel I deserve, given my disreputable past. I seem to spend almost as much time in Hampshire with them and their children as I do here. I can never thank them enough.'

Her expression had changed while she was talking. She looked thoughtful now.

'But although they were so similar – both kind and generous – there was one great difference between them. Underneath it all, Richard has a core of steel. I often wonder if he inherited it from his mother. I never met her, but by all accounts she was a woman of iron will, and absolutely unforgiving where Jack was concerned. When Richard began the process of taking over from his father, of gathering the reins of Jessup's into his hands, he realized that some heads were going to have to roll, especially in Hong Kong. Over the years Jack had let things slide to an alarming degree – his heart was never in the business – and Richard told me later he'd been appalled to discover the true state of affairs and how close the company was to bankruptcy. He had had to act quickly. The firings were wholesale and some of the people involved were old friends of Jack's; they had been with Jessup's for years. There was no question that radical action was needed; but it was something Jack could never have brought himself to do. It simply wasn't in him. But Richard sees things with a cooler eye. He's never been one to be blinded by sentiment. He can do what has to be done. I don't know about you, Mr Madden, but it's a quality I've come to admire and value.'

'But not one all of us possess.' Madden's smile was rueful.

'He gave me a hint of it when we talked about Stanley Wing. He said he had had to get rid of him.'

'Ah yes . . . Stanley Wing.'

Her gaze had clouded.

'Richard said you would want to ask me about him. Well, I wasn't altogether surprised when Jack told me he'd invited Stanley down to Foxley Hall for that weekend. He had always felt bad about him after Richard had insisted that the tie between Wing and Jessup's had to be broken. He didn't disagree with the decision – I think he knew in his heart that Stanley was a rotten apple – but having been moved to rescue him when he was a boy he had always felt some sort of responsibility for him. Of course I knew the whole story – how they came to meet, what Stanley's background was – before we went out to Hong Kong for the first time. But it still came as a shock when I realized that under all his surface politeness and formal good manners he obviously detested us.'

'*Detested* you?' Madden was brought up short by the word. 'What do you mean? And how could you know that if he didn't show it?'

'Oh, my instincts are seldom wrong: especially when it comes to men.' She caught his eye and smiled. 'I could see that he hated all of us, the British community as a whole, including the senior staff at Jessup's, even if he tried to keep it hidden. I'm afraid Jack was wrong about him. He believed that Stanley was grateful and even felt some affection for him. But I sensed he was cold, without what we think of as human feeling; cold and watchful. I don't know what his early life did to him; perhaps the damage he suffered was irreparable. But I felt instinctively that he was a dangerous man and it worried me that Jack was so attached to him.'

She paused, frowning.

'Mind you, Stanley had much to be bitter about. We British have such an ingrained sense of what we like to think of as our superiority to other races that we sometimes forget the effect it has on them; and Stanley being of mixed blood had the added misfortune of not being accepted by either community – British or Chinese. Wing isn't his real name, you know. His father was called Liang, and his mother gave him that name, partly out of defiance, Jack told me. Not that it did any good: the family turned their back on her. They refused to acknowledge any connection with Stanley. After Jack took him up he changed his name to Wing, which isn't a Chinese name, properly speaking. Perhaps Stanley wanted to distance himself from his father's people. But he found no great welcome from the British either, I'm afraid.'

'A touch of the chink . . .' Madden grimaced. 'I heard someone use those words about him recently, quite casually, and without thinking. I imagine it's the sort of thing he had to put up with.'

'You can be sure of it.' Mrs Castleton frowned. 'Mind you, Richard wasn't like that. He would never have spoken in that way. He took after his father. But he saw quite early on that Stanley was using the company for his own purposes, some of them illegal, and he was determined to get shot of him. It was a painful decision as far as Jack was concerned; but he knew Richard was right. Still, nothing would have made him turn his back on the boy he had saved from the streets, and when Stanley called that summer and asked if he could come and see us Jack agreed at once. I know that Stanley ended up in prison finally. I'm just thankful it didn't happen while Jack was alive.'

In the silence that followed her words the fluting warble of a thrush sounded from the shrubbery at the foot of the garden. Another of the species had been busy on the lawn for some time, stabbing at the grass with its beak in a cease-less search for insect prey. Mrs Castleton watched it for a moment. Then she turned back to her visitor.

'Forgive me. I've spent all this time telling you about my wicked past when what you want to know about is that weekend. But is it really likely that the police will reopen the investigation into the poor girl's death? Richard seemed uncertain.'

'And so am I,' Madden said. 'I haven't come across any-thing yet that would justify it. As he may have told you, I'm only doing this for a friend, a man I worked under at the Yard years ago, and I know from experience that once you start probing into people's lives and their behaviour, which is what happens in a police investigation, all sorts of odd and sometimes embarrassing things come to light which have nothing to do with the inquiry you're making.'

'Dear me. That does sound ominous.'

'I hope it won't be that bad.' Madden smiled. 'But from what I've been told it seems that even before Miss Blake's murder, that weekend wasn't entirely without incident. There was something in the air . . .'

'You're alluding to what happened at dinner the night before: that extraordinary performance of hers.' Mrs Castle-ton shook her head. 'I'd never seen anything like it. And the dress she was wearing – it would have turned heads in a Soho dive. We were all spellbound when she appeared downstairs; and from that point on, rather like grand opera, things only got worse.'

'According to Sir Richard, she seemed to make a point of tormenting Rex Garner. Was that your impression?'

'Yes, I suppose so.' Mrs Castleton took a moment to think before responding to the question. 'Mind you, she was sitting across the table from him, so in a sense he was her natural audience for all the byplay that was going on with the pendant. I felt she was quite aware that the rest of us were watching her, too, and rather enjoying the effect she was having on the party. Stanley, for one, was positively glaring.'

'The pendant – it was very much part of her act, was it?'

'It was quite central to it, I would say. She kept playing with it, swinging it from side to side like a pendulum. I couldn't think what she was up to.'

'Sir Richard said the effect was hypnotic: on Garner, at least.'

'Did he?' She smiled bleakly. 'I would have said he looked more dazed. He had his wife sitting almost beside him. I think that upset him more than anything. He kept glancing at her as if to reassure her; or at least suggest that he didn't know why Miss Blake was behaving in that way.'

'I asked Sir Richard if there had been anything between them in the past. He said that Garner had sworn to him that there hadn't; though he admitted to knowing the girl, or at least having met her.'

'So I gathered. Richard told me later they knew each other. If I'd known, I would never have invited the two of them down to Kent at the same time. But Miss Blake was a complete stranger to me. I heard her name for the first time when Jack told me that Stanley had asked if he could bring someone with him.'

'I have another question, though I don't know whether you can answer it.' Madden hesitated. 'Did Miss Blake know that Rex Garner would be there that weekend?'

Taken aback, she hesitated before replying. 'You're wondering whether she planned that scene with him.'

'That, and whether Wing might have put her up to it. He seemed to have some kind of hold over her. That's according to the woman she shared a flat with.'

'What a disagreeable thought.' Mrs Castleton brooded on the notion. 'Well, I can't answer your first question except to say that the invitation to Stanley Wing was extended *before* I decided to invite the Garners, so neither he nor Miss Blake could have known that Rex would be here at that point. However, Stanley and Rex had been acquainted for a number of years and if they had run into each other in London, which I believe they did, it's quite possible that Rex might have mentioned he would be in Kent on those dates.'

'It could have been after that that Wing got in touch with Sir Jack again.' He saw that his meaning escaped her. 'Sir Richard told me that Wing rang his father a second time only a week before he was due to come down to ask if he could bring Miss Blake with him.'

'I'd forgotten that.' She frowned. 'But you're right. Jack was captivated by the idea. He told me he'd never associated Stanley with a girlfriend and couldn't wait to see who he would bring with him. In the event Miss Blake, when she appeared, was quite a shock. She was a very pretty girl, and Jack simply couldn't get his mind around the fact that it was Stanley of all people who had brought her down.'

She paused.

'But as far as Wing being perhaps behind that display she put on during dinner, I think you're mistaken. After everyone had gone to bed I went to check on something upstairs and when I walked past Miss Blake's room I heard the two of them arguing – she and Wing. Only they weren't quarrelling exactly: it was more a case of Stanley reading her the riot act. I didn't pause to eavesdrop, but I heard enough to convince me that he was simply furious with her over the way she had behaved. That in itself was unusual; he so seldom showed emotion of any kind. But he was seething, fairly hissing with rage. "What is this game you're playing?" I heard him say. A few minutes later, when I came back, I heard her laughing. "Don't worry. They're in a safe place," she said. Then he muttered something which I didn't catch. But he sounded furious.'

She sighed then.

'It was a terrible shock for all of us when we heard what had happened to Miss Blake the next day; but particularly for darling Jack. He had a very traditional view of his role as host. That one of his guests – even if it was someone he barely knew – should come to such an awful end was a dreadful shock. As it was, he hadn't been well for some time – he had a degenerative heart condition – and the blow seemed to affect his health. He never really recovered after that and, as you probably know, he died the following year.'

'Then I can only say how sorry I am to have brought it all back.' Seeing the sadness in her eyes, Madden regretted the inadequacy of his apology. 'I should have realized.'

'You're not to think that.' She spoke firmly. 'Both Richard and I want this business cleared up. If there's anything more you need to ask me, please don't hesitate.'

'Then I've only one other question, but it's a delicate one.'

'Be brave, Mr Madden.' Her tone was teasing.

'It has to do with the Garners. How would you characterize their marriage?'

'Oh, dear!' The smile that had come to her lips vanished in an instant. 'Must I? Can it really have anything to do with Miss Blake's death?'

'It's possible.' Madden had to consider his reply. 'But only just. I'll admit I'm clutching at straws here. I gather she was a rich woman.'

'Yes, she came from a wealthy Scottish family. She was an only child.'

'And that Garner very likely married her for her money.'

'That was generally thought to be the case. There seemed no other reason for it. Rex is good looking, and a lot of women find him attractive. Personally, I've never cared for him, but Margaret was immensely flattered by his attentions. They made an odd-looking couple: the handsome pheasant cock and his dowdy hen. We could see the way things were going, Jack and I, but we were powerless to prevent it. Rex had her under his thumb from the start, and I know that as time went by she suffered more and more from the way he behaved.'

'Sir Richard told me how she died. Is it possible she took her own life?'

'Not according to the coroner.' Mrs Castleton shrugged. 'He ruled it a case of accidental death. I had my doubts, however; and so did others. Margaret was in the depths of depression. She seemed unable to face the prospect of what would certainly have been a squalid divorce case. I wasn't alone among her friends, though, in wishing she had grasped the nettle, if only to deprive Rex of what he eventually acquired.'

She caught Madden's questioning glance.

'He was left a lot of money in her will, though I'm told he's gone through most of it already. It meant he didn't have to look for a job, something he's never really had. However, I still don't see what his marriage to Margaret might have had to do with Miss Blake's death.'

'Probably nothing,' Madden agreed. 'In fact, this is what I meant by saying that inquiries of this sort have a way of delving into people's private lives, and not always appropriately.' He paused. 'And on that note I think I should take my leave. Thank you for all your help. You've been very patient with me.'

He prepared to rise to his feet, but checked his movement

when he saw that his hostess was distracted. She had looked away at that moment, frowning. He waited for her to say something, but she remained silent, and in the end it was he who spoke.

'I'm looking forward to telling Helen about our meeting. She was eager to have news of you.'

Mrs Castleton's face cleared at once. She turned to him.

'Will you tell her how very happy I am to hear that she did all she set out to do? And say I'd love to see her again.'

'I'm sure it can be arranged.' Madden smiled. 'In fact, I've a feeling she'll be writing to you very soon. If I know Helen she'll want you to come down to Highfield and spend a weekend with us.'

'Nothing would make me happier.'

She rose then and led him through the house, pausing in the sitting room to point out a framed photograph resting on a table by a window. It showed a man dressed in white duck trousers and a striped vest standing at the wheel of a yacht with a wide expanse of ocean behind him. Madden recognized his face from the painting and the snapshot he had seen in Richard Jessup's office.

'That's Jack,' Mrs Castleton said. 'We used to go sailing every summer. And there's Richard, with Sarah.' She pointed to another photograph. 'That was taken at their wedding.'

The couple stood arm-in-arm, Sir Richard in morning dress and his bride in a dazzling white gown. Slender, with fair hair that was cut short, Sarah Jessup, as she must just have become, faced the camera with a serious expression that was lightened by the hint of a smile playing about her lips. Although good looking enough in a conventional way, it was more the stamp of character that Madden fancied he saw in her face that impressed him.

'You'll hear people say that Richard, too, married her for

her money.' Mrs Castleton, standing at his shoulder, had noticed the direction of his glance. 'Jessup's was still in a bad financial state when they met and Richard was negotiating with the financial group headed by her father, Saul Temple. The war put a temporary stop to that, but later, when it ended, they made a substantial investment in the firm. It's what pulled Jessup's round in the end. You would have to know both Richard and Sarah to know how stupid and wrong those stories are. Richard fell head over heels in love with her and I fancy Sarah did the same. She's a wonderful partner for him; every bit his match.'

Having seen him out of the front door, Mrs Castleton accompanied her guest to the garden gate down a gravelled path bordered by flower beds and shaded, now that the sun was declining, by a tall box hedge. Reaching out to open the gate, she paused with her hand on the latch. Her expression was troubled. Madden recalled her distracted look earlier.

'I'm still thinking of what we were talking about a moment ago,' she confessed. 'I feel I can't let you go until I've unburdened myself. You hinted that if Rex had, in fact, had an affair with that young woman it could have had something to do with her death. Did you mean that Miss Blake might have been threatening to tell Margaret about it? That flirting with him in that theatrical manner was her way of warning him?'

'It was just a thought,' Madden responded cautiously. 'It might explain why she was dangling the pendant in front of his eyes in that way. He may have given it to her when their affair ended. But that's only a guess.'

'I see . . .' She bit her lip. 'So what you're wondering is whether Rex Garner might have been sufficiently disturbed by the thought of his infidelity being revealed to his wife to take drastic action.'

Madden hesitated. He was on delicate ground.

'It's something I've had to consider,' he admitted. 'Maybe I should explain. There are two possibilities: either Miss Blake had the bad luck to fall victim to a man who had already served time for attempted rape, and who in all likelihood was half drunk when they met by chance in that wood. In that case his conviction for murder stands and everything else falls away. But if there *was* a miscarriage of justice, as the two detectives who were in charge of the investigation now believe is possible, then there must be another explanation for her death, and it may well have something to do with her strange behaviour that weekend.'

Mrs Castleton nodded, understanding.

'Then what I can tell you is that Rex would certainly have been upset at that stage in their marriage to have Margaret made aware of his failings,' she said. 'She was very much his meal ticket, if I can put it crudely – she gave him a large allowance – and while he may well have strayed during the two years they had been married he'd been very careful up till then to keep his philandering a secret from her.'

She hesitated. Madden was silent. He sensed she had more to say.

'I didn't want to tell you this,' she went on after a moment. 'But since you're going to find out anyway you might as well hear it from me. Rex spent some time in Hong Kong when he was a young man. Jack sent him out there as a trainee.'

'I know about that. Sir Richard told me. He said Garner came back after only a year. Apparently it didn't work out.'

'That's true. But there was another reason.' She looked him in the eye. 'Rex was caught up in a scandal. Actually it was worse than that – he beat up a woman: quite savagely, I was told. She was Chinese, possibly a prostitute. The story was, he was drunk. I never knew the details – Jack didn't want to talk about it – and I don't know what happened to the woman, whether she ever recovered from the beating. But what I do know is that it was Stanley Wing who got him out of trouble. Somehow matters were smoothed over and Rex was put on the next boat back to England.'

'Did Sir Richard know that?' Madden asked.

'Of course, but he wouldn't have told you about it. He's like Jack was. He has old-fashioned notions of loyalty. He and Rex have known each other since boyhood. And although Richard finds their friendship a burden now – I think I can say that – he would still try to protect him if he could.'

She held his gaze.

'I feel no such loyalty to Rex,' she said. 'He's a selfish, calculating man who has always managed to live off others, mainly women. He's a sponger at heart. I don't wish him ill, but if he did have anything to do with that poor girl's death, he ought to answer for it.

10

'So you think it's a toss-up at best, do you, John? But surely there's still a chance the Yard might go for it?'

Angus Sinclair shifted uncomfortably in his chair. He had been immobile for some time sitting under the apple tree in his garden listening to Madden, and although his gout-ridden foot no longer rested on a cushioned stool as before, it was still encased in its padded felt slipper; still tender.

'They might.' Madden scowled. 'There's enough doubt now to make Charlie Chubb think again. I'm not so sure about Cradock, though. He's the one who'll make the final decision and he'll probably need more convincing.'

'But he can't deny that Garner's a possible suspect.'

'Possible being the operative word.'

Madden rose to stretch his legs and to move the hosepipe that had been playing on one end of the rose bed behind where he was sitting. It was the day following his meeting with Adele Castleton and he had stopped at the chief inspector's cottage on his way back from the farm to give him an account of their conversation. Not surprisingly, it was Mrs Castleton's opinion of Rex Garner's character and how he might have reacted to any threat to his marriage that had aroused Sinclair's suspicion.

'If the case were to be reopened, he could certainly be questioned about how well he knew Portia Blake.'

Madden returned to his chair and sat down.

'But whether that's enough in itself to prod the Yard into

action I can't say. There's nothing you could point to as evidence as yet. Garner's disappearance on the day following that dinner and the fact that he didn't show his face at the house again until after Portia Blake's body was discovered is open to question. But he told Mrs Castleton he was going into Canterbury to meet a friend and if he can back that up – if the friend, whoever it was, can give him an alibi – then presumably he's off the hook.'

The chief inspector growled.

'There's no avoiding the mistakes we made in the original investigation,' he admitted. 'We should have checked his alibi at the time; and we would have if Norris hadn't been arrested with Miss Blake's jewellery in his possession and if he hadn't confessed to the murder so soon afterwards.'

He shot a glance at Madden.

'Still, never mind – even if it was eleven years ago it's not too late. Garner can still be asked to name the friend he went to see.'

'But not by me.'

Madden had assumed they would get to this point and was ready with his response.

'I can't do that, Angus: checking alibis is a matter for the police; as would be tracking down the other members of the household – I'm thinking of the staff – which would probably be necessary if this turned into a full-blown investigation.'

'Oh, I can see that.' The chief inspector grunted. 'And as I think I mentioned before, you've already done enough. I'm more than grateful. But I'm sorry to see you so pessimistic. Surely even Cradock will be forced to recognize that there was a lot more going on among Jessup's guests that weekend than met the eye.'

'Yes, but does that add up to one of them having a guilty

secret? We've still no evidence of that. And if you're thinking of Garner as the possible killer, there could be a problem with that. Once you put the actual murder under a microscope it becomes difficult to imagine how Portia Blake could have been killed other than by the man who was sent to the gallows for it.'

'Explain, would you?' Sinclair frowned.

'It's a question of opportunity. How much time would someone other than Norris have had, first to kill her and then to make his escape? Not long, is the answer. Since Norris himself was already entering the wood and the young boys who found the body were coming up the hill from the other side, the murderer would have had at best only minutes to do what he did.'

'But it was still possible.' The chief inspector was insistent.

'I agree – though only barely. But that's not really the issue. The question is, could Rex Garner have done it?'

'I'm not sure I follow you.' Sinclair's frown deepened.

'I'm quite willing to believe he's a bad lot – grasping and dishonest, and quite possibly violent when drunk or angry. But his assault on that woman in Hong Kong sounds to me more like the act of a brutal bully than a cool-headed killer. Not the kind of man who could have strangled Portia in the few minutes he had available to him and then quietly made his escape without being seen. However, I haven't met Garner, so all this is theorizing. He doesn't sound the type, that's all. But he might be.'

'And if not, then there was someone else staying at Foxley Hall that weekend who would fit the bill even better.'

'You're thinking of Stanley Wing.'

Sinclair shrugged.

'Well, whether or not *he* murdered Portia Blake, he's certainly someone I'd look at carefully,' Madden agreed. 'If there was some plan afoot – some idea of blackmailing Garner – then it's likely he was involved in it. From what Jessup told me about him, there doesn't seem much he would have stopped at. But whether that can be *proved* against him is another question. Assuming he's still in prison, he can certainly be interrogated; but how willing he'd be to cooperate with a British police inquiry into a murder he might be involved in remains to be seen.' He glanced at the chief inspector. 'You're right, Angus. I'm not very optimistic.'

Sinclair's growl suggested he was none too sanguine himself.

'And there's something else we've lost sight of,' Madden went on. 'The note that was sent to Derry: the one that started this off. We've still no idea who was behind it, whether he or she actually discovered Miss Blake's pendant still lying in the wood, or came across it in some other way: whether in fact they really know something about the murder or are simply making mischief. I can't claim to have made any progress in that direction. It's still a mystery.'

Madden studied his old friend's face.

'What I'm trying to say is I think I've done all I can.'

'Poor old Angus. He was doing his best to put on a brave face, thanking me for the help I've given him. But I think he was secretly hoping I'd keep going; keep asking questions.'

Madden lowered himself into an armchair. He had a glass of whisky in his hand and he took a sip of it before sitting back with a sigh. Hamish, who was lying on the hearth rug, lifted his heavy head at the sound and surveyed his master for a long moment as though estimating his chances of being taken out for a walk, before lowering his head again and shutting his pouched eyes.

'I had to tell him I'd reached the end of the road.'

'But you haven't spoken to Rex Garner yet. Couldn't you go and see him?'

Lucy looked up from the dress she was working on, her darting needle still for a moment. She was sitting on the sofa beside Helen, who was occupied with her weekly accounts, running her pencil up and down the columns, frowning. Recently she had taken to wearing spectacles for reading and it was a source of wonder to Madden to see how a pair of simple horn-rimmed glasses perched on the end of her nose somehow added a new dimension to a face that had never ceased to hold him in thrall.

'I've thought about that and decided against it. If the Yard does move to reopen the investigation they'll want to tackle him cold. If I went to see him – and if he was involved in Portia Blake's murder – it would put him on his guard, and he'd have time to cook up a story.'

'Aren't you afraid that Sir Richard Jessup might warn him?'

'No, I'm not. I don't believe for a moment that he'd deliberately try to undermine a police investigation if one got under way.'

'But you don't think it will, do you?'

'Not as things stand.'

'Well, then . . .' Lucy's disappointment was plain. 'It's all been rather a waste of time, hasn't it?'

'Oh, I wouldn't say that.' Madden sipped his whisky. 'I've met some very interesting people, two of whom I really liked, which reminds me . . .' He glanced at Helen, who looked up at that moment. 'Have you written to Mrs Castleton?'

'I posted the letter today. I've asked her to come and stay

with us for a weekend next month. I left it up to her to choose the dates.'

'Was she like Violet said she was?' Lucy asked. She bit through the thread of cotton she was using and laid her sewing down. 'Doomed-looking?'

'Not that I noticed.' Madden chuckled. 'But I could see how fascinating she must have been to men. There's a quality of mystery about her.' He paused. 'No, that's the wrong word: it's a sense of depth, rather. She's someone you almost immediately want to know better.'

'But you escaped from your encounter unscathed?'

Madden eyed his daughter. She giggled.

'According to Violet, she used to leave all the men she cast a spell on . . . how did Violet put it, Mummy?'

'Alone and palely loitering.' Helen's gaze remained fixed on her columns of figures.

'You don't *look* pale, Daddy.' Lucy peered at her father. 'But I shall be keeping a close watch on you.'

'Watch all you want.' Madden downed the last of his whisky and stood up. 'I'm going to take Hamish for a walk before supper and see which trees in the orchard need pruning.'

'But are you really going to give up on Angus's case?' Lucy made a final appeal. 'It doesn't seem right just to drop it this way. What if something comes up . . . something new and unexpected?'

'Then Charlie Chubb will be ideally placed to spring into action. I'm going to see him when I go up to London next week. I'll tell him what I've learned about Garner and Wing and everything that went on during that weekend. After that it will be up to him and Cradock to decide what to do. I wash my hands of it.'

Whistling to Hamish he made for the door to the terrace, but paused when he heard his daughter mutter something.

'What was that?' he asked.

'Nothing, Daddy.' She offered him one of her brilliant smiles.

'What did she say?' he asked Helen.

She glanced up over her glasses.

'Like Pontius Pilate.'

Sundays began slowly in the Madden household. Early risers on every other day of the week, Madden and his wife seldom went downstairs for breakfast before nine o'clock, while Lucy, when she was staying with them, was capable of spending the entire morning in bed (to recover, she said, from the rigours of her London life). Thereafter the day was devoted to the enjoyable pursuits of leisure: to reading under the trellised vine that gave shade to part of the terrace or attending to small and undemanding tasks in the house and garden. Although strictly speaking on call as the village's only doctor, Helen rarely stirred from the house except in an emergency, while Madden went to the farm only when he felt his presence there was necessary; as it seldom seemed to be these days.

'The truth is, George can manage perfectly well on his own,' he had lamented, with a sigh, only the night before when Helen and he were preparing for bed. He was speaking of his farm manager, George Burrows. 'I'd like to think I was missed, spending all this time up in London seeing to Aunt Maud's house and trying to soothe Angus's fevered brow. But everything seems to be running quite smoothly without me. If things go on this way I'm going to find myself turning into what I've always dreaded most becoming: a gentleman farmer.'

Spurred on by these guilty thoughts, Madden armed himself with a saw next morning and walked down to the orchard at the bottom of the garden. He had marked out several branches on the older trees the evening before and was engaged in the agreeable business of removing them (and covering himself with sweet-smelling sawdust in the process) when he heard Helen calling to him from the terrace.

'John . . . John . . . you'd better come up.'

'What it is?' He shouted back to her.

'Just come up. There's something you have to see.'

Baffled, he lay down his saw and walked up the long lawn to the terrace. Helen was at the table under the trellis and when he got there he found that she had the Sunday newspapers on the table in front of her. Delivered by the Highfield newsagent's son, who made a leisurely tour of the houses outside the village on his bicycle, they included not only the *Sunday Times* for Madden and Helen but also the *News of the World*, ordered at the request of Helen's maid of many years, Mary Morris, who had taken up residence with them following the death of her mother two years previously and occupied a sunny room on the upper floor of the old, half-timbered house with a view of the long wooded ridge called Upton Hanger that rose like a green wave beyond the stream at the bottom of the garden. It was this last journal that Helen was looking at and as Madden approached she pointed to a story displayed on the front page.

Madden bent over her shoulder to peer at it.

'Oh, Lord!'

He stared aghast at the headline.

Murder of Actress Called into Question – Missing Pendant Found – Was the Wrong Man Hanged?

Further down, and in slightly smaller type, were the words *Society figures involved*.

A photograph of Portia Blake accompanied the story, which gave a full account of the murder and the trial that had followed as well as the names of all the guests who had been present at Foxley Hall that weekend. Clearly a picture taken for publicity purposes, it showed her in an off-the-shoulder dress sitting in a chair with her legs crossed and her hands laced about one knee. Her smile was suggestive.

'I can't believe Violet has been talking about it,' Helen said. 'She promised me she wouldn't.'

She glanced up at her husband. Madden's eyes were still glued to the page.

'Could it have been one of the people you've been speaking to: Sir Richard Jessup, perhaps? All it would take for the story to get out is one careless remark.'

'No, I don't think it was Jessup. It's the last thing he'd want to see happen.' Madden went on with his reading.

'What about that actress, Audrey Cooper?'

'I thought of her at once. She's spiteful enough to take pleasure in starting a rumour of this kind. But if it was she, I can't help feeling she'd make sure that her own name cropped up in the story somehow, if only for the publicity it would give her. And I was careful to tell her that the police weren't interested in reopening the case.'

'Tell me it wasn't Lucy,' Helen pleaded.

Madden shook his head, laughing.

'No, it's not Lucy.' His smile faded. 'I think it's the same person who sent Derry that note.'

'Why? I mean, why do you think that?'

'It's the language the reporter uses.' He pointed a finger at the page. '*Confidential sources have revealed that the jade pendant sent to the police is the same one that disappeared from Portia Blake's body in August 1938.*' Madden quoted from the article. '*There is a slight flaw in the figure that enabled it to be identified.*'

He looked up.

'That's almost word for word what was in Derry's letter: except now it's being stated as an established fact that the two pendants are one and the same. Whoever sent it to him hasn't got the reaction he was hoping for. There's been no sign of any renewal of police interest in the case. He's decided to take the bull by the horns and drag the press in. It's easy to see what he's up to. He wants to force the issue. But what is he *really* after?'

Madden's scowl had returned.

'And who the devil is he?'

11

'WELL, ANGUS HAS got his way.' Charlie Chubb eased himself into his chair. 'Cradock's had to accept that the case must be looked at again. I've just been speaking to him. Or been spoken *to*, I should say. He'd come from seeing the commissioner and if the way he talked to *me* was anything to go by I reckon he'd just had a bollocking. Oh, and he had a few words for you, too.'

The chief super pointed a finger at Madden, who had arrived only a few minutes before and was sitting in front of his desk beside Billy Styles, who had also been summoned to the meeting and who had greeted his old mentor with a smile and a warm handshake.

'"Tell Madden to keep his nose out of police business," he said. "This is not the first time he's interfered. But it had better be the last. And tell him to hand over that pendant as well."'

'Surely he doesn't think I had anything to do with leaking the story.'

Stung by the words, Madden pulled the object from his pocket and passed it across the desk to Chubb. He had intended paying a visit to Scotland Yard later in the week. But the story that had appeared in the *News of the World* had spurred him into ringing the chief super as soon as he got up to London that Monday morning. Chubb had asked if he could come down to the Yard right away.

'It looks to me as though the newspaper received the same

sort of letter as Derry did,' Madden went on. 'The language is similar. And it's equally obvious it was sent by the same person. Whoever he or she is, they want the case reopened.'

'It's partly my fault,' Chubb admitted. He held up the pendant to the light and peered at it. 'I told Cradock that at least we wouldn't be starting cold: that you'd been speaking to some of the people involved as a favour to Angus. That set him off. He said it must have been you that caused the leak to the press. I tried to explain about the note Derry had received and how some of the wording in the newspaper report was the same, but I don't think he was listening. Mind you, his mood wasn't improved by the way the dailies have taken the story up. Have you looked at them, John?'

He gestured to the newspapers spread out on his desk, two or three of which Madden had already glanced at on his journey up to London by train.

'The *Daily Mail*'s the one that really got him going. *Is there a murderer still at large among us? Yard tight-lipped.*'

The chief super chortled.

'One of their reporters rang up yesterday and got hold of the CID duty officer, who said he couldn't comment on the story in the *News of the World* and they'd have to wait till today for any reaction. That's being tight-lipped for you. I'll be issuing a statement later saying the investigation is under review.'

He shrugged.

'Anyway, the word from on high now is that we have to get this business cleared up once and for all. Styles has already told me about your visit to Kent and what Derry had to say. But you've seen a few more people since then, I gather, so if you wouldn't mind telling us what you've learned, and whether you think it amounts to anything, I'd be more than grateful.'

'I'll do my best, Charlie. But tell Cradock that if he's got any more remarks to make about me he can say them to my face.'

His words brought a chuckle from Chubb. He cocked his head on one side and peered at his visitor's scowling visage.

'I don't think he'd dare.'

Chubb settled himself in his chair.

'So if anyone's in the frame, it looks like being Garner. But does the fact that he might have had an affair with Miss Blake really constitute a motive? What's your view, John?'

'It could do, I suppose – if he thought his future was at stake.' Madden tugged unhappily at an earlobe. 'He was upset by the act Portia Blake put on at dinner the night before. You've got both Jessup and Mrs Castleton as witnesses to that. If, in fact, he did arrange to meet Miss Blake the following day so that he could have it out with her in private, I suppose you could argue that she might have pushed him even further; taunted him, and perhaps driven him to an act of violence. Both Derry and Angus thought at the time that Norris had probably killed the girl by mistake: that he'd tried to choke her into submission and gone too far.'

'Grabbed hold of her scarf in a fit of anger, you're saying, and killed her almost before he knew it?'

'Something of the sort.' Madden shrugged. 'But according to Mrs Castleton, Garner also displayed that kind of anger, that lack of control, before – when he assaulted the woman in Hong Kong. The same thing might have happened with Portia Blake, and if, in fact, Garner killed her – and if the pendant was a present he gave her – then it's easy to understand why he might have taken it from her body. But how could it have turned up again in this way? That's another unanswered question. Did he lose it? Did it fall into someone else's hands? Surely he would have wanted to get rid of it as soon as possible.'

The chief super stirred uneasily in his chair. He cleared his throat.

'But on balance, don't you agree that Garner is the most likely suspect?' he asked.

'Other than Norris, you mean?' Madden frowned. 'Yes, I suppose so. Although we still haven't dealt with the problem of opportunity: how little time there was for him to have committed the murder before Norris arrived on the scene. That's assuming *he* wasn't the killer. Either Garner's spurt of homicidal rage happened at just the right moment to allow him to escape unseen, or we may have to look for another explanation.'

'Or at someone else who was in the vicinity,' Chubb suggested. He cocked an eye at his visitor.

'You mean Stanley Wing.' Madden nodded. 'Angus said the same thing. Yes, I can picture him killing Portia in cold blood. But why should he do such a thing? We're still stuck for a motive there. And as I told Angus, if he is the man you're after I doubt you'll get him to admit it, no matter how hard he's pushed.'

Chubb muttered unintelligibly. He and Billy had listened to Madden for close on an hour while he gave them a detailed account of his interviews with Richard Jessup, Audrey Cooper and, finally, Adele Castleton. Now and then one or other had put a question. But for the most part they had stayed silent. Finally, at the conclusion of his long recital, Madden had taken a sheaf of folded foolscap paper from his jacket pocket and handed it to the chief super.

'This is a summary of the various conversations I've had. It includes all the points I think are significant, though you can make your own judgement as far as that's concerned.'

161

The chief super turned to his younger colleague.

'What's your opinion?' he asked. 'How do we go about this?'

'We should look at both Garner and Wing.' Billy had his answer ready. 'We can question Garner about any prior connection he might have had with Miss Blake now that this is out in the open. We can certainly ask him to confirm his alibi for that afternoon. As for Wing, I reckon we'd better get in touch with the Hong Kong police about having him questioned. Sending a detective all the way from London would be an expensive business. I can't see Cradock authorizing it.'

'While we're at it we can ask them about that business between Garner and the woman he beat up,' Chubb observed. 'It'd be interesting to find out if it's on their books, or if Wing was able to arrange things so that the police weren't involved.'

'As far as Wing is concerned, Jessup has offered to help,' Madden interrupted them. 'He said he would ask his people out there if they had any news of him.'

'Should we question him, do you think? Jessup, I mean.' Chubb asked the question. It brought a shake of the head from Madden.

'I don't think that's necessary: at least, not at present. He wasn't one of the guests that weekend. He was down there to talk business with his father, and he left well before Miss Blake was murdered. He's been very cooperative so far, with me at least. I noticed from the papers that his name has already come up, but only in passing, as it were. They still seem to be fixated on his father and the people he mixed with. Black Jack Jessup has a ring to it, after all; not to mention the Prince of Wales. I'm planning to ring him to explain how this business became public – how I believe the newspapers came to learn of it. I wouldn't want him to think I had anything to do with it; not after he was so helpful. He's still away from London on business, but he should be back by the end of the week.'

The chief super ruminated. He had been making notes on a pad while Madden spoke earlier and he glanced at his jottings now.

'What about this actress – Miss Cooper? Has she got anything more to tell us?'

'She might have,' Madden said, after a moment's thought. 'I'm not sure she was altogether truthful with me. There was a moment when I thought she might be keeping something back, though I'm not sure what. It was only a feeling, mind you.'

'How about Mrs Castleton?'

'I've told you what she told me. I doubt she has anything to add. But she might know what became of the staff at Foxley Hall after Jack Jessup died and she moved out. I imagine you'll want to track them down, if you can.'

The chief super made another note.

'Any other thoughts?' he asked.

Madden hesitated. 'Mrs Castleton said she doubted that Wing was behind the display Portia Blake put on at dinner and she instanced the remarks she overheard him make when she walked by Portia's room later. "What is this game you're playing?" she heard him say. He sounded very angry.'

'Yes . . . and?'

'I think she was right, but only up to a point. What seems to have angered Wing was that Portia took matters into her own hands: it sounds as though her performance at dinner was her own idea, one she hadn't consulted him about. But I think he was pulling the strings, just the same. I think he had a plan hatching. There's still no explanation for why he brought her down to Kent with him.'

'Unless it was what we've been talking about,' Chubb pointed out. 'Unless it was to blackmail Rex Garner in front of his wife: to put pressure on him. I know Garner wasn't rich in his own right, but he was married to a wealthy woman. Wing might have reckoned he could get his hands on a hefty sum if he needed to.'

Madden was slow in responding. Finally, he spoke.

'Look, there's a bigger problem here – for me, at any rate. I can't quite see what Wing was supposed to have been threatening him with. Even if Garner had been forced to admit to his wife that he'd had a fling with Miss Blake, would it really have been so serious? Granted, it might have made things sticky between them for a while, but he could have claimed quite reasonably that their liaison was brief and that he'd recognized his error and corrected it. He'd broken off with the girl. I just can't see that it's the basis for any serious blackmail threat.'

He looked questioningly at his two listeners.

'You're saying there must be more to the whole business?' It was Billy who spoke.

'Or nothing at all, and we've been making too much of it.' Madden shrugged. 'I just feel there's a large hole in the theory as it stands.'

Chubb's growl signalled his displeasure.

'What about that girl in Hong Kong, though? We don't know what happened to her. Could Garner have killed her? Was that something else Wing had over him?'

'It's possible, I suppose.' Madden scowled. 'But the only people who might be able to help you there are the Hong Kong police, and as far as we know they never took any action over the matter.'

*

164

'Well, at least it'll bring a smile to Mr Sinclair's face.'

Billy Styles lifted his glass of beer in a silent toast to the absent chief inspector. A grin accompanied his words.

'But I gathered from what you were saying, sir, that you don't think we've got much chance of overturning the original verdict.'

'Not as things stand, Billy.' Madden sampled his beer. 'You'll need more than a suspicion that Garner may have had a part in Portia Blake's death. The same goes for Stanley Wing. And the fact that all this happened eleven years ago only adds to the difficulty. Short of a confession by one or other, I can't see you making much progress.'

Following their meeting with Chubb – and since it was the lunch hour, and Billy was free to take a break – the two men had repaired to a nearby pub to exchange last thoughts on the problem that had occupied Madden's mind for the past fortnight and was now the CID's responsibility.

'But what will matter to Angus is that the effort is being made,' Madden continued. 'Once the Yard has announced that it's looking at the case again, he'll feel better.'

'Even if it changes nothing? Even if we decide that the right man went to the gallows after all?'

Madden shrugged. 'Norris is still the most likely culprit. Angus knows that. Nothing I've turned up points decisively to anyone else. It's possible that whatever scheme Wing was hatching was somehow connected to Portia's murder. But it may have had nothing to do with it.'

He looked at his watch.

'I must be off,' he said. 'I've got a couple of estate agents coming to look at the house later this afternoon. We're putting it on the market at the end of the month and they want to inspect it first.'

Billy emptied his glass.

'Well, you can give Mr Sinclair another piece of good news,' he said. 'I've already started putting a team together and Lily Poole's name is on the list.'

The young woman he was referring to, a detective-constable in the CID, had been one of the first of her sex admitted to the Met's plain-clothes division at the end of the war. A protégée of Angus Sinclair, she had quickly made her mark at the Yard and the chief inspector continued to take a lively interest in her career.

'So Charlie has finally come round to her, has he?' Madden smiled. 'Angus will be pleased to hear that.'

Like many of his colleagues, Chief Superintendent Chubb had long harboured doubts about the wisdom of employing women in the force, and not even Lily Poole's accomplishments to date – they had already earned her three commendations – had brought about a change of heart. Until now, it seemed.

'I wouldn't say he's come round exactly.' Billy grinned. 'Lil took the sergeant's exam recently and she's still waiting to hear the result. Charlie's digging in his heels. He told me the other day he's afraid it might have a "disturbing effect" on some of our longer-serving DCs if she was promoted over their heads. I said that short of putting a stick or two of dynamite under them, I couldn't think of a better way of getting them to move off their lazy backsides and do some work.'

12

No matter how many times he visited Rotterdam – and his duties brought him to the great port quite frequently – the sight of the devastation wrought by the German bombers in 1940 never ceased to impress Chen Yi.

This was the purest expression of violence he had ever seen – greater even than the damage wrought by the Japanese on the city of Nanking, where he had been born twenty-six years earlier. This was the iron fist made manifest.

The entire heart of the city had been flattened; obliterated.

They had to invent a new term to describe it. Carpet-bombing was the phrase used. A carpet of bombs had been laid on the old city, and with the work of restoration hardly begun, all that remained of its medieval heart was a ruined church; that and some other half-wrecked structures.

It was towards one of these last that Chen was making his way that evening through the grid of streets that remained like the bones of a skeleton, fleshless, devoid of the houses and shops that had once stood there, in the company of an older man whose name was Huang Wei. Coarse-featured, and boasting a crooked nose that had been broken more than once to judge by appearances, Huang was a famous street fighter and Chen treated him with all the deference due a Red Pole – for such was Huang's position in the family, an enforcer in the language employed by the brotherhood of which they were both members – while privately finding him somewhat comical. But that was true of most of the old ones, the long-standing members, with their quaint titles and arcane ceremonies dating from centuries back. Sometimes Chen wondered if they knew they were living in a new world now: that everything had changed since the war.

The building in question was near the edge of the devastated region and might in its day have been a warehouse of modest proportions. Still with its walls mostly standing, it lacked only a roof, and on reaching it Chen paused to look about him. The deserted street down which they had walked was empty, as was the intersection at which they had paused. However, as they stood there a young man with jet-black hair cut close to his scalp appeared in the doorway of the ruined warehouse. He bowed his head on seeing them.

'All is ready,' he said.

With a glance at his companion, Chen walked past the youth, who stepped to one side and then followed him in, staying a pace or two behind so that Chen could speak to him over his shoulder.

'Is everyone here?'

The question was superfluous. Not one of the score of men he saw standing in a circle near the centre of the warehouse would have dared to stay away. They were 49s – ordinary members only – but they had taken the oaths.

'All are present.'

Again the young man made a slight bow. Chen turned his attention to the scene before him. Although littered with debris, the floor of the warehouse had been cleared in one area and it was there that the group awaiting him had gathered around a man stripped to the waist who was kneeling on the floor with his head bowed and his hands tied behind his back. His flabby body was marked by several tattoos of an exotic nature which included a dragon that wound its scaly tail about his slumped back.

No words were necessary. All knew why they had been summoned there, and if what was to follow bore something of the nature of a ritual it was designed to deliver a message. No one who witnessed it would forget what he had seen. The guilty man had stolen from the family. Money received in payment for the precious white powder they trafficked in had been held back. The betrayal of sworn oaths was gross and unforgivable. Each of the spectators knew that he, too, might one day find himself in the same fatal predicament and it was with this in mind that Chen spoke once more, though only in an undertone.

'We don't believe that Liu was working alone. One or two others might have had a hand in his scheme. Watch their faces. See which ones sweat the most.'

The youth acknowledged the words with the faintest of nods.

'Let us begin.'

Chen turned and went back to the doorway where Huang had been waiting. The older man took off his jacket and handed it to Chen. His shirt and tie followed. Stripped to the waist, his stocky, well-muscled body bore tattoos similar to the ones marking the body of the bound man as well as two scars, one across his chest, the other close to his navel, both the result of knife slashes. Chen folded the clothes and carried them to a block of concrete which had been well dusted. Laying the garments down carefully, he picked up a woodsman's axe which was leaning against the block and brought it to Huang. Although the evening was well advanced there was still enough light in the sky to bring a gleam from the polished head as Huang swung it easily from side to side, testing the weight and balance. A murmur came from the lips of the men standing in the circle. It died as

Huang moved forward, approaching the kneeling man from behind, and then stepping to one side.

Measuring the distance with his eye, he lifted the weapon with both hands and then brought the edge down in one swift stroke on the neck of the kneeling man. The body bucked convulsively as his head was separated from his body and sent rolling across the cement floor. Blood spurted from the neck like a fountain. It continued to flow as the body slumped to the floor, spreading in a dark puddle that shone faintly in the last of the light. A sigh came from the lips of the watching men.

Huang handed the axe to Chen, who walked to where the head was lying. Affecting an indifference he was far from feeling – it was the first such execution he had witnessed – he picked it up by the hair and carried it to the door of the warehouse where another cube of cement stood ready. Laying the axe aside, he settled the head firmly on the block so that the face with its lips drawn back in a last rictus of pain and shock was clearly visible.

Huang, meanwhile, had retrieved his clothes. Taking his time, he put on his shirt and tie and donned his jacket.

Only then did he turn to the circle of men, none of whom had moved.

'Go,' he said. They were his first words. 'And remember.'

'The Deng brothers looked away when you struck the blow. I noticed they were sweating.'

Chen spoke in a toneless voice. Though careful not to show it, he had found the preceding spectacle somewhat absurd (or so he told himself, now that the initial shock had worn off) and the bloody finale overdone. Wouldn't a bullet in the back of Liu's head have done just as well? Couldn't they simply have cut his throat? These old men lived in a fantasy . . . a dream of the past.

Huang shrugged. 'I will arrange for them to be watched,' he said.

After the departure of the others the two of them had waited alone in the warehouse for the cleaning crew to arrive. Not required to attend the execution, they were only aspirant members, Blue Lanterns, not yet initiated into the family. Chen had given them their orders. The body was to be cut up and disposed of: all except the head, which was to remain where he had placed it. All traces of blood were to be washed from the floor, which was to be liberally sprinkled with dust afterwards. They were to keep silent about what they had seen and done on pain of death.

The orders having been issued, Huang had led his assistant outside. Darkness had fallen finally, but the summer night was warm.

'I have received instructions from Hong Kong,' he said, speaking in English. Up till then both men had used only Cantonese. 'There is more work to be done. I shall need an assistant. Is your passport in order?'

'It is.'

'Be at Amsterdam Centraal station on Tuesday, no later than a quarter to two. Bring clothes for at least a fortnight. Make sure they are suitable.'

Unsure what was meant by these last words, Chen simply bowed. The older man regarded him.

'You are not curious to know where we are being sent?'

'Does it matter?' Chen knew well how to frame his reply. 'We follow orders.'

'A good answer.' Huang's slate-coloured eyes were

unreadable: it was impossible to tell what he was thinking. 'But then you are a clever young man . . . or so people say. I will tell you anyway. We are going to London.'

PART TWO

13

'GO ON – a *detective*?'

Arms folded, Annie Potter eyed her visitor suspiciously. She was standing on her doorstep barring the way in, and to judge by the work-stained apron tied to her waist and the white flecks of soap suds attached to her tanned forearms it looked as though she was in the middle of her housework (and not best pleased with the interruption).

'Are you having me on? I've seen one or two women in uniform, but I haven't met one in plain-clothes yet. You got a warrant card and all?'

Though slightly built, she looked to have the lean strength of a whippet – or so it seemed to Lily Poole – and thus far she was showing no sign of being willing to admit a stranger through the front door of her small terraced house.

'Course I have,' Lily replied. 'She fished out her card demonstrating that she was indeed what she said she was, a bona fide detective-constable with the Metropolitan Police, and held it out for the other woman's inspection. 'I would have rung you in advance to say I was coming, but I couldn't find your number in the phone book.'

'That's because we haven't got one.'

Despite the sharpness of her tone, she seemed satisfied by the sight of Lily's card and she stepped aside.

'Come on in, then. But keep it down, will you? My youngest is upstairs, sleeping, and I'm warning you now he's a holy terror when he's awake.'

She led the way down a short passage covered with linoleum into a cramped kitchen where a small girl whose dark curls matched her mother's was sitting at the table with a colouring book open in front of her and a box of crayons beside it.

'This is Winnie for Winifred,' she announced. 'And this is Detective-Constable Poole,' she added, turning to the little girl. 'Believe it or not she's a copper, so mind your manners.'

The little girl giggled. Having examined Lily for a moment or two, she went back to her colouring.

'Fancy a cuppa?' Annie Potter asked her visitor. 'I was about to put the kettle on. Then we can sit down and you can tell me what brings you down this way. It wouldn't be about that story I read in the paper the other day, I suppose?'

Her glance had sharpened.

'It's not about that young lady that got herself strangled all those years ago?'

Truth to tell, Lily wasn't best pleased with the assignment she'd drawn. She had hoped for something a little more testing after learning that Billy Styles had been given the job of looking into an old murder case, one she remembered reading about before the war, and had chosen her to be part of his team. She'd been hoping he would make her his number two, but when she answered the summons to his office she had found that Joe Grace, one of the most experienced detective-sergeants on the Met's strength, was already there and waiting to receive his orders.

'The chief super wants this business cleared up quickly,' Billy had told them both. 'Read this file first.' He had tapped a hefty looking folder on his desk. 'There's a lot of detail you'll have to get clear in your minds. Some of the witnesses are dead now, and others may be hard to track down, but we'll be talking to as many of them as we can get hold of. It's pretty straightforward. Either the bloke that was hanged got what he deserved – his name's Norris – or there's been a miscarriage of justice. It's up to us to find out which. And, like I say, we've been told not to hang about.'

The case was a tantalizing puzzle – or so Lily had thought after a day's hard study of the evidence collected at the time and the additional information gathered since, mainly by Mr Madden, whom she happened to know personally, thanks to his connection with the man she was more indebted to than any other: former Chief Inspector Angus Sinclair. It was Sinclair who, on Billy Styles's recommendation, had overseen her transfer from the uniform branch to the CID shortly before his retirement some years earlier. Lily had never ceased to be grateful to them both and it was the favour that Styles had shown her since then – he had taken pains to include her in a number of important investigations, cases from which she might have been excluded on account of her sex – that had given her hope of taking a further step up the ladder at the Yard with this new inquiry that was about to be launched.

Thanks to her careful reading of the file she could see that the man they ought to be focusing on first was this Rex Garner bloke. The fact that he might have had an affair with the murdered woman and never owned up to it was reason enough to look hard at him; and then there was the question of his so-called alibi. Had he really driven into Canterbury that morning to see an old friend? Or had he arranged to meet Portia Blake in private later, after lunch? Was he the one who had strangled her?

Armed with this idea, she had gone to see Styles to suggest that they pay him a visit at his flat.

'You've got the right idea, Lil,' he had told her. 'But he's not in London at present. I've been making some phone calls and I've learned that he went up north a couple of weeks ago. You've heard of the Glorious Twelfth?'

'The glorious *what*?' Lily asked.

'It's the day the grouse-shooting season starts, mainly in Yorkshire and Scotland. The nobs go out with their guns, and I suppose Garner counts as one of them. His late wife had an estate up there. He went up to Scotland a fortnight ago – I got that from his daily – but he's due back in London any day now, so instead of us chasing up there after him I thought we'd just wait until he gets back.'

Styles had tapped the file on his desk.

'Meanwhile, there are some other people we can talk to. I've managed to run down some of the staff who were employed at the house. The butler was a man called Hargreaves. He's retired now and lives in Bournemouth. I'm sending Joe down there tomorrow morning to talk to him. I'm going to slip down to Canterbury myself. It'll give me a chance to talk to Tom Derry and I've learned that one of the maids called Daisy Davenport is working in a dress shop there. I'll have a word with her too. What I'd like you to do is go and have a chat with a woman called Annie Potter. She was another maid, the only one we've been able to track down who lives in London. I've got an address for her from Mrs Castleton. Ask her what she remembers about that weekend. See what you can get out of her. Servants tend to fade into the background – people forget they're there – and sometimes they notice things others don't.'

He'd been trying to encourage her, Lily supposed. (She liked Billy Styles. He had always stood up for her and was one of the few at the Yard who treated her like a copper rather than a butt for one of their pathetic jokes about women

178

in the force.) But talking to a former maid about what she might or might not have seen eleven years ago didn't strike her as much of a challenge and she had made her way down to Whitechapel, where this Potter person lived, with little hope of a fruitful outcome to the interview.

'That's right,' she said now, having accepted the offer of a cup of tea and taken a seat at the table alongside Winnie, who remained bent over her book, busy with her colouring. 'It's the Portia Blake case. We're taking another look at it. The pendant she was wearing at the time of her murder and which was lost has turned up unexpectedly. Do you remember her wearing it, Mrs Potter?'

'Call me Annie.' She turned to glance at Lily from the cupboard where she was fishing around for cups and saucers. 'You're from down this way, aren't you?'

'Not that far off,' Lily admitted. 'I was born in Stepney. My dad was killed in the first war and when my mum died of the flu I went to live with my aunt and uncle. He was a copper stationed at Paddington nick.'

She returned Annie's smile, feeling easier now. Although she was proud of her Cockney roots, Lily knew her accent had faded somewhat with the years due to her living away from the East End; yet Annie Potter hadn't been fooled and Lily hoped that she would prove to be just as observant in other respects.

'Basically, we're looking to see if anything was missed in the investigation,' she said. 'How well do you remember that weekend?'

'Well enough.' Annie shrugged. She put the crockery on the table and turned to attend to the kettle, which had just begun to boil. 'We weren't all that busy: it wasn't a big party. There was all that hoo-ha at dinner, though. You know about that, do you?'

She glanced over her shoulder again, this time with raised eyebrows.

'The way Miss Blake carried on, you mean?'

Annie nodded. 'Danny O'Grady said it was better than a floor show. He was one of the footmen.' She grinned. 'I never saw her in that dress, but Danny said it was so low-cut you could practically see her navel. It was all he could do not to spill the soup when he bent to serve her. He said it was like looking down the Grand Canyon.'

Lily waited until her hostess had filled the teapot with boiling water and brought it to the table.

'What was your job?' she asked.

'I was an upstairs maid. I did the bedrooms and cleaning with Mary Keen. Mary was sweet on Danny. They got married later and went back to live in Ireland. She's got two nippers herself now, like me.'

Annie settled herself at the table. Her brown eyes shone.

'I got hitched myself during the war. I was working in a factory up in Birmingham. We had an anti-aircraft unit stationed only a couple of streets away. Bert was one of the gunners. That's how we met. You married?' she asked.

Lily shook her head. 'Still looking.' She could see from her hostess's animated expression that she was enjoying the chance to reminisce and that the best way to proceed would be to keep chatting to her in a relaxed way. It was a trick she had learned from working with Billy Styles who himself had picked up the technique from Mr Madden (or so he said), the man who had taught him his trade. Except – according to Styles – it hadn't been a technique with his old chief. It was just the way he was; different from other coppers.

'How long did you work at Foxley Hall?' she asked.

'Seven years.' Annie lifted the lid of the teapot to check

the state of the brew and then filled their cups. She handed Lily the milk jug. 'I started when I was just a girl, doing the rough work: laying the fires, cleaning the oven, polishing the shoes. Later I got to be a proper maid.'

'And when did you leave?'

'At the same time Mrs Castleton did. That was in 1939, after Sir Jack died. She couldn't stay there any longer. I don't mean anyone was pushing her out. As far as Sir Richard was concerned she was as good as married to his father and Foxley Hall was her home for as long as she wanted it to be. But she couldn't stand to be there without Sir Jack, so the house was shut up and the staff went their way.' She sipped her tea. 'With the war on, I was ready to leave. I'd had enough of service. But all the same I felt sad. We were lucky to have worked there, all of us, and we knew it. It wasn't like being in service elsewhere; more like being part of a family. But I understood how Mrs Castleton felt. It could never have been the same without Sir Jack.'

She smiled to herself.

'The day I arrived to work there – I was all of fifteen – he had me brought to his study and he said, "I want you to be happy here, Annie. I want you to think of it as your home. If you have any problems, bring them to me. We'll sort them out." And he meant it too. I remember how he used to make a point of praising us and paying us compliments. It wasn't what you'd get in most places, I can tell you. "Oh, I like the way you've done your hair, Annie," he would say. That sort of thing: it was meant to make you feel better. When Mrs Castleton came to stay we thought things would change. But we needn't have worried. She just made everything run better in the house, like you'd expect a woman to, but quietly, with just a word here and there. And when the house was finally shut up she did her best to find jobs for everyone who wanted to stay in service. We're still in touch, her and me.'

Annie's smile blossomed.

'She gave us a lovely wedding present, Bert and me: a full set of cutlery. And she sends us a card every Christmas, and never forgets the kids' birthdays. That colouring book and those crayons are a present from her. Isn't that so, Winnie?'

The little girl looked up shyly, nodded, and then bent to her task again.

Annie added more hot water to the teapot. Lily handed over her cup for a refill.

'To get back to that weekend,' she said. 'The dinner apart, do you remember anything unusual happening? Anything to do with the guests, I mean: in particular Miss Blake, Mr Garner and that Chinese, or half-Chinese bloke, Mr Wing?'

'Oh, him?' Annie rolled her eyes. 'He was a strange one, all right. He'd look at you with those black eyes of his and you'd wonder what was going on in his mind. He gave Mary and me the creeps.'

'Were you surprised when he showed up with Miss Blake? They don't sound like the kind of guests you'd expect to find at a house like Foxley Hall.'

'Oh, well, as to that . . .' Annie Potter's tone was philosophical. 'I can tell you we had our share of rum ones over the years, people Sir Jack picked up on his travels. We had a bullfighter once, I remember. He used to chase Mary and me around his room if he caught one of us up there alone. Sir Jack had to turf him out in the end.' She laughed. 'But you're right – Wing and that Miss Blake didn't exactly fit in. Though she thought she did.'

'Oh . . . ?' Lily raised an eyebrow.

'She was trying to play the lady, making out she was at home, putting on airs.' Annie was scornful. 'It wasn't too bad the first evening they were there – Friday it would have been. From what I heard she didn't create at dinner that night; she saved it all for the next day. But I didn't take to her. You can always tell a real lady from the way they treat servants. But she didn't know how. She thought she was better than us, but I could see through her.'

'What about Mr Garner?' Lily realized she'd come across a shrewd judge of character. 'What did you think of him?'

'He was all right, I suppose.' Annie wrinkled her nose. 'He'd been a guest at the house often. When he first came down he was still single and he used to give us the eye – me and Mary, and Daisy Davenport, too; she was one of the downstairs maids. You could see he fancied the girls; but I reckon he was afraid of doing anything to upset Sir Jack. Then he got married and that stopped; he behaved better.'

'What did you think of him, though? Did you like him?'

Raising her cup to her lips, Annie considered the question.

'No,' she said finally. 'Not really. He was charming enough, and good looking, too. But it was all on the surface. Not like Sir Jack. You always knew where you stood with him. He never hid his feelings, never pretended. Everything about him was real. Like when that girl was murdered – you could see how terrible he felt. She was his guest, staying under his roof, and he couldn't forgive himself for allowing it to happen. Except, of course, he didn't: *allow* it, I mean.'

She paused to make sure that Lily understood her meaning.

'He hardly knew her. But that didn't make any difference in his mind. He thought he'd failed her in some way, and he took to his bed shortly after that. He wasn't well anyway – we all knew that – but it really hurt to see him getting worse by the day. I think it broke Mrs Castleton's heart. But there was nothing to be done and he died in less than a year, soon after the war started.'

Lily swallowed the last of her tea.

'So other than what happened at dinner, there was nothing special that you can remember?'

Annie shook her head. She gathered the cups off the table, placing them, with their saucers, one on top of the other. She looked questioningly at Lily. It was clear she wanted to get back to her work.

'Just one more thing, and then I'll leave you in peace. Think back to the day Miss Blake was murdered. I know Mr Garner went out in the morning and didn't return until after her body was found. But where was Mr Wing: what did he do after lunch?'

'Went up to his room to rest, most likely.' She shrugged. 'They all did. Except Miss Blake, of course: she went out.'

'One of the maids saw her leaving, didn't she?'

'That was Daisy. She'd been dusting downstairs and she saw Miss Blake leave by the side door and go into the garden.'

'Where did she go then – Daisy, I mean?'

'To the kitchen, where the rest of us were, having a break; chatting. Lunch had been cleared away and there wasn't much for us to do until tea time.'

'So if someone else – I mean one of the guests – had come downstairs and followed Miss Blake out, no one would have seen them?'

'You mean Mr Wing, don't you?' Annie eyed her shrewdly.

Lily shrugged. 'I'm not saying that. I'm just trying to get the lie of the land.' She paused, considering her next question. 'When did you first hear about the murder? What time was it?'

Annie thought. 'It was close to four o'clock,' she said, 'or maybe a bit earlier. They were starting to get things ready for tea in the kitchen. Old Pat Duckworth, the village bobby, rang the doorbell and Mr Hargreaves went to answer it. He didn't come back for nearly ten minutes, and when he did he told us what had happened. He had had to break the news to Sir Jack, who was still upstairs in his room, resting. He came down to talk to Pat and quite soon afterwards the other guests appeared from upstairs. Apart from Mr Garner, that is – he hadn't got back yet. Sir Jack got them together in the library and told them what had happened.'

'And Mr Wing was among them?'

Annie nodded.

'So as far as you knew he hadn't left his room?'

'That's right.' Annie squinted at her. 'But what you're thinking is he *might* have?'

'If he had, was there anyone else who would have seen him? What about the rooms upstairs, the bedrooms? Could he have been spotted from a window up there?'

Annie shook her head. 'If he went out of the garden the same way Miss Blake did he would have gone down the yew alley, and he couldn't have been seen in there. The branches grew together at the top; it was like a tunnel. It went all the way to the gate at the bottom.'

She studied Lily's face, as though expecting to see some change in her expression.

'When was the first time you saw him?' Lily continued to speak in a neutral tone. 'After lunch, I mean.'

'When the guests came down from their rooms and Sir Jack got us all together in the library – guests and staff – and told us about the murder. He looked terrible. He was that cut up.'

'How did Mr Wing take the news?'

'I don't know. I wasn't looking at him. I was looking at Sir Jack and at Mrs Castleton and wondering if there was anything we could do for them. I didn't take any notice of Mr Wing. In fact, I don't remember seeing him until a few minutes later when I went upstairs with a pile of clean linen and towels to put in the airing cupboard. Mr Hargreaves had told us we had to carry on as normal until the police arrived. He didn't want us sitting around in the kitchen gossiping.'

'You say you saw Mr Wing upstairs? Where was that, exactly?'

'In the passage. The guests' rooms were off it. He was coming towards me and we passed by one another. He didn't say anything. Just nodded as he went by.'

She sat back. Lily smiled.

'Thanks, Annie,' she said. 'You've been a great help. Sorry to have bothered you. I know you've got work to do.'

She glanced down.

'And it was nice to meet you, Winnie. I can see you're really good at colouring.'

The little girl blushed with pleasure. Lily prepared to rise, but then checked her movement when she saw that the look on her hostess's face had changed. Annie was staring out of the window at the back of the kitchen, where there was only the empty yard.

'Annie . . . ?'

She turned slowly towards Lily. Her face wore a puzzled look.

'I've just remembered something,' she said. 'He shouldn't have been there.'

'Who?'

'Mr Wing. It never struck me at the time. But I've just realized . . .' She stared at Lily. 'You see, the upstairs linen cupboard was at the end of the corridor, and Mr Wing came walking towards me from that direction. But he had no business being there . . .'

'No business . . . ?'

'*His* room was at the other end of the passage – his and Mr and Mrs Garner's. Sir Jack's other guests were a couple called Lord and Lady Cairns. Their room was near the cupboard and Miss Blake's was across the passage from theirs.'

She went on staring at Lily.

'So . . . so where could he have been coming from? That's what you're wondering?'

Annie nodded mutely.

'It couldn't have been from this Lord and Lady Whatsit's room?' Lily wanted to be sure she'd got it straight. 'He'd have had no business in there?'

'That's right. And anyway, they were still downstairs.'

'So there was only one other room he could have been coming from?'

Annie nodded mutely.

'He must have been in Miss Blake's room,' she said. 'But what was he doing *there*?'

14

'SO THE ASSUMPTION IS Wing went into the Blake woman's room to look for something?'

Angus Sinclair added a question mark to his statement.

'But it couldn't have been the pendant. She was wearing that when she went out.'

'Wing wouldn't necessarily have known that,' Madden pointed out. Having received a full report on Lily Poole's visit to Whitechapel from Billy Styles before he returned home from London for the weekend, he had walked down from the house to give his old friend an account of the latest developments in the reopened investigation. 'But I agree it's quite possible he was looking for something else.'

'But what, I wonder?'

The chief inspector snipped a blood-red rose off one of his bushes and added it to the stems lying on the grass behind him. Whether his gout was truly in remission – he was still moving about gingerly – or whether the Yard's decision to reopen the Portia Blake inquiry had sent a dose of adrenalin through his system, the chief inspector was looking more like his old self, alert and energetic.

'What else could he have wanted to get his hands on?'

'We discussed that,' Madden said. 'Mrs Castleton over-heard Miss Blake tell Wing she had put something "in a safe place". Billy was going to get in touch with Portia's sister. It was she who collected Portia's effects from the flat she was sharing with Audrey Cooper. There might be something among them that will shed light on the mystery.'

'Unless Mr Wing found what he was looking for and pocketed it.'

The chief inspector ran his eye along the line of roses, searching for another victim.

'You say some of those originally involved have been spoken to again? Did they offer anything new?'

'Not really, and Billy also talked to Tom Derry in Canterbury, but he had nothing to add to what he had already told me, and he also saw the downstairs maid, Daisy Davenport. But she could only confirm what she said at the time about Portia leaving the house after lunch. The butler, a man called Hargreaves, retired to Bournemouth. Joe Grace has spoken to him, but other than giving an account of that dinner that accords with Richard Jessup's, the only thing he had to say of any interest was that he thought Rex Garner was more disturbed than he let on by the way Miss Blake was behaving. He was trying to ignore it, Hargreaves said, but actually he was furious. At least that's what Hargreaves thought.'

'But Garner himself hasn't been approached yet?'

'He went up to Scotland for the grouse shooting. He'll be back in London next week. Billy plans to interview him then.'

The chief inspector snipped off a last rose. Bending to collect the others that were lying on the grass, holding the prickly stems in his gloved hands, he led the way up the short path to the front door of his cottage. Madden followed. The roses were for Helen and he assumed that the chief inspector was going in search of some paper to wrap them in.

'And what of Mr Stanley Wing?' Sinclair paused at the door. 'Have you anything more on him?'

Madden shook his head.

'But I'm wondering whether Richard Jessup might have something to tell me on that score. He's only just returned from his business trip; but according to the message Helen took he wants to see me as soon as possible. I'll know more by tomorrow.'

It was Mrs Castleton who had relayed the invitation. She had telephoned the previous evening to say that Jessup hoped both Madden and his wife would lunch with them that Sunday at his house near Petersfield. Helen had taken the call, and when she joined Madden in the drawing room he had seen from her expression that she was pleased.

'That was Adele,' she said. 'She hasn't received my letter yet, but that's because she's been down in Hampshire looking after the Jessup children. His wife had to fly back to America at short notice. Her father's unwell and her mother had asked her to return. Why Adele rang was to ask us both to drive down there on Sunday. She said Sir Richard was anxious to see you. The way she said it made me think it might be important. He'll be home later tonight – he's been away on business – but he wanted Adele to ring us as soon as possible so that we'd have time to decide. I accepted at once and told her I would only ring back if you felt we couldn't make it for some reason.'

There being no such reason – Madden had been as eager as she to accept the invitation – they set off in mid-morning with Sinclair's roses wrapped in newspaper lying on the back seat of the car, knowing that the journey would take the better part of two hours. Jessup's house lay beyond the bounds of Surrey, in the county of Hampshire, near a village called Hawkley, a famous beauty spot and one that the Maddens had visited more than once before the war, when weekend drives in the country had been commonplace: a time distant in memory now. Although the government had finally taken pity on the long-suffering population and re-instated the modest wartime petrol ration, there was little of the precious fuel to spare. As a doctor, Helen had always been able to obtain a supply for her work, but she was reluctant to use it for private purposes, so it had been down to Madden to provide the coupons for their trip. And since his own car, a venerable Humber which had spent the war years sitting on blocks in the family garage like a beached whale, was no longer regarded as reliable for a journey of any distance (it needed a thorough overhaul and new parts that were not presently available), it was Helen's Morris Minor that they took.

New on the market, the car had been heralded by its makers as the answer to the German Volkswagen and its distinctive jelly-mould shape and superior performance had made it an instant favourite with the public. Not many were to be seen on the roads as yet – most vehicles coming off the assembly lines were earmarked for the export market – and Helen's cream-coloured model drew more than one envious glance as they made their leisurely way southwards along the A3 until they were a few miles short of Petersfield, at which point Madden, who was acting as navigator, spotted the signpost for Hawkley. Ten minutes later, still following the minutely detailed directions Adele Castleton had given them, they turned into a pair of wrought-iron gates and up a long avenue flanked by elms that led to the house.

Late Victorian in design, it was fronted by a circular driveway with a lily pond at its centre. The high brick wall of a kitchen garden was visible on one side of the house and it was from that direction that a man wearing work clothes approached them. Short and ruddy-faced, his close-cropped hair seemed to mark him out as an old soldier and he strode briskly towards them, in spite of having a slight limp.

'Mr and Mrs Madden, is it? How do you do, sir – and you, ma'am?' He dipped his head to Helen. 'Lennox is my name. I'm Sir Richard's chauffeur. He's over on the other side of the house with the children, but he told me to keep an eye out for you. Mrs Castleton's hereabouts. I think she's in the kitchen garden. I'll just go and see.'

About to leave them, he paused as his eye fell on Helen's car.

'Oh, you've got one of those have you, ma'am?' His face lit up. 'Is it true they do forty miles to the gallon?'

'Quite true.' Helen was complacent.

'And the independent front wheel suspension . . . does it really make cornering easier?'

'Much easier.'

'I must say she's a beauty.'

He laid a reverent hand on the machine's bonnet.

'Don't encourage him, Helen.'

Turning, Madden saw Adele Castleton approaching. She had a basket on her arm.

'Ted's one dream is to drive in the Monte Carlo Rally. If you're not careful he'll be asking you if he can borrow it next.'

Garbed in a loose silk dress with a flowered pattern, she wore a wide straw hat that kept the sun off her face but did nothing to hide the warmth of her smile.

'Are those roses for me?' Laying down the basket, she enveloped Helen in a warm embrace. 'How lovely to see you again, my dear: it's been such a long time. Do you know, you haven't changed a bit?'

She turned to Madden.

'Richard was so pleased to hear you were coming today.

He would have driven up to Highfield himself to see you, but he hadn't set eyes on the children for more than a fortnight and with their mother away he felt he had to spend the weekend at home. Sarah rang from Philadelphia last night. It sounds as though her father has had a slight stroke: not a disabling one, I'm happy to say, but enough to worry them. She's going to stay there for a little while longer. Let's go round to the front and look for Richard. No, wait . . .'

She hesitated.

'Your car will bake sitting in the sun. Would you like to put it under the tree over there?' She pointed to a handsome oak whose spreading branches covered a corner of the drive.

'Perhaps Lennox would like to do that for me.' Helen turned to the chauffeur. 'The keys are in the car.'

'Of course, ma'am.' His face lit up at the prospect.

'But only as far as the tree, Ted.' Mrs Castleton cautioned him. 'No taking it out for a spin.'

'Oh, ma'am . . . you know I wouldn't do that.'

Grinning with pleasure, he opened the car door, and as they went off they heard the motor start.

'Ted served in the war with Richard,' she told them as she led the way up the side of the house. 'He was his company sergeant-major. When it was over Richard offered him a job. Officially he's his chauffeur, but he's far more than that. He does all sorts of things for us. He's a dear man. The children adore him.'

When they came to a door she paused.

'I must just put your lovely roses in water,' she said, relieving Helen of her burden, 'and take this into the kitchen, too.' She indicated the basket she was carrying. 'It's so difficult with rationing still, isn't it? There's a farm attached to the house and we get some stuff from it. But Richard doesn't like to bend the rules, especially when he knows he could do it so easily. But fortunately we've a lovely kitchen garden and I can promise you a good salad to go with our rabbit pie.'

She returned after a few moments and they continued to the front of the house where she paused so that they could take in the view. Before them was a garden boasting a wide, tree-shaded lawn bordered by flower beds and hedged by dense shrubbery, and beyond that a sweeping vista of beech-clad hills stretching for miles into the hazy distance.

At the bottom of the lawn two figures stood facing one another some yards apart. As they watched, the taller of the two moved forward, bringing his arm over in a slow arc. Madden saw it was Jessup, and that he was bowling to a boy who must be his son. The crack of a cricket bat striking a ball reached their ears, and at the same moment another, smaller figure, clad in white, darted like a sprite from the shadows cast by a giant beech and hared after the ball, which had disappeared into the shrubbery.

'Poor Katy.' Mrs Castleton sighed. 'They just use her as a fielder. She hardly ever gets a chance to bat.'

'Hello, there . . . !' Jessup called to them.

Raising his hand in greeting he came up the lawn to meet them, trailed by the children.

'It's so good of you to come all this way.'

He spoke while he was still some way off, and Madden and Helen had time to take in his lithe figure, dressed simply in a pair of shabby corduroy trousers and a flannel shirt with the sleeves rolled up to the elbow.

'Dr Madden . . . ?' He held out his hand.

'Please . . . call me Helen.'

'Adele has told me so much about you.' Jessup looked into her eyes as they shook hands. 'But I want to hear more . . . about both of you,' he added as he turned to greet Madden. 'First, some introductions, though . . .'

He beckoned to his son, who had paused behind him, bat in hand, waiting to be presented.

'This is Jack . . . John, actually, but he prefers Jack, just as his grandfather did. Come and say hello to Mr and Mrs Madden.'

The boy stepped forward. Dark-haired, like his father – and with the same high cheekbones with their promise of good looks – his face was burned brown by the summer sun. Eyes blue as sapphires examined them curiously as they shook hands.

'Now what have you done with your sister?'

Jessup bent to peer into his son's face, ignoring the presence of the little girl, who had held back and was standing some distance off, clutching the cricket ball to her chest and eyeing the visitors doubtfully.

'She's over there, Daddy.' The boy pointed. 'You can see her.'

'So she is . . . !' Jessup drew back in mock surprise. 'Come along, Katy. I want you to say hello.'

The girl approached them, head bowed.

'Shake hands now.'

Still clutching her ball with one hand, she extended the other. It was solemnly accepted, first by Helen, and then by her husband.

'There . . . that wasn't too difficult.' Jessup ran his fingers through her curls, which were fair like her mother's.

'And now I think it's time for your lunch, both of you.'

'It's waiting in the kitchen,' Mrs Castleton announced. She glanced at Helen. 'Shall we take them inside? Then we can settle down on our own. We've a great deal of catching up to do.' She had turned to Jessup. 'And I know you want to speak to Mr Madden. So why don't we all meet in an hour.'

*

195

'I might have guessed that would catch your eye. She dominates the room, doesn't she? Poor mother – she was afflicted by the worst of all curses: the unshakeable conviction that she was always in the right.'

Jessup spoke from the doorway. He had led Madden to his study, a pleasant book-lined room with a view of the garden and the rolling, wooded countryside beyond, and left him there while he went to wash his hands and put on a jacket. Madden had wandered about, glancing at the books and inspecting the paintings hanging on the walls which included a view of the Hong Kong waterfront busy with shipping, and with the well-known silhouette of Signal Hill rising in the background. He had stopped at a table in one corner covered with framed photographs, one of which had attracted his attention. Larger than the rest, and somehow managing to tower over them, its subject was a handsome dark-haired woman with strong features who gazed back at the camera without even a hint of a smile, seeming to challenge the lens, daring it to find fault with her.

'I never understood how she and Father came to marry. They were young, of course, which may partly explain it. I'm sure Mother was quite inexperienced; my father I'm not so sure. But they very soon found that they couldn't live with each other and parted on the worst of terms; though not before I was sired; obviously.'

Smiling, he came over from the door.

'And there's a snapshot of Rex and me. It was when we were at Eton. We rowed in the same eight.'

The two boys stood side by side, each holding an upraised oar. Easily recognizable in spite of the lock of hair that hung carelessly down over his brow, partly covering one eye, Jessup was half a head taller than his companion, whose hair was brushed back from his forehead. Both were smiling broadly.

'We were great pals in those days.' Jessup's voice was tinged with regret. 'It was only later that we fell out.'

His face brightened.

'And this is Sarah,' he said, picking up a photograph that was standing on his desk and handing it to Madden. 'It was taken on our honeymoon in Paris.'

The young woman whose face Madden recognized from the picture Mrs Castleton had shown him stood with her hands in her coat pockets. A beret tilted at a rakish angle crowned her fair head and a woollen scarf was wound about her neck. The cobbles at her feet shone with rain, but her smile lit up the damp day.

'My mother didn't *quite* approve of her. She didn't think any girl was good enough for her son. But they were starting to get on better when she died. It was soon after Father passed away. Mother had been diagnosed with cancer some time before, but she hung on grimly and managed to be present at our wedding in Philadelphia, something Father was unable to do. It was towards the end of 1938 and he was already too ill to travel. I've always believed that Mother was determined to see him in his grave before she went herself. As I think I told you, I began to spend more time with him as I grew older and she never really forgave me for it.'

Putting the photograph back in its place, he went to a cabinet and opened it.

'Will you join me in a bottle of beer before lunch, John? I've worked up a thirst.'

They had moved easily onto a first-name basis, the transition occurring naturally and without fuss, and Madden had found himself surprised at how quickly a feeling of ease and companionship had grown up between them. Naturally reserved, it was a new experience for him and he put it down to the absence of just that quality in the other man. The openness Jessup had shown him from the first had been like a bridge that they had crossed without effort.

Accepting the glass of beer offered him, he took his seat in a stuffed-leather armchair, one of two set on either side of a low table. Jessup stayed by the window looking out.

'You've been very patient.'

He turned with a smile.

'I was going to ring you when I got back from my trip on Friday and found an express letter from the head of our Hong Kong office waiting for me. It was in reply to the telegram I sent him about Wing. But then something else happened that made me think it would be better to wait until I could speak to you about both in person.'

'If I'd known you were back I would have rung you myself,' Madden said. 'I wanted to explain how this story had got into the newspapers. I think the same person who sent the pendant to Derry also sent a letter to the *News of the World*. Whoever it is seems to want the case reopened.'

Jessup grunted. 'I did wonder about that.'

He came over from the window to join Madden and sat down facing him.

'First let me tell you about Wing. To begin with, he was released from prison two months ago. He'd been inside for four years of a six-year term and there was nothing unusual about his early release, which was for good behaviour. You may wonder why I hadn't heard about it before. I certainly did. But it turns out that Stanley was far from an ordinary prisoner, and the manner of his release was equally unusual. No announcement of it was made by the prison authorities. In fact, it was kept a close secret, which explains why my people didn't find out about it until now. They also learned that he was able to leave the colony immediately, possibly with official help. They were given to understand that he went across the bay to Macau – it's a short ride by boat. But after that he disappeared.'

'What was so special about him?'

'The charge on which he was convicted – of collaborating with the enemy – was real enough. But there was an aspect of it which put him in a different category from others who were charged with the same offence. What he was accused of, in fact, was acting as an intermediary between the Japanese occupying forces and the triad gangs. I take it you know who I'm referring to?'

'They're a criminal society, aren't they?'

Jessup nodded. 'They date from the seventeenth century. Originally they were a secret organization opposed to the Manchu rulers, but later they turned to crime and became involved first in the opium trade and later in all kinds of skulduggery including extortion and drug smuggling; and murder, of course. They spread to Hong Kong a long time ago, but now with the Communists on the point of taking control of the whole of the mainland the colony is their centre of operations. According to police estimates there are upwards of 300,000 triad members active in Hong Kong.'

He saw Madden's look of amazement and shrugged.

'I had always assumed that Wing had triad connections. He could hardly have carried out his business in stolen artefacts without their help. But I hadn't realized until now the full extent of his involvement with them. According to our sources in the Hong Kong police, Wing was recruited by one of the biggest gangs, or families, as they like to call themselves – the Tang – and went through their initiation ceremony which, among other things, requires the sacrifice of a live animal and the drinking of its blood mixed with wine.

Unknown to us, he'd become a fully-fledged member and would have had to swear eternal loyalty to the brotherhood, it being understood that any infringement of the oaths he took carried the penalty of death. The triad gangs are absolutely ruthless when it comes to punishing betrayals, or indeed any perceived affront. Wing, it turns out, had transgressed on both counts, hence the special treatment he received in prison; and the protection he was given when he was released.'

'He became an informer? Is that what you're saying?'

'In effect. The police had evidence that he'd been quick to approach the Japanese when they occupied Hong Kong and point out to them the advantages of using the triads to control the local population and manage the labour force. His actions were treasonable beyond question, and if he hadn't offered to turn King's evidence when he was arrested he would have drawn a much longer prison sentence. But his willingness to cooperate with the police meant he was a marked man from then on: his name was on the Tang's death-list, and almost at once he was the target of an assassination attempt in prison, which led to his being kept in solitary confinement for the remainder of his term. He was still providing the authorities with valuable information about the gangs' activities, so it was worth their while to protect him. And apparently he managed to extract a further concession from them: it was agreed that his eventual release should be kept secret.'

'And now he's disappeared?'

'So it would seem.'

'You're not certain of that?' Madden had caught a slight change in the other's tone.

'This is that other matter I mentioned.' Jessup rubbed his jaw. 'This is what I wanted to speak to you about in person. It's a sensitive issue and it raises difficult questions – for me, at any rate. What I've just told you is information you're welcome to pass on to Scotland Yard. They can discover it for themselves in any case by getting in touch with the Hong Kong police. But this other matter . . . it's put me in a quandary. I'm not sure what to do about it and I'd like your advice, John.'

'Tell me about it. I'll see if I can help.'

'I got back from my trip late on Thursday and when I went into the office the next day I found the letter from Hong Kong waiting for me. I'd barely had time to digest its contents, though, when my secretary told me that an elderly Chinese businessman I'm acquainted with, a Mr Lin Jie, was asking to see me urgently. He had heard that I was back in London and telephoned from his offices in Soho to ask if he could call on me at the earliest possible moment. He'd been unwilling to divulge the reason for his request, except to say that it concerned a matter he could only discuss with me in person.'

Jessup hesitated.

'What I'm about to tell you now is not established fact,' he went on after a moment. 'It's merely a suspicion. But I've reason to believe that Lin was party to the illegal trade in Chinese artefacts I told you about earlier – the ones Wing sold to collectors in this country. Stanley would have needed some sort of cover for his business as well as some means of smuggling the art objects into this country, and Lin was in a position to provide both. He runs a successful import company here in London. I knew that they were acquainted, and from what I was able to learn I felt reasonably certain that they were partners. Given my suspicions, I've always kept Lin at arm's length and we've never done any business together. You can imagine my surprise then when I learned that he wanted to see me. But I was curious to know why and I told my secretary to invite him round. He arrived half an hour later – in some haste, I might add – accompanied by a young man who he introduced as his nephew. I could tell at once from Lin's manner that something unusual was afoot. Normally meetings with Chinese gentlemen of the old school proceed at a snail's pace. Polite inquiries as to one another's health and well-being, not to mention those of one's family, are considered de rigueur before getting down to business. On this occasion all formalities were dispensed with. Lin asked me at once if I happened to know of the whereabouts of Stanley Wing.'

Madden's eyebrows shot up.

'Precisely. I was equally surprised. Before I had a chance to respond, however, he went on to explain that although he was aware that Wing no longer had any connection with Jessup's, he knew that he had once been closely associated with the firm, and with my late father, and for that reason he hoped I might be able to help him in this matter. He was starting to sweat at that point and I noticed that he kept glancing at this young man he said was his nephew, as though seeking his approval. I guessed at once what must have happened: who had put pressure on him.'

'You mean the triads?' Madden frowned. 'I wasn't aware they were active in London.'

'They're not, at least not to any great extent, and not yet. But I've heard rumours that moves are under way to establish a branch here. It's the drug trade: big business for them. But quite apart from that their reach has always been long. Most of our Chinese came from Hong Kong originally. Nearly all of them have families living there. I couldn't ask Lin outright if his had been threatened. But that was how I interpreted the situation. And, of course, it made sense that the triads would come to him for information about Wing. They almost certainly knew of their pre-war connection.'

Madden scowled. 'Tell me about this so-called "nephew" of his. Can you describe him?'

'He was young, very sleek-looking, and wearing what looked like an expensive suit. He didn't speak during our meeting.'

'Could he have come from Hong Kong with orders to hunt Wing down?'

'Possibly.' Jessup frowned. 'But it's more likely he was sent from Amsterdam. There's a big triad presence there. A lot of the heroin that reaches Europe comes through the port of Rotterdam. But he looked too young to me to be an enforcer: a Red Pole in the jargon they use.' He grimaced. 'He's more likely to be his assistant; his jackal, if you like.'

He gnawed his lip.

'There's more,' he went on. 'I haven't finished yet. I thought it rich that Lin should be asking me where Stanley was, given their past association. But I told him the truth: that I had no knowledge of Wing's whereabouts, other than that he had recently been released from prison in Hong Kong; which, incidentally, seemed to come as no surprise to either of them. But then he said something that startled me even more. He asked me if I had any reason to believe that he might be here in London.'

Jessup studied his guest's face.

'You're not surprised?'

'Not really.' Madden shrugged. 'I thought from the start that he was probably the person behind all this. But when you told me he was in prison I had to abandon the idea. Now it's beginning to make sense. But tell me – was Lin fishing, do you think? Was he just trying out the question on you? Or did he have definite information that Wing was in this country?'

'I don't know.'

'It matters, you see.'

'Why?'

'Well, if we knew for certain that he was here, it would tend to support at least one theory the police are working on now.'

Madden stopped. He had forgotten who he was talking to.

'What is that, John?'

Madden hesitated. The ease he had felt in talking to his host had led him astray. But it was too late to back out now. Jessup was listening to him intently, waiting for him to speak.

'It's only a theory, Richard, an attempt to explain some of the facts as we know them. For heaven's sake don't take it as gospel.'

'Go on.' Jessup spoke tersely.

'Let's suppose for a moment that, eleven years ago, Wing tried to set up a blackmail scheme with Garner as its victim. He knew that he had married a wealthy woman and could probably get his hands on a large sum of money if pressed.'

'Why pick on Rex?'

'Well, for one thing, Wing had once done Garner a favour in Hong Kong. Isn't it true he got him out of a bad situation with a woman and put him on a ship back to England?'

Madden paused. Jessup's gaze had dropped.

'I'm sorry, John. My father told me about that. It was years ago. I should have passed it on to you. It was just . . . I didn't think it was relevant.' He looked up.

'No matter.' Madden shrugged it off. 'But the point is – did Garner ever repay the favour? Did he, for example, try and persuade you, his old friend, not to terminate Wing's connection with the firm?'

Jessup shook his head. 'Rex told me Wing had asked him to intercede with my father, but he'd turned him down flat. He said Stanley had made his own bed and could lie on it. He thought it was amusing to see him caught out for once. I always imagined that Rex would have to pay someday for the favour Wing did him. I couldn't see Stanley playing the Good Samaritan, ever. I'm sure he felt that Rex was in his debt.'

'That's what I thought.' Madden had listened closely to his reply. 'Well, if we follow the theory the police are looking at, it goes something like this. In order to make his plan work Wing needed to compromise Garner in some way. That was where Portia Blake came in. Wing was in England that summer and perhaps he found some way to engineer an affair between them. We know that he accompanied Portia to some of those parties you mentioned and he could quickly have seen the possibilities of involving her with Garner, who always had an eye for a pretty face. How he might have managed to persuade Portia to join in the scheme one can't say; but presumably she was going to benefit from it too, financially. So the hook was baited, and once Garner had taken it, Wing could have put the rest of his plan into action. He could have arranged things with your father so that he and the girl were invited to Foxley Hall at the same time as Garner and his wife, whose presence was essential if the plan was to work. Wing probably meant to apply the screw gently . . . delicately. He merely wanted to show Garner the danger he was in. But Portia Blake had other ideas, hence that scene at dinner, which pretty well blew the gaff on Wing's plan, which in any case was finally put paid to the following day when the girl was murdered.'

'I'm sorry, John, but I must interrupt.' Jessup sat forward. 'You keep saying the police think this, the police believe that. What do *you* believe? Does this theory of theirs hold water? Give me your honest opinion.'

Madden considered his reply.

'As I've already made clear to the detectives dealing with the case, I have a problem with it. I find it hard to believe that Wing would have devised such an elaborate plan when the success of it must surely have been in doubt from the start. For all he knew, Garner might simply have thrown it back in his face; he could have told him to do his worst and Wing would have been left helpless. According to Mrs Castleton, Garner had his wife well under his thumb at that stage in their marriage. He could easily have talked his way out of what was only a minor indiscretion. The question is – did Wing have something else on him, some other hold, and was he prepared to use both in an attempt to extort money from his victim? We don't know what happened to that girl Garner assaulted in Hong Kong. It's been suggested he might have killed her and that Wing helped cover up the crime. I take it you can't help with that?'

'Good God, no.' Jessup shook his head angrily. 'If my father had known he would have told me; and he would never have stood by and done nothing.'

'It's pure guesswork at this stage, but without it, or something like it, the theory I've been outlining to you doesn't seem to me to hold up. Mind you, that won't stop the police from considering it, at least.'

Madden paused to empty his glass. He saw that the expression on Jessup's face had changed. A frown had settled on his brow. It was hard to tell what it signified . . . disbelief, perhaps?

'Even if all you've said is true, what has it got to do with the present? There's no point in anyone trying to blackmail Rex now.'

'Not for being unfaithful to his wife – no.'

'What do you mean?'

Madden took a deep breath.

'Richard, I have to remind you again that this is all speculation, and I only bring it up because it's another line of inquiry the police may well decide to pursue. They don't know yet that Wing may be in London and could be the person behind this whole business. But once they do they're likely to reason as follows. Wing is on the run from the triads. Among other things he's short of money. He's never forgotten those months he spent in England, nor his failed attempt to blackmail Rex Garner, and at some point, perhaps when he was in prison, he realizes he can put the same plot, or one very like it, into operation again. Only this time Garner has money of his own, thanks to the legacy left him by his late wife; and the threat Wing can dangle over him now is far more dangerous than the mere disclosure of some piece of marital misbehaviour. By sending that pendant to the police, he's serving notice on Garner that he can tie him to the murder of Portia Blake.'

He stopped. He had seen the look of shock on the other man's face.

'Are you seriously suggesting that Rex might have killed her?' Jessup had turned pale.

'No, I'm merely explaining a line of reasoning that will almost certainly occur to the detectives examining this case.'

'But *how* . . . I mean, even supposing it's true, how could Stanley possibly have known that?'

'Well, for one thing, he might have followed Portia that day when she left the house. He was furious over the way she had behaved at dinner the previous evening. He no longer trusted her and might have felt the need to keep an eye on her. If he did witness the killing, it would have been very much in character for him not to intervene or report what he had seen to the police, but rather look to see how he could profit from it. And it may well have been *he* who took the pendant from Portia's body.'

'Why should he have done that?'

'Perhaps because he knew it was a gift from Garner and something he could use himself if he pressed ahead with his scheme.' Madden shrugged. 'In fact, the possibilities for blackmail must have looked even rosier to him in the wake of Portia's murder until the unexpected arrest of Norris, which happened very soon afterwards, and the even more surprising news that he had confessed to the murder. It left Wing in a quandary. It was too late for him to point the finger at Garner, and in any case there would be no advantage to him in doing so. Unless he could think up some new plan he would have to accept failure. For the time being there was nothing he could do but return to Hong Kong.'

'But if he was unable to move against Garner then, how is it possible he can do so now, more than ten years later?'

'I don't know.' Madden shook his head. 'Perhaps something has happened in the intervening years to change the situation, some new development, or perhaps he's simply desperate, ready to try anything.'

Jessup sat biting his lip.

'Could it really have happened that way?'

'I've no idea. It's only a theory, as I said.' Madden was surprised by the effect his words had had on his host. Although the colour had returned to Jessup's cheeks, his face still showed signs of the shock he had felt on hearing Madden's revelations. 'I'd suspend judgement on it if I were you.'

THE DEATH OF KINGS

'I just can't swallow the idea that Rex might be a murderer.'

'Then don't,' Madden urged him. 'There's no *evidence* as yet to suggest that he had anything to do with Portia's death. Because of those stories appearing in the newspapers the police have been forced to look at the case again, and this is just one of the ideas they're playing with. For my money, Norris is still the most likely killer and it may well be that the Yard will come to the same conclusion in the end.'

'But the pendant . . . these letters . . . someone must have sent them. And as you say, Wing could well have had a motive for doing so. And if he *is* in London and he *did* send them, then Rex is bound to come under suspicion.'

A further thought seemed to strike him then and he caught Madden's eye.

'My God, I wonder if he knows about this. He's been up in Scotland for weeks. Is he even aware of what's going on?'

'You haven't heard from him?'

'Not a word. As I told you, we don't see much of each other these days.'

'Well, the police know that he's due back in London soon. They mean to interview him when he returns. It might be best to wait until they've done that before you get in touch with him. And as far as the other matter you raised goes . . .'

'The other matter . . . ?'

'Your meeting with Lin. You said it raised difficult questions for you. What did you mean exactly, Richard?'

Jessup bit his lip. It was clear he was having difficulty answering the question.

Finally, he spoke. 'It's like this, John. I don't mind telling *you* my suspicions about Lin and his past relationship with Wing. But I'm not comfortable about passing them on to the police. They're not proven, as I said, and I wouldn't want to blacken Lin's name without being certain. Is there any way of keeping him out of this?'

Madden shook his head. 'I'm afraid not. Wing's possible presence in London can be inferred from the other information you've given me – I mean his release from prison in Hong Kong and his need to quit the colony in a hurry. The police here will quickly put two and two together, just as I did, and see that it was very likely he who sent the pendant and those letters to Derry and the newspapers. But the fact that triad killers may be actively searching for him here can't be kept from them. They must be told about your meeting with Lin. Why don't you leave it to me to talk to them first? I know the detectives who are working on the case. I can explain the situation to them.'

'Would you, John?' Jessup's relief was plain. 'I'd be more than grateful.'

He shook his head. He seemed at a loss for words. Finally, with a sigh, he glanced at his watch.

'An hour, Adele said. I think we'd better break for lunch.'

'You said Wing had offended against the triad laws in two ways, Richard. What did you mean by that?'

They were walking together along a valley walled by steep, wooded ridges. Madden had paused to put his question, and to glance back along the way they had come towards the house, where he could see in the distance the small figures of Helen and Adele Castleton walking arm in arm on the lawn as they talked. Lunch had been laid in a corner of the garden shaded by the spreading branches of yet another ancient oak and, seemingly relieved by the opportunity offered to switch to a different topic, Jessup had eagerly engaged Helen on the subject of her work.

'I'm all in favour of the National Health Service. In fact, I voted for the Labour Party after the war, much to the horror of my fellow club members, one or two of whom actually threatened to blackball me. But how is it working out in practice? I've heard mixed reports.'

In reply, Helen had outlined the changes the new system of health care had made to her life.

'On the whole it's functioning well enough,' she said, 'except that it tends to encourage people to drop in at their doctor's surgery on the slightest pretext now that it costs them nothing. I've had more than one stubbed toe brought to me for urgent attention. In fact, because of the added workload I've more or less decided to look for a partner to share the practice with me. I've got my eye on a young man who works at Guildford hospital, but would like to move with his wife and baby son to the country.'

The enjoyment which both she and Mrs Castleton were taking in renewing their acquaintance had been plain to see. They had been talking animatedly when the two men had joined them and it was with some reluctance – or so it seemed to Madden – that they had adjusted to the more general conversation that had followed. For his own part, he had listened with pride as Helen spoke in her usual forthright manner about her work. Dressed in a white linen frock – it was one of Lucy's creations – with only a red leather belt to lend a touch of colour, her beauty seemed no less compelling to him now that her hair was starting to grey than when they had first met, and he had taken quiet pleasure in the open admiration he had seen in Richard Jessup's glance as he listened to her.

Lunch done, his host had proposed that they go for a walk, and with Mrs Castleton having decided that she and Helen should remain at the house so as to be there when the children came downstairs from their afternoon rest, the two men had set off through a gate at the bottom of the garden, Jessup carrying a shotgun broken at the breech in the crook of his arm.

'It's more for show than anything else,' he had told Madden with a smile. 'Though I do pot the odd rabbit for the larder.'

The gate through which they passed had given onto a wide field where cows were grazing. Seeing Madden pause to cast an appreciative farmer's eye over the well-fed herd, Jessup, too, had stopped. He had pointed to a row of cottages at the far end of the meadow.

'That's where our farmworkers are housed. One of the first things Sarah did when we settled here for good after the war was to install new plumbing and otherwise bring them up to scratch. Her whole family is strong on social conscience and I've found that it's catching. I've got our management in Hong Kong drawing up plans to improve working conditions in the cotton mills we own. In some cases it'll require complete rebuilding and I've had some opposition to it from my board of directors. But Sarah's father, Saul Temple, came down strongly on my side. He's a very active partner in the business and one I've come to value greatly.'

'He's not seriously ill, I hope.'

'No, the stroke seems to have been a mild one; more of a warning to ease up a little, Sarah says. We spoke last night on the phone. I do wish she had been here to meet you and Helen. We'll have to fix another meeting soon.'

They had walked on, and it was not until they had left the open fields behind them and entered an area where the wooded hangers for which the district was noted rose on either side of the path they were taking that Madden had returned to the subject they had been discussing earlier.

'Wing was guilty of two mortal offences against the triads' code,' Jessup replied to his question. 'One was to turn informer; but the other was more personal, and in some ways graver.'

'More *personal*?'

'He committed the ultimate sin: he caused the triad leader, the head of the Tang, to lose face. The man was an acknowledged Dragon Head, the highest rank in the triad hierarchy.'

'How did he offend?' Madden was fascinated. 'And was he aware of what he was doing?'

'Only too well. But he was caught between . . . between Scylla and Charybdis, if you like. On orders from the triad boss he had managed to get on close terms with one of the most senior Japanese officers stationed in Hong Kong, a general. The man was something of a dilettante, an art collector, and Wing had been providing him with pilfered objects stolen from graves on the mainland and smuggled into Hong Kong in much the same way as he had done with Western collectors before the war. As chance would have it, he had come into possession of an exceptional jade piece, an unusual bas-relief depicting two lovers in a garden. Though carved by an unknown hand, it was clearly the work of a skilled artist. Collectors knew of its existence, but it had been lost to sight for more than a century.'

'Until it fell into Wing's hands?'

Jessup nodded. 'It was promised to the Japanese general, but unfortunately for Wing, the Dragon Head to whom he owed absolute loyalty had got wind of it and wanted the piece for himself. It was left to Stanley to decide which of the two should get it and, not surprisingly, he plumped for the general. The Japanese were in complete control of Hong Kong at the time. If he had reneged on the deal he would more than likely have been executed out of hand. Of course, he was in no less mortal danger from the triad chief, but as long as the Japanese were there he could count on their protection. Once the war ended, however, his days were numbered, and since there was no way he could escape from Hong Kong, he surrendered himself at once to the returning British authorities. Even so, the Tang leader wanted his head.'

Jessup eyed Madden meaningfully.

'I mean *literally*, John. He wanted Stanley's head removed from his body. Apparently it's the trademark of this particular triad boss: his signature, if you like. Where possible the victim's body is destroyed or disposed of, leaving only the head as a warning to others. I told you Wing was attacked in jail. The two prisoners who carried out the assault did their best to decapitate him, but they were attempting to saw his head off with the only weapon available, a makeshift knife, and they were stopped before they could complete the job. Even so it was a near-run thing. They apparently got to within a hair's breadth of Stanley's carotid artery before the guards intervened.'

Jessup stopped to look back.

'I just want to make sure the children aren't following us. Jack will be on our heels as soon as he realizes we've gone for a walk; and Katy won't be far behind him.'

He scanned the valley.

'She must still be resting. Adele's strict about that. She has to stay on her bed for an hour after lunch. They're not allowed to follow where we're about to go now. But there's always the temptation to break the rules.'

Satisfied, he went on, but after only a few steps veered to the right, leaving the path they had been following. Madden quickly caught up with him. Walking side by side, they ascended a grassy rise that formed a saddle dividing the ridge

into two wooded hillocks. Although it was late in the afternoon the sun was still hot and both men were sweating by
the time they reached the top of the slope, where they paused
to take in the view.

'I used to walk these hills when I was a boy,' Jessup said.
'I'd put a piece of bread with a lump of cheese and an apple
in a knapsack and disappear for a whole day. I'd take a book
with me and lie in the shade for hours, reading. Edward
Thomas lived not far from here for a time – at Steep.' He
pointed to a distant cluster of red roofs topped by a church
spire. 'Have you read his work?'

'I came across his poems after the war,' Madden said. 'The
first war, that is.'

'He was one of those who didn't come back. But you
did.' He caught his companion's eye. 'I bumped into Ian at
the club on Friday evening. He filled me in about your past;
or some of it, at any rate.'

'Did he?'

'War's terrible enough, but the worst thing for me, what I
found hardest to bear, was the knowledge each time we went
into action of how much I had to lose. In the end I had to
stop thinking about Sarah and Jack, who was just a baby
then, and about this house and these hills, about everything I
loved. I had to put them out of my mind. A wise old soldier
once told me that the only way to go on and hope to survive
was to think of oneself as already dead. Did you ever feel
that way?'

'More than once.' Madden smiled grimly. 'And I didn't
even have what you had to come back to. Not then.'

'But later, yes . . .' Jessup smiled in turn. 'Adele told me
something of what you told her . . . about yourself . . . and
Helen. You understand then . . .'

His voice tailed off and he turned his gaze back to the rolling tree-clad country in front of them. Madden waited for a moment before speaking.

'About Thomas's poems, though – I was struck by them. He had a voice all his own.'

'Do you remember the one about the weasel and the gallows?'

'And the gamekeeper . . . ?'

'Who shot the weasel, yes . . . and hung him on a bough.' Jessup's gaze swept the land around them. 'And left him to swing there in the wind and rain, without pleasure or pain. I read it when I was a boy. It was an image I couldn't get out of my mind.'

'Why won't you let the children come this way?' Madden asked.

'I'll show you,' his companion replied. 'It's not much further.'

They continued across the saddle until they came to a straggling line of holly bushes, where they halted.

'There's an old chalk quarry on the other side of this hedge,' Jessup said, 'and I'm always afraid that the children might forget about it one day and go dashing through. A couple of boys from the village who were bird-nesting tried to climb down the side of it last year and one of them lost his footing and was killed in the fall. The drop's all of two hundred feet.'

He picked his way through the tangled branches. Madden followed. The short stretch of turf beyond ended abruptly and he found himself looking down the almost vertical side of an old chalk pit.

'We're at the very edge of the Downs,' Jessup said. 'There are plenty of quarries still active south of here. But this one hasn't been worked for years. I've told the county council they ought to fence it off for safety reasons, but nothing's been done yet, as you can see.'

They retraced their steps, and as they crossed the saddle and came down the slope they saw a figure standing, as if held back by an invisible barrier, rooted to the path below. It was Jessup's son. He was barefoot. Catching sight of his father, he sprang into life and came running up the slope towards them, calling out:

'Daddy, you said you'd tell us when you were going for a walk.'

'Did I? I must have forgotten.' Jessup looked back towards the house. 'Where's your little sister?'

'I don't know.' The boy stood panting.

'Has she fallen down a rabbit hole?'

'No, of course not.' He turned to scan the way he had come. After a few seconds he pointed. 'There she is.'

Madden made out a small figure sitting on the grass beside the path some distance away. Jessup waved to her.

'Come on, Katy,' he called to her.

The little girl showed no sign of having heard. She stayed sitting where she was, head bowed.

'What have I always told you, Jack?' Jessup rumpled his son's dark hair. 'You must look after Katy. I can't be here all the time. You have to keep an eye on her until she's old enough to look after herself.'

'But she's only *five*.' The boy was despairing. 'It'll be *years*.'

'All the same . . .' His father patted him on the head. 'Now run along and see what the trouble is.'

Listening to them, Madden chuckled.

'You'd better not mention it to Jack,' he said as they followed in the boy's footsteps, 'but when our son Rob joined the navy in the last war he told us with a straight face that it was the act of a desperate man. He said if he didn't take the chance to escape then, he knew he'd spend the rest of his life getting his sister out of one scrape after another. Mind you, he had a point. Lucy was particularly trouble-prone.'

'I know all about your beautiful daughter.' Jessup smiled at him. 'I made Ian tell me everything he knew about you and your family. It was the least I could do after burdening you with the history of mine.'

They had reached the spot where the children were. The little girl's cheeks were wet with tears and Madden saw that she was nursing a bloody knee.

'What have we here?' Jessup got down beside her. 'A wounded soldier? Oh, I think we'll need a bandage on that.'

Taking a handkerchief from his pocket, he dabbed her tears dry and kissed her. Then he bound the piece of material about her knee.

'Do we need to call for stretcher-bearers, do you think?' He addressed the question to his son, who shook his head scornfully.

'Of course not. She's all right. She can walk. See . . . !'

The little girl was already on her feet, her tears forgotten.

As Jessup rose, Jack spoke again, this time in an urgent whisper.

'Look, Daddy . . . rabbits! Over there . . . !'

Turning, Madden saw a dozen or so feeding on the grass at the bottom of the ridge not far from where they were.

'Shoot one of them!'

Jessup picked up his shotgun from the ground and slipped a cartridge into the open breech. He fired a shot. The rabbits scattered.

'You missed! Daddy, you're *hopeless*. Lennox is a much better shot than you.'

'You're right, he is.' With a grin Jessup broke the gun and

extracted the spent cartridge. 'Dead-Eye Dick. That's what we called him. But you don't even like the taste of rabbit, do you?'

Jack shook his head.

'Then why did you want me to kill one?'

Stumped for an answer, the boy was silent. He shuffled under his father's questioning gaze.

'Think about that, and give me your answer tomorrow.' Settling the shotgun in the crook of his arm again, he ran his fingers through his son's hair, pushing it back from his forehead.

'Can I carry it?' Jack looked longingly at the gun.

Jessup shook his head. 'Not until you're older.'

'You always say that.'

'Not until you're this tall.' He held his hand an inch above the boy's head.

'You always say that, too, and you keep moving your hand higher.'

Jessup laughed. 'All right. I promise you can carry it when you're ten.'

'But I've only just turned nine.'

'That means you've only got a year to wait.'

'A *year* . . . !'

The enormity of it left the boy speechless.

'Off you go now, the two of you. Tell Grandma we'll be back in time for tea.'

He watched as the two children set off down the path, Jack in the lead, his sister following at a trot. Then he glanced up at the sky.

'Have you noticed that kestrel?' he asked.

Madden nodded. 'I spotted it earlier. He's been circling for some time.'

'We're old friends.' Jessup watched as the bird glided above them, dipping first one wing, then the other, soaring on the thermals. His face was alight with pleasure. 'He hunts this valley. He won't be best pleased today, though. He probably had his eye on one of those rabbits.'

With their shadows lengthening now, they walked on in companionable silence until Jessup spoke again.

'After you tell the Yard what I've told you they'll start looking for Wing in London, won't they?'

'Unquestionably.'

'Then perhaps I should send them that snapshot I showed you in my office: the one of Wing standing with my father and those others. He was a lot younger than he is now, but it might help.'

'I wish you would, Richard. The more I hear about Wing, the more important I think it is that he should be located as soon as possible.'

'I'll ring Miss Harmon at home this evening,' Jessup said. 'I have to go to Paris for two days, but I'll get her to send it over to the Yard first thing tomorrow.'

Glancing at Madden, he saw that his face had settled into a heavy frown.

'But why are you so concerned about this, John?'

'It comes from something Mrs Castleton said to me when we talked,' Madden replied. 'The only thing she seemed certain of where Stanley Wing was concerned – and I would call her a good judge of men – was that he hated the people he worked with at Jessup's, the British I mean, all of you. We've tended to assume that this whole business has to do with blackmail. But that may be a mistake, or not the whole truth. There may be more to it than that.'

'What are you saying, John?' Jessup had stopped in midstride. He was peering at his companion.

'Wing has spent years in prison, more than enough time to nurse his grievances. He must know that sooner or later the triads will catch up with him. He's living on borrowed time. He did Garner a great service once, and was never repaid. This could be his way of taking revenge. The pendant, the letters to Derry and the newspapers, the implied threat to reveal the true identity of the murderer . . . they're like . . . like . . .'

'The Chinese water torture?' Jessup's smile was bleak. 'The death by a thousand cuts? I take your point.'

'Not altogether, I think.' Madden hesitated. 'I've found it hard to get a picture of the man. Just how dangerous is he?'

The question seemed to disconcert Jessup. He looked away, staring into the distance. Twice he seemed about to speak, but each time thought better of it. But at length he turned to face Madden again.

'There is something else I can tell you about Wing. I ought to have done so before, but didn't because of the feeling of loyalty I have towards my father and the memory of how he always tried to give Stanley the benefit of the doubt. I should add that I have no proof of it. Bear that in mind.'

Madden waited.

'I learned about it when I was investigating his activities – before his ties with the company were severed. I already suspected him of having triad connections, as I told you, and I hired a private inquiry agent to look into his background. He found no evidence of any link to them, which is interesting in view of what we know now. They must have kept it very quiet. But he was told a story about Stanley dating from his earlier life, when he was still on the streets, before he broke into my father's house, which certainly gave me pause. He ran with a gang of boys and one of them told this agent that Stanley had killed a man once.'

'Murdered him, you mean?' Madden's eyes widened.

'Not with forethought – at least not as the tale was recounted to this detective I employed. It wasn't premeditated. But it seems Stanley was lured into the shop of a Kowloon rug merchant, a notorious pederast, on the pretext of being offered work. The man apparently tried to rape him, but Stanley was able to stop him by stabbing him in the ribs with the knife which he carried. Fair enough, you might say. But when he realized the man was still able to cry out for help and could identify him he cut his throat.'

'How old was he then?' Madden was appalled.

'Twelve, I believe.' Jessup's tone was dry. 'You asked how dangerous Wing was, John. I think he's capable of anything.'

'What a lovely day!'

Helen waved for the last time to the group gathered in front of the house: Jessup and Adele Castleton lifted their hands in response; the two children waved back vigorously; Ted Lennox gave them a smart soldier's salute. The chauffeur had a broad grin on his face.

'I do wish Sarah had been here, though. I'd love to meet her. Adele's going to visit us sometime in September. But I'd like to have the whole family over for lunch before then.'

'You two looked as though you'd had a good talk.'

Madden smiled at her as they started off down the long elm-lined drive.

'It was wonderful. I heard her whole life story – what she told you, and more. She still misses Jack Jessup, but all things considered I think she's as happy now as she could be. She loves being a grandmother to the children.'

She glanced at Madden.

'You and Richard really get on, don't you?'

Madden nodded. 'I don't know what it is about him. But it's not charm, though he has that. It's more a sort of grace. He's one of those people unusually blessed by nature, but makes no show of it. I get the impression he'd rather give than receive. I felt it as soon as we met. It seems as though we've known each other for years, but that's thanks to him . . . to his openness. Heaven knows it's not a gift I have.'

'I should say not.' She teased him gently. 'I remember it took me ages to break through the shell.'

Laughing, he touched her hand.

'Did he tell you anything useful?' she asked.

'Rather. I got the full story on Stanley Wing: it turns out he's been a member of a triad gang for years. He's in trouble with them now, deep trouble. They mean to kill him. It seems he may be in London.'

'Oh, Lord!'

'But that wasn't all we talked about. I didn't mean to bring Rex Garner into it, but somehow the conversation turned that way and I ended up by having to tell Richard that he's a suspect; at least as far as Billy and Chubb are concerned.'

'How did he take that?'

'He wasn't happy. In fact, he was more upset than I would have imagined, given that they're not close friends any longer. I tried to explain that there wasn't a strong case against Garner, and that I wasn't altogether persuaded by the theories the police were playing with. But Richard didn't seem to be taking it in. He kept insisting that Garner couldn't possibly have murdered the girl. It wasn't in him.'

He saw Helen's questioning glance.

'But I wonder if he really believes that.'

15

'IT COULD BE HIM, couldn't it?'

Detective-Sergeant Joe Grace peered at the grainy, ill-lit photograph he was holding, which at first glance seemed to show a naked woman sitting alone on the end of a bed. On closer examination, however, the figure of a man lying under the sheets behind her with his face buried in the pillow could just be made out, and it was on this near shapeless form that the sergeant had fastened his gaze.

'The trouble is, it could be anyone.'

Grace clicked his tongue in disapproval. He glanced at Billy. The two of them were sitting in the back of a police car on their way to Rex Garner's Mayfair address. Earlier that morning, knowing that the individual they wanted to interview was due back any day, Billy had rung his number and found he had finally returned from Scotland.

'Still, at least we know who the lady is: Miss Portia Blake in the altogether – and a nice bit of crackling, too. A pity she had to go and get herself topped.' Joe sounded regretful. 'What a waste.'

The photograph, cropped to focus on the two figures – more of the room was shown in the print Grace was looking at – and with Miss Blake's breasts and lap decorously blacked out, had been splashed across the front page of the *Daily Mirror* that morning. According to the story that accompanied it, the snapshot had been received by the editor through the post together with a note, not typed this time but written in printed capitals, stating baldly that the man lying face down on the bed was in a position to reveal 'valuable information' about the young woman's murder. *I will say no more at this stage*, the brief letter had concluded ominously. Both note and photograph had been sent to Scotland Yard at Chubb's insistence.

Coming as it had on the heels of the information about Stanley Wing furnished by Sir Richard Jessup and relayed to the Yard by Madden, this latest development had spurred Chubb to summon the detectives involved to his office for a council of war.

'We've got to put a stop to this nonsense,' he had declared. 'We're being led by the nose and I won't have it. I've sent a telegram to Hong Kong asking for confirmation of what Jessup told Madden, not that I doubt it. I think Wing's here in London all right, and it's odds on he's the one behind this. I want him found, and quick. How's the photo lab doing with that picture Jessup's office sent us this morning?'

'We've got a shot of Wing's face ready to be copied and distributed.' It was Billy who replied. 'I've already put his name out and I've asked for a check on all hotels and boarding houses. But if the triads are after him it's likely he's travelling under a false name. If he is – if he's using a forged passport – that's an offence and we can detain him. Otherwise we've nothing to hold him on for the moment. We could still take his prints, though. We've managed to lift several different sets from the photo. Some of them will belong to whoever handled it at the *Mirror*, but we might find Wing's as well. If so, we can ask him what he's up to. I think we should also get in touch with the Amsterdam police. If Jessup is right about the triads possibly sending a killer from Holland, they might know something about it.'

'I'll see to that.' Chubb had made a note. 'As for the rest, this bloke Garner must be spoken to. I've already asked Hong Kong if they know anything about that woman he's supposed to have beaten up. I'm still waiting for their reply. But I want the question of his alibi cleared up. If he satisfies us on that score we can cross him off the suspects list and Mr Wing may have to work a little harder to get our attention. Find out exactly where Garner is. If he's still in Scotland, one of you will have to go up there and talk to him. I'm not prepared to wait any longer. Neither was the commissioner after he saw that photo in the *Mirror*. He sent word via Cradock this morning that we were to pull our fingers out; only he put it less politely.'

It was following this meeting that Billy had made his call and, having finally located the man they wished to question, he had delayed only long enough to give Lily Poole her orders before setting off with Joe Grace to conduct their interview with Garner.

'Portia's not the only one without any clothes on,' Grace remarked now. He was still peering at the photograph. 'There's a painting of a woman on the wall behind the bed. You can just make it out. She's lying on her back.'

'It's a print of a famous painting by some Spaniard,' Billy said. '*The Nude Someone-or-Other*. Lil told me she'd seen a reproduction of it in a book. Maybe it was put there to lend a little atmosphere to the place. It looks to me like a tart's bedroom.'

'Borrowed for the occasion, you mean?' Joe was intrigued.

'That's my guess.'

'Do you reckon he's seen it?' Grace tapped the photograph with his finger. They were approaching Hyde Park Corner, only minutes away from Garner's house, which was situated in a street off Park Lane bordering on Shepherd Market.

'I shouldn't think so.' Billy grimaced. 'He drove down from Scotland and only got home late last night. Somehow I doubt he has the *Daily Mirror* delivered to his doorstep.'

'You didn't mention it when you called?'

'I think I woke him up. I just told him we wanted to speak to him. He tried to put me off, said he had an engagement this morning, but I told him it was urgent and couldn't wait.'

'Do we hit him hard?' Grace asked. 'We could just shove this under his nose and ask him if the bloke in the bed is him. If he's still half asleep we might catch him off-guard.'

Billy shook his head. 'I'm going to take him back to the day when Portia was killed. I'll tell him we're checking on everyone's movements, and that includes his alibi. Depending on how he answers, we can ask him about that girl in Hong Kong. We'll save the photograph till last.'

Billy glanced at his colleague. Lean, narrow-eyed, and with a pock-marked face that would have sat well on an axe murderer, Joe Grace was one of the Met's most experienced detectives; more to the point, he could also be one of the most disagreeable when it came to dealing with anyone he regarded as a less than truthful witness, which Rex Garner might well prove to be, Billy thought, having already had a sharp exchange with the fellow on the phone a little earlier; especially if it turned out that he had lied about his alibi.

'Let me say at once that I resent this intrusion, Inspector. You've no right to barge in here with hardly a by-your-leave and start firing questions at me for no good reason. I intend to have a word with your superiors. I warn you now I'm not without friends in high places.'

If Rex Garner was trying to present a threatening front,

he was making a poor job of it, Billy thought. Still in his pyjamas and wearing a silk dressing-gown and felt slippers, he looked like a man who had just been dragged from his bed to answer the doorbell; and given that he had probably gone back to sleep after being woken by the call he'd received earlier that might well be the case. His lank dark hair was uncombed and, although he had the kind of good looks that the newspapers liked to compare with a matinee idol's, his bloodshot eyes were bleary and his cheeks unshaven. Nor had he improved the impression he was making on the two detectives when, having led the way into his drawing room, he had poured himself a whisky and then sat down heavily in an armchair. Joe Grace had glanced ostentatiously at his watch. It was barely eleven o'clock.

'I know that the investigation into the murder of Miss Blake is being reviewed. I saw something about it in a newspaper up in Scotland. But I can't imagine why.'

His face set in a belligerent expression, Garner swallowed a mouthful of neat whisky. His gaze moved restlessly about the room, which was large and airy with tall sash windows giving out onto the street, and a ceiling higher than most, which afforded space for a handsome wooden staircase at the back of the room leading up to a gallery lined with books. Despite its elegant appearance, however, there were abundant signs of neglect all about them. Magazines and old newspapers lay strewn around along with ashtrays that must have remained uncleared for weeks, given that Garner had only returned the night before. A thin patina of dust dulled the polished surface of a sun-bathed table near the window.

'There's certainly nothing I can tell you. I was nowhere near Foxley Hall when the girl was murdered. As I told the police at the time, I was in Canterbury for most of that day.'

'Lunching with a friend?' Billy asked. Yet to be invited to

sit down, he and Grace had settled for standing side by side in front of Garner, only a step or two away from him.

'Precisely.'

'Could you give us his name, please?'

'His *name*?' Garner flushed. 'Of course I can give you his name. But I don't see why I should. I was interviewed by the police years ago and they were perfectly satisfied with the answers I gave them then.'

'His name, if you don't mind, sir.' Billy held the other's gaze.

'I do bloody mind. His name was Peter Carrick.'

'And he can confirm that you had lunch together that day?'

'I rather doubt it. Poor old Peter didn't survive the war. His plane was shot down over Germany. He was a bomber pilot.'

Garner's lips twitched in a near smile. He seemed to feel he had scored a point.

'What was he doing down in Kent that weekend?'

The blood returned in a rush to Garner's cheeks.

'How is it you two came to meet for lunch in Canterbury on a Sunday? Is that where he lived?'

'My God, you've got a nerve! Are you accusing me of lying?'

The man seemed intent on working himself up into a fury, but Billy wasn't impressed – and neither, he saw out of the corner of his eye, was Joe Grace. The sergeant's thin lips were drawn back over his teeth. The effect was wolf-like.

'No, I'm simply asking you questions, Mr Garner, the same questions that everyone who was staying at Sir Jack Jessup's house that weekend will be required to answer. We need to trace people's movements that Sunday afternoon.

This is normal police procedure. If Carrick wasn't one of Sir Jack Jessup's house guests, what was he doing down there?'

'His people have a place nearby.' Garner was breathing heavily. 'He was spending the weekend with them and we agreed to meet in Canterbury. I rang Mrs Castleton to tell her I wouldn't be back for lunch. If she hasn't confirmed that yet, I'm sure she will.'

'Thank you.'

Billy took out his pad and made a note in it. Garner watched him with narrowed eyes.

'Will that be all?' he asked.

'Not quite.' Billy put his pad away. 'I've got a more general question for you now. How well did you know Miss Blake?'

'How *well* . . . ?' Like a cartoon character, Garner's face seemed to inflate with renewed rage. 'I barely knew the woman: that's to say I had run into her once or twice during the summer. She was always with that Chinaman, or whatever he is.'

'You're referring to Mr Stanley Wing?'

'You know bloody well I am.'

'With whom you were also acquainted?'

'What of it?'

'Has he been in touch with you recently?'

'The man's in prison, for Christ's sake. Don't you even know that?'

'Are you sure you've had no communication with him?'

'Quite sure.' Garner mopped his sweating brow with the sleeve of his dressing-gown.

Billy took out his pad again and made a further note.

'We've been given an account of the dinner that took place on the evening before Miss Blake was murdered. Can you explain why she behaved in the way she did?'

'Of course I can't bloody *explain*.' The bloodshot eyes bulged. 'She was putting on some kind of act; don't ask me why.'

'An act that was directed at you, it seems. Or so we've been told. According to one account, she appeared to be trying to embarrass you. Would you agree?'

'I don't know what she was doing. And no, I wasn't embarrassed, I was just annoyed. I didn't know what had got into her.'

'Was that why you decided to absent yourself from lunch the next day? Was it because you didn't want to have to sit through the same performance again?'

Garner glared at them, but said nothing.

'Turning to another matter now . . .' Billy consulted his notepad. 'Could you tell us about the incident that took place in Hong Kong some years earlier – it was well before the war – involving you and a Chinese girl? Apparently you assaulted her – so badly that the affair had to be hushed up and you were sent home at once.'

Garner swallowed. He had turned pale.

'We'd like to hear your account of that incident. Also, could you tell us what happened to the girl? Did she recover from the attack?'

'Of all the damned nerve . . . !' Garner found his tongue. But the sudden look of panic Billy saw in his eyes spoke louder than words. 'I want you both out of here. *Now!*'

Billy ignored the outburst.

'And there's one final matter we need to raise with you. Did you see today's *Daily Mirror*? No? It carried a photograph on the front page.'

He nodded to Grace, who produced the snapshot with a flourish and thrust it in front of the seated man's face.

'Recognize anyone?' The sergeant bared his teeth in earnest.

Garner's jaw dropped. Unable to disguise his astonishment he stared transfixed at the photograph.

'That's your friend, Miss Blake, sitting there.' Grace's grin suggested he was enjoying himself. 'But who's the bloke in the bed behind her? That's what we want to know. Any ideas?'

Seemingly struck dumb, Garner's eyes remained fixed on the glossy print. Twice he opened his mouth as though to speak, but each time he closed it without uttering a word. Finally he tore his gaze from the photograph. The two detectives watched as he fumbled for the whisky bottle beside him. He filled his glass with a shaking hand.

'I refuse to answer any more questions.' He sat blinking. His gaze had lost focus. It seemed his thoughts were elsewhere.

Billy cocked his head on one side. He wasn't sure what to make of the man's reaction. He studied the slumped figure in front of him.

'Do you know that room?' he asked.

'What . . . ?' Garner awoke from his reverie. 'No!' He half shouted the word.

'Are you sure you don't recognize it . . . that painting on the wall behind the bed? You can tell us if you were ever there with Miss Blake. You can admit it. It doesn't mean you killed her. We know she had a lot of men friends.'

Swallowing the last of his whisky, Garner grasped the arms of his chair. He rose unsteadily to his feet, forcing them to shuffle backwards.

'I've already told you: I won't answer any more questions.' He stood swaying before them. 'I want you to leave.'

'Fine. But I ought to explain something first. We've been

looking at this case again, going through all the statements, reviewing the evidence. And if we were wrong first time round, if Miss Blake's killer got away with it, then I have to tell you that the facts we're collecting now seem to point to you as a possible suspect. Unless you're willing to answer our questions honestly, unless you're prepared to clear the air, then the next time we question you it will be under caution, and if you refuse to answer you may find yourself facing charges of obstructing the police and perverting the course of justice. Do you understand?'

'Perfectly.'

Garner pointed a quivering finger at the door.

'Now get out.'

'He was scared . . . pissing himself.' Joe Grace snorted, then drew on his cigarette. 'I reckon he was lying, too. He'd been in that room. I'd stake my life on it. The way he stared at the photo . . .'

'He certainly looked stunned,' Billy agreed. He tugged at an earlobe. 'Maybe he realized for the first time what sort of trap he'd walked into back then. But we still can't be sure it was him in the bed, not without more evidence. Mind you, there must be other photos. Whoever's behind this is dragging it out.'

They were standing on the pavement outside Garner's house. Their car with its driver stood waiting, but Billy had paused to mull over the interview they had just conducted.

'My money's on Wing.' Joe nodded. 'He set this up: the room, the snapper. But Portia was in on it too . . . sitting there at the end of the bed, looking so innocent.'

'It seems they were working together,' Billy agreed. 'But what happened to the photographs after she was killed, that's what I want to know? Where have they been all these years? And why has this one suddenly appeared now?'

'Maybe Wing has had them all this time. He went into her room right after she was killed, didn't he? He must have been looking for something. But the war came, and then he went to prison. This may be the first chance he's had to use them.'

'Maybe . . .' Billy gnawed at his lip. 'But I'm still finding it hard to put all this together. It's like Mr Madden says: there are gaps . . . things that need explaining.'

'But it still looks like blackmail.' Grace tossed his cigarette into the gutter. 'And that means Garner's still in the frame. But why was he so bothered? He must know we haven't got the evidence to pin Portia's murder on him. Then again, it was mention of that Chinese girl that really got him going. You scared him. Topping young women who get out of line could be a nasty little habit of his, one that's coming home to roost.'

Billy shrugged. 'As far as that's concerned we'll have to wait to hear from Hong Kong.' He glanced at his watch. 'The person we really need to talk to is Stanley Wing. Let's get back to the Yard and see if Lil has come up with anything. We have to find him before the triads do.'

16

LILY TAPPED ON the door and stuck her head in.

'Excuse me, guv. Can I have a word?'

Lofty Cook looked up from his desk, scowling. When he saw who it was at the door, however, his face cleared.

'Hello, Lil.' He beamed. 'What are you doing up here? Haven't you got enough to keep you busy at the Yard? Don't just stand there looking bashful. Come on in.'

All of six feet and then some, he rose from his chair and reached across the desk to shake her hand.

'Take a pew.'

A chief inspector stationed now at West End Central, Lofty had been a DI at Bow Street, Lily's old stamping ground, when she had first known him, and one of the few officers – she could count them on one hand – who had never held her sex against her. It was he who had paved the way for her move from the uniform branch to the CID, recommending her to Billy Styles when they had worked together on a murder case during the war. Styles in turn had brought her to the attention of Angus Sinclair, who had made it his business before resigning to see her transferred to the Yard's plain-clothes division. Given the task of tracking down Stanley Wing and finding out what she could about any triad presence in London, Lily had decided that Soho was as good a place as any to start. And knowing that the area was now on Cook's patch, she had made the short journey from the Embankment up to Savile Row to pick her old guv'nor's brains.

'You could do worse,' Lofty said, having heard her out. Lily had given him a quick summary of the case and shown him the photograph of Wing that she had in her handbag. 'Though there's been no real Chinatown in London since the war; not since the Blitz. They used to congregate in Limehouse, as you know, but the bombing put an end to that. The community was scattered. Now they're starting to gather again, and Soho is one of the areas where you'll find new Chinese restaurants popping up. If there are any triad visitors in town, word will have spread. You might pick up a whisper there.'

He grinned then. It was as if he knew what she was going to say next.

'You wouldn't have a good snout, would you, guv?'

'A Chink snout? You'd be lucky to find one you could even converse with.' His grin widened. 'Usually it's a case of no spikee English.'

He watched as her face fell.

'I'm just pulling your leg, Lil, though it's not that far from the truth. They don't have much to do with us. They're a close-knit lot and they tend to sort out their own problems. As it happens, I do know someone who might be of help. But it'll be up to her whether she's willing to talk to you or not. And you've got to promise to keep schtum: no passing her name around among those layabouts at the Yard.'

'Word of honour, guv.' Lily grinned.

'I won't come with you.' Lofty hoisted himself to his feet. 'I don't meet her in Soho. They know my face there. But I'll go with you part of the way. I fancy a cuppa.'

*

'She's got a shop off Gerrard Street. She sells silk scarves and trinkets, lacquer-work, that sort of stuff. Anna Wu is the name she goes by. She anglicized it when she came here from Hong Kong. That was before the war.'

Lofty poured some of his tea into a saucer, blew on it, returned the tea to his cup and took a sip. He had led Lily to a cafe near the police station. They were sitting at a table by the counter.

'She's not your run-of-the-mill snout, as you'll see; she's got a mind of her own. But she hates the triads. Her father was a gang member – a low-ranking figure in one of the families. He was killed in a street fight in Hong Kong twenty years ago. She's known to them, of course, and triad couriers use her shop now and then as a meeting place. There's nothing she can do about that, and I turn a blind eye to it. She's too valuable to me.'

'Are they here in numbers, then?' Lily asked. Cook shook his head.

'Not yet. But I reckon they will be. Extortion's one of their dodges. The Chinese restaurants here will soon find themselves paying protection money once a triad branch is established. But drugs are their main business. We can see it coming, but there's not much we can do about it for the present.'

'Does the term Red Pole mean anything to you?' Lily sipped her tea.

Lofty shook his head. 'Should it?'

'That's what they call an enforcer – a killer, if you like. Or so we've been told.'

'And you're wondering if one of them has been sent here from Holland to do this bloke Wing?'

Lily nodded.

'Well, if so, Anna might have heard something about it –

a whisper, as I say. But don't try to push her too hard, Lil. She won't take it.'

Cook was serious now.

'She walks a fine line, and I don't want her put in danger.'

'I understand.'

'And I doubt she'll be able to tell you anything about Wing.'

'Why's that?'

'Because if I was him, Soho is the last place I'd show my face. Once word gets out that the triads are looking for him there'll be any number of people hereabouts ready to shop him. They may not like these thugs, but they know better than to cross them. If I was Wing I'd stay well away from the city centre. I'd stick to the outer suburbs.'

Lofty rose to his feet. Lily followed suit.

'And I'd keep on the move, too.'

The shop, Happy Thoughts, was next to a restaurant named the Jasmine Inn which, like others of its kind nearby, had a row of ducks' carcasses hanging in the window.

'You could do worse than have a bite there afterwards if you feel peckish,' Lofty had told Lily when he'd given her directions. 'I've been getting a taste for Chinese grub since I moved over here from Bow Street.'

As she opened the door a bell tinkled and a woman dressed in a long gown made of black silk decorated with silver flowers and butterflies appeared from behind a curtain at the back of the store. Small in size, her golden cheeks were smooth and Lily could see no hint of a wrinkle around the dark brown eyes that regarded her without expression. According to Lofty, Anna Wu was in her early forties.

'Yes, Miss . . . ?'

Lofty had prepared her in advance for the encounter. He had given her the magic words, as he'd put it, and Lily saw no reason not to plunge right in.

'Your shop was recommended by a friend of mine,' she said. 'He bought a silk scarf from you not long ago.'

'A red scarf?' The yellow face remained blank.

'No, a blue one.'

A crease appeared in the smooth forehead. 'You no detective.' It was an accusation.

'Yes, I am.' Lily had her warrant card ready. She slid it across the glass-topped counter. Miss Wu studied it.

'Who send you here?'

'Mr Cook. He said you might be able to help me.'

'Why he no come?'

'This isn't his case. And he said you two never meet in Soho.'

'Ah . . .' Miss Wu seemed to find these last words reassuring. She glanced at her wristwatch. 'Closing time.'

She came around the counter and went to the glassed door where a sign reading CLOSED hung from a hook. Reversing it so that it faced outwards, she locked the door.

'Come . . .'

She led the way past the curtain at the back of the shop. Lily followed, and found herself in a small storeroom lined with boxes. A brass lamp suspended from the ceiling gave off a faint smell of incense. In the centre of the room were two chairs on either side of a lacquered table. Miss Wu gestured to her to take one. She sat down facing her.

'Why you detective?' She looked hard at Lily, frowning. 'Why you not home?'

'Home . . . ?'

'Young woman stay home, take care of husband.'

'I haven't got one,' Lily said. 'I'm not married.'

'Why not?' Miss Wu's frown had grown fierce.

'I don't know.' Lily scratched her head. 'Maybe because no one's asked me.'

The flicker of a smile crossed Miss Wu's solemn face. 'I have husband. He no good. I throw him out.' The smile vanished. 'Why you detective?'

She seemed determined to find out. Lily shrugged.

'I joined the police when I was eighteen. I always wanted to be a copper. I don't know why.'

'You catch bad men?'

'Sometimes.'

'Good . . . too many bad men.'

Miss Wu studied her hands, first the palms, then the backs. Lily felt she was being weighed in some balance and she waited for the verdict to be delivered. Finally the other woman looked up.

'So . . . ?'

'We're trying to find a man called Stanley Wing. He's from Hong Kong and we think he may be hiding out in London.'

'Why hiding?'

'One of the triad gangs is looking for him.'

'Ah . . .' Miss Wu's glance sharpened. 'Which family?'

'The Tang . . . ?' Lily wasn't sure she'd remembered it correctly, but her questioner showed no surprise on hearing the name. She merely nodded.

'Man's name is Wing, you say . . . Stanley Wing?'

Lily nodded.

'Stanley Wing not Chinese name.'

'He's half Chinese, half English.'

Miss Wu looked thoughtful.

'Someone came to my shop last week,' she said. 'He also

looking for man, but not Wing: man called Lee. This also not Chinese name.'

'Did you know him, the man who came to your shop?'

Miss Wu shook her head. 'He tell me his name is Chen Yi.'

'Was he from Hong Kong?'

Miss Wu shrugged. It appeared that she didn't know.

'Or perhaps from Amsterdam?'

Miss Wu cocked her head on one side. For the first time she looked at Lily with respect.

'Is good guess ... yes, maybe ... Amsterdam. Very smooth young man. He show me photograph.'

Lily dug into her handbag and took out the snapshot of Wing she'd brought with her. She handed it to Miss Wu, who nodded after only the briefest glance at it.

'Is same man. Chen Yi say he has scar on his neck now.' She put a hand to her throat. 'I tell him I don't know this man.'

Lily retrieved the photo and put it back in her bag. She was thinking.

'Chen Yi – could he be what they call a Red Pole?'

Miss Wu's eyebrows shot up. She said something in Chinese.

'Where you hear about Red Pole?'

'From someone who knows Wing's background: someone who has been in touch with the Hong Kong police. He said this triad family might send a man to London to kill Wing: a Red Pole.'

Miss Wu brooded in silence.

'Chen Yi not Red Pole.' She sounded positive. 'He man who asks questions.'

'You mean he works for the Red Pole?' Lily wanted to be

clear about this. 'Would *he* be in London too?' They had to know.

'Must be.' Miss Wu shrugged again. 'But you not find him. He waits . . .'

'Until Wing has been located?'

Miss Wu dipped her head in silent acknowledgement.

'And then?'

'You *sure* is Tang family that look for Wing?'

Lily nodded.

'Then they chop head off.' Miss Wu brought the edge of her hand down sharply on the table, making Lily jump. 'Like that. Is Tang way.'

17

'Is that it? Have you got it?'

Chubb grabbed the snapshot Billy was holding out to him.

'Does it tell us anything more?'

The chief super peered at the new photograph.

'Garr . . . !' A growl of disgust issued from his lips. He slapped the print down on his desk where a copy of the *Daily Mirror*, displaying the same picture on its front page, but in cropped form, lay on the blotter. Like the previous one it featured the naked image of Portia Blake, this time seen from behind, but with her buttocks modestly veiled by the now familiar black rectangle, standing beside the bed on which a man was sitting. Bare from the waist up, he was on the other side of the nude woman and leaning forward so that his head was hidden by her body. The picture, which had appeared in that morning's edition, had been sent to the editor through the post as before, but this time without any accompanying note. It had been forwarded at once to the Yard.

Chubb read out the banner headline: '*MYSTERY DEEP-ENS*. They're getting their money's worth, aren't they? The editor must be cock-a-hoop. The commissioner hasn't seen it yet, but Cradock has.' He glared at Billy. 'What's he on about, this bloke? Is he just winding us up?'

'Not us, sir. We're coincidental. It looks to me like he's holding a sword over someone else's head: he's telling him he's got more pictures.'

'Coincidental . . .'

The chief super fumed in silence. Billy coughed.

'We're still working on Garner's alibi. Grace has tracked down the parents of that man Carrick who was killed in the war, the one Garner said he had lunch with in Canterbury, but unfortunately they seem to be away. Apparently they have a house in the South of France. Grace is trying to get hold of the phone number there.'

'Do you seriously believe either one of them will remember what their son was doing that day? It was more than ten years ago.'

Billy could only shrug.

'What about this so-called Red Pole? Do we know that he's in London?'

'We can't be certain, sir, but it's likely. We know that Wing's using the name Lee and that a young Chinese bloke called Chen Yi is looking for him. It's odds on he's working for the Red Pole.'

'Damn silly name.' Chubb glowered.

'I'd be a lot happier if we knew his real one.' Billy grinned. 'Have you had any word back from the Amsterdam police on that?'

Chubb shook his head. 'Only that they're looking into it for us.'

'How about Hong Kong?'

'The same. It's been several days since I sent them a telegram asking about that girl Garner is supposed to have beaten up. My guess is they haven't found anything in their records, which makes me think it wasn't reported at the time.'

'So perhaps only Wing knows what happened to her.' Billy rubbed his chin thoughtfully. 'That could put him in a strong position vis-à-vis Garner.'

Chubb hoisted himself to his feet.

'I'd better go and talk to Cradock. There'll be hell to pay when the commissioner sees today's *Mirror*, and we'd better be prepared. They'll both want to know what we're doing about Garner. Have you spoken to him again?'

Billy shook his head. 'But he knows we'll be back. I told him so. I thought I'd give him a day or so to stew and then call on him again. By then I hope we'll have managed to check his alibi. He's got a meeting fixed with Sir Richard Jessup tomorrow evening.'

'Has he now?' Chubb's eyes lit up.

'I spoke to Mr Madden yesterday. He's up in town again. He'd had a call from Jessup just before he went off to Paris yesterday. Jessup said Garner had rung him and asked if they could meet. He said he wanted to see him urgently. They're having dinner at Jessup's club tomorrow night after he gets back. He told Mr Madden that Garner sounded "agitated".'

'Agitated . . .' The chief super rubbed his hands. 'That's more like it.' He picked up the photograph and newspaper from his desk and tucked them under his arm. Then he cocked an eye at Billy. 'What do you think? Will he crack?'

'He might.' Billy himself had been weighing the same possibility in his mind. 'But it all depends on his alibi. And, like you say, will anyone remember that far back?'

As Billy entered his office he heard a phone being slammed down, followed by a muttered curse. Joe Grace was sitting at the desk across from his, glaring at the instrument.

'What's up?'

'Carrick's parents aren't at their house in France. They were until a few days ago. Now they're driving back to

England. But they're stopping off in Paris and nobody knows what hotel they're staying at.'

'Nobody . . . ?'

'I got hold of the hall porter at the block of flats where they live. They rang him from France a week ago telling him not to forward any more post to them and that they'd be back this week. But they didn't say when. He gave me the name of their daughter, a Mrs Hill. She lives in London.'

'And . . . ?'

'Do you know how many Hills there are in the phone book?'

'No, and I don't want to. Keep trying, Joe.'

Billy himself had a call to make, and as soon as he'd sat down at his desk he dialled the number. The phone rang for some time and he was on the point of hanging up when Madden answered.

'Sorry for the delay, Billy,' he said, after they'd exchanged greetings. 'Alice is moving out today and it's proving to be a wrench. She's lived in this house for thirty years, poor old dear. At this moment she's having a quiet cry in the kitchen. I wish Lucy were here. She'd be better at this than I am.'

'If it's a bad time, sir . . .'

'No, it's not that. But if I have to break off suddenly it'll mean the taxi is here. I'm going to take Alice down to Waterloo and put her on a train for Hastings. It's the least I can do. Tell me – is it something to do with Garner?'

Madden already knew about the meeting Billy and Grace had had with the man the day before. But he was unaware of what Lily Poole had learned in Soho and Billy quickly brought him up to date.

'It sounds as though Sir Richard was right,' he said. 'The triads have got someone here already looking for Wing.'

'And meanwhile the executioner's waiting offstage . . .' Madden hummed thoughtfully to himself.

'We're still in the dark about Garner's alibi. We might hear something later today, but either way I'm going to talk to him again. He's hiding something. Grace and I both felt he wasn't being honest with us.' Billy paused. 'I'd like to be a fly on the wall when he meets Jessup. Why do you think he wants to see him, sir?'

'Probably to ask his advice. Sir Richard's not looking forward to the encounter.'

There was silence between them. Looking across the room at Joe Grace, Billy realized that he, too, had not spoken for some time. The sergeant was sitting with the telephone pressed to his ear. He was writing busily in his notepad.

'What will he do if Garner confesses to the murder and asks for his help?'

'He'll tell him to go to the police.' Madden's response was unhesitating. 'He'll advise him to make a clean breast of it.'

'But what if Garner doesn't take his advice? Will he shop him?'

Madden sighed. 'I can't answer that question, Billy. Only Jessup can. But I don't believe he'd protect him: not if he knew he was a murderer.'

He hesitated.

'Look, he said he'd call me after their meeting tomorrow evening, Jessup, that is. Why don't you come up here and have supper with us? We can wait to hear from him.'

'I don't want to put you to any trouble—' Billy began, but was quickly cut off.

'You won't. We've still got several tins of Aunt Maud's illicit hoard to finish off, and Lucy would love to see you. She'll be here. Why not bring Lily Poole with you, too. Angus is always asking me for news of her.'

'Well, if you're sure, sir.' Billy beamed. 'It'll be a pleasure. Elsie and the kids are still away. But I expect you guessed that.'

As he hung up he caught Grace's eye. The sergeant brandished a clenched fist.

'Yes, Mrs Hill.' He spoke for the first time in a while. 'That's very helpful. And you're sure of that, are you – the dates, I mean?'

He listened in silence.

'Yes, I quite understand. There couldn't be any mistake. We may need a statement from you later. I'll be in touch about that. And thank you again.'

He put down the phone.

'Wouldn't you know it?' Joe's smile was triumphant. 'Alibi, my eye! Garner was lying in his teeth.'

'How could he think he'd ever get away with it?' Chubb shook his head in wonder.

'Well, he did first time around.' Billy settled himself in his chair. He and Grace had hurried down to the chief super's office to give him the news. 'No one was interested in his alibi once Norris was arrested, and especially not after he confessed. Garner had already told Mrs Castleton earlier in the day that he was lunching with a friend in Canterbury and he stuck to the story when the police interviewed him. He was up in Scotland when he learned that the case was being reviewed. He had time to think of who he could name and came up with what he probably thought was the brilliant idea of choosing someone who was dead. I got the impression he wasn't very bright.'

Chubb turned to Grace. 'How could this Mrs Hill be so sure after all this time? Tell me exactly what she said.'

'The whole family was down in France, including Peter Carrick,' Grace replied. 'They've got a house near Nice. They didn't hear anything the Sunday Portia Blake was killed, naturally. But the next day she and her brother went into Nice where they bought the continental edition of the *Daily Mail*. The story was front-page news and since they knew Jack Jessup well – their house in Kent wasn't far from his – they read every line of it. Not only that: Peter Carrick actually knew that Garner was staying there. They'd had lunch together in London shortly before Carrick went off to France and he told his sister he remembered Garner telling him he was going down to Kent that weekend. Carrick was in France the day Portia was killed – there's no doubt of it – and Mrs Hill is prepared to make a statement to that effect.'

'So Garner's put himself right in it.' Chubb still couldn't credit what he'd heard. 'He's practically handed us his head on a platter.'

'We still need more evidence,' Billy responded cautiously. 'But if his face appears in one of these photographs it's going to put him into a near impossible position. He's always denied that there was anything between him and Portia. Wing's the key to this, though. He may be the only person who can prove that Garner was the killer. But will he do that? If it's money he wants, he'll keep us in suspense, at least until Garner coughs up. But if it's revenge he's after, which Mr Madden thinks is possible, he could deliver him into our hands. And if Garner knows that, he might decide to act first and confess. It would look better for him if he did. He could claim he acted in the heat of the moment and killed her by accident.'

Chubb pondered in silence.

'Now that we know his alibi is false, you could arrest him and question him under caution.'

'I know, sir, and I mean to if he sticks to his lies. But it might be wise to let him have this meeting with Sir Richard first. Mr Madden thinks Jessup will press him to come clean about whatever it is he's hiding, and he may have more influence on him than anyone else. It only means waiting another day. We can afford to do that. Meanwhile, we can keep looking for both Wing and this Red Pole bloke and tie up any other loose ends.'

'Loose ends?' the chief super growled. 'I don't want any of those left hanging, not again. What have you got in mind?'

'If you remember, Mr Madden thought that actress Portia shared a flat with, Audrey Cooper, hadn't been entirely frank with him. He had the feeling she was keeping something back. I'm going over to Chelsea with Poole this afternoon to question her again.'

18

BILLY GLANCED AT his watch.

'How did she sound when you rang her?'

'She didn't seem surprised, guv.'

Lily wound down the window. The two of them were sitting in the back of a radio car that must have been standing in the sun all morning. It felt like an oven. The busy traffic in the King's Road had slowed their progress to a crawl.

'In fact, she said she'd been wondering when we'd get around to her.'

'According to Mr Madden she's got a sharp tongue. He didn't care for her. Isn't this the end of the King's Road?' Billy had leaned forward to speak to their driver. 'Are you sure we haven't gone too far, Carter?'

'No, sir, it's next on the right . . . Langton Street.'

Slowing the car as he spoke, he turned across the on-coming traffic, and then braked.

'Crikey! What's going on here?'

The narrow street in front of them was blocked by a small crowd which even as they watched was being added to by people spilling out of doorways on either side of the road. They were gathering around a spot where a blue-clad figure could be seen lying stretched out on the road surface.

'Jesus!' Billy grabbed for the door handle. 'He's one of ours.'

Lily already had the door on her side open. Springing out

of the car, she raced down the street and forced a way through the crowd.

'Stand back . . . police . . . !'

The constable was lying on his back. A young man, his eyes were wide and staring and as Lily went down on her knees beside him she saw his mouth open and close as though he were trying to speak. A man wearing a postman's uniform and cap was kneeling on the other side of the prone body. He was trying to get the buttons of the officer's jacket undone. A stain darker than the blue material surrounding it showed beneath the ribcage.

'I think he's been stabbed.' The postman was out of breath. 'I saw it happen. I was just behind him.'

'Has anyone sent for an ambulance?'

Billy barked out the question. He had arrived on Lily's heels and was crouching down beside her. Lily had taken over the task of undoing the injured man's buttons. When she pulled his blue jacket open they saw the spreading red stain on his white shirt.

'Not as far as I know.' The postman panted his reply.

'Carter . . . !' Billy shouted over his shoulder to their driver. 'Call for an ambulance . . . on the double. And tell dispatch we've got a PC down injured here and we need some officers on the scene.'

Lily was searching through her pockets and her handbag.

'I need a cloth or a scarf . . . anything.'

She called out to the crowd. After a moment a handkerchief was thrust into her hands, then another. Folding them into a pad, she tugged the bloodstained shirt open and pressed the makeshift dressing against the narrow wound oozing blood which she could see in the young man's stomach.

'Anyone here had first-aid training?'

Billy shouted the question, and a voice answered.

'Yes. Me.'

The crowd parted and a woman appeared, elbowing her way forward. Middle-aged and stocky, she wore a confident look.

'I drove an ambulance during the Blitz,' she announced. 'I know what to do.'

Kneeling down beside Lily, she took hold of the make-shift pad from her, keeping it pressed firmly to the wound. 'Edie . . .' she yelled over her shoulder and a young voice answered. 'Run into the house and fetch me two clean hand towels from the linen cupboard; fast as you can.'

Billy rose to his feet. The postman followed suit. His leather satchel had been resting on the ground beside him and he hoisted it on to his shoulder.

'What did you see?' Billy asked him. 'How did it happen?'

'I was walking down from the King's Road a few paces behind this officer when we heard a scream.'

His words brought an answering murmur from the crowd. A voice called out: 'That's right. We all heard it.'

'The officer stopped. He wasn't sure where it had come from; neither was I. Then that door there opened' – he pointed to a nearby house – 'and a man came running out. The constable shouted to him to stop, but the bloke tried to run past him and when the officer grabbed him he hit him in the stomach. At least, that's what it looked like.' The post-man winced. 'But your chap went down at once clutching his gut and the other fellow ran off that way.' He pointed in the opposite direction to the King's Road. 'I don't know what happened to him after that. I saw your man was hurt and I thought I'd better stay and help him.'

'Can you describe the man who stabbed him?'

The postman shook his head. 'I didn't really get a look at

253

his face. It all happened so quickly. Dark hair – that's all I saw.'

Billy bent down.

'Can he talk?' he asked Lily.

'I wouldn't advise it.' It was the woman tending to the injured man who answered. 'He's in shock. Best to leave him quiet for the moment.'

Billy beckoned to his driver, who was standing by the police car. He came running.

'I got through to dispatch, guv. There's an ambulance on its way. And they're sending more officers. There should be a Flying Squad car here any moment.'

'We're going into that house. Someone in there may be hurt. Wait for the other officers to arrive. Tell them what happened. Lil . . .' He touched her on the shoulder. 'Come on.'

With a last glance at the young constable, Lily got to her feet and followed Billy along the pavement towards the house the postman had indicated. She stopped when the saw the number on the door.

'Guv, look.'

Billy followed the direction of her pointing finger.

'Number 8. This is where she lives: Audrey Cooper. Her flat's on the first floor.'

'Christ!'

Billy was up the steps and through the door, which had been left standing open, in a flash. Lily stayed on his heels. A narrow hallway, empty apart from a bicycle leaning against the wall, led to a flight of stairs. When they reached the first landing they found yet another door standing ajar. Billy stuck his head in.

'Anyone home?' he called out.

There was no reply.

He led the way inside and the two detectives found themselves in an untidy sitting room, carelessly furnished, and with the chairs and settees, most of them showing signs of age, strewn with discarded items of women's clothing. When Lily half stumbled on something and looked down she saw it was a pile of what looked like play scripts. The air was sour with the smell of stale cigarette smoke.

Spotting a door open at the back of the room, Billy hastened to it.

'Miss Cooper . . . ?' He called out her name. When there was no reply, he disappeared through the doorway.

Lily went to the other side of the room where there was a large picture window overlooking the street. A big purple sofa, splitting at the seams and stained with wear, stood away from the wall. Nearby was a small writing-desk. Its drawers had been pulled out; one of them was lying on the threadbare carpet at her feet. As she bent down to pick it up her eye was caught by the sight of a broken vase and some strewn flowers on the floor near the wall. She also spotted something else protruding from behind the sofa.

It took a moment before she realized what she was looking at: it was a bare foot encased in a slipper.

'Guv . . . !' she yelled out. 'In here . . . !'

Billy was back in seconds. He found Lily down on her knees and peering behind the sofa.

'What is it?'

'Miss Cooper, I reckon.' She glanced up at him. 'And there's blood, too . . . lots of it.'

Lily felt a tap on her shoulder. She looked up. A burly PC was standing there holding out a cup of tea. She took it from him with a nod of thanks.

'Drink this.' She offered it to the young woman sitting beside her on the bed. 'You'll feel better.'

The girl showed no sign of having heard. She sat with her blonde head bowed and her arms hugging her chest, sobbing quietly.

'Who'd do a thing like that . . . ?'

Lily barely caught the muttered words.

'Come on, Pixie.' She spoke more sharply this time. 'You can't go on like this. I need to ask you some questions. Have a sip of this tea.'

The girl sniffed. She accepted the cup and saucer offered her, but made no move to drink from it, and after a moment Lily took it back and put it down on the bedside table. Pixie du Pre was the name the young woman had given her, and only after being pressed by Lily had she admitted that she had adopted it for the stage and that her real name was Gladys Wainwright. Escorted upstairs by a bobby posted in the street outside, she had entered the flat almost unnoticed. The forensic squad and fingerprint crew summoned from the Yard had been hard at work for half an hour. They had moved the sofa further away from the wall, giving the pathologist, also called to the scene, room to examine the body, which was stretched out on the floor. The carpet had absorbed a lot of the blood, but there was still a large pool of it standing untouched on the bare boards where the actress's head lay. Pixie's shriek, uttered as she took in the scene from the doorway, had made everyone jump.

Seemingly unable to speak, she had screamed in hysterics for several seconds until Lily had taken hold of her shoulders and shaken her, and when that proved ineffective slapped her on the cheek. Quietened finally, she had allowed herself to be led through the sitting room to one of the two bedrooms

at the back of the flat where she had identified herself as
Audrey Cooper's flatmate and, like her, an actress. She had
gone out that morning, she said, to do some shopping and
after lunching with a friend near Covent Garden had taken
part in an audition for a new musical. She had no idea what
her flatmate's plans for the day were, but as far as she knew
she had not been expecting any visitors.

'She's been so strange lately . . .'

A new note sounded in Pixie's voice, and Lily pricked
up her ears. Up till then the young woman had been locked
in her grief, unable to focus on what had happened. Now it
seemed as though she was speaking her thoughts aloud.

'Since when?'

'Since that man came to see her.'

'What man?' Lily reacted quickly. 'What was his name?'
And then, as a new thought struck her. 'Was it a Mr Madden?'

'How'd you know that?' The girl turned a teary gaze on
her. Lily ignored the question.

'What happened?' she asked. 'What did Miss Cooper say
about their meeting?'

'Not much.' Pixie shrugged. 'Only that he was a dark
horse and that he wasn't telling her everything. But she began
acting funny as soon as he left; she started searching for
something, going through the drawers of her desk, talking to
herself, saying "Audrey, you idiot!" when she couldn't find
it. But then she remembered . . .'

'Remembered . . . ?'

'Where she'd put it. It was in the box where she kept her
jewellery. And when she found it there she seemed really
pleased. She said bingo!'

'Bingo . . . ?' Lily blinked. 'Yes, but what *was* it?'

'I don't know.' Pixie shook her head. 'She didn't say.
She just took the box with her into the bedroom and when

she came back she had her handbag with her and said she had to go out. I was going out myself and Aud said she'd walk with me to the bus stop. It's in the King's Road. But she left me there and went on and I saw her go into the chemist. Then the bus arrived and I had to get on so I didn't see where she went after that.'

The words were tumbling from her mouth now.

'But after that she started to behave differently . . .'

'How differently?'

The girl frowned. Her tears had stopped. She seemed to be concentrating now . . . trying to remember.

'You know what it's like when someone knows something you don't know and won't tell you what it is?' Pixie's wide blue eyes were fixed on Lily's face.

'I think so.'

'When they're pleased with themselves about something and can't hide it?'

Lily nodded.

'Well, she was like that. She was up to something, I could tell, but she wouldn't say what it was, and it hurt. I'd thought we were close . . .'

Tears shone afresh in the blue orbs.

'She did say one thing, though . . .'

'What was that?'

'It was after she went off one afternoon and didn't come home till late. When she did, I could see she was even more chuffed. She was like . . . like a cat that had swallowed the cream. "I've been to the far north in search of treasure, Pixie," she said. "I rather think I found it."'

'To the far north . . . ? And back the same afternoon?' Lily was baffled.

'That's how Aud talked,' Pixie explained. 'She had this

flowery way of speaking; theatrical, I suppose. She probably just took the tube somewhere.'

'And what was the treasure?'

'I asked her that, but all she said was, "I speak in meta-
phors."' Pixie waved her hands helplessly. 'She said the
treasure would come later, and with any luck I'd be able to
buy myself some fancy new clothes. "We could take a trip to
New York together," she said. "Or would you rather have a
week in Monte Carlo?" I didn't know what she was on about.'

The far north . . . ? Lily stared at the slumped figure
beside her. Pixie's words had started a train of thought in
her mind. Pieces were starting to fall into place, like bits of a
jigsaw puzzle . . . jewel box . . . chemist . . . treasure. As the
picture became clearer Lily pursed her lips in a silent whistle.

Was that it? Had she guessed right?

But before she could take her idea any further there was
something she had to do. She touched Pixie's hand.

'You don't want to be here on your own,' she told the
disconsolate girl. 'Have you got a friend you could stay with,
at least for a day or two? You shouldn't be alone.'

While Pixie made a call on the bedside telephone, Lily
went next door to seek Billy's approval for the arrangement
she was making.

'They were more than flatmates,' she told him. 'And more
than friends, too, I reckon.'

'Aye, aye . . .' Grace, listening in, had winked knowingly,
but Billy had simply shrugged.

Her duty done, Lily watched as the police car drove off,
and then went back up the stairs. She was ready to share her
thoughts with her two male colleagues now.

She just hoped she had it right.

✳

'So Miss Cooper found something in her jewel box which she thought was worth a few bob.' Billy scowled. 'But how do we know it had anything to do with Portia Blake?'

'Because she started looking for it the minute Mr Madden left. He must have said something that got her thinking. And all they talked about was Portia and that Wing bloke.'

While she waited for her guv'nor's reaction, Lily looked about her. The sitting room was starting to empty. The work of the specialist squads sent from the Yard was over. The crews were packing up their gear and preparing to leave. Still waiting to do their job, a couple of ambulance men stood by ready to load Audrey Cooper's remains onto a stretcher for transporting to the mortuary at St Mary's Hospital in Paddington where the post mortem would be carried out. Mingled with the musty smell of tobacco and old cigarette butts there was another odour, one Lily had learned to recognize: the metallic scent of blood.

'How's the PC who was stabbed?' Lily asked. She had joined Billy and Joe Grace in the corner where they stood observing the proceedings.

'Stable, according to the ambulance blokes,' Billy told her. 'That lady did a good job tending to him. We ought to send her a note of thanks. You just missed the pathologist,' he went on. 'He confirmed that Miss Cooper had her throat cut. She also had wounds on her hands, which suggest she tried to defend herself. She must have realized he was going to kill her: that could have been when she screamed. Joe and I have been trying to work out whether this was random, or if it's linked to the Portia Blake murder. You're telling us now that it must have been Wing who killed her. Why?'

'Well, for one thing, according to Sir Richard Jessup, he carried a knife in the past. And he wasn't afraid to use it. But mostly because Miss Cooper had something he wanted.'

'Which was . . . ?'

'The photographs . . . or rather the negatives . . . the ones Portia had taken of herself and the bloke in the bed, who we think could have been Garner.'

'Are you sure about that?' Billy's eyes bored into hers. 'Up till now we've been working on the assumption that it was Wing who had possession of those photos.'

'Yes, but what if we've been wrong, guv? What if Portia showed them to Garner in the wood, and when he tried to take them from her they fought and he ended up killing her in a rage? He would have destroyed the pictures, naturally, but there were still the negatives. Maybe Wing didn't find them when he went into her room later because Portia had left them behind in London as insurance. That's how they could have come into Miss Cooper's hands. She could have gone through Portia's things after she heard about the murder. There wasn't much love lost between them. She might have put them aside and forgotten about them until Mr Madden showed up that day.'

The two men stared at her. Grace's narrow features were knotted in a scowl – of disbelief perhaps. But Billy's expression was harder to read. He seemed to be at least considering the idea.

Lily took a deep breath.

'If Wing really had found the photos when he went into Portia's room, why did he go home to Hong Kong? Why didn't he put pressure on Garner right away? Strike while the iron was hot? It doesn't make sense him leaving the country, not if he had evidence pointing to the real killer.'

'What about the pendant?' Grace broke in. 'He had that all right.'

'Did he?' Lily looked at him. 'We don't *know* that it's the same one, Sarge. All we know is it looks like it. Whoever took the photographs off Portia's body must also have taken the pendant. Nothing else makes sense. But how can we know that Wing didn't go back to Hong Kong and have another one made just like it, with the same sort of flaw? Even if he witnessed the murder, even if he knew Garner was the killer, he needed to concoct some evidence before he could put pressure on him. But instead the war came and everything changed, particularly for him. Now he's in deep trouble, near the end of his rope. He's desperate. He comes back to England hoping to put his blackmail scheme into operation again, but he's got precious little to back it up with; only that pendant. He sends it to Mr Derry along with a letter, and when that gets no reaction he writes to the editor of the *News of the World*. He's trying to whip up interest in the case, but he's out of ammunition. Then a miracle occurs – at least from his point of view. That first photograph appears in the *Mirror* – and not with a typed note, by the way; this one was written by hand – and Wing knows instantly who must have sent it. It can only be Audrey Cooper. If Portia didn't have the negatives with her in Kent, she must have left them behind in London and somehow Miss Cooper had got hold of them. So he came calling . . .'

Lily paused for dramatic effect. She could see that what she was saying was finally having an effect on one of her listeners. Billy Styles was rubbing his chin; he looked thoughtful.

'Joe found that jewel box,' he said. 'It was on the floor near her body with some stuff beside it . . . a bracelet and some beads and other odds and ends. I had it dusted in case the killer left his paw prints on it. What happened to it, Joe?'

'It's on the table over there.'

Grace crossed the room and returned with the item in question.

'What I don't see is how she could have missed whatever she was looking for, how she had to go searching for it.' The sergeant's scowl was back. 'All she had to do was open the flipping lid.'

'Yes, but when we found it there was a drawer sticking out of the bottom.' Billy examined the object. 'What happened to that?'

'Search me.' Joe shrugged. 'The fingerprint lads must have shut it. I can't see how it opens.'

'May I, guv?' Lily reached for the box. 'I've seen one of these before.' She ran her fingers along the bottom rim. 'There should be something here . . . yes there it is. There's a spring or something . . .'

She pressed with her two fingers on either side of the box. A shallow drawer slid out.

Grace grunted. 'It's empty.' He frowned. 'There's nothing there.'

'But there might have been,' Lily insisted. 'If it was open when you found it, then maybe Wing took whatever was inside.'

'You couldn't hide much in there.' The sergeant was unimpressed. 'There's no room. A letter maybe . . . ?'

'Or a bunch of photos.' Silent up to now, Billy spoke up. 'But why do you think they were negatives?' He put the question to Lily. 'They could have been another set of prints.'

'That's possible,' she agreed. 'But right after Miss Cooper found what she was looking for she went out. She walked Pixie as far as the bus stop in the King's Road and then carried on down the street. Pixie saw her go into the chemist.'

She paused. The two men were looking at her.

'Well . . . ?' Grace growled.

'Well, apart from buying medicine, what else do you go to a chemist's for?' Lily was grinning.

'To get your negatives developed.' Billy supplied the answer. 'All right, Lil, you've made your point. And we can easily check it. They'll certainly remember handling a set like that. What about the "far north" then? What does that mean?'

'It's only a guess, guv . . .'

'Did you hear that?' A glint had appeared in Joe Grace's eye. 'She's guessing. She must be human after all.'

'Go on, Lil.' Billy smiled.

'Well, Pixie said Miss Cooper was exaggerating the way she always did. She reckoned she'd probably just gone somewhere on the tube – probably to north London. I was trying to think what was there – what might have interested her – and then I remembered the newspaper library at Colindale. That's right near the end of the Northern Line.'

'And what do you think she was doing there? Go on. Tell us.' It was Grace who was egging her on now.

'Again, it's only a guess, but what if she was trying to identify that bloke in the photographs. If she had all the photos, it's odds on his face must appear in some of them. But she probably didn't know who he was. Garner may fancy himself as a ladies' man, but his face isn't known to the general public – at least not to me, and probably not to her. It's possible she wanted to check the newspapers published at the time of Portia's murder. All the guests who were at Jack Jessup's house that weekend were named and most of the papers carried photographs of them. She would have seen Garner's face, and compared it with the photos she had. I'm betting she had the same idea as Wing: to put the squeeze on him for money in return for the photos. She told Pixie they were going to be flush soon. She was talking about them taking a trip to New York.'

Lily went silent. She'd said all she had to say.

Joe was still looking at her – but in unfeigned wonder now.

'Do you know what?' He turned to Billy with a wide grin. 'She's a bleeding marvel.'

19

'JUST TELL ME one thing – are we getting close? That's what I want to know. More to the point, it's what the commissioner wants to know. Are you certain that this latest murder is connected to the case you've been reviewing? It sounds to me as though there's a lot of guesswork involved. Above all, can you assure me that at least we'll be spared the sight of another photograph of Miss Portia Blake with no clothes on splashed across the front page of the *Daily Mirror?*'

Eustace Cradock fixed his two listeners with as fierce a glare as he could muster. A small man with little to mark him out – his most prominent feature was a pointed nose that had a tendency to redden in moments of stress – the assistant commissioner had appeared initially to have grown several inches since their last encounter, and it was only after Billy had stolen a glance beneath his desk and twigged that he was perched on a particularly well-stuffed cushion that morning that the mystery had been resolved.

'Yes, on both counts, sir.' Chubb offered his reply in the blandest of tones. 'We're now certain that this fellow we've been looking for, Stanley Wing – the man connected to the Blake murder – was Audrey Cooper's killer. Confirmation of that was obtained this morning. I'll let Inspector Styles explain.'

The chief super turned to Billy, who was seated beside him in front of Cradock's desk. The two of them had been summoned to appear together, and as luck would have it

Billy had received the information he was seeking only minutes before the call came.

'The Chelsea police have gone door-to-door down Langton Street, where she lived, and also along the street at the bottom of it, which is where the man who stabbed the constable ran off to,' Billy began. 'They found three people – a man and two women – who got a good look at him as he went past, and all of them agreed that he was Chinese, or at least an oriental. I sent DS Grace over there this morning with a copy of that photograph Sir Richard Jessup supplied us with, and one of the women made a positive identification. She saw the man face to face as he ran towards her and she's ready to swear it was Wing.'

'That means we can give his picture to the newspaper now along with his name. We can start a hunt for him. That would be something, at least. Do I need to keep reminding you that the commissioner wants *action*?'

Cradock glared at them both.

Chubb coughed.

'Yes, sir, but doing that would create a new problem – two, in fact. Not only would it tip him off that we're on to him, it would also tell these Chinese gangsters who are out for his blood that he's definitely in London. Wing will be aware of that and it might just be enough to persuade him to drop his blackmail scheme and flee the country. In which case we'd be left with an unsolved murder – Miss Cooper's, I mean – and one of our PCs lying in hospital with a stab wound. I can't see the commissioner being pleased about that. Also, if we keep Wing's name out of the papers for the moment there's a chance the press won't link Audrey Cooper's murder to the Portia Blake case; at least, not at once. I don't recall that anything was made of the fact at the time that they were flatmates. But give the press Wing's name now and we could be letting ourselves in for a three-ring circus.'

Cradock made a noise difficult to interpret: not one of approval, certainly, but possibly a sign of grudging acceptance.

'As for the other point you raised, sir – about the photographs of Miss Blake that have been appearing in the *Mirror* – we're confident that won't happen again. Grace was also able to get confirmation from a chemist near where she lives that Miss Cooper had given them a batch of negatives to be developed. They weren't happy at having to handle them and told her they wouldn't accept any more of the same kind. They included the pictures of Miss Blake and that man that have appeared in the *Mirror* as well as others, some more explicit. There's no doubt that Miss Cooper was the person who sent them to the paper, and since she's dead . . .' He spread his hands in silent explanation.

'But can we be sure that this man Wing won't do the same thing now that he has them in his hands?' Cradock scowled.

'Not a hundred per cent certain, sir. But we're inclined to doubt it. Wing's at the point where he'll have to put pressure on his victim. He's running out of time. The longer this game goes on, the more danger he's in from his triad friends. I'd expect him to get in touch with Garner directly and let him know he has the pictures in his possession. He might even send *him* one or two of the choicer items. I mean those with his face clearly shown in it.'

'And what are *we* going to do in the meantime?' The AC seemed to be spoiling for a fight that morning. 'Just sit on our hands?'

'Not at all, sir.' Chubb's tone remained soothing. 'We're in a position to threaten Garner with arrest now, even if we haven't got enough to charge him as yet. We know that he lied to us about his alibi. Styles and Grace are both of the opinion that he's close to cracking. He's got a meeting set with Sir Richard Jessup this evening, one he asked for. It could be crucial. Jessup's promised to let us know what passes between them.'

'He'll get in touch with you, will he?'

Chubb coughed. 'No, actually it's Mr Madden he's promised to telephone.'

'Madden again!' The tip of the AC's nose turned red. 'I thought he'd agreed to leave this inquiry to those whose job it is to deal with it. Now you tell me he's meddling again—'

'He's not meddling, sir,' Billy broke in hotly. 'He's trying to help. The only reason we are where we are is because of the trouble he's gone to on Mr Sinclair's behalf. He's given us invaluable information, and most of it has come from Sir Richard Jessup, who obviously trusts him. That's what's got us where we are. If it wasn't for the two of them – Sir Richard and Mr Madden – we'd still be floundering.'

'All right, Inspector . . .' Chubb made a calming gesture. 'Keep your hair on.'

Cradock glowered at Billy. For a moment it seemed that he might react. Instead he turned to Chubb.

'What do you plan to do now, Chief Superintendent? The commissioner will want to know.'

'Keep looking for Wing, sir. We've sent copies of his photograph to all the police stations in the Metropolitan area along with the two names, either of which he may be using. I'm hoping we'll have him in custody soon.'

'What about Garner?'

'Depending on what Jessup has to tell us, I plan to call on him first thing tomorrow morning with DS Grace.' It was Billy who replied. He'd had time to cool down. 'He'll

be asked to explain why he gave us a false alibi for the day
Portia Blake was murdered. Unless he can provide a satisfac-
tory answer, we'll bring him in for questioning.'

Cradock muttered something unintelligible. He glared at
them both.

'Well, I only hope you know what you're doing . . . both
of you. But I'm warning you again – I want to see some
action. So does the commissioner. This business has dragged
on long enough.'

'Someone got out of bed on the wrong side this morning.'
Chubb chuckled. 'And someone else has been twisting his
tail . . . the commissioner, I expect. But Cradock's got a point.
Even if we can't charge Garner in the end – we may have to
accept that there simply isn't enough evidence to convict him
– we have to find Wing, and quickly. If the triads get too
close to him he may well throw in the towel and skip the
country.'

Billy's grunt was non-committal. They were walking
down the corridor away from the AC's office and they went
on in silence until they came to the door to Chubb's office.
There the chief super paused.

'I was expecting to hear a little speech from you, Inspector.' He shot a sly glance at Billy. 'I thought we'd get a few
words from you on the subject of Detective-Constable Poole
and her latest contribution to the investigation. Mind you, I
don't mind admitting that was a smart bit of work she did
yesterday, putting it all together after she'd spoken to the
girl.' He shook his head ruefully. 'It's not a gift everyone
has. Most of us have to sweat out the details and then try to
make sense of them. But now and again you come across
someone who seems to sense how the dots are joined up.

John Madden had that gift, I remember.' He peered at Billy. 'Why didn't you say something when you had the chance? You should have spoken up.'

'Not with Cradock in that mood,' Billy growled. 'It would have been a waste of breath. But I mean to see that her work gets recognized. When this is over I'm going to write her up for another commendation. She's already earned it.'

'Good.' Chubb nodded approvingly. 'And while you're at it, you might recommend her for sergeant again. You were right – we've got too many idle DCs around here working out their pensions. It might be time to throw a cat among the pigeons.' He frowned. 'What's she doing now?'

'I sent her out to Brent Cross this afternoon. We had a report from the police there that an oriental answering to Wing's description had been reported staying in a local boarding house. He moved out a few days ago, but he's been seen since in the same general area and I thought we'd better check it. Even if he doesn't know yet that the triads are looking for him here, it's likely he'll stay away from the city centre. I haven't heard from Lil, but I'll be seeing her later this evening. We're having supper with Mr Madden in St John's Wood. Depending on what he hears later from Sir Richard Jessup, I might have some news for you tomorrow.'

Lily checked her wristwatch.

It had just gone nine o'clock. She wondered how much longer they would have to wait. What time did nobs sit down to dinner? (She was thinking of Sir Richard and his guest.) Surely later than she was used to doing. Left to her own devices, Lily usually had something to eat soon after she got home to her flat in St Pancras, which was around six o'clock as a rule, unless she was kept late at the Yard. It was the same when she went over to Paddington to see Aunt Betty and Uncle Fred, the couple who had raised her after she had lost both her parents, one to a bullet in the trenches, the other to the influenza epidemic that had swept the world in the wake of the Great War. Aunt Betty always had them sit down at six-thirty on the dot for what she called either supper or high tea, depending on her mood. Here, as guests of Madden and his daughter, they had eaten at half-past seven. But whether this was the family's normal practice, or done as a favour to their two visitors, it was impossible to say. Nothing about the evening had been familiar to Lily. She had seldom felt more out of her element, but the funny thing was she had enjoyed every moment of it.

It had started when she rang the doorbell . . .

Knowing that she was late – Billy Styles had told her to be at St John's Wood by six – Lily had hurried from the bus stop in the Finchley Road where the ponderous double-decker she had caught at Marble Arch had deposited her. Behind her was a largely wasted afternoon spent in the wilds of Brent Cross, one of the more distant London suburbs, near the end of the Edgware line. It had taken her half an hour to get out there and the same amount of time to get back. In between she had been forced to spend a long after-noon following up a lead which in the end had yielded next to nothing in the way of useful information.

Not that the local plod hadn't been helpful: the station commander, a grey-haired Irishman, had detailed one of his PCs to accompany her to the boarding house where Stanley Wing had, until recently, been staying.

'You were right about him using the name Lee,' he had told her. 'That's how we got on to him. He'd been staying there for a fortnight, according to the landlady. He couldn't produce an identity card, naturally, but he showed her a passport when he registered and gave an address in Hong Kong. She never got a chance to chat with him, she said; he was hardly ever there and took all his meals out. About the only thing he told her was that he was in London on business and wasn't planning to stay long.'

'What about the report that he'd been seen later in the same area?' Lily had asked. 'It might mean he'd just moved to another boarding house. He wouldn't want to remain in one place for too long.'

'I thought of that.' The commander had nodded sagely. 'But we've already checked other boarding houses and hotels and drawn a blank. If he is still hereabouts he's probably found a room to rent. Mostly they're advertised in tobacconists and newsagents, and we're checking those. But there's also word of mouth.' He had shrugged. 'We're doing our best, but the last sighting we had of him, the one you're talking about, happened a week ago and for all we know he may have moved on since then.'

Wing's landlady, when Lily finally spoke to her, had little to add. Sharp-eyed and businesslike – she seemed sure of her facts – she had described her erstwhile lodger as a 'strange one' but 'no trouble at all'.

'He was quiet as a mouse,' she told Lily. 'I can usually hear when anyone's coming down the stairs and going out through the front door, but he used to slip by without a sound. He wouldn't even stop for breakfast, and although I serve supper for them that want it, he was never here. You couldn't tell what he was thinking, either. He'd look at me with those black eyes of his and I wouldn't have the first idea of what was going on in his head.'

She'd had no hesitation, however, in identifying Wing from the photograph she'd been shown and had added a crucial detail about his appearance which disposed of any doubt that might have remained in Lily's mind.

'He had a scar on his throat. I only saw it once. He used to try to hide it by wearing a scarf, which seemed an odd thing to do, given this hot weather we've been having. But one morning he must have forgotten to put it on because when he went past me to the door I saw the mark. It looked like a nasty gash.'

With nothing to show for her afternoon's efforts other than this one small grain of information, and aware that she was a good half-hour late for her evening appointment, Lily had arrived hot and panting at the address she'd been given in St John's Wood. Pausing only to run her fingers through her hair and button the blazer-type jacket she generally wore for work, she had pressed the doorbell . . .

Rapid footsteps sounded from inside, and after only a moment the door was flung open. Expecting to see the tall figure of John Madden, Lily was confronted instead by a young woman about her own age wearing an apron and holding a bowl in the crook of her arm.

'Excuse me, Miss . . .' She had got no further.

'Not Miss . . . Lucy.'

'I'm sorry . . . ?'

'That's my name . . . Lucy. And you're Lily . . . Lily Poole.' A smile had illuminated the young woman's face. 'I know all about you. Angus is forever singing your praises.'

'Angus . . . ?' Lily wasn't sure how to respond. But the young woman, whom she'd guessed must be Madden's daughter, was already stretching out a welcoming hand and she'd allowed herself to be drawn into the house.

'I should have said Chief Inspector Angus Sinclair, formerly of the Metropolitan Police.' Lucy Madden's expression had become grave and her voice had dropped several registers as she intoned the solemn words. 'But, you see, I've called him Angus since I was eighteen. It started when I joined the Wrens during the war. Daddy was shocked. He said I ought to be more respectful to my elders. But Angus insisted. In those days I was stationed at the Admiralty and he used to take me to lunch at the Savoy now and then. I loved it. It was the first time anyone had treated me like a grown-up.'

She led Lily down a short passageway from the bare, uncarpeted hall.

'I'm sorry the house looks so abandoned. It belonged to my great aunt, but she died recently and it's up for sale. Nearly all the furniture has gone. But we've still got chairs and a table in the kitchen. Daddy's gone out with Billy to a pub round the corner. He said they were going to buy some bottles of beer but I expect it was because he wanted to talk to him about this case you're all working on. I read in the paper this morning about that poor woman being murdered in her flat – the one Daddy went to see – and I wanted to hear what Billy had to say about it. But as soon as he arrived they decided they had to go out, and I'm sure it's because they didn't want me to hear what they said. It's *so* frustrating . . .'

They had reached the kitchen, where Lily had her first chance to study the golden-haired girl. She'd been told that Madden's daughter was good looking, but saw now that that was an understatement. 'Stunner' would have been closer to the mark.

'I'm so pleased to meet you at last, Lily.' The radiant smile had returned. 'Can you help me choose something for supper? We've got all these tins' – Lucy waved her hands at the assortment of objects lined up on the kitchen table – 'which we simply have to get rid of before we move out.

Actually, I shouldn't even have mentioned them to you.' She giggled. 'They're terribly illicit. Aunt Maud bought them off a spiv called Sid during the war – poor Sid, he ended up in jail – but never ate any of them except the caviar.' She frowned. 'We could have some of that I suppose . . .'

'Caviar . . . ?' Lily had only ever heard of the stuff.

'Or perhaps not.' Lucy shook her head. 'I think it's dreadfully overrated . . . just, well . . . fishy. But we've got one tin of pheasant left, and some foie gras, which isn't the best thing for one's complexion, but never mind that, and an absolutely delicious Stilton which is sitting in the larder. What do you think?'

She looked inquiringly at her guest. Then her expression changed.

'What lovely eyes you've got, Lily.'

'Me . . . eyes?' Lily was struck dumb again.

'You must do something with them.'

'*Do* . . . ?'

'Come on. This can wait.'

Seizing her visitor by the hand, Lucy pulled her out of the kitchen and up an uncarpeted echoing flight of stairs to the landing above and from there to a bathroom. Positioning Lily in front of the mirror, she rummaged in a cloth bag standing on a table by the basin and brought out a stick of mascara.

'Stand still,' she commanded.

Minutes had gone by. Madden's daughter worked busily. Finished with the mascara, she fished out a compact from the bag. Lily felt the feather-light touch of a powder puff on her cheeks.

'There, now . . . !' Lucy had stood aside. Lily gazed at herself in the mirror.

'Crikey!' she said.

'You see? All it takes is a touch here and there.'

Lucy had put her face beside Lily's and the two of them had gazed at the mirror together.

'Your boyfriend will get a surprise.' Lucy caught Lily's eye in the mirror and smiled. 'Have you got one?'

'There's a young copper stationed at Paddington nick.' Lily couldn't stop herself. She'd never come across anyone quite like Lucy Madden before. 'I met him through my uncle Fred.'

'And is he your boyfriend?'

'He thinks he is.'

'That's the way to handle them.' Lucy was warm in her approval. 'Keep them guessing.'

She cocked an ear.

'I can hear Daddy's voice. They must be back. We'd better go down.'

'So it all depends on what Rex Garner has to say for himself.' Lucy Madden pondered the question. 'He might just decide to confess. It could all be over this evening.'

She turned her eager gaze on Lily.

'But doesn't it seem a little too easy to you?' she asked.

Lily awoke with a start. It had been a long day and after two glasses of wine (which was one more than she was used to drinking at any one time) she was starting to feel drowsy sitting there at the table.

'Easy . . . ? I wouldn't say that.'

'Nor would I.' Billy met Madden's glance and smiled. 'I'll let you into a secret, Lucy. As far as any copper is concerned, the easier the better. But I wouldn't count on Mr Garner coming clean, just like that. Chances are he'll look for a way out. If he's smart, which I don't think he is, he'll realize that we don't have enough to charge him with as yet. Not on the Portia Blake murder, anyway. But there's still that business in Hong Kong. That's hanging fire . . .'

Glancing at his watch, he shrugged.

'Still, I wish they'd get a move on.'

Supper was over and they had been sitting round the kitchen table for some time drinking coffee and sipping wine, waiting for the phone call that Madden was expecting. Initially reluctant – or seemingly so – to discuss the case, Billy had quickly yielded to the pressure which Lucy exerted on him, and which had begun after she witnessed the way her father greeted Lily Poole.

'Billy's been telling me about your work.' Madden had shaken the young policewoman's hand warmly. 'He explained how you put the pieces together yesterday. You were right, of course. That's what Miss Cooper failed to tell me when I spoke to her. She's the one who had those negatives all the time. She must have pocketed them before Miss Blake's sister came to collect her things. Poor woman: look what they brought her to in the end.'

'What did Lily do?' Lucy had pounced on her father's words. 'And why is she blushing like a beetroot?'

'Oh, I can't discuss that.' Madden had adopted a distant air. 'What I really want to do is hear Lily's news.' He had seated their guest at the table beside him. 'Mr Sinclair will demand a full report. He hasn't been able to get about for a while, as you probably know. I've had to be his eyes and ears.'

'Billy . . . !' Lucy had rounded on their other visitor. 'I *insist* on being told. I've seen the *Daily Mirror*. I know all about the photographs.'

'Sorry, luv.' Billy had taken his cue from Madden. He contrived to appear regretful. 'I'm afraid I can't talk about it. Police business, you know . . .'

'Police business! I've never heard anything so ridiculous. You know very well you're going to tell me in the end, so stop teasing me, both of you.'

Catching sight of Lily's expression, she had burst out laughing.

'Don't be shocked. I can say anything I like to Billy. I've known him all my life. He used to take me for long walks in the woods when I was small. I can still remember those afternoons.'

'So can I.' Billy caught Lily's eye and winked. 'I learned a lot, especially about the flora and fauna. You see, when Lucy realized I was a city boy and didn't know a warbler from a water-rat she made up a lot of names to tell me and I went off thinking I had it all sorted out. It came as a bit of a shock later when I learned there was no such thing as a hooter bird and that stoats didn't really build their nests in trees. Or anywhere else, come to think of it. I see she's already been to work on you.' He looked pointedly at Lily's eyes. 'So a word to the wise: mind how you go with this young lady.'

'Billy, you promised!' Lucy's cheeks had turned scarlet. 'You swore you'd never tell anyone about that.'

'No, I didn't. I said I'd think about it.'

He had started to laugh then.

'But I know you're curious about this case – your dad told me – and if you ask me nicely, I might just tell you a little more about it over supper.'

'Billy, Billy . . .'

Madden had shaken his head in despair.

Lily glanced at her watch again, and as she did so the telephone rang.

Madden got to his feet.

'That must be Jessup, he said. 'Do you want to speak to him?' He put the question to Billy, who shook his head.

'I don't think so, sir. You can tell him I'm here, if you like. But he's always been open with you, and he might feel he has to choose his words carefully if he's speaking to a police officer.'

With a non-committal shrug, Madden left them. They heard him pick up the phone in the hall, but his voice was barely audible as he spoke to his caller and he quickly fell silent. A long pause ensued. Then they heard him speak again, and this time they caught the words.

'Thank you, Richard. I'll pass that on.'

He returned to the kitchen looking thoughtful.

'Well, it seems Lucy may be right. It could be over.'

He sat down.

'It sounds as though Garner's in a bad way. According to Sir Richard he was half drunk when he got to the club and in even worse shape when he left a few minutes ago. But he's come to a decision. He's going to get in touch with you tomorrow morning.' He looked at Billy. 'He wants to make a statement, Jessup says. But he'll do it in the presence of a solicitor.'

'Ah . . .' Billy took a deep breath. 'That could be it, then. Did he say anything else – Garner, I mean?'

'Only that he'd heard from Wing.'

Billy pursed his lips in a silent whistle. 'That must have come as a nasty shock.'

'Garner declined to say what had passed between them. But it had clearly upset him. "I thought the bastard was in prison." That was his only comment, according to Jessup. He said Garner was very much the worse for drink by that time and not making much sense. But it was clear he was worried sick.'

'Did they talk about Portia Blake?'

'Her name certainly came up.' Madden frowned. 'But Garner didn't admit to killing her, if that's what you're wondering. What he did say was that he'd given you a false alibi for the day she was murdered. At that point Jessup urged him to make a clean breast of things and told him it would be best if he went to the police on his own initiative and set the record straight. He offered to put him in touch with his solicitor. My guess is you'll hear from Garner in the morning.'

'And if we don't, Joe Grace and I will pay him another visit, like we planned to.' Billy's eyes narrowed. 'I take it there was no reference made to the girl in Hong Kong?'

Madden shook his head. 'Sir Richard didn't mention it.' He paused, frowning. 'I'm just wondering what it was that got Garner so worried. Was it something Wing said to him?'

'He could have told him about the photos,' Billy suggested. 'That would have been enough to send Rex reaching for the bottle.'

'Always supposing the man in the bed is him,' Madden pointed out. 'But it's not *evidence*. It doesn't link him to the killing.'

He pondered the question in silence for a few moments. Then he turned to Lily. 'What do you think?' he asked.

Caught off-guard, Lily collected herself quickly. She hadn't expected to be asked her opinion.

'Well . . . well, we don't know what Wing knows, do we?'

It sounded like a feeble reply to her, but Madden appeared to think otherwise.

'What cards he may be holding, you mean? Yes, that's very true. We shouldn't forget that. For all we know he may be in possession of other evidence incriminating Garner. He may even have enough to tie him to Portia's murder.'

281

'Or to that girl in Hong Kong,' Lily pointed out.

'Who may or may not have survived the assault she suffered at his hands.' Madden nodded thoughtfully. 'To one or other, you mean?'

'Or both.'

20

'WHERE THE DEVIL is he? He can't just have disappeared.'

Chubb glared at Billy from behind his desk.

'You've tried ringing the house, have you?'

'Several times, sir, but there's no reply. According to Jessup, Garner was going to get in touch with us after he'd spoken to a solicitor. But there's been no word from that quarter either.'

'Could he have changed his mind, do you think?' Chubb's face darkened. 'Sobered up?'

'We'll soon find out. I've asked Lofty Cook at West End Central to send a bobby round to his house to ring the doorbell, and to keep on ringing if he doesn't respond. Of course, he could still be sleeping it off. According to Jessup he was reeling drunk when he left the club last night.'

'Perhaps he never got home,' Chubb suggested. 'But whatever the explanation is, I want answers fast. I've already had a call from Cradock asking if Garner has been brought in for questioning yet. Get cracking.'

Happy enough to obey – answers were what he lacked at the moment – Billy left to return to his own office. He was thinking he might have to take the bull by the horns and ask Richard Jessup for the name of his solicitor. The fact that they hadn't met made it difficult and he wondered whether he could turn to Madden for yet more help. He had still not resolved the question in his mind when he reached his office and found that Lily Poole was on the phone.

'Hang on, guv.' She spoke into the instrument when she saw Billy, and then beckoned to him urgently. 'It's Mr Cook,' she said.

Billy took the phone from her. 'Lofty . . . ?'

'Hello, Billy. I've got news for you. I've just heard from the bobby I sent round to that bloke's house . . . what's his name?'

'Garner . . . Rex Garner.' Billy had caught a note in the other man's voice that alerted him: something was up. 'Did he speak to him?'

'Hardly. If it's the same bloke you want to talk to, he seems to be strung up inside.'

'*Strung up* . . . ?'

'Hanging by his neck.' Cook's tone was dry. 'You'd better let me explain. The constable rang the doorbell, like he was told to, and went on ringing until it was plain no one was going to answer. The curtains at the front of the house overlooking the street were drawn, but there was still a small gap between them. By pressing his nose to the glass the bobby was able to peer inside the room, and what he saw gave him a shock. There was a man hanging from some sort of balustrade at the back of the room. He returned to the front door and tried to break it down with his shoulder, but it wouldn't budge, so he rang the station. I've got a locksmith on his way over to the house now. I'll meet you there.'

With the bell on their police car ringing, Billy and his two colleagues forged a passage through the scattered crowd of onlookers that had gathered in the street outside Rex Garner's house. They drew up in front of the door, which stood ajar. As Billy climbed out of the car a uniformed officer with a sergeant's stripes on his sleeve approached him.

'Mr Cook's inside, sir. He told the rest of us to stay out here.' He pointed to the three other men posted on the pavement. 'He said you'd be the officer in charge. Let me know if there's anything we can do.'

'Just clear the street for now, Sergeant. I'll have a word with you later.'

Followed by Grace and Lily Poole, Billy went into the house. He found Lofty Cook standing just inside the door to the drawing room where he and Joe had interviewed Rex Garner only two days earlier. Beyond him was a grisly sight. The body of a man was suspended by his neck from the balustrade of the book-lined gallery which Billy remembered from his earlier visit. His feet were a foot or so off the floor and his body had twisted slightly away from the door so that his face wasn't visible. Billy had little doubt that it was Garner, and when he walked past Cook to the other side of the room and looked up at the contorted visage he knew for certain.

'It's him, all right, Lofty.' He reached up to touch the black rubber-sheathed wire that had cut so deeply into the man's throat it was only partially visible. 'What did he use, do you reckon?'

'It looks like electrical flex.' Cook had crossed the room to join him. 'And you can see he doubled it.' He pointed higher to where the separation between the two lengths of cable was clearly visible. 'He must have decided that a single strand wouldn't take his weight. Have you any idea why he did it?'

'Quite a few, as it happens. He was our new prime suspect for the Portia Blake killing – and he knew it. I had the feeling he might be close to cracking.'

Lofty whistled.

'Does that mean your case is wrapped up?'

285

'Not quite. We're still looking for Stanley Wing, the chap Lily talked to you about.'

Cook looked reflective. 'I know this is a Yard case, Billy. I'm not going to stick my nose in. But this is my patch, so if you don't mind I'll stay for a while and see how things work out.'

'Please do, sir.' Billy grinned. They had joined the Met at the same time, right after the end of the First World War, and although initially Billy had led the way in the race for promotions – he had secured his inspectorship earlier than Cook – Lofty had lately inched ahead; he was now a chief inspector. None of which had affected their friendship, which had remained solid over the years. 'By the way, I called Richard Jessup before I left the Yard,' he said. 'He's on his way over here now. He can formally identify Garner for us. And I rang Mr Madden, too. You remember him, don't you?'

'I should say so.'

'He's in London at present and I thought he might want to come down here and see this. He began looking into the Portia Blake murder before we did as a favour to Mr Sinclair. They're neighbours in the country now.'

'Wheels within wheels, eh?' Lofty rubbed his chin thoughtfully. 'Well, it sounds as though you're in luck, Billy. I wouldn't mind having John Madden at my shoulder if I was working a case. He was special, wasn't he? One of those blokes you don't forget.'

'I can't say he was happy when I saw him last, sir. He was muttering to himself in the back of the car all the way from Pall Mall. I couldn't hear what he said, except it seemed to be about some "damned Chinaman", as he put it. And I had a hard time seeing him into the house. He was the worse for drink, but he wouldn't accept any help. Each time I tried to take his arm he pushed me away. But I finally saw him to the door and after some bother with his keys – he couldn't seem to find the right one – he finally let himself in. And that's how I left him.'

Every inch the old soldier, and looking smart in his chauffeur's uniform, Ted Lennox stood to attention as he made his statement. At Billy's request he had been summoned by his employer from the car outside to give an account of Garner's movements the night before, after Jessup himself had revealed that he had detailed his chauffeur to take his dinner guest home.

'I'm afraid Rex was quite drunk and I didn't want to send him home in a cab.'

Sir Richard had arrived a few minutes after Madden, who had caught a taxi down from St John's Wood. Together they had watched in silence as the body of the dead man was lowered gently to the floor. Billy had had to wait for the arrival of the police photographer before the operation could be carried out, but once he had done his work two detectives from the forensic crew who had been standing by had jointly taken hold of the corpse as one of their colleagues loosened the double strand of wire tied to the balustrade above. Clearly appalled by the sight of Garner's livid features, Jessup had looked away.

'I had been planning to return home to Hampshire myself,' he told Billy, 'but it had got so late that I changed my mind and decided to spend the night at my club. My chauffeur was standing by with the car, so I asked him to make sure that Mr Garner got home safely.'

When the pathologist arrived soon afterwards to examine the body – and after Lofty Cook had taken his leave of them

– Billy led both men to a smaller sitting room on the other side of the entrance hall.

'We're going to need a statement from you, sir,' he told Sir Richard. 'The coroner will want to know what Mr Garner's state of mind was when you saw him last night. We can do that later – I'll send a man over to your office – but it would help if you gave me some idea of how he was behaving.'

Jessup had needed a moment to collect himself. Pale and distraught, he had been standing a little apart from them, staring at nothing, hardly aware of what was being said. 'Rex arrived a little after eight,' he said, 'and since it was clear he'd already been drinking I thought it best to go into dinner straight away. He was angry . . . fractious and belligerent . . . we'd hardly sat down when he started complaining about what he said was police harassment.' He caught Billy's eye. 'Don't worry, Inspector, I wasn't taken in by that, but I let him ramble on for a bit, and then I asked him if there was anything he'd like to tell me – anything he wanted to get off his chest. Well, I'm afraid that set him off again, and he turned on me, accusing me of being on "their side" – he meant you, the authorities – and demanding to know why I wouldn't stand by him. I assured him I'd do whatever I could to help, and it was then that he admitted he had given you a false alibi for the afternoon when Miss Blake was murdered. He hadn't met the friend whose name he gave you; he had simply driven into Canterbury and spent the next few hours on his own. He and his wife were due to drive back to London later that afternoon and he timed his return to the house to coincide with their planned departure.'

Jessup rubbed his forehead.

'I was shocked to hear that. I asked him why he'd done it. He said he had told Adele Castleton the same story years ago and thought he'd better stick to it . . .'

'The same story . . . ?' Billy broke in.

'Exactly.' Jessup had spread his hands. 'It was no sort of explanation. I could understand why he concocted an excuse to tell Adele. I'd always thought it was possible that he knew Miss Blake better than he admitted and had simply wanted to avoid seeing her again after her behaviour at dinner the previous evening. But I couldn't believe he'd been so stupid as to tell the police a lie just to cover up what was only a small fib, after all. It was at that point that I began to get worried. I wondered if he had more to conceal.'

'Did he at any point mention the woman he beat up in Hong Kong?' Billy asked. 'I believe you knew about that.'

Jessup nodded. 'Rex didn't refer to it directly, but it might have been on his mind . . .'

'Why did you think that, Richard?' Silent up till then, Madden had interrupted. Jessup turned to him.

'It was when he told me that Wing had been in touch with him. I had asked if he'd seen the photographs published in the *Daily Mirror* and what he made of them. That set him off on another rant. He said the police were trying to frame him. But then he quietened down and admitted that Wing had telephoned him earlier that day and tried to get money out of him.'

'Because of the photographs?'

'I don't know. Rex didn't say. He was cursing Wing as he told me about it. He said he was a leech, a bloodsucker, and he'd never be free of him.'

'And you wondered what he was talking about – whether it was the photographs, or something else?'

'The thought did cross my mind.' Jessup sighed. 'We had left the dining room by then. Fortunately, there weren't too many others there last night, but even so Rex had made something of a spectacle of himself, banging the table with his fist and creating a disturbance. I had managed to get him downstairs where there's a small waiting room by the entrance hall, and after I'd ordered him a brandy – he insisted on it – I told him what I thought he ought to do.'

'Which was to speak to us?' This time it was Billy who put the question.

Jessup nodded. 'I told him there was no way his false alibi would stand up and the wisest thing he could do would be to go to the police at once before they came to him and put the record straight. Then I added that if there was anything else he had to tell you he'd be well advised to take the opportunity to do so and if he wished I could put him in touch with my solicitor.'

Jessup's smile had a bitter edge.

'I was expecting another explosion then, but to my surprise he gave in. He said he would do that. He said he'd had enough.'

'Enough . . . ?' Billy intervened quickly. 'What did he mean by that?'

'I can't say for certain, Inspector. But it sounded as though he'd thrown in the towel. That was my impression. I should tell you that things had been going from bad to worse for some time in Rex's life. He was deeply in debt. This place is mortgaged to the hilt. He owes money left and right. I was just wondering how I was going to get him home when I remembered that Ted was outside with the car. I got him to bring Rex here and to see him inside his front door safely; which I believe he did. But you can ask him that yourself. He's waiting outside.

'What will the police make of this, John?'

Jessup stood on the pavement looking about him. The crowd that had gathered in the street earlier, drawn by the police presence, had largely dispersed and those bystanders still tempted to remain were being gently but firmly moved on by the uniformed officers posted outside.

'What will they read into it? Will they take it as confirmation of their theory that it was probably Rex who killed Miss Blake?'

'They might.' Madden had come outside to accompany the other man to his car, where Lennox stood waiting with the door open. 'They certainly regarded him as a suspect. I told you that. But they were some way from making a case against him. However, there's still that woman in Hong Kong to be considered. They're waiting for word from the police there. So far they've found no trace of her in their records. It's possible she didn't survive the assault she suffered at Garner's hands and somehow her body was disposed of; and it's equally possible that Wing knew that and could pin the crime on him. We don't know what passed between them when they spoke on the phone yesterday.'

Jessup pondered in silence. Although he appeared to have recovered from the shock of seeing Garner's body lowered to the floor, he still seemed troubled.

'Will the question of Miss Blake's murder come up at the inquest?' he asked. 'I expect I'll be summoned to appear as a witness.'

'It may well do.' Madden nodded. 'As Inspector Styles said, the coroner will try to establish Garner's state of mind prior to his suicide, and your testimony will be crucial. He'll want to know why he was so upset. There's no way you can avoid the subject.'

'And what will the police say about it?'

'Not a great deal, I imagine, and not until they have either found Stanley Wing, or are satisfied that he has left the country. At that stage they might issue a statement to the effect that the inquiry remains open, or, if they're satisfied that Garner was Portia's killer, that they're no longer looking into the case.'

'I just hope they tread carefully,' Jessup said. 'I don't like the idea of branding a man as a murderer when he can't defend himself. It's not as though anyone will ever know for sure who killed Miss Blake.'

'Not unless the police catch up with Stanley Wing,' Madden observed. 'He's the one person who might be able to answer these questions.'

Jessup reflected on his words. Then he sighed.

'I can't help feeling I let Rex down. I should have done more for him.'

'Perhaps he was past help, Richard,' Madden said gently. He sensed the other man's distress. 'It looks to me as though he'd backed himself into a corner, and took the only way out.'

Having seen Jessup off, Madden went back inside the house to find that Billy had returned to the drawing room and was standing to one side with Grace and Lily Poole. They were watching the pathologist, who was still busy. On his knees now he was bending over the body and peering closely at the dead man's throat.

'Isn't that Ransom?' Madden asked. It was years since they had met, but he recognized the pathologist's face and recalled that he'd been regarded by the Met's squad of detectives as something of a card.

'It's him all right.' Billy chuckled. 'Do you remember how he used to get the chief inspector's goat? Mr Sinclair couldn't be doing with his shafts of wit. I can't say he's changed all that much. We're wondering what he's going to come up with today.'

As he spoke, the burly figure shifted. Sitting back on his heels, he hoisted himself slowly to his feet and then turned to face them.

'I see business is picking up, Inspector. Am I right in thinking this is your second corpse in . . . how many days? Three, is it? I'm only thankful I was spared the most recent offering: I understand the lady met an unpleasant end.'

His solemn expression changed; his face brightened.

'Isn't that Mr Madden standing beside you? Don't tell me you've returned to the force, sir. I thought you were happily retired.'

'And you were right.' Madden smiled. 'I'm here on behalf of Mr Sinclair, who I'm sure would send you his regards if he could.'

'I very much doubt it. The good chief inspector and I seldom saw eye to eye. But you can give him my best wishes if you like. Now, Inspector, as to your body . . .'

He turned his gaze back on Billy.

'Death was caused by strangulation, as you can see, and I would estimate that it occurred some twelve hours ago: say between eleven o'clock and midnight.'

He bent to buckle the straps on his bag.

'And it was quite straightforward, was it?'

'Straightforward . . . ?' Red in the face from bending over, Dr Ransom stood up. 'Well, that depends on your definition of the word; but yes . . . straightforward . . . after a fashion.'

'Don't be like that, Doctor.' Billy heaved a sigh. 'Just give me the authorized version: did the man hang himself?'

'Once again, I very much doubt it.' The pathologist chortled. He seemed to be enjoying a private joke. 'Seeing as how he was almost certainly dead at the time; strangled, as I said.'

'Strangled . . . ?'

'Prior to being strung up, I mean. And since he could hardly have done it to himself, I'm inclined to think he was murdered.'

'How's it going, Lil? Have you found anything?'

Billy went over to the foot of the staircase leading up to the gallery where Lily Poole was down on her knees.

'Yes, I think so, guv. There are scuff marks at the edge of the carpeting – do you see?'

She pointed. Billy bent over her shoulder to look, and Madden, who was standing on the other side of the young policewoman, followed suit.

'It looks like something was dragged up the stairs.'

'Like a body, you mean?' Billy nodded. He saw where the pile of the carpeting had been brushed back. 'He must have been pulled up by his armpits. He would have been quite a weight.' He glanced at Madden. 'What do you think, sir?'

'I agree. The scuffing could have been caused by the heels of his shoes catching on each step.'

Billy straightened.

'We know that the curtains were drawn, so I don't suppose anyone outside noticed anything.'

Having listened to Ransom's explanation, Billy had directed Joe Grace to organize a house-to-house inquiry using the uniformed officers stationed outside.

'Joe has already spoken to a woman who lives across the street and saw Garner come home last night,' he told Madden. 'She confirmed what Lennox told us: she heard a disturbance in the street and saw Garner, obviously drunk, being shepherded to his front door. But I want people asked about what they might have seen earlier in the evening as well, since whoever killed him may have already been in the house when he got back.'

The pathologist had been succinct in his depiction of how the dead man met his end.

'To put it bluntly, he was strangled twice. There are two separate marks on his throat. They lie at different angles, and are quite easy to spot. I would say that the first one was caused when he was throttled from behind. If Garner was standing or sitting when that happened, the mark would have been more or less parallel to the floor. And it's thinner than the other one, which suggests he was first choked using a single strand of flex. The second mark, the one caused by hanging, lies at a quite different angle – it slants up towards his ears. I think he was either killed or rendered unconscious down here and then taken upstairs to the gallery and hung by a double strand of flex from the balustrade. I will so state at the inquest.'

With the investigation headed in a different direction now, Billy had ordered the fingerprint specialists summoned from the Yard, who up till then had been standing idle, to go over the drawing room inch by inch.

'I want the banisters and the balustrade covered in particular,' he told them. 'Lift all the dabs you can find. Take Garner's prints before the body is removed.'

He glanced at Madden, who was standing beside him, observing, but saying nothing.

'I'd say this was Stanley Wing's work,' he said. 'It's the only thing that makes sense.'

'What I'm wondering is how it came about,' Madden said. 'Why exactly did Wing kill him – and why now?'

Billy pursed his lips. He gave the question serious thought before replying.

'Suppose Garner had already seen the photographs, ones

with his face in, I mean, when he met Jessup last night. The chemist who developed the negatives told us he made two prints of each at Miss Cooper's request. So Wing must have a spare set, and he could have put them in the post right away, that same afternoon, and they would have been delivered next day. We have to remember he's pushed for time. Garner told Jessup that Wing had phoned him. If so, then Wing would almost certainly have demanded money from him and that could explain Garner's state of mind when he met Jessup later.'

Although Madden showed no reaction, Billy saw he was paying close attention.

'And what if Garner told him there wasn't any – money, I mean?' He continued with his train of thought. 'That he was broke? Maybe Wing decided there was only one thing left he wanted to do, and did it.'

At that moment Billy became aware of a figure hovering at his elbow. It was one of the detectives from the forensic squad, a DC named Travis.

'I've got something to show you, guv.' He nodded towards the far end of the room where several armchairs were grouped around a fireplace.

Billy accompanied him to the spot, with Madden at his heels. Travis bent down. He had a pair of tweezers in his hand.

'I noticed there were some ashes in the grate,' he said, 'and that seemed strange. I mean, lighting a fire in this hot weather. So I had a look at them. I reckon they were photos.'

He reached into the grate with his tweezers and extracted a triangular shape, charred along its base. He showed it to Billy, who was bending down, peering over his shoulder.

'That's a piece of a photograph, all right. There's part of a woman's face there . . .' Billy peered closely at the fragment

Travis was holding. 'And a bit of her arm, too. Hang on! I think I've seen this.'

He stood up straight, looking round as he did so.

'Lil . . . !' He called to her across the length of the room. 'Come over here.'

Lily hurried over from where she was standing at the foot of the stairs, watching the fingerprint crew at work on the banisters.

Billy stood aside so that she could see what the detective held in his tweezers.

'Isn't that the same face that was in that painting at the back of Portia's bedroom? You said you recognized it.'

'*The Nude Maja*?' Lily brought her eyes up close to the fragment. 'Yes, that's it, that's her . . . well done, Mike.' She patted Travis on the shoulder.

Billy looked at Madden.

'We can assume it was Garner who burned them,' he said. 'But if Wing rang him like Garner said he did he would have told him that he still had the negatives and there was no way Garner was going to escape this time.'

Madden mused in silence for a moment. 'What I'm wondering is how Wing gained entry to the house last night,' he said.

'I thought about that.' Billy nodded. 'I had the windows checked. They're locked from the inside. They don't seem to have been fiddled with. I reckon he simply knocked on the door and Garner let him in. Granted, he wouldn't have been pleased to see Wing. But he might have thought it worthwhile trying to reason with him: to explain that he couldn't pay up.'

'What about the flex Garner was hanged with, though? That's got me puzzled. Do you think Wing brought it with him?'

Billy scratched his head. He could see that the question was bothering his old chief.

'It's more likely he found it here, in the house,' he said. 'I sent a couple of men downstairs to the basement. They said there was a lot of stuff lying around, including some tools. I think Wing found what he wanted down there.'

'Leaving Garner up here in the drawing room on his own, do you mean?' Madden was still dubious.

'On his own, but most likely passed out, or close to it. That's what we're forgetting. Garner arrived back here dead drunk. It wouldn't have been hard for Wing to deal with him once he'd been let in. He can't have been pleased when he found all his efforts had gone for nothing; that Garner wasn't going to pay. He may not have come here intending to kill him. But he wasn't going to let him off.' Billy shrugged. 'And who knows? Perhaps in the end Wing did him a favour.'

'Meaning what?' Madden frowned.

'If Garner was guilty of Portia's murder – and Wing knew it, and could prove it – then it was odds on Rex was going to end up the same way sooner or later: on the end of a rope.'

21

CHARLIE CHUBB STOOD with his arms folded staring out of the windows of his office. His gaze was fixed on the sky, where a mass of white clouds, tinged with grey, had been gathering in the west all afternoon.

'I keep hoping we'll get a storm,' he said, with a sigh. 'Something to break this heatwave we've been having. The clouds build up, but nothing happens. My lawn's dying of thirst. You're a gardener, aren't you?'

He swung round to face Billy, who was seated in a chair in front of his desk.

'I've got the same problem as you, sir.' Billy looked glum. 'My grass is turning brown. What's more, I saw something in the paper the other day about a hosepipe ban being introduced unless we get some rain.'

Chubb snorted. Two days had passed since the body of Rex Garner had been found hanging in his drawing room and the chief superintendent had summoned the officer assigned to the case to report on the progress of the investigation.

'I've got a meeting fixed with Cradock and the commissioner in half an hour,' he announced as he took his own seat. 'They're not happy with the way things are going, and I can't say I blame them. We've got the press practically accusing us of withholding information from the public, of trying to cover up our mistakes.'

He fumed.

'They know who Garner is – or was. They know his name was linked to the Portia Blake murder and they know we've been looking into the case again. They've put two and two together and think he committed suicide because we were on to him. They want us to admit that the wrong man was sent to the gallows. I'm only grateful that they haven't made the connection to Miss Cooper's murder yet. But they will.'

Billy shrugged. 'They won't be quite so cocky when they learn that Garner didn't kill himself: that he was topped. I wish we could put that out now, but we'll have to wait for the inquest, and that won't be till next week.'

'And what then . . . ?' Chubb glared. 'They'll be jumping up and down, wanting to know who killed him, and I don't fancy the prospect of having to announce that our prime suspect has probably skipped the country. Speaking of which, have we *any* idea where Stanley Wing is?'

'Not for certain, sir. But I doubt he's made any attempt to leave as yet. If he had, I think we'd have heard about it. His photograph and the names he's using are in the hands of the immigration authorities and all ports have been warned to keep an eye out for him.' He paused. 'Of course, there are other, illegal ways of making himself scarce. It could be Wing will try to slip aboard a cargo vessel on the sly. He doesn't know yet that we're after him, but he must suspect that the triads are on his trail and he may feel that that's his best option. But it's not something that can be arranged on the spur of the moment. He'd need time to set it up, and we've warned our snouts on the docks to keep their eyes and ears open.'

Chubb growled unintelligibly. He shifted in his seat.

'I can tell you now – none of this is going to make the commissioner feel any better. He won't accept the idea that a man wanted for two murders might slip through our hands. Perhaps it's time we made his name public and gave his picture to the newspapers.'

'We can if you want to.' Billy weighed the option. 'We still haven't picked up any trace of him beyond the report Poole brought back from Brent Cross. Maybe if we show his picture to the public someone will spot him. But the drawback is it'll tip him off, and that might be enough to persuade him to skip the country while he still can. On balance, I think we should wait a little longer.'

'A few days, then, but no more.' Chubb shook a warning finger.

Billy frowned. 'And we have to think about the future, too. We can certainly arrest him, but can we make a case against him? As of now, the only hard evidence connecting him to Audrey Cooper's murder is the identification provided by that woman who saw him run by her in the street. It was what any defence counsel worth his salt would call a "fleeting glance" and I doubt we could get a conviction on that alone.'

'What about the constable who was stabbed?'

'I'm glad to say he's doing well in hospital, but he can't identify Wing from his picture. It all happened too quickly. He heard the scream, saw the man run out of the house, tried to intercept him and got stabbed in the gut for his pains. He didn't get a clear picture of his face.'

'How about the Garner murder? Can we link Wing to that at least?'

'Not positively. Not as yet. We're still sorting through the fingerprints lifted at the house. Other than Garner's own, there are two other sets that we found in the drawing room that we've been tentatively able to identify . . . One of them belongs to his housekeeper, a Mrs Adams. Ex-housekeeper,

I should say, since she quit her job before he went up to Scotland for the grouse shooting. When she read about his murder in the paper yesterday she rang us. He hadn't paid her wages for a couple of months and she finally got fed up and handed in her notice. Grace went round to see her. Her prints match one of the sets, as I said, and it seems likely that the other one belongs to a maid who was in Garner's employ until a couple of months ago, when he dismissed her. It sounds as though he was having trouble making ends meet. But there were two other sets we found, made by the same person, which remain unidentified, and given where we found them are definitely suspicious.'

'Were they in the drawing room?' Chubb asked.

Billy nodded. 'They were on the banisters, in fact: the only ones we found there. Maybe Garner didn't spend much time with his library. One print was halfway up and the other near the top, and they were both made by a left hand, which was significant.'

'How so?'

'If whoever killed Garner was dragging his body up the stairs, he was most likely holding him under the armpits and leaning back himself as he pulled the body up. It looks to me as though he lost his balance a couple of times, and instinctively grabbed at the banister to steady himself. Both of the prints were left-handed, which fits with that idea: the banisters are on the right going up.'

'Ingenious, Sherlock!' Charlie's doleful visage brightened momentarily. 'You'll make a detective yet.'

'Needless to say, we're hoping these prints will match Wing's. I've sent a copy of them by express mail to the Hong Kong police. They must have his dabs on record. We should hear from them before long, though I'm hoping we'll have caught Wing by then.'

'If he hasn't scarpered, you mean.' The chief super's mood had quickly soured again. 'You do understand what we're facing here? It's not just that we could end up with two unsolved murders and a wounded officer and no suspect to lay the blame on. There's also the Portia Blake case to consider. You can be sure the press will go on pestering us about that. We could always tell them that we stand by the original finding, I suppose, but that's not something I'm willing to do, given what we've learned in recent weeks. And neither, I might add, is the commissioner.'

22

ELEGANT IN HIS silk suit and new Charvet tie – he had
bought it at a shop in Bond Street only the day before –
Chen Yi strolled down the Mall, enjoying the warm summer
weather. He had come from viewing the changing of the
guard at Buckingham Palace – a ceremony he had always
wanted to see but had only read about – and paused long
enough on his way back through St James's Park to feed the
ducks in the ornamental pond.

His appointment was for noon and his way took him
beneath Admiralty Arch and around Trafalgar Square to St
Martin's Lane and Charing Cross Road. It was his first visit
to London – but not, he hoped, his last – and he was getting
to know the city centre; in particular the area around Soho.
It was no secret that the brotherhood would shortly be
expanding its operations and with his excellent English and
good record to date Chen had hopes of being posted to the
capital in a position of responsibility. As yet only an ordinary member – a 49 in the triads' code – he was due for a
promotion, or so he believed, and could see himself being
named White Paper Fan, or administrator of the newly
established branch; or if not that, then perhaps Straw Sandal,
which would put him in charge of liaison duties.

Nor did his ambitions end there. The climb to the top
could be slippery – and treacherous. But Chen was confident
of his abilities and believed that one day he might even

ascend to the uttermost pinnacle: he had it in him to be a 489, he believed; a Dragon Head, no less.

His unhurried steps, meanwhile, had taken him past Trafalgar Square and up Charing Cross Road, and presently he turned off it and entered the lower reaches of Soho. He had explored the area several times and called in at a number of shops and restaurants, all run by Chinese, in order to show the photograph he had brought with him from Amsterdam. Up till now his inquiries had met with no success. Nor had the word which Huang had put out among his own contacts borne fruit. But Chen had reason to believe that today would be different. The telephoned message he had received had come as a surprise: he had thought that particular avenue a dead end. Now it seemed that the road to their goal might be open after all. His caller had claimed to be in possession of valuable information.

Soon he had crossed Shaftsbury Avenue, and after walking a short distance up Wardour Street he reached his destination: a building fronted by several windows through which half a dozen young men, all of them Chinese, could be seen working at desks. A glassed door with a board beside it bearing the words NEW CHINA IMPORT COMPANY in gold lettering gave access to the building. Chen went in and crossed the carpeted floor of the lobby to a desk at the rear where the receptionist, a young woman dressed in black, watched his approach without expression.

'I am here to see Mr Lin,' he announced, speaking in Cantonese.

He took a business card from his jacket pocket and slid it across the desk to her.

'He is expecting me.'

*

Chen walked to end of the alleyway, taking care not to step on any of the refuse strewn over the cobbles in front of him. The alley ran past the back of a restaurant and the rubbish bins behind it were, as usual, overflowing with bits of rotting fruit and vegetables which were spread like a minefield across the slippery walkway.

Near the end of the street he came to a door, which he opened using a key. As he started up the narrow stairway the figure of a Chinese woman wearing a soiled dressing-gown emerged from the gloom at the back of the hall. She nodded when she saw him. Chen said nothing. He continued up the stairs.

Though he knew better than to reveal it, he had been shocked by the lodgings to which Huang Wei had led him after they had crossed the Channel by ferry from Ostend and taken the train to Waterloo station. Situated south of the River Thames in a rundown district whose seedy aspect was further marred by numerous unfilled bomb craters overflowing with weeds, the building where they were staying seemed little better than a slum to him, its sour-smelling rooms occupied by the lowest sort of Chinese immigrants, most of them labourers to judge by their clothes and rough manners. Presiding over the establishment was a woman of indeterminate age, who appeared to know Huang. At all events she had greeted him respectfully. But after having shown the two visitors to their respective rooms on the first floor she had left them to their own devices, and Chen at any rate had not had occasion to exchange another word with her.

As he walked down the uncarpeted passage towards Huang's door he heard a high whining sound, steady in note and quickly cut short. After each brief pause, it resumed at the same even pitch. When he knocked on the door, the sound ceased.

'Come.' The terse order was uttered in Cantonese.

Chen entered and saw Huang, barefoot and clad only in trousers and a white vest, sitting in a cane chair by the window. He had a long axe balanced across his knees and held a whetstone in his free hand. His slate-coloured eyes were expressionless as they took in Chen's appearance.

'A handsome piece of neckwear.' He spoke in English. His glance was fastened on the tie Chen was wearing. 'Where did you get it?'

'The tie . . . ah . . . in a shop.' Chen stumbled over the words.

'Has it not occurred to you yet that we did not come here to be noticed?' Though Huang's tone was mild, his eyes told another story. They had hardened in the last few seconds. 'Why do you think we are staying in this . . . ?' He switched back to Cantonese, employing a vulgar term for a lavatory bowl and its likely contents. 'Our purpose is to remain invisible. But you advertise your presence like a . . . like a . . .' Again he turned to his native tongue, this time using a common term for a male prostitute. 'I blame myself. I should have guessed from the silk suits you wear. I should have known a peacock when I saw one.'

He paused. Chen stood with bowed head.

'Do not take offence at these words of mine. Learn from them. You are a clever young man and you will see that what I say is worth listening to. Appearance is nothing. Let others think less of you. That way you will learn more of them; you will see their weaknesses. In time they will come to fear you. All will follow from that. Keep it in mind and you may rise in the brotherhood. Forget it and you will surely fall.'

'Your words are precious.'

Chen stood with head bowed. Although he was trembling with suppressed rage, he knew better than to show it. He saw now that he had misjudged the enforcer. He had seen him simply as a thug: a man with iron fists and an indifference to physical pain. But there was more to Huang than he had imagined, and he would do well not to forget it.

'I will remember each one.'

Huang returned to the task he had been engaged in, drawing the whetstone along the edge of the axe, setting off the same high, keening note as before. Chen stared at the implement. He knew that Huang hadn't brought it to London with him. His luggage had been confined to a single small suitcase. He had obviously acquired the axe locally, but not from a hardware shop. Although the gleaming head looked new, the handle had been used. It was clear that he had connections here; there must be people he was acquainted with apart from the woman who ran the lodging-house. For all Chen knew the embryo of a new Tang branch already existed. His hopes of attaining a post of importance in the new order had begun to shrivel under the sharp edge of Huang's tongue.

As he stood there another thought came to him, equally disagreeable. Earlier in the day he had allowed himself to indulge in pleasant dreams of the future; he had seen himself rising through the organization, gaining steadily in importance and influence as his talents were recognized, even to the point where one day the leadership might beckon.

But now, watching Huang as he drew the whetstone across the gleaming axe head, Chen was aware for the first time of a flaw in the image he had of himself, a weakness he had not acknowledged before. There was one position in the triad hierarchy that he could never aspire to, and it might be enough to damn his hopes. The cold purpose he sensed in the scarred figure of the enforcer was foreign to his nature. Although the thought was like gall, he knew that the iron that dwelt in some men's souls was not his to command. He would never have it in him to be a Red Pole.

As though reading his thoughts, Huang paused in his labour.

'You looked pleased with yourself when you came in.' His tone was neutral. 'Have you fresh information?'

Swallowing, Chen nodded.

'The old man has news of our bird.'

'Does he know where he is?' Huang showed no reaction. Only his eyes had narrowed slightly.

'No, but he has learned his plans. Wing means to leave the country as soon as possible.' Eager now to placate his superior, Chen ventured a smile. 'With luck we can set a trap for him.'

Huang stroked the head of his axe with a scarred fore-finger. Chen could see that he was thinking.

'This is good.' His eyes bored into the younger man's. 'But how do we know Lin is telling the truth?'

Sweating now, Chen replied.

'He is too afraid to lie.'

Huang nodded with satisfaction.

'You see, I am right. It starts with fear.'

PART THREE

23

'AYE, AYE . . . DO you hear that?'

Hammer raised, George Burrows paused mid-stroke as the rumble of thunder sounded in the distance. Busy shoeing their old mare, he was standing in the stable yard with the animal's foreleg held firmly between his thighs and his hammer raised, ready to drive the nail in.

'We could have a spot of rain later on. The ground could do with it. I'd like to see it softened up a little before we start with the autumn ploughing.'

He bent to his task again. Madden, who was holding the horse's head still, watched as the nail was hammered home, meanwhile musing on the words he had just heard. Aware that the speaker had given no real thought to what he had said, or to who might be listening, he realized that they reflected a simple reality: namely that the farm was coming more and more to be George's responsibility, while his own role was growing increasingly marginal. It was time either to reassert his authority, or to make a graceful retreat. He watched as Burrows took a fresh nail from his mouth and the operation was repeated.

'There – that'll do you for now, old girl.' He stood up, stretching.

The mare, Daisy by name, filled a number of roles on the farm, none of them taxing. Madden used her now and then to ride around his acres, while at other times she was employed to pull a cart carrying vegetables and other produce to the village grocer who was a good customer.

'The autumn ploughing . . . yes, I must give some thought to that.' Madden decided it would be as well to put down a marker at once while the opportunity presented itself. 'I know I've been away a lot lately, George. But it was unavoidable, I'm afraid. Never mind. We'll soon be back to normal.'

'That's good to hear, sir.' As though aware of his employer's unworthy train of thought, Burrows showed every sign of welcoming the news, smiling broadly. 'May was saying only the other day that the place doesn't seem the same without you here.'

May was George's wife, a woman Madden had known since girlhood and believed to be incapable of falsehood. Suitably chastened, he surrendered the bridle he was holding and prepared to leave.

'Well, I only have to go up to London once more,' he announced as he donned his tweed jacket, an ancient garment patched at the elbows, which was draped over the side of a dog cart. 'We'll be clearing out the very last pieces of furniture from the house in the next couple of days. After that it'll be in the hands of an estate agent and ready for viewing. Lucy will stay with friends until we find a flat to buy which she can move into.'

He had not seen fit to mention the other business that had kept him away – George knew nothing of the inquiries he had been making on Angus Sinclair's behalf – but as he made his way along the stream towards the chief inspector's cottage he was only too aware that he wasn't done with it quite yet. Although they had spoken on the phone during the week, his old friend was yet to receive a first-hand report on the latest developments, which included the murder of both

Audrey Cooper and Rex Garner, and as likely as not would be champing at the bit for further details.

'It's as good as over, then, is it? Done with? All wrapped up?'

The chief inspector seemed less than happy with the verdict he had just delivered. Madden had found him where he had so often been these past weeks, sitting in his garden under the apple tree with a book in his hand.

'I can't help thinking it was a pity Garner was murdered. If he had hanged himself as was first thought, Charlie Chubb and his myrmidons could have laid Portia Blake's murder at his door with a clear conscience. Now it's still open to question . . .'

'Not necessarily,' Madden pointed out.

Seated in a garden chair close to Sinclair's, he had spent close on half an hour filling his eager listener's ears with a detailed account of the events of the past few days. The part played by Lily Poole in making sense of Audrey Cooper's actions prior to her death had brought words of warm approval from her old backer. But it was the second murder committed in the course of the week that had evoked the sharpest reaction from him.

'Wing might well have been trying to blackmail him over Miss Blake's murder,' Madden explained. 'He obviously thought those photographs were valuable enough to kill for and he didn't waste any time letting Garner know they were in his hands. But as we've learned, his victim was penniless, or as good as, and he probably told Wing that, which may explain what followed.'

'Still, it's curious about the flex, don't you think?' Sinclair was assailed by the same doubts that had troubled his visitor earlier in the week. 'After all, Wing had a knife, and was only too ready to use it, as we know. Was he trying to disguise the murder, do you think? Make it look like suicide?'

'It's possible. But there could have been another reason. He might have thought that if he used his knife the killing would be linked to Miss Cooper's murder and the police would start putting two and two together.'

Stretching, he sighed.

'But that's been the trouble with this case, Angus. I've never felt easy about it. It's full of unanswered questions, and some of them may never be resolved. For what it's worth, I think they're all tied up in one way or another with the person of Stanley Wing. We've heard a lot about him, but for me he's still a puzzle. Mind you, given his background that's no surprise. None of us can pretend to imagine what it must have been like growing up as he did. While it's true that Jack Jessup rescued him from the streets, I think his character was already formed by then. He saw the world as a jungle; no one was to be trusted, not even his benefactor. I think Mrs Castleton was right. He's driven by hatred. But beyond that there's nothing I can say about him with any certainty. The man's a mystery to me.'

Glancing at his watch, Madden made to rise from his chair.

'I must be getting home. We've got Violet and Ian coming for a drink. I want to be there before they arrive so that I can impress on Lucy the need for discretion. She knows far more about this case than she ought to, which is my fault, and is altogether too eager to talk about it. Luckily we've had some news that might distract her. Rob has written to say he'll be back in England soon and that he's due some leave. Lucy is already organizing several parties in London for his benefit, and with any luck that will keep her mind busy; at least for a while.'

*

As he unlatched the gate at the bottom of the garden, Madden heard the sound of his daughter's voice.

'It's all very well you saying it's a nautical tradition, Mummy, but it simply won't do. If Rob wants me to introduce him to my girlfriends, he'll have to make some sacrifices. I'm going to insist on it. The beard must go.'

Emerging from the orchard, he saw her standing a little way off beside Helen, who was on her knees by a flower bed, busy with a gardening fork. Lucy held a snapshot in her hand. It was one that her brother had sent them when he had written to say that he would soon be back in England. Madden and Helen had admired the photograph, which showed their tall son in full naval uniform and sporting a handsome, bushy beard.

'Daddy, don't you agree . . . ?' Spying her father, Lucy turned to him for support. 'Rob simply can't present himself in decent society looking like a savage.'

'I don't see why not.' Madden went over to join them. 'Your mother and I think he cuts a fine figure. The beard is particularly impressive.'

'Well, I'm sorry to say you're mistaken.' Lucy flushed with annoyance. 'I can't see any of my friends wanting to dance cheek-to-cheek with that great hairy thing.'

'Should this be of concern to Rob?' Madden affected an air of bewilderment. 'Not that your friends aren't charming, I'm sure, but why are you so convinced he'll want to dance cheek-to-cheek with them?'

'Oh for heaven's sake, Daddy!' Lucy lost patience. 'He's been at sea for the last six months. What do you think he'll want to do? I'm going to give him an ultimatum. Either the beard goes, or . . . or . . .'

Unable to think of a suitable threat, she stalked off, heading up the lawn towards the house, with Hamish – her ever-faithful shadow – trotting at her heels. Madden and Helen looked at each other.

'It sounds as though the battle lines have already been drawn.' Madden ventured a comment. 'Lucy seems almost to relish the prospect.'

'Rob will be just the same.' Helen was in no doubt. 'There's nothing they enjoy more. It's a struggle to gain the upper hand, and it started in the nursery, if memory serves. You'd better prepare yourself. We could be in for a lively few weeks.'

Shedding her gloves, and helped by the hand Madden offered her, she rose from the lawn. He collected the tools she had brought.

'How was your talk with Angus?' she asked as they set off up the lawn. 'Is he satisfied with the outcome of this case – or at least resigned to the fact that there's nothing more anyone can do about it?'

'Not entirely,' Madden replied. 'But he knows better than anyone that not all investigations end happily. With Garner dead, I doubt the police will ever know for certain who killed Portia Blake, while if Wing had any hand in her death, that's likely to remain a mystery too unless the authorities can lay hands on him, which seems increasingly unlikely. I wouldn't bet much on his chances of survival with those triad killers after him, so whatever secrets he might harbour will probably die with him. And of course the irony is that in spite of all that has happened in the past few weeks, the police may have got it right first time around. There's still no real evidence to suggest that it wasn't Norris who murdered the poor girl.'

'But your part in this is over?'

'I certainly hope so. There's really nothing more I can do

for Angus. I've asked Billy to keep me abreast of developments so far as the search for Stanley Wing is concerned, but that's for Richard's benefit. Garner's death has hit him hard. They grew up together. He's still trying to cope with the idea that his old friend committed suicide and I'm not in a position to tell him that the police are treating it as a case of murder. They don't want that news released before the inquest.'

They had reached the terrace, and there they parted – Helen to go upstairs and change, Madden to take the gardening tools he was carrying to the potting shed at the side of the lawn. On returning to the house he heard the phone ring in the study and went to answer it.

'Richard . . . ?' He recognized his caller's voice.

'I'm sorry to bother you, John, but will you be up in London next week?'

'Just for a day or two. We're moving out of the house for good on Wednesday. Is there something I can do for you?'

'I was hoping you could join me for dinner at my club.'

Madden hesitated. He had caught an alien note in the other man's voice.

'Is something the matter, Richard?'

'You mean something apart from the frightfulness of this whole sordid business?'

The bitter outburst took Madden by surprise. He was still trying to think of a suitable response when Jessup spoke again.

'No, it's just that I'd like to have your company, John. Would Tuesday suit?'

24

As MADDEN CLIMBED out of the taxi he noticed a man in uniform standing on the pavement; he was looking up at the sky, which was already darkening with the onset of night.

'Hello, Lennox,' he said. 'Are you checking the weather? It looks as though we could have a storm before long.'

'Mr Madden, sir . . .' Jessup's chauffeur turned to him with a smile. He doffed his peaked cap. 'I've just dropped Sir Richard off. He was late getting away from the office. I'll be driving him down to Hampshire later, and I was thinking we'd probably run into some rain.'

As he spoke a flash of lightning showed in the blackness. It was still some distance off and the accompanying rumble of thunder took several seconds to reach their ears.

'Being a farmer, I'll be glad to see it. But I hope for our sake it's not too heavy.'

With a wave Madden went up the shallow steps and through the doors into the club. He found his host standing at the reception counter with his hat in his hand and a raincoat over his arm.

'There you are, John . . .'

Despite the smile of greeting he offered his guest, Madden noted the dark shadows under his eyes; sure signs of sleeplessness, he thought. It looked as though the strain of the past few days was taking its toll.

'We appear to have been abandoned. They're building a

new cloakroom downstairs and we're supposed to drop off our things here, but there's no one about.'

As he spoke the sound of laboured footsteps reached their ears. They were coming from a stairwell at the back of the lobby and after a moment the figure of an elderly porter dressed in the customary black garments of his calling came shuffling into view. He was breathing heavily.

'I'm sorry, sir.' Panting, he addressed Jessup, whom he had just caught sight of. 'I was just making sure the back door was locked. What a mess those builders make. They leave everything lying about. The passage to the bathroom is like an obstacle course. I've had complaints from the members. I meant to have a word with them about it this evening, but they slipped out before I had a chance.'

'That's all right, Tom.' Jessup handed him their hats and coats. 'We haven't been waiting long. This is a guest of mine, Mr Madden. Have you got the visitors' book handy? I ought to sign him in.'

As the porter reached beneath the counter for his ledger. Jessup pointed to the row of campaign medals pinned to his jacket.

'Those date from the Boer War, John. Parsons was at the siege of Mafeking.' He was making an effort to sound cheerful. 'Isn't that so, Tom?'

'Quite right, sir.' Still pink in the face, the old man's cheeks flushed a deeper red.

'Mr Madden here was in the first war, and I was in the second. Together we make quite a trio. Someone ought to take our picture.'

The suggestion was well received. Parsons chuckled richly.

'Tom's been at the club longer than anyone.' Jessup bent to sign the book. 'I can recall the first time my father brought me here, when I was still a boy. I can't have been older than fifteen or sixteen. It was to have lunch. You were on duty that day, Tom. Do you remember?'

'Very well, sir.' The porter beamed. 'Sir Jack said he was going to propose you for membership in due course and that I was to keep an eye on you. "See he doesn't get into any mischief," he said.'

'I'd forgotten that.'

As though a magic wand had been waved across it, the strain vanished from Jessup's face in a moment. The smile he offered the old man was full of affection.

'Well, I'm not sure how successful you were, Tom, but you certainly did your best.'

'I've got some news for you, Richard. It'll be welcome in its way, at least I hope so.'

They had paused only briefly in the bar for a glass of sherry before going into the dining room, where Jessup, who seemed more troubled than ever, sat drumming his fingertips on the table while the waiter brought their food and filled their wine glasses.

'I spoke to Billy Styles today,' Madden began. 'The police here have had word from the Hong Kong CID. They've finally tracked down that woman Garner assaulted years ago. She was a prostitute, but she's married now with a family and doesn't want the matter brought up again. The point is, she survived the beating.'

'So Rex didn't kill her.' Jessup's face cleared momentarily. 'Well, thank God for that.'

'It's the first piece of solid information the police have had. So much of this case has been supposition. Unfortunately it tends to strengthen the case against Garner as far as

Miss Blake's murder is concerned. It's the only other thing Wing could have had over him. And we're assuming it was he who sent Garner those photographs. It could hardly have been anyone else.'

Silence fell as Jessup pondered his words.

'Look, John, I realize that the police think Garner killed Miss Blake, but will they take it any further now? Will they make that public? As I said before, it seems hard to condemn a man when he isn't alive to defend himself.'

Madden saw what was troubling him.

'Truthfully, I can't answer that, Richard. It's not for me to say. But I don't believe they will, partly for the reason you give and partly because there are still missing links in the chain of evidence and without them they can't prove that Garner was guilty. It's my belief they'll let the matter drop. At worst they may say that they're not looking into the Portia Blake case any longer and leave the public to draw their own conclusions.'

Jessup sat brooding. He had hardly touched his food.

'I can't tell you how hard I find it, thinking about Rex,' he said at last. 'We were such friends when we were boys. My mother thought he was a bad influence on me, but she was wrong. We both liked breaking the rules and we egged each other on. But there comes a time when you have to grow up, and poor Rex never realized that. He thought he could live life on his terms, bend it to his will. But it broke him in the end and he began to drink more and more. He became a sad figure and people tended to avoid him. I'm ashamed to say I was one of them, and he felt the betrayal keenly. There's a particular pain that comes from shedding old friends. Do you know what I mean, John?'

His glance pleaded for understanding, and Madden dipped his head in silent acknowledgement.

'I'm going to tell you something I shouldn't,' he said, 'but it may help ease any guilt you feel about Garner. He didn't commit suicide, as was thought. He was murdered.'

'Good God!' Jessup was dumbfounded.

'You must keep this to yourself. It can't come out till the inquest. But the pathologist who examined the body is confident that Garner was strangled before he was strung up, and with the same length of flex.'

'But . . . but who by?'

'The betting is on Stanley Wing. He had a motive of sorts. It's clear that Garner wasn't in a position to meet his supposed blackmail demands – we know that from you – and it also seems likely that Wing hated him. There's no proof as yet that Wing was ever in Garner's house, but that may change in the next few days.'

'Change . . . how?'

'There were some fingerprints left on the banisters which don't match Garner's or any of his staff's. It's likely they were left by the killer when he dragged the body up to the gallery to hang it. The police are expecting to receive a copy of Wing's prints from the Hong Kong police any day now. If the two sets match the police will know he was there.'

'And if they don't?'

'Then the police will be faced with another puzzle.' Madden shrugged. 'But that's been a feature of this inquiry from the start. All it's ever done is raise more questions than it answers.'

He caught his host's eye.

'As far as the inquest is concerned, at least you won't have to answer questions about the conversation you had with Garner here at the club before his death. In fact I doubt that the name of Portia Blake will even come up. You'll only be asked to help establish his movements, to say how he got home, which is something Lennox can confirm. You will have to say he was drunk, I'm afraid. That can't be avoided. It may explain why he was unable to defend himself.'

Jessup shook his head hopelessly.

'God, I wish Sarah were here.' The words burst from his lips. 'I miss her terribly.'

'Will she be returning soon?' Madden asked.

'By the end of the week, she says. We talk every evening by telephone, but it's not the same.'

'As soon as she's back and settled you must all come over to Highfield. Helen is counting on it.'

Jessup brightened on hearing the words. The cloud on his face seemed to lift.

'I can't think of anything I'd like more.'

Madden searched his memory to see if there was anything else he could tell his companion that might serve to ease his mind.

'I do have some news about Wing,' he said. 'He was staying in a boarding house in Brent Cross a fortnight ago. The landlady remembers him. But he's disappeared since then. He probably found a room somewhere, the sort that are advertised in tobacconist's windows and don't involve any record being kept.'

'He's a fool to have stayed here so long.' Jessup's tone had turned grim again.

'I believe you're right. It seems certain those triad killers are on his trail. At least one of them – not the enforcer himself, his assistant, the young man who came to your office with Lin – has been asking questions and showing Wing's photograph to members of the Chinese community. They seem to know he's here.'

About to continue, he paused. Jessup's expression had changed. He was looking past him and when Madden turned he saw a black-suited figure standing at the entrance to the dining room. It was Parsons, the porter from downstairs. He was peering about him. When his eye fell on Jessup he hurried across the room to their table.

'I'm sorry to interrupt, sir.' He bent to murmur in Sir Richard's ear. 'There's a phone call for you – it's a Detective-Inspector Styles, of Scotland Yard. I tried to explain that you were having dinner with a guest, but he insisted on speaking to you.'

'Thank you, Tom.'

Jessup rose. He shot a glance at Madden, who shook his head.

'I'm sorry, Richard. I've no idea what it's about.'

'I'd better have a word with him.'

Madden watched as he left the room and then gestured to the waiter, who was standing beside the table with a wine bottle in his hand waiting to fill his glass. He couldn't imagine what might have prompted Billy to call at this hour, but it had to be something important or he would have waited until the morning. Casting his mind back, he recalled the look on Jessup's face when he had watched the body of Rex Garner being lowered to the floor: the pain he must have felt at that moment. All he could hope now was that what-ever Billy had to say wouldn't add to his distress.

The sight of Tom Parsons bending to whisper anxiously in his host's ear a moment before reminded him of the scene downstairs, when Jessup had made much of the old man, putting his own cares aside to cheer him and bring a flush of pleasure to his cheeks. It had been the action of a man, as he himself had put it to Helen, who would rather give than receive, and the memory brought a smile to Madden's lips as he sipped his wine. Just then, though, another thought occurred to him, an idea so startling – and unwelcome – that instinctively he thrust it from his mind.

'John . . . !'

Madden looked up with a start.

'Richard . . . what is it?'

Jessup stood beside him. His face had paled in the few seconds he'd been absent from the table.

'They've found Wing.'

'The police . . . where . . . ?' Madden pushed back his chair.

'In the docks . . . that's to say, they think it's him. They want me to go over there.'

'Do you mean they've found his body?'

'Not exactly . . .'

Jessup looked away. For a moment he seemed he might be unable to speak. But then he forced the words from his lips.

'All they have is his head.'

25

A bolt of forked lightning split the sky above them. It was followed by a peal of thunder that echoed like a roll of giant drums for long seconds before it died away. The rain that had started to fall in scattered heavy drops a few minutes earlier just as they entered the dock gates turned suddenly into a downpour. The long-awaited storm had finally arrived.

Madden and Jessup had already opened the two umbrellas which Lennox had retrieved from the boot of the car, but Lily Poole, who had been waiting at the dock gates to meet them, had only a raincoat to protect her and Madden drew her into the shelter of his. Leaving car and chauffeur parked at a spot a short distance from the gates, the two men had set off with their guide, but had hardly taken more than a dozen paces when the heavens opened.

'It's only about five minutes from here, sir.'

Lily had to shout into Madden's ear, so loud was the drumming of the rain on their spread umbrellas. She was leading them down a narrow lane walled on either side by darkened buildings, some of them whole, others damaged beyond repair. Lying well downriver on a tongue of land called the Isle of Dogs, which was enclosed on three sides by a great loop in the Thames, the docks had been heavily bombed during the war, as Madden was well aware, and although a programme of reconstruction had been under way since the end of hostilities, with funds in short supply, many sheds and office buildings still stood derelict.

Little had been said during the drive across London. Although Jessup had taken it for granted that his guest would want to accompany him, he had sat silent as they followed the course of the river, past his company's offices on Cheapside and on through the deserted night-time streets of Wapping and Limehouse, heading for the great dock complex. He had already told Madden all he knew before they left the club.

'The murder was reported more than an hour ago, according to Inspector Styles, but it took a while to get a squad of detectives assembled and then to find out what had happened. The best guess seems to be that Stanley was making a run for it, trying to smuggle himself out of the country aboard a freighter, and somehow the triads got wind of it.'

Madden for his part had failed to rid himself of the disturbing notion that had come to him while he was sitting on his own at the table waiting for Sir Richard to return. Although he had tried to dismiss it from his mind – it had been prompted by an incident so trivial it hardly seemed worth thinking about – the thought continued to nag at him.

Lily tugged at his sleeve.

'There we are, sir.' She pointed to a lighted doorway ahead of them. 'You'll find everyone inside.

A few seconds later, ushered out of the rain and relieved of their umbrellas by a waiting constable, they found themselves standing in the shell of a large warehouse empty of goods whose high roof was all but lost to view in the darkness above. What light there was came from a pair of standing lamps whose long cords snaked across the cement floor to an electrical outlet. Like stage spotlights, their beams were trained on an area in the middle of the cement floor where a round object lay. Although they were still too distant from the scene to make out any details, Madden had little doubt that it was a decapitated head they were looking at and his presentiment was confirmed moments later as they approached the spot and he saw the face distorted by a hideous grin and the wide pool of dried blood surrounding it.

Instinctively he glanced at Jessup, who had come to a halt beside him. He was staring at the object with a look of mingled horror and disbelief.

'Sir Richard . . . !'

Billy had just noticed their arrival. He had been standing with a group of detectives at the edge of the illuminated area, watching as a police photographer circled the spot snapping shots from different angles. He hurried over to them.

'I'm sorry to drag you out on a night like this, sir.' He addressed his words to Jessup, though with a quick glance at Madden. 'But we can't be sure it's Wing from the photograph you lent us.' He tapped his breast pocket. 'The features are twisted and . . .'

'It's him.' Jessup's gaze was riveted on the ghastly spectacle in front of them. 'That's Stanley Wing.'

'Ah . . .' Billy let out a sigh. 'It's settled, then. We had to be sure.'

He caught Madden's eye.

'I didn't expect to see you, sir.'

'I was having dinner with Sir Richard when you called. Who found the head, Billy?'

'The river police. They've got a station near the dock gates. A couple of their officers were on a routine patrol around the North Dock. It's where imports are offloaded and the police check the warehouses as a matter of course. This shed we're in is a new one. It's not in use yet. The builders are still putting the finishing touches to it and the officers would probably have walked right past it if one of them hadn't heard faint noises coming from inside. They stopped and shone their torches in. At first they didn't see anything; then one of them spotted something lying on the floor and they went over to investigate.'

Billy shrugged.

'They realized they must have just missed whoever did this.' He gestured towards the head. 'The warehouse was empty. But there was another door on the other side from where they'd come in – that one there.' He pointed. 'They went over to have a look, but they couldn't see anyone outside. It was dark and the area behind this shed is still pretty much as it was at the end of the war: just a lot of damaged buildings. They decided the best thing to do was to report their find, so one of them stayed here while the other ran back to the station. The news was telephoned to the Yard quick enough and when the duty officer heard about the head he rang me at home and I came over here at once. It seemed likely that the victim was Wing, but I didn't know how to get hold of you, sir.' He looked at Jessup. 'So I rang your number in Hampshire and spoke to Mrs Castleton. She told me to try your club.'

Jessup was silent. He had been standing motionless for long minutes, seemingly unable to tear his eyes from the grisly sight before him.

'We'll have to wait for the pathologist, but it looks like a clean blow to me.' Billy felt he had to say something. 'At a guess, I'd say an axe was used.'

Jessup stirred.

'What about the body?' he asked.

'River police officers are searching the area now, but what with it being dark and a lot of these buildings still in ruins it won't be easy. And the rain isn't helping either.' He beckoned to Lily. 'Get hold of an umbrella, Lil, and see if you can locate Joe Grace. I want to know if they've found anything.'

331

He turned back.

'As I understand it, sir, you told Mr Madden that this particular gang gets rid of its victims' bodies.'

'That's correct, Inspector.' Jessup spoke in a dead voice. 'They leave only the head. It's intended to instil fear in their own ranks: to warn backsliders what may lie in wait for them if they break their oaths. Ideally, they like to make a ceremony of it and conduct the execution before a select audience, or so I've been told. I dare say it wasn't possible in this case. They must have felt they had to kill Wing on the spot. But word will get out: the discovery of his head is bound to be reported, and that will be enough to send out a message.'

'On the spot, you say, sir?' Billy frowned. 'So you agree he was probably trying to flee the country?'

'It does look that way, doesn't it?' Jessup shrugged wearily. 'I expect you'll find there's at least one freighter in the docks due to weigh anchor in the next few hours; if it hasn't slipped its moorings already.'

'We thought of that, sir. There's a Chinese vessel, Hong Kong registered, due to cast off in a couple of hours. I sent DS Grace aboard to question the captain, but he swore he knew nothing about it. All his crew were aboard, he said. He brought them up on deck for Grace's inspection and showed him a list of their names. That doesn't mean anything. I doubt Wing's would have been among them, or any other name he might have been using. But what I don't understand was how he could have arranged it. He can't have that many contacts in London.'

'All he needed was one, Inspector.' Jessup's tone was bleak.

Billy studied his face. He shot a questioning glance at Madden.

'Are you saying you know who that might be, sir?'

Jessup opened his mouth to reply, but then seemed to change his mind. He stood biting his lip.

'Sir . . . ?' Billy prompted him.

'This is only a guess, Inspector, and I wouldn't want you to take it as gospel.' Jessup spoke finally. 'I dare say Mr Madden told you about the two Chinese men who called on me recently asking if I had news of Wing. One of them was a businessman called Lin Jie. Although I've no proof of it, I've reason to believe that he and Wing were involved in importing Chinese relics into this country illegally some years ago. And given that it was Lin whom the triads chose to approach when they began searching for Stanley, it does seem likely they had a past connection.'

'So what you're suggesting is it might have been this Lin fellow who arranged for Wing to slip out of the country, and that somehow the triads got wind of it.'

Jessup nodded. 'But don't imagine for a moment that he'll admit to anything. He'll plead complete ignorance and nothing you or I or anyone else might say to him will alter that. He may have been hoping that if the triads learned that Wing had left the country they would leave him alone.'

Billy turned to Madden.

'What do you think, sir?'

Madden came to himself with a start. His mind had been wandering.

'I really can't say, Billy.' He forced himself to concentrate on the moment. 'But I'm wondering how Wing got into the docks.'

'There's a passport control office at the gates,' Billy explained. 'They told us that a number of Chinese came through tonight, all merchant seamen, and their papers were checked. Wing could have been among them. Even if he was travelling on a false passport, it might have been good enough to pass muster.' Billy scratched his head. 'But it's these killers who really puzzle me – how did *they* gain entry? They couldn't have just walked through the gates with the others. And there's a twenty-foot wall around the whole dock complex.'

'I can tell you that, guv.'

Billy swung round to see Joe Grace standing behind him in a puddle of water with Lily at his side. She skipped away smartly as he shook himself like a dog, sending a spray of water from his dripping hair and coat.

'Watch it, Sarge!' she protested. Joe grinned.

'Me and some of the lads have just found a gate at the top of the docks that ought to be locked, but isn't. According to the river police it's open during the day, but locked at night with a chain and padlock. Someone's gone to work with a bolt-cutter. The chain's been cut. That's how they got in, and they left the same way. In fact, they were spotted.'

'By who?'

'A bloke who's got a fish-and-chip shop across the road. He stays open late because of seamen reporting for duty, but he'd closed for the night and gone upstairs to his flat when he saw half a dozen men coming out of that gate which he knew was usually kept locked, which was why he noticed them. They had a bakery van parked there . . .'

'*A bakery van . . . !*' Billy was disbelieving.

'That's what he said.' Joe flashed his wolfish grin. 'But he didn't take a note of the name, more's the pity. Anyway, just before nine, which is when we think Wing was topped, he saw these blokes come out through the gate, and they were carrying something.'

'Like a body?'

'Could have been.' Joe shrugged. 'There were two of them toting it. But it was wrapped in something, cloth or canvas is my guess, and that's all he saw. The men stuck it in the back of the van and off they all went. And before you ask, guv, he couldn't describe them, couldn't even say if they were Chinks, it was too dark. But they were all dressed in black.'

'A bakery van . . .' Billy repeated the words. 'Well, it's a start at least. We'll get on to it right away.'

He looked around him. The photographer had finished his work. The other detectives he had brought with him were standing idle.

'You'd better fetch those officers in out of the rain,' he told Grace. 'There's no point in them searching any longer.'

He turned to Jessup.

'I'm just waiting for the pathologist to arrive before we remove the head, sir. There's no call for you to stay any longer. And again, I'm sorry for having dragged you down here.'

'Don't apologize, Inspector.' Jessup rested his tired gaze on Billy. 'I can't help feeling this was always going to happen – if not here, then some other place.'

'You mean the triads were bound to catch up with him sooner or later?'

'That's always been their reputation. Stanley must have known he was living on borrowed time.'

He turned to Madden.

'John . . . ?'

'Yes, I'm coming, Richard.'

Madden turned, more than ready to leave now, but then paused when he saw that Jessup hadn't moved. Once again he was gazing down at the bloodied object lying on the floor at his feet.

'I can't deny I'd hoped to see this man arrested and stand trial for what he's done.' He lifted his eyes to meet Billy's gaze. 'But I wouldn't wish an end like this on anyone.'

26

Big Ben was chiming the hour as they turned off the Embankment and drove past the Houses of Parliament towards Whitehall. Although the storm had passed, the streets, still wet, shone like mirrors in the lamplight. Looking at his watch, Madden saw that it was midnight.

'At least you won't have to drive me to Hampshire, Ted.' Jessup spoke from the back of the car where they were sitting. 'I'm going to sleep at the club. We'll go down tomorrow.'

He turned to Madden.

'I'm sorry, John. I had no idea the evening would turn out this way.'

Madden was silent. He'd not spoken since they had left the docks. Jessup examined his face.

'You look worried,' he said.

'I've been trying to work out how those men got hold of Wing.'

It wasn't altogether true. His thoughts had been on another track. But the two questions weren't unrelated.

'I'm sorry . . . ?' Jessup didn't understand.

'How did they manage to overpower him and get him to that warehouse? The docks weren't exactly deserted. There were river police stationed there and those merchant seamen who passed through the gates must have walked down the same road Wing would have taken to get to the freighter he was supposed to board. Any sort of rough stuff between him and these triad thugs was bound to have been noticed by someone. At least, you would think so.'

'So what's your conclusion?'

'That it's far more likely he went there of his own accord.'

'To an empty unused warehouse . . . ?' Jessup frowned. 'But why should he have done that?'

'I can only make a guess, Richard.' Madden glanced at him. 'But it could be because he had an appointment there.'

'With Lin, do you mean?'

Madden shrugged.

'He's the most likely person to have set something up. You said so yourself. He might have told Stanley that either he or someone he'd send in his place would be there to ensure that the arrangement with the ship's captain went smoothly. But whatever Wing was told, whatever was arranged, it was almost certainly a blind.'

'A *blind* . . . ?'

'It's only an opinion, mind.' Madden searched the other's face. 'But I doubt that any passage on a freighter was ever fixed for Stanley Wing, no matter what he'd been led to believe. I think the aim was simply to get him to the docks, and then into that warehouse . . .'

'Where the triads would be waiting for him?'

Jessup had understood.

'What you're saying is that he walked into a trap.'

'I'm worried about him, sir, and that's the truth. I haven't seen Sir Richard look this tired since the war.'

Ted Lennox's homely features were a picture of concern as he nursed the big Bentley around Hyde Park Corner.

'Mind you, then he had reason: we were up against it more than once, and he was always worried about us, the men. Is it because of Mr Garner dying that way? Is that what's upset him?'

'Mostly, I think.'

Madden was sitting beside the chauffeur in the front of the car. When they dropped Jessup at the club Lennox had opened the back door for Madden to climb in, but his passenger had declined the offer.

'I'd rather sit up with you, Ted.'

'Sir Richard does the same whenever we go down the country. He likes to chat.'

It was Jessup who had insisted that his guest accept the offer of a lift up to St John's Wood instead of getting the night porter to ring for a taxi, as Madden had suggested.

'The very least I can do is see that you get home safely after what I've put you through tonight.'

Lennox, too, had been quick to add his support to the plan. All three of them had got out of the car and were standing on the pavement.

'I'll be driving up that way in any case, sir,' he had assured Madden with a smile. 'I've got a room in Bayswater for when Sir Richard spends the night in London, and there'll be no traffic this time of night.'

Madden had accompanied Jessup to the doors of the club, which had been locked, and Jessup had rung the bell for the night porter. While they waited he had asked Madden for a favour.

'If the police need to talk to me could you tell them I'll be down in Hampshire? Sarah is due back on Thursday. I'll have to come up to London for the inquest – Rex's that is – but otherwise I'll stay in the country.'

When he heard the porter unlocking the door he had held out his hand.

'Thank you for being there, John. It meant a lot to me. Pray God I never witness another sight like that.'

Madden could see he was exhausted.

'Try and get some sleep, Richard,' he said.

Standing a little way off, Lennox had eyed his employer with concern.

'He'll feel better when his missus gets back,' he confided to Madden now as they drove up Park Lane. 'Don't you think so, sir?'

'I'm sure he will, Ted.' Madden had noticed the chauffeur's worried look. He cast around in his mind for a subject that might distract him. 'I understand you and Sir Richard met during the war?' he said.

'That's right, sir. It happened soon after I'd volunteered for the Parachute Regiment. I was assigned to his company and the first thing he said to me – he was a lieutenant then – was that I should have known better.' Lennox's frown had faded. He was chuckling now. '"Never volunteer for anything," he said. "Didn't they teach you that in basic training?"'

Madden smiled. 'Did you see a lot of action together?'

'Enough to go on with: North Africa, Sicily, Normandy . . . and then Arnhem, of course. By that time I was company sergeant-major and Sir Richard was our captain. We'd been through a lot together by then, and we all felt the same about him. He was one of those officers you'd follow anywhere.'

Lennox glanced at his passenger.

'You were in the first war, weren't you, sir? Sir Richard told me. I reckon you know what I mean.'

'Yes, I know what you mean.' Madden returned his glance. 'Tell me about Arnhem. I've read accounts of the battle, of course, but Sir Richard doesn't talk about the war and I've never spoken to anyone else who was there.'

Lennox sighed.

'Ah, well they tried to make it sound like a victory afterwards, but you could have fooled us. We jumped into a hornets' nest, sir, and that's the truth. It turned out there were a couple of Panzer divisions refitting in the neighbourhood which nobody seemed to know about and we hadn't been long on the ground when all hell broke loose. There was a bridge over the Rhine we were supposed to take so that the troops moving up from the south could cross it, but we never did, and after that things began to fall apart. The weather was bad so we didn't have the air support we were expecting and most of the supplies dropped to us ended up in the Jerries' hands. We'd been there more than a week and were running out of ammunition and taking heavy casualties, too, so in the end the colonel had to call it a day. But word went out to the men that they didn't have to surrender if they could find a way of escaping. There wasn't much left of our company, just a handful of men, but we were posted on the outskirts of Arnhem – we were holding the flank there – and the captain decided it was worth having a go at joining up with other units who were in a neighbouring town.'

He fell silent for a moment as he navigated the turn from Marble Arch into Oxford Street.

'Well, just about then I got hit in the leg by a stray bullet, and I reckoned that was my lot. I'd just have to wait until the Jerries arrived and hope they would take me prisoner and not just shoot me out of hand.' His chuckle had taken on a wry edge. 'I'm not saying anything against them, mind. They were good soldiers, but street-to-street fighting is the worst kind and you don't like to leave any wounded enemy behind you. But the captain took one look at me lying there on the ground and said, "You're not getting out of this that easily, Ted Lennox." Next thing I knew he'd hauled me to my feet and strung my arms around his neck. "Hang on tight," he said, and from then on he carried me.'

He shook his head ruefully.

'We got out of Arnhem all right, and into the next town, but the Jerries were hot on our heels. We could hear them: they were only a few streets away. But I wasn't the only casualty and our wounded were slowing us down. Then, just as we thought we'd be caught, a man appeared in the doorway of a house just ahead of us. He started waving to us and calling out in English: "This way, Tommies, this way!" We'd had a lot of help from the Dutch civilians. They'd taken in our wounded and given us food, so we didn't hang about. We headed straight for his house and he hurried us all inside and told us to go up to the floor above and stay quiet. "The Germans are coming," he said. We could hear them ourselves. It sounded as though they were in the next street. "Don't make any noise. I will say you went past." He spoke good English.

'We went straight up the stairs into a bedroom and waited. We could hear the Jerry soldiers calling out to one another. They were coming closer. The captain had put me down on the bed with another bloke who was also wounded, and while I was lying there I noticed something hanging on the wall. It was a painting of an old-fashioned shield with a funny looking design on it: a sort of hook with a line drawn through the middle. I'd never seen anything like it. I noticed that the captain was looking at it too; staring, I should say. Then suddenly, in a flash, he was gone—'

'Gone . . . ?' Madden cut in.

'He just ran out of the room and we heard his feet on the stairs; then another noise, a sharp cry, more like a yelp, and the sound of a door being slammed. Some of the men went after him, but I had to stay lying there on the bed and only

341

heard later what had happened. This Dutch bloke had been going to shop us to the Jerries and the captain had grabbed him from behind at the front door just in time. It was that shield he had seen . . .'

'It must have been a *Wolfsangel*,' Madden said.

'That's right . . . that's the word.' Ted Lennox looked at him in wonder. 'The captain told us about it afterwards. I was trying to remember the name.'

'It was a simplified design of a wolf trap from German heraldry,' Madden explained. 'The Dutch fascists used it as their symbol before they switched to the swastika. Sir Richard must have recognized it.'

He was riveted by the tale.

'So you all escaped?'

'Only in the nick of time. This chap had a whistle to his lips when the captain grabbed him. I saw it lying there beside his body when we came downstairs. He was about to blow it.'

He shrugged.

'Anyway, we left by the back door double quick, and a short while later we joined up with some of our blokes who were holding positions in the town. There was already a plan in operation to withdraw as many men as possible and that same night we made it back across the Rhine.'

'And was Sir Richard still carrying you?' Madden asked.

'Right up to the moment he dumped me on a raft.' Lennox shook with laughter. 'Later, after we were back in England, he came to see me in hospital. I was up and about by then, but still on crutches. "You'll have to get rid of those," he said, "if you're going to be my chauffeur." I didn't know what he was talking about. "Well, you'll need a job after the war, won't you?" he said. "And I'll need a chauffeur. Think about it and let me know."' Laughing, Lennox shook his head. 'Well, I thought about it,' he said, 'for a few seconds anyway.'

Madden had been so caught up in the tale that he saw with surprise that they had already rounded the top of Regent's Park and were turning up Avenue Road towards Aunt Maud's house.

'The truth is, we all owed him our lives, I reckon.' Lennox's voice had altered. He spoke in a solemn tone. 'All of us who were with him that day.'

The car drew to a halt.

'I can't say for sure what would have happened if the Jerry soldiers had trapped us in that house.' Lennox looked at his passenger. 'But something tells me it wouldn't have ended well. Still, it can't have been easy for the captain, having to grab that Dutch chap from behind and break his neck. But it was him or us. The captain knew that. So it had to be done.'

27

Madden awoke in darkness. Peering at the luminous dial of his watch, he saw that it was just after four o'clock. His brief sleep had been troubled by dreams, none of which he remembered clearly other than the last, in which he had found himself walking down seemingly endless passages which had turned first one way then another and which had ended in a small room where a man was sitting at a table. His face seemed familiar, but it was only after he awoke that Madden realized the features were those of Tom Parsons, the club porter.

Half an hour later, finding that further sleep eluded him, he rose and donning his slippers and dressing-gown went quietly down the uncarpeted wooden stairs to the floor below, where he proceeded to roam about the empty rooms retracing the tangle of thoughts that had kept him awake, a winding maze that called to mind the passages he had stumbled through in his dream.

Finally, worn out by his restless pacing, he sought refuge in the kitchen, where there was still a table with a chair beside it. Settling down there, he sat with his elbows on the table and his chin resting in his cupped palms, staring into the darkness . . .

'What on earth are you doing here, Daddy? Have you been up all night?'

Madden lifted a heavy head. He had fallen asleep in the kitchen. His daughter had found him still sitting at the table with his head resting on his folded arms. He blinked at her.

'This isn't like you at all.'

Looking unusually elegant in a beautifully cut suit which she had acquired in Paris two years before while supposedly studying French, Lucy seemed bent on making the most of her discovery.

'Did you remember to strip your bed? Shall I do it for you? I'm coming back in my lunch hour to collect the bed-clothes and any other odds and ends we've forgotten.'

Madden saw that she had a suitcase with her. It had been their last night in the house. Lucy was moving temporarily into the flat of a friend who was away for a few weeks and whose absence meant that Rob, whose ship was due to dock at Plymouth in a few days, would also be able to stay there with her when he came up to London.

'Thank you. I'll strip my own bed.' Madden clung as best he could to the shreds of his dignity. 'I must get dressed,' he said.

'I don't know what Mummy will say.'

'Nothing, if you don't tell her,' he growled.

'And what were you up to last night? I wanted to hear about your dinner with Sir Richard. I stayed up for ages, but you never came back. Why were you so late?'

'We were busy . . . occupied.' Rubbing his eyes, he dragged himself to his feet.

'Is that all you're going to say?' His daughter was dis-believing. 'After everything we've been through together on this case? I can't believe it . . .'

Madden scowled. Gathering himself, he addressed her in a different tone.

'I've said all I'm going to say, Lucy. I have nothing to add. You're just going to have to accept it. Is that clear?'

She stared at him, open-mouthed.

'You're using your "voice",' she said accusingly.

'My *what* . . . ?'

'That's what Rob and I used to call it. Daddy's speaking in his "voice", we'd say. We'd better do as we're told.'

'I wish I'd known that. I would have used it more often.'

'Well, you're not to take advantage of it now, just because I told you.'

He tried to maintain a serious air, but it was hopeless. All he could do was laugh at her.

'There – that's better.' Satisfied, she kissed him. 'You were looking so sad.'

'Was I?' He put his arms around her and held her close.

'That's my cab,' she said as the doorbell rang. 'I have to go.' She kissed him again. 'But you're not to look sad any more. I forbid it.'

It was true. His spirits had sunk to a point so low he could barely bring himself to attend to the business that had brought him to London. He was faced with a dilemma he didn't know how to resolve. The more he thought about it, the more intractable it seemed, and it stayed with him as he went upstairs to strip his bed and get dressed. When he returned to the kitchen to make himself a cup of tea he was interrupted by another ring at the door. The callers proved to be a pair of removal men and for the next twenty minutes he was occupied watching as they carried the last pieces of Aunt Maud's furniture out of the house.

There being nothing further to do – a set of keys had already been placed in the hands of the estate agent – he was about to call for a taxi to take him to Waterloo station when the phone rang at his feet. It was due to be disconnected at the end of the week. He bent to pick up the receiver.

'Ah, I've got you, John! I was afraid you might have left already. Styles told me you'd be going home today.'

Charlie Chubb's voice sounded loud in his ears. The chief super seemed to be in good spirits.

'What a night you must have had! I've seen a few things in my time, I can tell you, but a severed head all on its own: that's something I've never clapped eyes on, not in forty years on the job. I hope it didn't spoil your sleep.'

'What can I do for you, Charlie?'

'Nothing, really, but if you're heading for Waterloo, as I imagine you are, I thought you might like to drop in here on the way.'

'Why should I want to do that?'

'I'd rather tell you in person. I want to see the look on your face.'

It was clear the chief super was enjoying himself.

'What do you mean, Charlie? What are you talking about?'

'Well, if you insist . . . Wing's body. It's turned up.'

'Good God!' Madden was struck dumb. Seconds passed before he could speak again. 'Where did you find it – in the river? Was it fully clothed?'

'Fully clothed . . . ? That's an odd question. I don't know. But I can tell you it was unearthed in Bow Cemetery. Styles has just called me with the news. But he'll be back here presently, so if you want to hear the full story you'd better look in as I suggested.'

Madden didn't hesitate.

'I'm on my way,' he said.

*

Billy cleared his throat.

'The first I heard about it was just after I arrived for work. I got a call from the police in Tower Hamlets. One of their bobbies had received a report from a bloke who was walking his dog late last night and saw what looked like some men digging in the cemetery there. He was on the other side of the railings, of course, and some way off from where they were.'

He paused to take a sip from his cup of tea. He had arrived in Chubb's office accompanied by Grace and Lily Poole to find Madden already there, and the chief super in the process of pouring out tea from the pot he had had his secretary make for them.

'He didn't think anything of it at the time – he just went home to bed – but when he took out his dog again this morning he bumped into one of the local bobbies and told him what he'd seen. They went to the cemetery, which was open by now, and he showed the bobby where he'd spotted the men. There was a fresh grave there all right, and when the bobby made inquiries he was told that a body had been buried at the same spot a couple of days earlier; it was all above board. But that still didn't explain what this chap with the dog had seen . . .'

Billy paused for another sip.

'. . . so the bobby got hold of the grave diggers who work there and asked them to take a look at it. They said they couldn't be sure, but it looked like it had been messed with. The mound of soil wasn't how they had left it; and it seemed bigger. That was enough for the bobby. He rang the station and a detective-sergeant came over to take a look for himself. He decided to have the grave dug up again and warned the diggers not to disturb the coffin. He knew he'd have to get permission from higher authority if they had to remove it and look underneath. But in the end it wasn't necessary. They hadn't even reached it when they found a body lying in the earth, and when the DS saw it was headless he got on the blower to me. He had read the report I put on the telex the night before. We went over at once. It was Wing all right.'

'How could you be sure?' Chubb asked.

'The body was dressed in seamen's clothes. There was nothing in the pockets, but we found a money belt strapped around the waist under his shirt which the people who buried him must have missed. Along with some cash it also contained a passport in the name of Wing, which meant he must have got into the docks using the other one he had in the name of Lee. That was missing.'

Billy grinned.

'And that wasn't all,' he said, 'though we didn't realize it at first. It was only after we'd got the body to the local mortuary and I had a chance to examine the passport that I found it had a handful of negatives clipped to one of its pages. They'll need to be developed before we can be certain, but even looking at them now there's not much doubt they're the same ones Audrey Cooper had; the ones that got her killed. I've sent them up to the lab.'

'Were there any prints with them?' Chubb asked.

Billy shook his head.

'I reckon Wing must have sent those to Rex Garner,' he said. 'And Rex got rid of them double quick, in his fireplace, if you remember. But that was no skin off Stanley's nose as long as he had the negatives. But when Garner couldn't pay him and he topped him it must have seemed like a lot of trouble for nothing. And I can't see that they're going to be much use to us now, not unless we decide to name Garner as Miss Blake's killer. What's your feeling on that, sir?'

Chubb shrugged.

'I can't see it happening myself,' he said. 'We still can't prove it. But it's not my decision, thank God, and I'm not even sure it'll be Cradock's. The commissioner seems to have his own opinion on the subject. We'll find out soon enough. I've got a meeting fixed with them both for this afternoon.'

He turned to Madden.

'Well, John, I hope you don't feel I dragged you down here for nothing. But after the part you've played in this – for which I'll thank you again, even if Cradock won't – I thought you ought to be in on the final act. And of course Angus will want a full report too. Let's not forget that.'

'Indeed not, Charlie.' Head bowed, Madden had listened in silence to Billy's account. Now he gathered himself to leave.

'We're near enough to lunchtime for me to invite you upstairs to the senior officers' canteen, if you care to stay. I might say the cuisine there has improved somewhat since your day.'

'Tempting as the offer is, Charlie, I'm afraid I must decline.'

Madden rose with a heavy sigh.

'I've a train to catch.'

28

THE WIND HAD got up suddenly in the last few minutes and now Madden felt the first drops of rain on his cheek. A change in the seasons was under way. The blue summer skies of the past month had given way to broken cloud, and the weather forecast he had glanced at in the paper coming down to Petersfield had held out the promise of further rain.

Just then a rumble of thunder prompted him to glance up at the sky, and as he did so he caught sight of a kestrel hovering above him, banking against the wind. He wondered if it was the same bird he and Jessup had seen when they had walked up this way together. Lowering his gaze, he saw a figure in the distance. Someone was following him up the path from the house. He recognized Ted Lennox's stocky figure and limping stride. Madden waited for him to catch up.

Although he had given them no warning of his visit he had been warmly greeted by Mrs Castleton when he had arrived by taxi from the station. Shown into the drawing room by one of the maids, he had found her busy arranging flowers in the vases placed there.

'I'm so pleased to see you, John.' She had shaken his hand. 'Richard said you might come down from London today.'

'Did he?' Madden had been surprised.

'He told me you would probably turn up. Do you mean you didn't mention the possibility to him?' Now it was she who looked puzzled.

'It was a last-minute decision.'

Madden had spent some time on the train coming down from London thinking up a plausible excuse for his visit and he offered it to her.

'I was at Waterloo intending to catch a train to Highfield when I changed my mind and decided to come down here instead. There's something I want to discuss with Richard. Has he told you what happened last night?'

'You mean about Stanley Wing?' She winced. 'What a dreadful business! Richard told me about it when he got back this morning. He said he had to go to the docks to identify what was left of the poor creature, but that you were with him, and that made it easier.' She smiled. 'You've been a great support to him, John. Rex Garner's death upset him terribly. But I expect you know that.'

She had paused to place some flowers she was holding in her arms into one of the vases.

'Sarah will be back tomorrow,' she said over her shoulder. 'I want the house to look its best for her.'

Drying her hands on a rag she turned to him again.

'Still it is strange that Richard seemed so sure you would come down today. I don't mean to pry, but is what you have to discuss with him so important?'

Madden hesitated. He wanted to be as frank with her as he could. But there were things he could not say.

'I was at Scotland Yard earlier today and was told they had discovered Wing's body. I felt Richard should know.'

'Oh, that explains it, then.' She seemed relieved. 'Why he thought you might be coming down. He knows, you see.'

'Knows . . . ?'

'A police inspector rang this morning, a Mr Styles from Scotland Yard. Richard came back from London quite exhausted and he'd gone upstairs to rest. But he came down to take the call and afterwards he told me that Stanley's body had been found. I think it was a relief to him.'

'A *relief* . . . ?' Madden was incredulous.

'Of course, it's an awful thing to contemplate, but he did say something that made me think that in some way it was a comfort to him. "At least it's all over now," he said, "nothing more can happen . . . nothing terrible." I thought then that he'd go back to his bedroom to rest, but he decided instead to go out.'

'For a walk, do you mean?' Madden was even more puzzled now.

'He said he wanted to see whether the council had started work on fencing off a piece of land not far from here – it overlooks a disused quarry – which he feels is dangerous.'

'I think I know the spot.' Madden frowned. 'He showed it to me.'

'He said he'd take the children with him. I wish he hadn't. It's going to pour with rain. Anyway, off they went, and so did I. Lennox took me into Petersfield to have my hair done. If only we'd known, I could have delayed my appointment and met you at the station.' She smiled. 'Now, have you had any lunch, John? We can easily fix you a sandwich.'

Madden hesitated. He was baffled by Jessup's behaviour.

'And you're sure he took the children with him?' he asked.

'Without doubt, I'm sorry to say.' Mrs Castleton laughed. 'I'm afraid they're going to get soaked. I was about to go outside to have a look for them. Would you like to come with me?'

She had led the way out through the door onto the flagged terrace where they found Lennox busy with a chore. Dressed in rough clothes, he was down on his knees varnishing a bench. When he heard their voices he looked up.

353

'Hello, sir.' He greeted Madden with a smile. 'I wasn't expecting to see you today.'

Mrs Castleton was already scanning the field beyond the wall at the bottom of the garden.

'There they are,' she said. 'The children, at any rate. I can't see any sign of Richard.'

Madden followed the direction of her gaze; Lennox, too, paused in his work to look up. Two small figures could be seen making their way across the meadow towards the house.

'Jack's carrying something,' Mrs Castleton said, shading her eyes. The sun had come out for a moment. Lennox followed her example.

'I reckon that's Sir Richard's shotgun,' he said after a moment. 'What's Master Jack doing with it, I wonder?'

Mrs Castleton was already moving towards the steps that led down to the lawn and Madden followed her. Together they walked towards the gate, but before they got there it opened and the children appeared. The little girl ran towards them, calling out.

'Look what I found, Grandma!' She was brandishing a large mushroom.

Mrs Castleton bent to kiss her. 'You mustn't put it in your mouth, Katy darling. It might be poisonous. Where's Daddy?' she asked.

'There . . .' The girl pointed back towards the wooded valley down which they had walked.

Her brother, as though conscious of the importance of the mission he'd been entrusted with, followed at a more sedate pace. He held the shotgun cradled in his arms.

'Daddy told me I could carry it back to the house,' he announced importantly. 'He said I was to give it to you, Lennox.'

The chauffeur had materialized at their side. Solemnly he took possession of the weapon.

'You have to put it in the gun room, Daddy says.'

'Of course, Master Jack – that's where it belongs. We'll do it right away. Would you like to come with me?'

'Just a moment, Jack . . .' Madden checked them. 'Did your father say how long he'd be?'

The boy shook his head. 'He just said he wanted to walk some more, but that we should go back because it was going to rain.' He pointed at the dark clouds that were massing overhead.

Madden turned to Mrs Castleton.

'I think I'll go after him,' he said.

'Must you?' She was unhappy with the idea. 'You'll only get wet yourself. I can't think why Richard didn't come back with them. Just look at the sky.'

'I can't stay long,' Madden said. 'I have to get home. If I don't go now I may miss him.'

Trying not to reveal his growing unease, he turned to leave, but then paused.

'Jack . . . !' He called to the boy, who was already walking away up the lawn with Lennox. They both turned to look at him.

'Did your father say anything else?' he asked.

The boy thought for a moment.

'Only what he's always telling me: that I have to look after Katy and see that she doesn't fall into any rabbit holes.'

Grinning, he gestured at his sister, who was sitting on the grass at Mrs Castleton's feet picking at her mushroom.

'He said I must remember to take care of her.'

*

Heralded by a roll of thunder, the rain arrived all at once, changing without warning from a sprinkling of drops to a sudden downpour that blurred the outlines of the landscape and reduced the approaching figure of Lennox to little more than a shape. Madden pulled up the collar of his raincoat and altered the angle of his hat in an attempt to ward off the lashing drops which were being driven by a high wind.

'What is it, Ted?' He called out to the chauffeur, who had neither a coat nor umbrella and was already drenched from head to foot. 'Is there a problem?'

'Not that I know of, sir.' As he came up to Madden he brushed the water from his face. 'I just thought I'd come with you.'

'You should have brought a coat, man.'

'You're right, sir. But it's a bit late now.' The brief smile he showed flickered and went out. 'The thing is, I'm worried about him, sir, and that's the truth.'

Madden was silent.

'Coming down from London this morning he never said a word. And he didn't sit up in the front with me like he always does. He sat in the back looking out of the window most of the time. I could see he was miles away.'

'He's been under a lot of strain, Ted.'

Madden turned to look up the valley.

'I don't see any sign of him.'

'Maybe he's gone up into the trees for shelter.' Lennox pointed to the wooded ridge above them. He sounded hopeful.

'He'll spot us if he has,' Madden replied. 'I think we should go on. He told Mrs Castleton he was going to the quarry.'

They continued up the valley, Madden walking with head bent against the driving rain, Lennox following in his footsteps. The path they were on had become a rivulet. Water flowed over their shoes as they trudged on. Looking up, Madden saw they had reached a gap in the ridge on their right, a grassy saddle that broke the otherwise uninterrupted march of beech and chestnut.

'We walked up there, I remember.'

He pointed, and heard Lennox's answering grunt behind him.

'That's the spot, all right.'

With one accord they veered off the path and started up the slope. As they neared the top the rain stopped as suddenly as it had begun and the wind died down. The leaden light that had enveloped them like a veil brightened and as they came to the hedge of holly Madden recalled from his earlier visit sunshine broke through the clouds, lending a glint to the dark green foliage.

'We'd better have a look on the other side,' Lennox said.

Stepping past his companion, he picked a way through the spiky leaves. Madden followed.

'Mind your step now, sir,' Lennox cautioned him as they came out on to the strip of turf Madden remembered. It was sodden underfoot. 'You don't want to slip here.'

The drop into the quarry beyond was only a few yards from where they stood.

Both men peered left and right along the empty stretch of grass.

'There's no sign of him.' It was Madden who spoke. The 'thank God' he muttered beneath his breath went unheard by his companion.

Lennox's gaze hadn't shifted. It remained fixed on a point a little way to their left.

'Just a moment, sir.'

When he moved in that direction Madden saw that his

attention had been caught by something on the ground. A strip of mud had been gouged out of the wet turf. It led to the brink of the quarry. Lennox approached it cautiously. Heart thumping now, Madden did the same. Just short of the mark the chauffeur went down on his knees and peered over the edge.

'*Christ, no . . . !*'

His anguished cry brought Madden to his side. Doing what the chauffeur had done, he went down on his knees and leaned forward as far as he dared.

The body was close to the white cliff-side. Richard Jessup lay sprawled on his back with his limbs spread-eagled. Despite the distance between them, Madden could see that his eyes were wide open. They seemed to be staring at the sky, and when he looked up he saw the kestrel hovering above them, motionless in the suddenly still air.

It was late in the afternoon before Madden had a chance to speak to Billy. On returning to the house – and before sending one of the maids upstairs to rouse Mrs Castleton, who was resting in her room – he had rung the police in Petersfield to report the accident, and to tell them that Sir Richard's chauffeur would be waiting by the body of his employer for their arrival.

He had hardly completed the call, made from Jessup's study, when he had heard the door open and saw Adele Castleton. She was in her dressing-gown. She stood in the doorway.

'John . . . ?'

One look at his face had been enough. Even before he spoke he had heard her catch her breath and turn pale. She listened to him in silence, eyes wide, but unseeing. Only when he had finished did she move, and then with a stagger, prompting him to come swiftly to her side. He had taken her arm and led her to one of the armchairs where he had sat with Jessup; there they had talked.

'An accident . . . ? Where . . . how . . . ?'

Like arrows drawn from wounds, the questions had appeared to cause her pain, and Madden had drawn his chair up close to hers so that he could take her hands in his. He had told her all he could.

'It looks as though he slipped. There was a mark in the ground. He must have gone too close to the edge of the quarry.' He paused. 'We must think about the children,' he had added gently.

She had stared at him for long seconds. And then, like a swimmer emerging from a deep dive, she had caught her breath with a gasp and he had seen from the steadiness of her glance that she was in possession of herself again.

'I can't tell them now.' She spoke calmly. 'We must wait until Sarah comes back. Her plane lands tomorrow morning. Richard was planning to drive up to London to meet her. I'll go with Lennox and we'll take the children with us. It's the best way, the only way.'

Her gaze had shifted to the table in the corner where the photograph of the fair-haired young woman wearing a beret and smiling in the rain stood.

'Poor darling,' she had murmured. 'What a homecoming.'

Soon afterwards the police in Petersfield had rung to confirm that they had collected Jessup's body from the quarry and to say that it had been taken to the town's mortuary. Half an hour later Lennox had returned to the house. Pale and still stricken, he had seemed bereft of words and Madden had led him to the kitchen where the cook and housemaids, already apprised of the tragedy, took him into their care. By that time the two children had come down from the nursery where they had been resting after their long walk and Mrs Castleton, who had had time to get dressed before they appeared, had taken them into the drawing room, where a fire had been lit. She had told them that their father would not be home that evening, but that she had a surprise for them. They would both be coming with her and Lennox to welcome their mother when she returned the following day.

'It means a trip to the airport,' she had told them. 'You'll be able to watch the planes landing and taking off.'

While they were together in the drawing room Madden had seized the opportunity to ring Scotland Yard. The news of Jessup's death had not yet reached London and Billy had been dumbfounded when he heard what had occurred.

'You say he fell into a quarry, sir?'

'That's how it looks. He seems to have slipped in the mud.'

'*Seems*, you say . . . ?'

Billy had dangled the question in front of Madden, hoping perhaps that he would take the bait. If so, he was doomed to disappointment.

'You called the house earlier, I believe, Billy?' Madden had responded with a question of his own.

'I wanted to speak to Jessup, sir. He had some questions to answer.'

'I take it you've had those negatives developed.' Madden saw no point in keeping up the charade any longer.

'You mean you know about them, sir?' For the first time in his life, Billy had sounded angry with his old mentor; well put out. 'You knew it was Jessup in that room with Portia Blake?'

'I only guessed. And it never occurred to me until last

night. I'd been trying to decide what to do about it. That's why I came down here. I wanted to speak to Richard: to hear what he had to say. But I never got the chance.' He paused. 'Jessup's wife – widow, I should say – is coming back from America tomorrow. Mrs Castleton is going up to London to meet her plane. I'll return home. Why not come down to Highfield? We can talk about it then.'

'I don't know, sir . . .' Billy had been far from mollified. 'What about this so-called "accident" then? Do you buy that?'

At that moment the door to the study had opened and Lennox appeared.

'Not now, Billy. We'll talk later, I promise.'

Madden had hung up.

29

'IT WAS STARING me in the face all the time, but I never saw it. I didn't want to. It's the only way I can explain it. I was drawn to the man. I admired him. I still do.'

Madden stared into the fire that was burning in the chief inspector's grate. Sinclair watched him closely. Catching Billy's eye, he saw he was about to speak and he held up his hand. *Wait!*

'*He* was the one with everything to lose, not Rex Garner, but somehow I managed to blind myself to the fact. I never could understand why Garner should have killed the girl. Even if he'd been in a rage over the way she had behaved the previous evening – carrying on that way at the dinner table – it still wasn't enough to provoke him into murder; or so I thought. And on top of that there was something that maid, Annie Potter, told Lily Poole that ought to have aroused my suspicions.'

'What was that, John?' The chief inspector was unable to obey his own admonition.

Madden met his gaze.

'She told Lily that Garner and his wife had arrived at the house in Kent on the Friday, as had Wing and Miss Blake. But that evening nothing untoward happened. Dinner went off without incident. It was only on the following evening, when Jessup came down from London, that Portia put on her act with the pendant. And of course it was directed at

Richard, as he very well knew, not at Garner, because it was Jessup who had given it to her.'

'How do you know that, sir?' Billy couldn't contain himself any longer.

'I don't,' Madden said bluntly. 'Most of what I'm telling you is guesswork. I'm simply reading between the lines. You don't have to accept it as fact, Billy.'

They had gathered at the chief inspector's cottage following Madden's return earlier that day from Petersfield. He had rung Helen the night before to tell her what had occurred, but although he had suggested that she might like to join them as soon as Billy came down from London she had decided it would be better if the three of them met on their own.

'Properly speaking, this is police business.'

No less shocked than Madden had been by the tragic end of a man whose worth she had never questioned, brief though their acquaintance had been, she told her husband she would rather hear the full story from him when they were on their own.

Consequently, when Billy arrived in his car soon after four o'clock, Madden had taken him down to Sinclair's cottage at once. One look at Billy's face had been enough to tell him that his erstwhile protégé was far from happy.

'The chief super's getting it in the neck,' he told Madden. 'Both Cradock and the commissioner are saying this would never have happened if he hadn't allowed you such a free hand with the inquiry.'

'An inquiry no one at the Yard was inclined to take up,' Madden reminded him.

'They're all saying you should have informed us the moment you realized that Jessup had been our man all along.'

'I was far from certain, Billy. It was only a suspicion. And what I'm going to say to you now is in confidence. Mr Sinclair already knows and accepts that.'

They had found the chief inspector, fully recovered from his attack of gout now, impatiently awaiting their arrival, and after both had declined the cup of tea he offered them they had all three settled down in front of the fire.

'Jessup told me he met Portia with Wing at a party that summer. He intimated it was a casual encounter, but I suspect it was a meeting Stanley Wing took pains to engineer. Jessup had been engaged for some months, but he hadn't seen much of his fiancée, who lived in America. Wing guessed correctly that he might be ready for a last fling before settling down to marriage and, if so, Portia Blake would have seemed ideally cast for the role: beautiful, and quite clearly available. She was privy to the scheme, too, I'm convinced. That business of showing off his jade jewellery was hogwash, just as Richard supposed, though he didn't know yet what was behind it: that all along Wing had him in his sights. We spent a lot of time wondering whether Wing was bent on making Rex Garner pay for that business with the Chinese woman in Hong Kong when he had got him out of trouble and was never rewarded for his pains. But we should have realized – *I* should have realized – that it was Jessup he really hated. It was Richard who had put an end to his connection with the company, who started him on the downward spiral that would lead to him falling foul of the triads and ending up in prison. And he knew just how vulnerable Jessup was.'

'Vulnerable?' Sinclair was paying close attention.

'Richard was in the process of pulling Jessup's back from the brink. His father had run the company into the ground, but thanks to Saul Temple's decision to invest in the firm he was managing to put things right. I don't believe his engagement to Temple's daughter had anything to do with the deal:

he wasn't that sort of man. But he must have known that if he became involved in a sexual scandal – one that would certainly have made headlines in the press, given his name and position – there was no telling how it would end. Not only could it have led to his engagement being broken off, it would also very likely have put an end to the partnership he was establishing with Temple's investment group. It could have spelt the end of Jessup's.'

'Even so . . .' Sinclair was frowning. 'Could that have prompted him to go so far as to *kill* the girl?'

Madden was silent. He gaze had gone back to the fire. He stared into the flickering flames.

'Mrs Castleton is as good a judge of men as I've ever met. She told me he had a core of steel inside him. She intended it as a compliment, and she was right. But it meant that in the last resort there was nothing he would shrink from, and once I began to think about this case in a different way, what she had said chimed with something that had bothered me earlier about the notion that Garner had murdered the girl in a fit of anger. It simply didn't fit the facts. If, indeed, Norris wasn't the murderer, then whatever happened in that hut must have happened in a very short space of time: minutes only. They would have had to have had a fight, she and Garner; he would have needed time to work himself up into a rage. It seemed to me that whoever killed Portia had decided in advance to commit the act, and that seemed to point to Wing initially. It was something he seemed capable of. But what reason did he have to kill her? I couldn't think of one, and later when it became clear that the murderer had taken not only the pendant she was wearing but probably also the photographs, I was forced to return to our original theory: that she'd been killed by someone she'd been involved with, who seemed to be Garner. But it wasn't he whom she went to meet in the wood that day. It was Jessup, and by that time, though she didn't know it, she had already made her fatal mistake.'

'What was that?' Billy asked.

'She'd decided to tackle him on her own. Up till then Wing had been pulling the strings. I'm sure he'd already been in touch with Richard. He would have told him that he was aware of the affair and might even have mentioned the photographs that had been taken of the two of them together. We'll never know for certain what he wanted: money, perhaps – he had to pay off Portia – but more likely reinstatement as a consultant to the company. It was his entrée into circles that were otherwise closed to him. But he would have applied the pressure gradually: he would have allowed Jessup time to see that his position was hopeless and that his best option was to give in to Wing's demands. Portia ruined all that. She had decided to act independently. It's clear that the performance she gave at that dinner playing with the pendant was her own idea. It was her signal to Jessup that he was dealing with her now. Wing was furious. Mrs Castleton heard him berating Portia afterwards in her room. But she carried on with her plan nevertheless and met Jessup alone the following day with the idea of showing him the pictures. She thought they were her trump card.'

'What did *she* want out of him, do you think – money?'

'That, of course.' Madden shrugged. 'But possibly even more. Audrey Cooper told me she had once tried to frighten one of the men she got involved with by telling him he had made her pregnant. Did she try the same trick on Jessup? Did she perhaps imagine she could force him into marrying her? We'll never know now. Miss Cooper didn't give her high marks for intelligence: she told her she was losing touch with reality. But the thought of the damage Portia could do to him if she went public was probably enough to doom her in Jessup's eyes. He saw with absolute clarity what the stakes were and knew there was only one way to deal with the danger. His chauffeur, Lennox, told me a story the other night of how Jessup had killed a civilian with his own hands during the war, a Dutch fascist. It was necessary; the man had been about to betray them to the Germans. But he did it in an instant. He didn't hesitate. He broke his neck. How many men do you know who could do that? I know I couldn't.'

'Yes . . . yes, but he returned to London after lunch that day.' Billy dragged them back to the issue he was wrestling with. 'Mrs Castleton had to send for him after Portia's body was discovered.'

'He went back, yes, but we don't know what time he arrived. The porter in the Albany who took Mrs Castleton's message was never questioned. Jessup had to wait until after lunch for his date with Portia. Heaven knows what time he got back to London. But thanks to the arrest of Norris none of the guests' alibis was checked, and his subsequent confession must have seemed like a godsend to Richard. He knew what a tightrope he was walking. If his connection with Portia Blake was revealed he would have been high on the list of suspects.'

'How did he keep it secret, though?' This time it was the chief inspector who posed the question.

'Ironically, I think it was Wing who helped there. The room they were photographed in together looked like a tart's bedroom, and may have been used for that same purpose before. I mean as a place where couples could be snapped without their knowing it. It was a world Wing was familiar with, or so I imagine, the sort of thing he was quite capable of arranging, and no doubt Portia went along with the idea. And I expect Jessup was more than happy to meet her in a place where they wouldn't be spotted. It might even have added spice to the sense of illicit adventure. But my point is, the last thing Wing wanted was for their brief affair to attract any attention. It would defeat the whole idea of catching Jessup in a trap of his own making. I'm sure he impressed on Portia the need to keep it to herself, which is why he was so angry over the act she put on later.'

'And after Miss Blake was murdered Wing went to her room to try to recover the negatives of the photographs, but found they weren't there.' Sinclair nodded. 'Do you think he witnessed the murder?' He cocked an eye at Madden. 'Did he know that Jessup was the killer?'

'It's highly likely. He already knew he couldn't trust Portia any longer, not after her display at dinner the night before. He was probably keeping an eye on her and may well have followed her out of the house when she went to meet Jessup. But if he did witness the murder, it's no surprise he didn't report it to the police. What benefit would that have been to him? He wanted to use the fact to his advantage. But when Norris confessed to the murder he must have seen that his chance had slipped by. Now he would have to find some other way of putting the screws on his victim. All he could do for the time being was go back to Hong Kong and think things over – and in the meantime get another pendant made similar to the one Jessup had taken from the girl's body.'

'He knew it was Jessup who'd given it to her?' Billy was intent on getting all the facts straight in his mind.

'Portia would have told him that. It was probably Jessup's farewell gift to her when he ended their affair. And it's more than likely he bought it in Hong Kong – perhaps as a present for his fiancée. Wing might even have known the shop it came from. He could easily have got them to make another like it. But then the war came and everything changed.

Caught between the Japanese occupiers and his triad friends, Wing's life began to fall apart. One can only imagine the bitterness he must have felt towards Jessup. He probably saw him as the author of his misfortunes. And even when he finally came out of prison his problems were far from over. The triads had marked him down for execution. He needed to get away from Hong Kong; he needed to disappear; above all he needed money.'

'And there was only one source he could go to for it?' The chief inspector rubbed his hands together. He was warming to the tale. 'Somehow he had to make Miss Blake's killer pay for what he'd done.'

'It would seem so.' Madden frowned. 'But all he had by way of ammunition at that stage was the false pendant he'd had made, and all he could do with that was send it to Derry along with a note suggesting there'd been more to the murder than met the eye. He was hoping the police would reopen the case so that he could begin to put pressure on Jessup again. But when there was no sign of that he sent a second letter to the *News of the World* saying essentially the same thing – that there'd been a miscarriage of justice – and that had the desired result. The police were finally forced to admit they were reviewing the original investigation.'

'We hadn't much option at that stage,' Billy agreed. 'The press were breathing down our necks.'

'What Wing failed to anticipate was that almost at once the investigation began to focus on the wrong man – Rex Garner.' Madden shook his head. 'That was my fault – or rather Jessup's doing. It was he who told me that story about Portia performing with the pendant at dinner, how she dangled it in front of Garner's eyes and seemed to be taunting him. That's what put us on the wrong track.'

369

'What about Garner, sir? If he wasn't mixed up in this business at all, how did he come to be murdered?'

Madden was slow in answering. Finally, he shrugged.

'In the end he had only himself to blame,' he said. 'It began when he saw that photograph you and Grace showed him of Portia and the man in the bed. It wasn't him, as we know, it was Jessup, and he either knew that – knew that Jessup had had an affair with her in the past – or he guessed it.'

'You mean he himself was never involved with Miss Blake?'

'Oh, I think he was,' Madden responded forcefully. 'That's to say he'd had the same sort of casual fling with her that Jessup had. He probably gave her name to Richard. As Miss Cooper said, the men were passing her around. He might even have done it at Wing's behest. They were all bumping into each other at parties that summer. We'll never get to the bottom of that. But having given a false alibi to the police at the time of Portia's murder, Garner knew he might be in difficulties, and when you showed him that photo he saw he could at least derive some benefit from it. You thought his reaction was strange, didn't you?'

Billy nodded.

'Joe reckoned it was because he knew it was him in the bed, but I didn't agree. It looked to me as though he was thinking of something else.'

'And you were right. He got in touch with Jessup right away. They had dinner at Richard's club the following night. We'll never know exactly what passed between them. But I suspect Garner told his old friend what he knew, or had guessed, and asked for money in return for keeping his mouth shut. He was broke, as we know. You'll recall that Jessup's account of their conversation was rather different.

He told me Garner was ready to call it quits: that he was going to make a statement to you the following morning in the presence of a solicitor.'

'And an hour or so later Garner himself was topped.' Billy's gaze had hardened. 'I'm beginning to get a nasty feeling,' he said.

Madden caught his eye and nodded. 'I'm afraid it was Jessup who killed him, not Wing, and you may be able to prove that, for your own satisfaction at least. I believe he told Garner he would pay him what he wanted and then got Lennox to drive him home. He knew he could slip out of his club by the back door, the tradesmen's entrance. It was kept locked at night, but I expect Jessup knew where the key was kept. He could have walked up to Shepherd Market. It wouldn't have taken him more than twenty minutes. All he had to do was rouse Garner, who hadn't even gone to bed, as it turned out, and was far too drunk to have put up much of a struggle.'

Madden quelled a shudder.

'Jessup couldn't trust him any longer, you see. Once the blackmail started it would go on. The same was true of Wing. He had to die, too. After he killed Miss Cooper it was Jessup to whom he sent that spare set of prints: care of his club, most likely, and by hand. His blackmail scheme was a lot stronger now that he had the negatives in his hands. But he had to move fast. The triads were hot on his trail. The fragment of the photograph you found in Garner's grate was from one of the prints. Jessup must have left it there to incriminate Rex.'

Sinclair stirred. He'd been silent for some time.

'You say that can be proved?'

'The evidence would be circumstantial.' Madden shrugged. 'It has to do with that length of flex we talked about which was used to strangle Garner and then hang him. It never seemed likely to me that the killer just happened to find what he needed in Rex's basement. I think Jessup brought it with him from his club. They've got workmen in building a new cloakroom downstairs. It seems they're careless with their tools; they leave things lying around. I heard one of the porters say so. A piece of flex that long is bound to have been missed. If the workmen are questioned I expect they'll confirm the theft.'

He saw Billy shake his head.

'Is *that* what put you on to Jessup, sir? You told me yesterday you'd only just twigged to him being the man in the photos. Was it hearing what that porter said?'

Madden nodded. Billy saw the sadness in his eyes.

'We were having dinner together, Richard and I. He'd been telling me how guilty he felt about Garner, how he felt he'd let him down. I think now that he was longing to tell me the truth. He'd been able to cope with the murder of Portia Blake – in his mind, I mean. Perhaps he'd found some way to justify it to himself. But killing a man who'd been his closest friend in boyhood was more than he could stomach. Perhaps he was already thinking of ending it all. The discovery of Wing's body with the negatives on it merely hastened the process.'

'Do you think he arranged for Wing to be killed?' Again it was Sinclair who put the question.

'I'm sure he did, though with the help of that Chinese businessman, Lin Jie. I don't imagine Jessup had any direct contact with the triads, but Lin certainly did, and both of them had good reason to want Wing out of the way. As far as I know Jessup and Wing didn't meet, but they must have spoken on the phone after Jessup received the photographs. Wing would have made his demands then. Since there was no prospect of his ever being linked to the firm again, I imagine what he wanted was money, and a good deal of it. That and safe passage out of the country, which he knew Jessup could arrange through the company's shipping contacts. I expect they were due to meet at the docks, where Jessup would hand over the money. It's possible that Wing promised to give him the negatives in exchange, but I doubt Jessup trusted him to do it. He knew Wing would probably keep back one or two as insurance. He staked his hopes on the triad killers disposing of Wing's body and anything he might have had on him, which would include the negatives. It was all he could do. He was already very close to falling off that tightrope.'

A log crackled in the fire and part of it rolled out of the grate onto the hearth. Madden was on his feet before Sinclair could move. The other two watched as he replaced the burning log and added a fresh one to the blaze.

Billy had been thinking. 'I still don't see why he took his life – Jessup, I mean?'

He hesitated when he saw the look in Madden's eye.

'You're not going to say he fell into that quarry by accident, are you, sir?'

'As far as anyone knows that's exactly what he did.' Madden's altered tone signalled a change in the atmosphere. 'Both Lennox and I saw a mark made in the mud that could have been where he slipped. Richard always said it was dangerous to leave that area unfenced. He wouldn't allow his children anywhere near it. I'll be appearing at the inquest in Petersfield next week, as you know, and if asked my opinion I'll say I believe it was a tragic accident.'

'I don't know, sir . . .' Billy flushed. 'That doesn't seem right to me. Ten years ago a man was hanged for a murder he didn't commit. I understand you might want to protect

Richard Jessup's name. But what about Owen Norris? What about *his* name?'

Madden was slow in answering. Watching him, the younger man saw it was only with difficulty that he brought himself to reply.

'I've no good answer to that, Billy. All I can say is I won't be party to any attempt to lay Miss Blake's murder at Richard Jessup's door; nor Garner's, if it comes to that. You'll have to prove it for yourself.'

He met the other's gaze.

'Remember, everything I've said to you has been in confidence, and I won't repeat it elsewhere. Of course you're free to make your own inquiries and deductions, but before you and Charlie Chubb decide whether you want to take this further, ask yourselves what you'll achieve by it. You can't prove that Jessup committed either of those murders; you can only show he had a brief relationship before he got married with a young woman who later fell victim to a man who was subsequently convicted of her murder and hanged.'

'What about Garner, though, sir? There's that length of flex to consider.' Billy wasn't ready yet to give in.

'Circumstantial, as I said. You'll need more than that to make a case.'

'How about the fingerprints left on the banisters? I'm willing to bet they'll turn out to be Jessup's.'

'I expect they will. But as any barrister would point out, the two men were friends of long standing. What could be more likely than for Jessup's prints to be found in Garner's house? As for Wing's decapitation, in order to prove that Richard had any hand in setting that up you would need Lin Jie's cooperation, and I very much doubt you'll get it. He'll say he has no connection whatsoever with the triads and doesn't know what you're talking about.'

Billy was at a loss. He had never come into conflict before with his old mentor, the man who had taught him his trade and whom he respected above all others. Nor did he appreciate the look of sympathetic understanding which the chief inspector was casting his way just then.

'What do you think, sir?' He turned to Sinclair.

The chief inspector considered his reply.

'All this has come about because I asked John to look into the matter on my behalf.' He spoke after a long pause. 'He's been good enough to share his conclusions with us, though he wasn't obliged to. And, as he says, he can offer next to no proof of what he has said: it's simply how he interprets the facts. In the circumstances I feel it only right to leave any final decision to him.'

Frustrated, Billy turned back to Madden.

'Well, if we couldn't have got a conviction against him, why *did* he go and top himself?'

Madden lifted his gaze from the fire.

'If you want my opinion – and that's all it is – it was because in the last resort he couldn't live with himself any longer. Even before I guessed the truth I sensed there was something eating away at him. And as I said before, he saw things with frightening clarity. Once he learned that Wing's body had been recovered with the negatives on it he knew that the police would launch a new investigation into Portia Blake's murder, one that might result in him being brought to trial. It wasn't just to protect his own reputation that he'd killed the girl. She was threatening to destroy everything he valued: not only his company, but his marriage to a woman he was deeply in love with. The same danger hung over him now; only it was worse. Even if the police couldn't mount a successful prosecution, a murder trial would do terrible damage, both to him and to the people he loved, including his children. It would leave a smear on the name of Jessup and everyone connected to it that would last for years, perhaps for ever. There was only one remedy, and he was ready to accept it.'

Madden looked Billy in the eye.

'He did what had to be done.'

EPILOGUE

'Has Billy forgiven you yet?' Helen took her husband's arm. 'I saw the two of you having a word after the service. I didn't realize he would be there. Was his presence official?'

'No, he came of his own accord,' Madden said. 'He told me he thought he ought to be there. He said he wanted to close the book on the case. And yes, I think he's forgiven me.'

'It's definitely closed then, is it?' She looked at him.

'So Billy said. There was simply no point in pursuing it. Even Charlie Chubb accepts that, though *he* hasn't forgiven me yet. I shall have to make my peace with him. I'll take him out to lunch. That should do the trick.'

The two of them had caught the train up to London that morning to attend a memorial service in honour of Richard Jessup organized by his widow. The occasion, held at St Lawrence Jewry, in Guildhall Yard, had been well attended, not only by City grandees and friends of the dead man, but also by more than a score of men Jessup had served with in the war. A mixed bunch, some of them hard-looking, and most dressed in cheap suits, they had gathered in a group with Lennox at the back of the beautiful Wren church where they stood throughout the service and the speeches that followed. At Mrs Castleton's request, Madden and his wife had kept her company in the row behind where Sarah Jessup sat with her parents and her children. Later, they had been introduced to the widow.

'Adele has told me how close you and Richard became.'

As good-looking in the flesh as she had appeared in the photograph he had seen in Jessup's study, and offering him the same open smile she had shown on that damp day in Paris, her straight glance had carried no hint of unspoken thoughts, nor of any suspicion that her husband's tragic end might have been other than it seemed.

Turning to Helen, she had added: 'I hope we can all get together very soon.'

It was only as they were about to leave that Madden had spotted Billy standing in the courtyard, hat in hand.

'I thought I ought to turn up, sir, just for form's sake.' Billy's handshake had lacked nothing in warmth. 'Quite a gathering, isn't it?' He had nodded at the crowd thronging the courtyard, which included a number of well-known faces.

'The chief super sends his regards. He thought I was bound to find you here and said I was to tell you he still had a bone to pick with you.' Billy chuckled. 'Oh, and by the way, you might be interested to hear that we picked up that fellow, Chen Yi.'

'I remember the name.' Madden was intrigued. 'He was the Red Pole's assistant; his jackal, Jessup called him.'

'He was stopped going through immigration at Ramsgate – he was about to board the Ostend ferry – and brought up to London. I questioned him myself. He was a smooth article.' Billy shook his head ruefully. 'Spoke English beautifully; said he was part owner of a restaurant in Amsterdam and had come over to London to visit a cousin. What cousin? I asked. I thought we might have him there, but blow me if he didn't produce a young Chinese bloke working in a laundry who was ready to swear on a stack of bibles that they were related. So we had to let him go.'

'What about the enforcer himself, Wing's killer?'

'We never saw hide nor hair of him. But then we didn't have either a name or a description.'

Before they parted Madden had put the same question to his former protégé that Helen would ask him later.

'Am I forgiven, then?'

Billy's chuckle had been answer enough. But that hadn't been quite the end of it, as he made plain.

'Still, it might not have turned out this way if he'd been anyone else.'

'Meaning what, Billy?'

'He was too important, Jessup was, too big a name to drag through the mud. The commissioner said as much. It was best to let things lie, he said.'

'And you don't agree?'

'I wouldn't say that exactly.' Billy weighed his hat in his hands. 'But I can't help thinking that all this started because some silly girl got ideas above her station. She wasn't much cop in the brains department, our Portia. You might even say she brought it on herself.'

'And your point is . . . ?' Madden eyed him keenly.

'She didn't deserve to die on that account.' Billy met his gaze.

'No, she didn't.' Madden had put a hand on the younger man's shoulder. 'Hold fast to that,' he said.

He smiled then. 'Oh, and there's one other thing. It's about time you stopped calling me sir, Billy. I'd rather you made it John.'

'So, you had your knuckles rapped?' Helen had enjoyed hearing the story. 'Good for Billy. He's always been a bit too respectful of you.'

Madden laughed. It was early evening and they were

walking arm-in-arm down the lawn to the bottom of the garden.

'Do you think he had a point?' she asked.

'More than ever.' Madden was rueful. 'The trouble was, we became too close, Richard and I. That's something we were always warned about when I was with the police.'

'But you're not any longer, my dear, and you never regarded him as a suspect.'

'True. But I can't help thinking he used our friendship to steer me in the direction he wanted. It almost worked, too.'

'Don't hold that against him.'

Surprised by her words, Madden stopped to look at her.

'Don't think of him that way. He cared for you, John. I could see that. Your friendship meant a lot to him. In the end it was probably what he clung to.'

'I'd like to think so.' Madden sighed. 'But then I find myself remembering something a fellow I met down in Kent said to me. He was an old boxer who ran a pub. He had known Norris, the man they hanged for Portia's murder, and didn't think he had it in him to kill. But then you never know anyone, do you, he said – not really.'

He felt her hand on his shoulder and he turned to face her.

'You know me,' she said.

Madden looked into her blue eyes for a long moment and as he did so felt his heart swell, just as it had years before when he had realized for the first time that she loved him. He took her in his arms.

'Yes, I do. Thank God for that.'

Unknown to them, they were being observed. Standing by the balustrade fronting the stone-flagged terrace, Lucy

Madden and her brother had been watching their parents for some time.

'Look at them!' Rob was scandalized. 'They're just like lovers.'

He shot a glance at his sister.

'What are you giggling at?'

'Nothing . . .'

'Come on.' He knew her too well. 'Spit it out.'

Head cocked on one side, Lucy considered her reply.

'Do you remember that spot down by the stream where we used to go when we didn't want anyone to find us?'

'Where we hid whenever the Mitchell twins came over because we didn't want to play with them?' He scowled at her. 'That patch of grass surrounded by bushes? What about it?'

'When they first met – it was during that big murder case when Daddy was still a detective – Mummy fell in love with him almost at once. She was sure that he felt the same, but he wouldn't say anything. It was because of what happened to him in the war. He was still too locked up in himself. He couldn't talk about his feelings. He thought he wasn't a whole man any more . . .'

She paused.

'So Mummy invited him to lunch. She got Mary to make up a picnic basket and she took him down to the stream, to that same spot, and laid a blanket on the grass . . .'

She fell silent.

'Good God!'

It had taken Rob some moments to find his tongue. He was staring at their parents in disbelief.

'Are you saying she *seduced* him?'

Lucy said nothing.

'How do you know that?' His scowl had turned fierce.

'Mummy told me once . . . woman talk . . .' She smiled.

'Woman . . . *you*?'

'Yes, *me* . . . !' She speared an elbow into his ribs, making him gasp. 'And when are you going to shave that horrible beard off? Poor Annabel was in a terrible state this morning. The whole side of her face has come out in a rash.'

'Annabel . . . ? Which one was she?'

'Which one . . . ?' Lucy aimed for his ribs again, but this time he managed to dodge her flying elbow. 'You spent half the night dancing with her.'

'She loved every moment of it.' Rob was enjoying himself. 'Couldn't get enough of my beard, she said.'

'She did *not*.'

'You're just jealous. You're longing to know what it feels like. Here, let me give you a taste . . .'

He grabbed for her, but she was too quick – 'No, you won't' – eluding his outstretched hand, and then turning and running down the steps from the terrace onto the lawn, pursued by Hamish, who'd been sitting nearby.

Her brother set off after her and caught up after only a few steps. Wrapping his arms around her, he tried to press his cheek against hers, but Lucy resisted, kicking at him with her heels, and when that didn't work, falling to her knees on the ground and tucking her head in her arms.

'You beast . . . !'

'Come on . . . at least try it . . . girls tell me it feels warm and furry.'

Bending down, Rob tried to prise her hands from her cheeks while Hamish, beside himself with excitement now, danced around them in a circle. It was the basset's frantic barking that caused Madden and his wife to break off their embrace and look back.

'Good grief!'

Madden stared open-mouthed at the sight of his two children locked in combat. As he watched they lost their balance and fell over, still wrestling as they rolled about on the grass.

He turned to Helen for support, but saw no help would be coming from that quarter. She was laughing helplessly. He was left to shake his head and say the one thing that seemed fitting in the circumstances, even if no one was listening.

'Do you think they'll ever grow up?'